Acknowledgements.

For all of those who know who you are ... and even if you don't.
I thank you and appreciate you.
Even if you die and come back.
I promise I'll take care of you myself.
Maybe.
If you're not too scary looking.
And smelly.

LZR-1143: INFECTION

A Zombie Novel

By:
Bryan James

Prologue

Then they took away the stone from the place where the dead was laid. And Jesus lifted up his eyes, and said, Father, I thank thee that thou hast heard me.

And I knew that thou hearest me always: but because of the people which stand by I said it, that they may believe that thou hast sent me. And when he thus had spoken, he cried with a loud voice, Lazarus, come forth. And he that was dead came forth, bound hand and foot with graveclothes: and his face was bound about with a cloth. Jesus saith unto them, loose him, and let him go unto the world.

The Gospel of John 11:41-44

Thus did Jesus prove unto us his power and righteousness, but to what end? Lazarus walked, but with the walk of the damned. His eyes possessed no light of the living, but stared as if dead. And his body moved, but he did not speak. Dumb, he struck about him so that those who came to see must restrain him lest they suffer pain as he did cast about, seeking to devour those with whom he had previously loved.

When Jesus did depart, was he again subdued. And the tomb was again sealed, and his sisters did wail upon the sand of the earth. Those of whom he had touched with his mark did die, and their rising was like unto death, the touch of God not upon them.

Unknown author, believed to be a resident of Bethany.
Written approximately 35 A.D.

And the smoke of their torment ascendeth up for ever and ever: and they have no rest day nor night, who worship the beast and his image, and whosoever receiveth the mark of his name.

Revelation 14:11

CHAPTER 1

I'm used to people telling me I'm crazy. But until today, I wasn't used to agreeing with them.

I had been watching events unfold on the television for the past hour, and as I sat there, remote control in one hand, empty soda bottle in the other, I became a believer.

In the best of times here, television had been a closely guarded and carefully monitored luxury. It was an award system that I had shunned since my first day of residency, realizing quickly that the only programs awarded to my special class of society were reruns of Saved by the Bell and whatever channel constantly replayed "Homeward Bound." Until today, I thought that those were the only channels the damn thing received.

I had found the remote control lying haphazardly on the counter that was normally staffed by a candy striper with an infuriatingly jolly smile and hundreds of vials of various sedatives and anti-psychotics. The drugs, normally in neat, orderly stacks behind the counter, were strewn on the floor. A half-eaten peanut butter and jelly sandwich lay on a piece of wax paper next to a full bottle of soda, which I had quickly confiscated. We weren't allowed caffeine.

A fellow incarcerate, not appreciative of, or more likely incapable of appreciating, our new found liberty, crouched behind an outdated sofa near the hallway, rocking on his heels and incessantly humming the theme song from what sounded suspiciously like the A-team.

From the East wing, a loud, constant hammering noise filtered through the cement walls. At first, I had naively attributed the thumping to renovations. They were always fixing this place, this bed and breakfast for the insane. Always making room for more of our kind.

My freedom was a serious breach in psycho-jail house protocol. I wasn't supposed to be privy to the remote control, and I sure as hell wasn't supposed to be wandering about unsupervised. Don't get me wrong: I wasn't exactly unappreciative of the liberty; it just concerned me. But when I figured out that the television "channels" we were allowed to watch were actually looped reruns on a CCTV network, and I switched over to the cable news networks, my curiosity proved to be well founded.

I watched, spellbound. Unbelieving.

Gone were the talking heads discussing the travails and indiscretions of minor celebrities and absent were the inane debates on whatever scandal had slithered its way to the forefront of the morning media. In their place was live coverage—actual raw footage—that identified my liberator. No sir, no celebrity brouhaha or overblown vanity trial here.

This was, apparently, quite real.

My own celebrity trial had been surprisingly short, although the build up to it—and the media circus that surrounded it—had not. I would say that it had been blessedly short, but in hindsight I doubt my seemingly hastily made decisions with the same level of circumspection that, for the last few months, I have now doubted my sanity. I'm not absolutely convinced that I'm crazy, but the events of the last hour have been making a compelling case for it.

My current home is King's Park in Long Island, New York. More specifically, I'm a ward of the state. In line with my title, my accommodations are top of the line: three square a day, galvanized steel cot, and all the sedatives you can choke down.

Seriously, my digs on their own are enough to give you nightmares. My lawyer gave me the history of the place before I landed, and its story matches its appearance step for step. Appropriate to its name, King's Park was built in 1890, originally to house lepers and the mentally deranged. It's a vast campus of dilapidated buildings in various states of disrepair, some of which are reportedly connected by a series of underground tunnels.

In the early 1900's, it was a hot spot for the cutting edge of psychiatry: frontal lobotomies and electro-shock therapy. The reputation has gone downhill from there. It was closed for about a decade, but reopened 6 years ago. During the years it was inactive as a hotel for the crazy, it was a refuge for transients, sexually exploratory teens (and adults), and a destination royale of sorts for ghost hunters and paranormal investigators. Hundreds, possibly thousands, of its past residents have expired behind these walls; some of them of natural causes. That kind of history just begs to be exploited and investigated. It also stinks of fear.

What a logical place to send convicted killers for rehabilitation.

Did you know that when you plead insanity, you're not telling the jury that you're innocent? Nope. What you're really saying, in legalese, is not what you appear to be saying in human talk. You're not saying "I'm innocent because I'm crazy."

No sir. What you're really saying is "I'll concede that I'm guilty as hell. But I don't deserve to go to jail because I'm crazy." Big difference there. Trust me.

I was admitted six months ago after pleading insanity to a charge of first-degree murder. I suppose it's also relevant to mention that the victim was my wife.

In my previous life, I was an actor. And I was famous. A certified celebrity action hero. Right before it happened, I had been on a location shoot in Vancouver, a popular spot for American filmmaking. I used to know why, back when it mattered.

We had just finished a film involving aliens and some sort of government conspiracy. Typical stuff. I think there may have been a talking dog, but consider the source before taking my word for it. My role, as always, was the delivery of bullets and pithy clichés, all while walking that delicate line between fantastic egoism and endearing self-deprecation.

I returned on a Sunday night. The airline had tried to bump me from First to Business on the four o'clock flight. The gall! I still remember being appalled at the nerve of the desk clerk, who told me to my face that I'd have to ride with the cattle, and to whom my celebrity seemed to mean very little. Oh, she recognized me, but acted as if I was just another passenger and seemed to think that, as a normal person, I would have to accept my situation and deal with it. Talk about foreshadowing. Nevertheless, with nothing left do but renting a private jet (don't think I didn't consider it), I elected to drink myself into a stupor in the lounge, and wait for the eight fifteen.

The flight was early, and I got home just after 4 in the morning. I actually expected to cross paths with Maria on my way in; she worked at a biological research facility outside the city, and commuted from our place in Manhattan four days a week. She only worked four days a week, but the drawback was an early start and a late finish. I still don't understand the drive to work those long hours. She absolutely hated getting up in the morning, and God knows we didn't need the money.

I should rephrase. I understood her drive; she loved the job, was always telling me about the stuff she did and how it was going to be the next big thing in medical advancement. The next penicillin. She couldn't get into too much detail, not because my eyes started to glaze when she got into the technical stuff, which they did, but because it was government stuff. Classified, apparently.

But she was allowed to share the enthusiasm. God, how her eyes lit up when she was talking about the implications of her work. Even when she kept the talk to vagaries, you could tell that this was something important. To her, if not to the person she was talking to.

So it was odd when I got in that morning, and the light was on but there was no movement in the kitchen. She should have been boiling water for tea, listening to the news, carrying on the normal early morning routine.

That should have been my first clue. But the alcohol and the exhaustion numbed my senses just enough to keep me oblivious to the little anomalies.

I remember as much now as I remembered at trial: the blood on the covers and on the walls; the noises coming from the bathroom; the police breaking down the front door. Then sitting at the kitchen counter, reeking of alcohol, covered in her blood, and holding the "murder weapon": a Titlist putter that I kept behind the bedroom door and used to practice my putting down the hallway. I don't even remember seeing her face.

But I remember the pictures at trial. Her face, grossly distorted and gray, the wounds on the left side of her head from the repeated impacts of the club, and the shots that ultimately convicted me—yours truly, covered in the blood of his wife, holding a bloody club in a limp hand, a vacant, lost expression, staring at the camera. These are the memories I wake with every morning. These are the memories I woke up with this morning.

But when I opened my eyes and looked around my room, I noticed immediately that today was different. First of all, it was mid-afternoon. They usually had us up pretty early, and by the light coming through the window set high in the exterior wall, I could tell we were off schedule.

Mentally, I felt drastically different. I didn't remember much from before I went to sleep, which was also unusual. What I could recall was a struggle, which was easily confirmed by a bruise I noticed on my left arm. I was normally drugged up, which most of the time put me into a trance-like daze that put a fuzzy corner on everything I saw and heard. But I could usually remember the previous day; vaguely at least. The only memories I had now were confusing images and sounds, along with the memory of having something pumped into my arm. I checked my right arm, locating and brushing my finger lightly over a pinprick bruise near my vein.

Yep, that was real.

I tried to concentrate on the sounds and images that I only vaguely recalled, but all that was left was the impression of anxious voices and loud noises. No cognizable words or sentences. Nevertheless, I felt like I had gotten a good, long sleep. Despite that foggy delirium that comes with oversleeping, my mind felt ... lighter. It wasn't as hard to formulate my thoughts, to piece together my surroundings.

Looking around the room, I took in the depressingly familiar surroundings: whitewashed walls marred by brackish-colored water damage and slight cracks in the cheap paint; a heavy metal door with a small integrated window; a bolted down bed frame covered in dirty white sheets and a limp pillow; and a bedside table—also bolted to the floor. I noticed that the cup next to my bed still held pills, and that the glass of water was full. Yet another oddity.

I was usually nuzzled gently awake by a Conanesque orderly who held me close and tender as he force fed me my continental breakfast of neuroleptics and water. Whoever complained of bread and water as a prison meal was clearly never on this diet.

The drugs normally kept me docile: not in a stupor, but just kind of numb and lacking the energy or initiative to act on my thoughts or desires. So, when I woke up this morning, saw the inappropriately open door, wanted to go through it, and was able to follow-through on that most extraordinary thought, I knew something was up.

I slowly stuck my head out of the doorway to my room, and checked for Conan. No one was around.

I couldn't even hear the normal sounds of squeaky cart wheels or inmate agitation that I had become accustomed to during my tenure.

"Odd" I said softly to myself, and quickly made a mental note not to speak unless necessary. The echo of my own voice combined with the unfamiliarity of the circumstances was simply too eerie.

I made my way down the hallway, passing open cell doors and vacant cells. A cart was turned over at the end of the hall, where dozens of individual Jell-O cups, having fallen victim to gravity in a tumble from their overturned food cart, lay prone and inert like so many stranded, colorful jellyfish. Mid-afternoon light streamed through a bank of barred windows in the rec room, illuminating the orange and brown 1970's decor. The double doors to the main hallway, my first doorway to the outside, stood shut. I checked the handles. They weren't locked.

I looked around, considered my situation, and locked them with a jaunty turn of the deadbolt. I may not be free for long, but every minute counts. Whatever happened here, they were going to come back. It was just a matter of time. May as well enjoy my R & R for as long as I could.

Then I found the remote.

The news was full of it. At first, I thought it was some sort of prank— some sort of television version of Orson Wells' duping of the American people in 1938. I changed channels and found only four other stations on the air; the rest had already shifted to the emergency broadcast network. I left it on one channel and sat on the couch for an hour, taking in what was being reported. There were inconsistencies to be certain, and no real idea of cause, or how the government was going to react. Even doubts that the government could react. Apparently, it had happened fast and most of the active military was overseas. I kept it on one channel and listened to what little was known.

The television recounted details of the impossible: reanimated recently deceased, attacking the living, bites caused death and subsequent reanimation. Obviously, I couldn't believe it.

But then I looked around.

Something caused the evacuation of this building, something caused me to be ignored in the flight of the authorities, and something was keeping everyone gone for a long time.

Someone should have returned by now. Even if there was a fire, or a gas leak, the firemen should have been here. I should have heard sirens and voices. Maybe helicopters. The clock above the nurse's station read four o'clock when I finally switched off the television and, after realizing how eerily quiet it was (save for that constant hammering, which appeared to have gotten faster and more insistent), turned it right back on again for the comfort of the extra noise. My friend hadn't budged from his station behind the couch, and he didn't seem to mind the extra sound.

That was definitely the theme song from the A-team.

Man, that song was gonna get stuck in my head.

CHAPTER 2

They kept me in Building 13. Innocuously named Wisteria, 13 housed the most dangerous inmates in King's Place. Murderers, rapists, and wife-killers all, we were held in individual cells controlled by a master switchboard in the security booth at the front of the building. I was guessing that switchboard was to thank for my freedom.

I lived on the first floor, but there was at least one more floor above me. Sometimes, mostly at night, I could hear a rapid staccato of beats on the ceiling above my head; an orchestral madhouse performance usually consummated by a crescendo of shouting, the hurried opening of a cell door, and a sharp, cracking thud that I imagined to be either a nightstick hitting a head, a head hitting the floor, or both.

At the moment, I was in the rec room, which was connected to the front of the building by a long, marble-tiled hallway ending in front of a Plexiglas antechamber, which in turn housed the security booth and the vending machines. The antechamber was normally locked on both sides, and the security booth controlled ingress and egress from the same panel that housed the electronic releases for the cells.

How do I know so much about the security set-up, you ask? A clever combination of pre-narcotic observation, and information overheard in a drugged stupor. Oh, and I was beaten to within an inch of my so-called life when I tried to make a run for the doors once.

Yeah, it only took once.

This highway to freedom was on the other side of the set of doors I had flippantly locked after discovering that our little hotel had some vacancies. But after having watched the news reports, I was a little wary about springing to freedom before figuring out where my jailers had disappeared to and, more pressingly, why they had disappeared. If those news reports were true, I thought I had a pretty good idea, but I still wasn't prepared for what I might find outside those doors.

Besides, my head was still foggy from yesterday's round of drugs and my prolonged nap, and I had no idea where I'd go if I made good on my escape. Almost absent-mindedly, I noted that the pounding from the East wing had stopped. For the record, I was no longer convinced it was anything as innocent as construction.

I turned my attention to my surroundings, searching for information. The desk normally occupied by the drug-dispensing nurse was, like the shelves behind it, in complete disarray. Papers were everywhere, looking as if they had been hastily rifled through and quickly discarded as either useless or irrelevant. I was famished, so I swallowed my pride and took a bite from the PB and J that sat on the desk.

My pride was the only thing I swallowed, quickly realizing that the mealy texture and sour taste were either the product of a piss poor sandwich maker or an extended period of exposure. Either way, and despite feeling like I hadn't eaten in days, I spit out the large bite I had taken. I dropped the soggy bread to the dirty desktop, smearing peanut butter on a large desktop calendar in the process. Maybe I could find a vending machine.

I pushed the rest of the sandwich aside and scanned the binders still set back against the credenza; most seemed to be visitor and patient logs. Some were medical manuals dealing with recommended dosages for various diagnoses. Only one binder lay open on the desk. It was today's intake chart complete with the intake notes from the last nurse on duty.

I scanned the list. It was like reading a plot summary for one of those television crime dramas. Or at least the writers' collective brainstorming for the criminal de jour.

September 15, 0415: Sykes, Trevor. *Multiple personality disorder; double murder; one personality extremely violent, other personality female. Latter personality friendly but no awareness of disorder. Convicted felon. 2F, 202E.*

This guy would fit right in.

September 15, 0805: Williams, Seymour. *Acute schizophrenia; murder, rape; requires constant sedation; use caution when handling needles. Patient has exhibited violence toward orderlies, nurses and all other authority figures. Patient has violent sexual impulses. Convicted felon. 2F, 206W.*

Seemed harmless enough.

While I read, I caught myself wondering vaguely what the alphanumeric codes at the end of each note meant. I read on.

September 15, 0930: Hickman, Travis. *Suspected bipolar; triple murder, attempted cannibalism; animalistic ideations. Patient seemingly identifies as wild animal; keep isolated. Admitted from County Sheriff for holding; pending arraignment. 1F, 126E.*

Attempted cannibalism and animalistic ideations? Now this was something. If the news reports were true, there were people out there infected with some sort of sickness that made them act like this. Because I was an adult, I didn't exactly buy the "risen dead" angle, but the shots they showed on the news of the infected really made a case for some seriously fucked up people on the outside.

Maybe this guy had it, and they admitted him before the psychotic crap hit the societal fan. The last entry on the log was the illustrious Mr. Hickman. At nine thirty in the morning.

I checked the clock again. Seven hours since they admitted the last patient, and still neither hide nor hair of another person. Other than A-team, of course.

Even if Hickman had the disease, it wouldn't take a whole facility to subdue him, and they sure as hell wouldn't have sprung the rest of us to do it. So he wasn't the entire reason for the deserted wing. More likely, whatever was going on outside had caused some sort of spur of the moment campus-wide evac, and rather than rounding us dangerous criminals up by the book and spiriting our rowdy asses away to safety, they just popped the gates and let us fend for ourselves, leaving the doors wide open. Much more plausible. Also much more disturbing.

The power flickered briefly, as it did on occasion; the wiring in this place was probably reaching its centennial. The brown-out caused the television to flick off, plunging the room into silence.

My head jerked up in surprise. Something was moving outside the doorway to the hall. I almost wrenched my arm out of the mental socket patting myself on the back for locking the doors.

Whoever it was, they were moving slowly. I scanned the room, looking for something to use as a weapon in case it was one of those lunatics.

I laughed as I examined my name-calling hypocrisy. Dear Kettle, you are surely as black as midnight. Love, Pot.

Of course there were no weapons. Rule number one in housing violent psychotics: don't leave anything laying around that you wouldn't want to see used as an incidental murder weapon, such as forks, knives, sporks, cotton candy, rolled up newspapers...well, you get the drift. The furniture was bolted down, the desk held only papers and binders. Even the trashcan was attached to the wall.

I turned in place, looking around somewhat frantically. I walked past the orderly's desk again and realized that in my initial giddiness at being released, I had failed to notice a faint—but quite clear—hand print on the wall. It wasn't unusual to find out of place marks or stains in the Park, especially in this room, where my compatriots were often allowed finger paints, water colors and canvas. But this was different.

I moved closer to the print, which bore the appearance of an elementary school Thanksgiving project where you press your hand in a blob of paint and make a turkey out of the hand print. But this was slightly different. I was fairly sure this picture was pressed in blood.

I picked up the pace at that point. I remembered the utility closet I had seen across the hall from my cell. It was probably locked, but worth a shot. We didn't exactly have free reign of the place, so I hoped that someone had been careless and left it open. I skirted around the edge of the desk (it sat precipitously close to the frosted glass windows spanning the tops of the locked doors) and walked quickly and quietly back down the hallway toward my room. I naively hoped that whoever was shuffling around outside would just pass right by, not recognizing that the adjacent room was occupied.

Trying the door to the closet, I realized my trust in the incompetence of my fellow man was misplaced. Locked. Just like it was supposed to be.

The hallway dead-ended in a glass block wall that allowed the ghost of daylight in, but not a view of the grounds below. No way out that way. The bricks were too thick, and I couldn't see how far it was down, even if I could break them. I turned back toward the rec room and my eye caught on the sign adorning the door frame to my cell: McKnight, Michael. 1F, 132W. First floor, West wing, room 132. Now those codes on the log made sense.

Shit. Now those codes on the log made sense. The last new intake was on this floor, East wing. Room 126. If he did have the disease, he was as loose as I was, and very close. I was starting to grow ... concerned.

I walked slowly back to the rec room, putting each foot down slowly on the marble tile, trying to mute my progress as much as possible. The A-team theme song continued to infuse the room with an audible sense of absurdity, and I resisted the ludicrous urge to join in as I evaluated the windows, judging their suitability for an escape route. Unfortunately, owing to my home's unique internal security features, the windows were barred, and the glass was unbreakable.

As I scanned the room frantically, I suddenly noticed that I couldn't hear anything from the hallway, and for a moment thought that the potential danger had passed. It was a fleeting moment.

Our tenuous calm was shattered by a pounding from the hallway on the doors to the room. Delivered in the same implacable cadence as the hammering I had heard when I first awoke, a body was being slammed with considerable force against the gateway to our temporary sanctuary. A-team didn't like this new development, and he loudly shrieked his objection.

Distraught, he shot up from his crouch behind the sofa and bolted to the doors, frantically making a play for the deadbolt. Bolted to the ground in shock like a piece of loony-bin furniture, I watched, unable to move. I couldn't believe my eyes; there was no way to get between him and the doors, and no way to stop him from damning us both.

He struggled with the locking mechanism for a split second, and yanked on the brass handle at the same time the doors were being shoved inward from the other side. His foot caught in the corner of the rapidly opening door. He fell to the floor awkwardly, still wailing his displeasure.

Our guest stood in the doorway, illuminated by the light from the barred windows.

I dropped instinctively to a crouch behind the desk, which blocked his view of me but afforded me a sheltered observation of our new friend. Too stunned to move, and with no chance to impede his progress into the room, I stared.

His skin had a light gray cast to it, and his face, fixed in a rictus of what could only be described as ravenous hunger, with the mouth slightly agape, and the cloudy eyes unblinkingly focused on A-team, wore no expression found on a living man. He was dressed in white pants and a white shirt, both articles straining to cover his massive girth. A bite wound adorned his massive neck, with the remnants of a crude bandage hanging lazily from his collar.

It was Conan.

His white canvas sneakers, one of which was stained with a dark red fluid, stood awkwardly cockeyed to one another, as if the two were acquainted but had never formally been introduced. He didn't pause when his gaze fixed on A-team; his massive bulk simply fell heavily on the hapless lack-wit with a speed not befitting his shambling gait.

A-team screamed once, before the creature brutally severed his jugular vein with his teeth and tore into the tissue around his neck, pulling skin from flesh as blood poured onto the floor. His jaw moved slowly as he chewed the first bite, blood trickling down the side of his jaw, eyes staring forward and unblinking, hands pressing down on the still-twitching shoulders of A-team.

"Fuck. That."

Conan looked up, dull glazed eyes searching slowly for the source of the distraction.

Had I said that?

Shit. That was genius. I ducked my head and cowered behind the nurse's station, hoping that I had hidden myself quickly enough. Fearful and confused, I listened intently for the sounds of a shuffling approach.

Then a moan and the sound of sniffling, like the thing had a cold. Then nothing. Could these things smell? Like a dog? For several long seconds I waited, holding my breath. I knew that if I moved, if I even twitched, I'd meet the same fate. My neck itched suddenly, anticipating dull incisors pressing into my arteries.

Finally, after what seemed like an eternity, I heard the horrific sound of Conan returning to his meal. Like a large dog gnawing blissfully on a bone, the gruesome sounds of flesh being sloppily pushed into an open mouth reached my ears clearly. The blood pooled across the floor, and I stared at its spreading stain as it intruded into my space, making its way toward me under the desk. There was so much blood.

My head split in two, fire from inside cracking my skull like a hammer blow to the forehead. Pain ripped through my consciousness.

Maria's face was suddenly before me, her mouth and eyes bearing the vacuous look of that thing on the other side of the desk, as she leaned toward me in a crude semblance of a lover's embrace. My hand was on something: a flashlight dropped under the desk. How did I miss that?

I was on my feet, and in the distant clouded vision of my mind's eye, I saw that I had been discovered. Maria's ID badge, still fashioned to her lapel, flashed in front of my eyes. Her eyes, unblinking, stared at me with no light of recognition as she came for me. The flashlight came up. The face I no longer recognized disappeared in an explosion of color. It was suddenly dark, and I was alone.

Again.

CHAPTER 3

The words on her badge were stenciled into my awareness as I struggled against the darkness. Starling Mountain. For the second time in the last two hours, I woke up. This time, I was sprawled in a pool of blackened, sticky blood, with the name of Maria's employer barely and inexplicably beating out a crushing headache for dominance of my skull.

I hadn't been out long. Light still streamed across the floor, casting shadows against the far wall and highlighting my unique predicament.

Conan lay atop my legs, his massive, crumpled torso trapping my feet, his head laying inert against the cool tile of the floor. A large flashlight was on the floor next to my hand, slick with blood and other matter.

I gently probed my head, feeling through my overgrown hair for contusions or bumps that would explain my nap, but I discovered nothing. I looked back down at Conan, slowly and laboriously removed a foot from beneath his massive chest, and rolled his weight off of my legs.

As the body flopped to the floor, the head pivoted to the side, allowing a glimpse of the trauma that had felled this tree of a man. He bore a massive head wound on the left side of the head.

This was too much. I must have blacked out when he attacked me, either from fear or exhaustion, or both, but still managed to hit him hard enough to drop him. But why did I remember seeing Maria's face? A voice that lived in a foggy corner of my mind was whispering to me, but I suppressed it.

Even if the voice was right, and I was imagining everything, even if this wasn't real, even if, as I lay here, feeling the pain, staring at the blood, I was in my cot, back in my room, doped up on meds, I lost nothing by surviving the hallucination. I lost everything if it was real, and I did nothing. I shook my head.

Escape first, existentialism later.

Rising slowly and shakily to my feet, I stuck the flashlight into the pocket of my standard-issue scrubs, and moved to the doors leading to the exit hallway. I was dizzier than a drunken sailor at the end of three days' leave, and the room spun until I managed to grab hold of a desk for several minutes. This was really bizarre.

No head wound, but I was blacking out and getting dizzy? Either I was really crashing hard from being doped up, or I was as crazy as they said I was.

Looking down at the crumpled bodies before me, I decided to reserve judgment for a later date.

The passage to the front exit stretched in front of me; corridors to more rooms extended to either side. I stared towards the exit, to the Plexiglas antechamber, and tried to make out the movement I could see in the distance. I looked to either side hallway, but discarded them as an escape option, the corridor to my left dead-ending in a wall past several rooms, the corridor to my right culminating in a stairwell, unpromisingly lacking the magic red Exit sign that I was searching for.

Nope, no doors to the outside that way, my friend, and it was the greener pastures of the good outdoors I was headed to right now. As I moved toward the security room, a fire extinguisher hanging from the wall caught my attention, and I ripped it from its mounting bracket. Oh, yeah. Now you're a bad ass.

In my movies, I always seemed to find a grenade launcher, a man sized pistol, or a shoulder mounted tank at the last (and most opportune and convenient) moment. Like during a romantic dinner, or while on the john.

No such luck today. I guess if I want some help, I need to write it in to the script. The little voice in the back of my mind tried to add to that thought, and I heard amused chuckling sound from the recesses of my brain.

As I approached the plastic chamber, I could see through the open exterior doors that there were definitely people moving around outside, some of them in the white uniform of the facility, some in street clothes. They were all moving very, very slowly. Either very unconcerned, or very sick. I wasn't liking my odds on it being the former.

While I still couldn't bring myself to buy into the story on the news, the pictures made for a compelling case of some seriously f'd up individuals on the outside. But there still had to be a better explanation for this than reanimated corpses. Rabies, maybe? People act weird all the time—it doesn't take some sort of zombifying plague to cause that, right? More likely a whole shit load of people just got their tax bills or their alimony was due or something.

Tax bills. Definitely. I could stick with that for comfort's sake. For now, at least.

I half-heartedly checked the door to the guard's booth to my right which, naturally, was locked. Not only locked, but keypad controlled. I needed a code. I glanced back toward the rec room; I could ask Conan, but I doubted he'd be much help. I checked the door to the antechamber on a whim, but no go on that front either. How much did I want to go outside anyway, given that it looked from here like at least twenty of those things were wandering in the yard? I walked back to the crossroads between the hallways, contemplating my next step.

Why had Starling Mountain come to mind? I know Maria worked there, but what the hell did that matter? She had worked there for years before it happened, and I never gave it much thought. Despite the many discussions we had about her work, I really didn't have a good idea what she did there. So why wake up with it in my head after beating a zombie to death.

I just used the word: zombie.

Jesus, I was crazy. No other excuse. I chuckled to myself. At least I least I was where I belonged.

The place was so damn quiet, especially since I had lost my theme-song soundtrack, that at first, I thought I was hearing things. From the hallway to the right, I thought I heard the faint sound of voices. Half-believing I made them up in my desire to normalize this oh-so-fucked up situation, but for lack of a better option, I moved cautiously down the hall to investigate. I stepped carefully to avoid the squelching sound my blood-soaked sneakers were making on the well-polished tile floors.

Definitely voices; real, live voices too. Not moaning or shrieking or an imbecile humming television theme songs. Sounded like two people having a conversation. I moved to the outside of the room and looked through the observation glass in the door. Sure enough, two men, seated in chairs facing a television, were tuned to the cable news. An anchor was interviewing a disheveled older gentleman in a uniform of some sort. The volume was up high enough to carry into the hallway.

The door was closed and latched, but unlocked, and moved easily enough when I depressed the latch that I could push it open with a toe and step in without calling attention to myself. Against the wall to the right, a chair lay overturned, and a remote control lay broken on the ground, having apparently fractured when it hit the floor.

Suddenly, a thought that should have come much earlier: Where had Conan come from? And why had he stayed when everyone else had fled?

I instinctively stepped backward, and my foot caught the leg of the overturned chair, slamming the back of the chair against the wall. The two men jerked, as if a noose around their necks had been pulled abruptly back, the spell of the television broken; their heads turned toward me, almost in unison.

He hadn't stayed, I realized too late. He had been left. Along with these two.

I backpedaled too fast and tripped, sprawling on my back in the hallway. I scrambled to my feet, as the creature on the left rose from his chair and shambled to the doorway, and his companion simply crawled over the back of his chair, sending he and the chair to the ground in the process. They each bore hand-cuffs that at some point been attached to the wooden chairs, but which now hung loose from their graying wrists. I caught the name on the breast pocket of the guy on the left: it was Mr. Hickman.

I sprinted, or did my best to sprint, down the hall, passing the rec room on the right, where Conan's body still lay inert, but A-team's had struggled slowly into a seated position, legs twitching. Vacant eyes tracked my stumbling, clumsy progress past the open door, and the sound of his struggling to get up reached my ears, even as I fled.

I shook my head and sped up, now convinced that this whole thing was some sort of mind-fuck, but not willing to slow down and find out.

The stairwell, my only option, was at the end of the hallway. I stumbled to a hasty walk as I reached it in order to navigate the narrow flight. The walls on either side of the narrow passageway were peeling, the bone-white top layer of paint revealing a light green underlayment the color of brackish ocean water. A chain link divider separated the stairwells from one another, and as I reached the bottom, two floors down, I met an iron door.

I had struggled to reach the end of the hall, muscles unused to activity and shoes slick with blood, so I had failed to outdistance those things by much, despite their slow movement. Low-pitched groaning and a putrid smell announced their proximity, as they reached the door to the stairwell and shuffled through. As I reached for the handle to the door I realized I had dropped my fire extinguisher in my haste to leave the party upstairs.

Not as much of a badass as you thought, eh McKnight?

The handle moved easily but the hinges squeaked something terrible. The pursuit from above quickened, if that was possible, and through the chain link barrier, I saw the shuffling feet descending the flight directly above me. I flew into the open doorway, nearly splitting my head on the low-hanging door frame, and slammed the heavy iron door shut behind me. I felt for some sort of locking mechanism, and found a rusty latch that I threw into place just as the first body slammed against the thick metal.

I was breathing harder than I thought possible. They let us exercise, but we got very little in the way of cardio training. The anti-psychotics constricted the lungs, and made any kind of excessive cardiovascular exercise painful. Those of us who were sane enough to do so got to do light weight training; enough at least to keep fit, if not maintain the muscle mass some of us started with. Exercise releases endorphins, endorphins make us happy, and when we're happy, we don't crap in the rec room. Good theory, and based on actual research done by the guy down the hall from me who would engage in the latter activity if not allowed the former.

I couldn't wait to write my memoirs.

Once upon a time, I had been a muscular fellow. No Schwarzenegger or Stallone, but certainly larger than your average Gold's Gym toolbox. I still had a decent amount of size to me, but nowhere near the imposing figure I cut in my last film.

Either way, breathing was a happy place for me right now as my lack of aerobic exercise caught up to me.

As the pounding on the door kept up, I pulled the still wet flashlight from my pocket and for the first time, thought to check to see if it worked. A glorious beam of light shot from the lens, and temporarily blinded me as I adjusted to my surroundings.

I was in a narrow, low-hanging chamber, and large, corroded pipes led from my little room down a narrow passageway to a terminus unknown. The walls here were brick, probably the original stuff from the 1890's. I moved slowly down the passageway, looking over my shoulder to check that the latch was holding strong against my pursuers. Water dripped slowly from the low ceiling, and as I moved further into the dark hallway, the dank, centuries old walls illuminated by the fluorescent glow of my flashlight, it took more and more effort to quell the sense of growing claustrophobia.

Shadows created by the severe contrast between light and dark masqueraded as solid entities before me.

I walked for what seemed like hours through the maze of subterranean passages. At times, I would pass side chambers, formerly devoted to storage or some other inane function. Several times, I passed more sinister looking rooms; even a morgue, complete with yawning stainless steel cavities and vacant examination tables. To say that, after my ordeal upstairs, I was less than excited about wandering these dark tunnels with such sights was an understatement.

Eventually, the passageway terminated where a boiler room began, and I faced a grouping of massive furnaces and steaming pipes. I took in the room, checking it from floor to ceiling for potential weapons. No luck on that count, but I did take the opportunity to chuck my blood soaked scrubs and don a dark blue janitorial jumpsuit I found in a locker, being careful to avoid the blood and wipe as much off my skin with the discarded clothes as possible. I checked my hazy reflection in the stainless steel of a water heater, ran a hand through my hair, grabbed my flashlight, and started up the stairs to the only door in the room.

I didn't know where I was, where I was going, or what the hell I'd do when I got there. The most important thing to me was the sign over the door that promised simply: Exit.

CHAPTER 4

I opened the door slowly, not knowing what was waiting for me on the other side. It moved easily, making only a brushing, metallic sound as the steel hinges worked against the frame. Quietly, I listened for movement before slowly peering into the hallway. No shuffling, no moaning.

I looked slowly around the corner of the door, ready to slam it shut in an instant. I was in another hallway, identical to the one I left in the last building. Moving cautiously out of the doorway, I made sure not to let it slam shut behind me. The sign on the door frame to my right read "Boiler Room", surprisingly enough, but gave no further indication of my location. The corridor stretched out straight ahead of me, with closed doors lining the sides. I moved further down the hall, tiptoeing past seemingly empty rooms and abandoned nursing stations. No sounds of movement came from behind the doors, and if the state of my own building was any indication, this place was vacant too. Of life, that is.

In the middle of that thought, a soft whisper of air against the back of my neck and the sudden, quiet presence of another body made me jerk upright. My neck cringed in anticipation of a sudden jarring bite, and I froze in terror.

"Say something." Then a loud click.

Relief flooded washed over me like warm water; recognizing that I at least had a chance with a living human, my baser instincts took over. I had always been a smart ass. Family, friends, teachers—anyone that knew me growing up remembered me for that. Not a good heart, or a kind soul, but a smart-ass punk kid. In a situation like this, you go with that first, wise-ass instinct. You stick with your roots.

"You got a spare pair of shorts?"

A pregnant pause, and then a woman's voice and a breath of air against my neck as she chuckled. I turned around and faced her. She wore a stylish pants suit, much the worse for wear, covered by a white lab coat with spots of red and gray sprinkling the chest. Her name tag read Katherine Whitmore, followed by "M.D. Psychiatry", all in that same corny, loopy lettering they use to embroider hospital clothing.

Crap. You gotta be fucking kidding me!

Of all the psych wards in all zombie-invasions of the world, I get one that was still staffed by a damn doctor; a shrink no less. Why couldn't I have come out from my hole into a strip club or a pole-dancing academy? After putting in my time, was that too much to ask? And maybe a beer...I would kill for a beer.

"Get many tourists this way, or am I your first?" I asked, snapping back to reality and hoping for another laugh while I searched the hallway for signs of more activity or people. She kept her eyes trained on my face, flicking her gaze once to my chest. Her look was curious and slightly confused. She was tall, almost my height, and very attractive. Her brown hair, disheveled by what must have been a day's worth of running or fighting, fell around her shoulders. A pair of ratty sneakers, clearly not part of the original outfit, stuck out from the rest of the ensemble.

"You're my first...Joe," she replied with a slight somehow knowing grin, tucking the small, snub-nosed revolver in her lab coat pocket. I started, suppressing the urge to look over my shoulder for Joe ... until I looked down and remembered the nametag sewn proudly over my chest. Right, I was Joe. No problem.

She looked past me. "You alone?"

"Yeah, so far. What's going on here?" I belatedly added, "Doctor."

"It's Kate," she said, walking past me.

"And to be honest, you got me; I'm just trying to get through the next hour." She turned around, gesturing forward for me to follow.

"We'd better move back. There are more of those things in the next hall over, and the mops and brooms we stuck through the cafeteria door handle aren't going to last long."

She nodded her head to the right, and I followed her down the hall and around the corner, where I could see at the end of the adjoining hall a waiting area, occupied by three other people: a young man, an older man, and a young woman, who sat in various states of disarray.

"Where'd you come from?" she asked over her shoulder as we walked, "We thought we were on our own. We've been holed up in the cafeteria for the last three days, but we had to run when those things broke in through the kitchen. I was just looking for some food before we tried to get out of here."

Three days? Jesus! That must have been some fucking cocktail they served me last night. Rather, two nights ago.

"I, uh, was doing maintenance in the halls below ground and got stuck in the halls below the boiler room. Lost my keys." She had never been down there, how would she know what was or wasn't possible, right?

"Should have stayed down there, apparently," I said, believing every word.

"Do you know what's going on here?" she asked with a touch of exhaustion in her voice.

I nodded, not untruthfully. "When no one answered my radio calls, I found an FM radio. Heard about these wackos on the radio."

"Remember the company you keep when you're throwing that word around," she remarked quietly as we entered the waiting room. She smiled wryly, and turned to the waiting triplet.

"Everyone," she announced slightly louder than necessary, "this is Joe. He's a friend and he's going to be coming with us. Can everyone say hello?"

Taking in the room and paying closer attention to the occupants, I sighed. Of course. My luck keeps getting better and better. No pole dancing school or strip joint for me. Instead, I found a shrink toting three inmates, each of whom looked wackier than the guys that just tried to have me for brunch. Three faces, displaying varying degrees of stupor, tuned in on me.

"Pancake," said the young man, nodding his head in greeting. The young woman grunted, and the older man stared at me, then at the floor.

"That's Fred, and that's the only word he'll say," Kate explained before I could ask, gesturing to the young man with breakfast on the brain. She moved to the nurse's station against the far wall, rifling through drawers and searching through the discarded personal belongings. "He was admitted a few months ago; apparently he saw his father brain his mother with a frying pan while she was making breakfast. Since then, that word has been the full extent of his conversation skills."

I nodded back at Fred, looking at the other two expectantly. Neither spoke.

"That's Erica," she said, gesturing to the young woman.

Erica mumbled something incomprehensible and promptly stuck her hand in her mouth, rocking slowly back and forth in her chair, staring past me into the hall. She was young, maybe twenty-five. Her round, simple face was frightened and her pants were stained with various fluids, her left foot missing a shoe. The older man at her side, long ratty hair framing a narrow, worn face, perched on the arm of a tattered sofa. He simply stared at me, as if daring me to talk.

"I don't know his name; Fred and Erica were in my group, but he must be new." As if in response, No-Name grunted, rolled his eyes, and scratched his crotch vigorously. I suppressed the urge to laugh, instead turning back to Kate.

"How'd you end up here? With your friends?" I asked. I looked out the window against the wall behind the nurses' station. This was a low security ward, and had only the normal window frames, no glass bricks, no bars, no cloudy, unbreakable glass. In the courtyard below, I could see dozens, maybe even hundreds of those things wandering about. I wasn't completely prepared to bandy about the "z" word, but they sure as hell weren't human anymore.

In the distance, several plumes of smoke rose to the sky, highlighting a sunset that was starting to light up the horizon. Under different circumstances, it might have been beautiful. Today, it simply marked a quiet end to a surreal day.

"I'm a psychiatrist, and I was running a group a couple days ago. We were in the front courtyard," she canted her head toward the window I was staring through while I listened, "and a guy wandered up real slow, arms twitchy, kind of drooling on himself, with a funny look in his eyes. Given the locale, I didn't think twice, and the orderly that was out there helping me ride herd on my charges went to help him back inside." She struggled with a desk drawer, which suddenly came open too quickly. She caught herself on the edge of the desk, and looked down into the drawer, still talking.

"When the orderly, I can't remember his name, got to our slow-motion visitor, he grabbed for the orderly's throat. He tried to wrestle him down, but the crazy bastard bit him on the neck." She grimaced.

"It got serious at that point, and I called for help. A couple nurses from inside ran out as three or four more of those things came up the driveway from the street. We still didn't know what was going on, but they all had that look about them, so we got most of our people inside and locked the front door, just in time for the Head to order an evacuation." She picked through the contents of the drawer and abruptly pulled out a purse that was lodged in the back of the open drawer.

"I was about to leave with the rest, but noticed we came up short on the low security head count; we were five down, but no one wanted to wait around and find the last ones." She made an exasperated and resigned face.

"But you did," I filled in, impressed.

"Those things were already surrounding the buses, and it was getting pretty hairy. The Head gave me a set of keys to the last bus in the yard, had the driver pull up next to a fire escape, and bid me good hunting." She made a disdainful face.

"Selfish ass. They sped off toward the expressway, and I found my five. Three of them were in the cafeteria. I found Fred here wandering around one floor up, and this guy," gesturing to No-Name, "was actually two buildings over, between the max security ward and the gym."

"So you holed up in the cafeteria?"

She shook her head slowly, agreeing and disgusted at the same time. "Yeah. Someone had left them there, unsupervised. The rest of them were eating their damn breakfast when I found 'em."

"Pancake!" This from Fred, who hadn't even looked up, but was focused intently on untying and retying his left shoe.

She spared a glance in his direction, and dumped out the contents of the purse on the desk. With a gasp of success, she picked out a key ring and moved on to the wallet, flipping through various cards until she found an insurance card, which she stuck in her pocket. She discarded the rest.

"So we just barred the exterior doors and hunkered down. They didn't even realize we were in there until I made a loud noise this morning dropping a damn can of beanie wienies. That did it. They were all over the doors like white on rice. Took 'em no time to get through the barrier. So now we're here." The sound of beating on a door filtered up from the hallway we had vacated. "For now."

"What are you looking for?" I asked, although I was fairly sure I knew the answer.

"I lost the keys to the bus when we had to bolt from the cafeteria. We've got no other way to get out of this place, and those things are everywhere. They started streaming into the campus after everyone else took off." She looked outside, seemingly unconsciously.

"They're attracted by at least sight and noise, and when our patients started screaming in terror, they just started...well, not running, but they did some pretty speedy shuffling toward anything that moved. I lost two people in the cafeteria when they got in." Her face was serious and her eyes widened. She gripped the edge of the desk tightly as she spoke.

"They fucking tore into them with their teeth! I've been dealing with crazy people—clinically and criminally crazy, sick bastards—for years, and I've never seen anything like it. They didn't just bite them, they were chewing and fucking swallowing!" She shuddered briefly. I remembered A-team and the blood. So much blood.

She kept on. "There were ten or twelve of them that got in. I was lucky enough to pick this up," she patted her lab coat pocket, "from a guard booth downstairs before we locked down, and got off a couple shots, but it was like they didn't even feel it. I got these three out, but the other two didn't know any better. What a cluster fuck it was down there. Those things moaning and groaning, my people screaming and falling down. When we left the cafeteria, two of us were down, and five or six of those ... things ... were on each of the unlucky bastards."

She smiled wanly, "You'll have to excuse my language, but when I get excited, I tend to curse. Bad habit I suppose, but I think that the unique nature of the situation calls for it."

I looked at her and grinned. "Fuckin' A," I said.

She shot me a quick smile, looked past me to her charges, and held up the keys she had found.

"I got the plate number from the insurance card. All we need to do is find the car that matches these keys, and we're in business." Her ballsy claim was punctuated by the sound of crashing metal and tearing wood. No-Name sat bolt upright, staring down the hall. Erica continued to stare, spittle running from the corners of her mouth, where her lips failed to fully surround her hand, which was now in up to mid-palm.

The barrier from the cafeteria broken, and nothing but stale air separating us from the lunatics with a hankering for human flesh, we moved toward the double doors leading from the waiting room and away from the intruders.

Must lead to the parking garage or parking lot, I thought, not wanting to betray my ignorance of the building by asking. Although I couldn't see that it mattered, all things considered, I wasn't excited about revealing my identity to this doctor. While she seemed decent enough, I didn't want her to think of herself as a caretaker for four, instead of three. And I sure as hell didn't want her to be afraid of getting bludgeoned in the head while she slept.

The voice that had until now remained quiet, spoke up. Should she be? Afraid of being bludgeoned, I mean?

I had no answer for it. It didn't ask for one; it simply chuckled softly and retreated for the time being.

We spilled through the double doors in front of us, as at least ten of those things slowly came into view behind us. They caught sight of our group, and immediately turned the corner in pursuit. As we ran down the hall toward the dubious safety of a vehicle, I couldn't stop trying to fill in the gaps from what I had seen on television.

What the hell had happened?

CHAPTER 5

According to the news reports I had seen, it started somewhere on the eastern seaboard, and spread.

Fast.

Apparently, the first morning of the infection had been a morning like any other, albeit with strange reports filtering in from the initial infected cities and some small surrounding towns. But by the mid-afternoon of that same day, as I would soon bear witness, the shit got real.

No one had a bead on where it actually started, but the consensus was that it was mid-Atlantic East Coast. Probably D.C., New York, Baltimore or Philly: areas that saw the first cases. But because it apparently spread through the blood stream quick, and the things were hardwired for aggressiveness, it went through the densely populated areas like wildfire. And when every person killed was another person added to the ranks of the killers, society was facing a pretty real threat in a very short time.

The vast bulk of the military was in Iraq, but what was left stateside of the Guard was called out.

They had apparently attempted ad-hoc evacuations of the cities, with barricades keeping the infected in and trying to weed the healthy out. Most of the news footage that I saw was from outside the barricades looking in. I even caught a helicopter shot of a huge throng of the bastards pressing against a barrier set up on an interstate, catching healthy humans between the collective mass of creatures, while the Guard opened fire. They cut from that shot pretty quickly after that. Still had standards of decency to uphold, I guess. What really struck me from that video was the numbers. It looked like a hundred to one ratio—and it wasn't in favor of the living.

The news channels also seemed to be making a lot out of the response times; apparently, those areas with local emergency plans were faring a hell of a lot better than those that were waiting for FEMA and what was left of the Army. The Guard was able to work pretty quickly in conjunction with the local guys, who had drilled emergency plans since the terrorist attacks in '01, and the Katrina debacle in '05.

Boy, if that mess didn't teach you that you have to watch your own back, nothing will, huh?

A small town in Jersey was highlighted; they had evacuated their whole township in under two hours, and were locked tight in a local stadium, complete with a contingent of Guard and the whole damn police force. Compare that with one of the stories about a shelter opened by FEMA in DC to keep some inner city neighborhoods safe and secure; someone had left a back door wide open when loading water into storage, and the doors were all dead bolted from the inside. Those things wandered right in, following the water boys, and the guy with the key went missing. The next part was predictable, and the only survivor could barely get out the story before collapsing in front of the interviewers. Of course, the small towns only had 5,000 people to handle, and DC had a few more bodies to contain. But still.

The rural areas might be faring better, but they weren't on the news. The populated areas were hit hardest and fastest; the denser the population, the faster it spread, and the more resulting converts there were to infect others.

I remembered seeing a program on the internet when I was younger. It was put up by a math student at a university in Boston, and it purported to simulate a zombie invasion, and the rapidity with which an infection like that would spread. A joke at the time, probably inspired by an obsession with that director who made all those zombie movies, it illustrated how fast a disease like this would spread. It was just a simple maze with hundreds of little dots milling around aimlessly. The gray dots were zombies and the green ones were humans. You start out with five or six gray ones, and hundreds of greens. When the zombie dots touched the human dots, they turned to gray, and the infection rate accelerated out of control. In a matter of minutes, the box was totally gray.

It was interesting at the time but now, as the theory was put into play, it seemed too real. If that was any indication of how fast this plague could move, we were looking at a shit load of gray dots. Humanity's fate, summed up online, and in a matter of minutes. Will the wonders of the internet age never cease?

I snapped back to the present as we hung a left at the water fountain and toward the back exit, which through the window on the door looked to open into a garage of some sort. Given the number of those things I had glimpsed from Wisteria, seemed to be very little to recommend this course of action, this headlong plunge into the known unknown. But I wasn't about to hang around here. We weren't. We couldn't. So better the devil you don't know, right? Whatever.

We reached an external door with a red and white striped handle: the kind that is keyed to an alarm, so that anyone within a half mile knows when the door is opened.

"The only way to disarm this alarm is from the guard booth on the other side of the building," said Kate, "and I don't think any of us want to make that trip." She indicated back the way we came.

"So this door is going to scream bloody murder when we touch that bar," I filled in, not really a question. She nodded. We shared a look that conveyed our mutual uncertainty. We had no idea whether the ones outside would be attracted by such a noise, or if they needed to see their prey to be drawn to us.

"On the other side of this doorway is a parking garage, but we have no way of knowing what's out there." The sounds of pursuit filtered to our position from further down the hall. Slow, but persistent. "But we don't have a choice, and our options are limited. We're looking for plate number XLJ 920, Jersey tags." She looked out the window in the door, which afforded a very narrow view of the exterior. No-Name grunted, and Erica stared down the hall the way we had come. Fred, sensing the tension, bounced quickly on the balls of his feet, looking excitedly first to me, then to Kate. Two of our followers rounded the corner and, seeing us clustered at the end of the hall, shuffled forward hungrily.

They looked like Conan did: gray, pallid skin; shuffling feet; vapid, empty expression. But it was eyes that got to you. Not in a weird, Discovery channel kind of way, but I mean really got to you. They were bloodshot and wide open, staring forward - always trained on you, never blinking, never looking away. And there was nothing there but pain. No shred of humanity, no flash of cognizant thought or human comprehension. These fuckers were just hungry.

"OK, time to go now," I said, pushing forward and slamming the door open. A high-pitched squeal cut through the air; a red light above the door flickered to life and flashed insistently over our heads like a damn Wal-Mart special. Free meat! it screamed.

"Move!" I shouted, as Erica stopped in the door frame to cover her ears, crouching in an upright fetal position. Kate, Fred and No-Name bolted across the intervening space and into the garage, Kate turning and stooping to examine license plates as she ran.

Erica wouldn't move from the door frame and I struggled to pull her after me. The pack behind us had grown to ten or twelve, and the first creature was barely five feet from her cringing figure, its bare feet squeaking loudly against the tile floor.

I looked over my shoulder to the garage, seeing Fred looking at plates, apparently imitating Kate. No-Name was following Fred, walking unconcernedly behind.

Back to Erica. Three feet. I pulled as hard as I could, and she shouted in pain as I jerked her off her feet, and physically dragged her through the exit.

I threw her to the ground as the first creature's arm plunged through the opening. I slammed home the door, but too late. The fleshy resistance obstructed a complete lock and I struggled to push it shut.

The arm moved, fingers searching in vain for purchase on my arms. Gray, flaky skin came off on the door and the frame as the arm moved up and down along the gap. Brown fluid smeared against the white paint and a horribly rotten burst of air blasted into my face as the creature pressed its face inches from my own and I pushed harder, my weakening legs straining for leverage. Suddenly, the door shifted inches inward, and the obstruction vanished. Three neatly severed fingers fell to the ground as the alarm stopped wailing. I turned toward Erica, pulling her weeping frame from the ground into the garage.

"I've got it, Joe! Let's go!" Kate's head disappeared from behind a small Korean sedan. No-Name and Fred followed closely after. Dragging Erica behind me, I staggered to the car, weary legs, unused to such activity, bearing me stolidly forward.

Kate flew into the driver's seat, plunging the key into the ignition. I pushed Erica into the backseat, and Fred piled in after me. No-Name crowded into the front seat, seeming now to sense the urgency of the situation. Erica laid her head against the glass of the passenger side window, staring unseeing ahead. The ignition turned. The engine came to life. Gears ground loudly as Kate threw the car into reverse and her head whipped around.

"Where to?" she asked anxiously, looking at me.

"Don't you have a plan?" I replied, still trying to catch my breath.

"I didn't expect to get this far," she yelled, fear and adrenalin making her voice shrill and her words tumble over one another in rapid succession.

Suddenly, from the front of the car, a shadowy form shambled into view. The look in my eyes, or perhaps a reflection, betrayed the sudden appearance of a business suit-clad creature, rounding the corner between the hood of the car to our left and the concrete barrier, and Kate turned back to the windshield. His tie hung from a bloody neck, face slack-jawed but for the now-familiar glare of hungry malevolence. Shuffling forward, he clambered against the passenger side of the car. Kate, glancing once in his directly, slammed her foot on the accelerator. The car powered backward, the small engine humming in surprise. The creature fell forward, suddenly bereft of his support, sprawling forward into our now vacant space.

"Son of a bitch!" Kate screamed, more startled than angry, throwing the car into first and accelerating forward, into the hunched-over figure.

I braced myself against the back of both front seats, arms flying from my sides and elbows locking in anticipation of impact. Not against the target, but against the wall behind him.

The front fender caught him in the jaw, just as the head turned ignorantly upwards to meet the coming challenge. The head was separated from the body instantly, landing prominently on the hood of the car and rolling off to the side. I caught a fleeting image of the blank stare and then secondary impact. Kate slammed the brakes as soon as the decapitation had been achieved, but given the fifteen feet or so of lead space she had used to accelerate, it looked like we needed at least three feet of braking space. We had two.

We all jerked forward as the airbags in the front seat deployed, and the car came to a stop, the front end crumpling back slightly into the engine compartment. The airbags abruptly deflated. I peeled my fingers from their grips on the front seats, and looked to both sides groggily. Fred and Erica had both hit the seats in front of them, but they looked fine. Kate shook her head and looked back at us. I tentatively reached up to touch my forehead, feeling the warm sensation of blood heating my fingers as I did. They came away sticky and red from a small laceration above my right eye. A single tear of blood dripped off my eyebrow as Kate turned around.

"Shit. Look at your head. Sorry about that, I ... "

Whatever she was going to say was interrupted by the shattering of glass on the passenger side of the back seat. I turned to the sight of Erica's

head being pulled violently back over the shards of remaining glass, and a
mouth firmly attaching itself to her jugular, clamping down firmly as she
screamed, blood spraying against the roof of the car in spurts. Two more
creatures followed her attacker, stymied in their own approach only by the
narrow passage afforded between our car and the adjoining vehicle, which
pathway was currently blocked by the dining intruder.

I grabbed the hair of the creature and tried to dislodge its toothy grip.
Erica continued to struggle, her scream now garbled by the intrusion of teeth
into her larynx; hair matted with crusted blood fell across her face, as the
intruder's head ground slowly against her neck. In frustration, I balled my
fist, striking the back of the creature's head as hard as I could and forcing it
from its meal. I grabbed the hair on the top of Erica's forehead, pulling her
head back into the car as forcefully as possible.

"Drive!" I screamed, as her head snapped forward, tears streaming
from her eyes, and her lifeblood pooling in the hollow of her neck and
trickling down her torso, relocating to a stain of widening moisture on the
chest of her scrubs. Her attacker's hand was still clamped on the back of her
neck as the ignition stuttered, catching on the third try, and the car rocketed
backwards.

Erica screamed again as her neck became the prize in a tug of war
between the creature and the car, the latter prevailing only as the creature's
arm was sheared off at the shoulder, our car slamming its side into the
adjoining SUV and scraping the thing off on the corner of the monstrous
vehicle. I pressed my hand against her neck, which was a fountain of blood,
as Kate navigated the rows of parked cars and sped toward the exit.

The engine was protesting too much, stammering when given gas;
steam rose faintly from the crumpled front end, ghosting past the front
window in a modest but constant trail of condensation. No-Name was
crouched bravely against the now limp airbag, having distanced himself
manfully from the conflict behind him. Fred was petrified, flattened against

his door, simply staring at Erica and at me, as I futilely tried to prolong the inevitable.

"I'm going to head for the Expressway," Kate threw back, as she turned the final corner into a straight away ending in the exit. "It was where the Head was told to go when they evac'd the facility; apparently the police had set up a safe house of sorts in the Merchant Marine Academy and they were directing traffic to take the expressway to the academy for the time being," she explained. "How is she?" She glanced back and grimaced, her medical training likely answering her own question before I could respond.

I had little experience with gushing neck wounds. Real ones, at least. In my movies, people could come back from anything. A shot to the forehead with a twelve gauge could be a flesh wound, the victim reappearing in the final act with a band aid and a margarita.

Unfortunately for Erica, this wasn't one of those times.

"I'm no authority, but this isn't looking good." I replied. In fact, it was over. I looked at Erica's face and cursed silently.

Roll the credits; turn up the lights.

The flow of blood had slowed to a trickle, and her eyes were closed. There was no pulse under my red fingers, sticky with her blood. I moved my hand away from the wound, and had to repress a gag reflex—a massive parcel of flesh was missing from her neck, and a thin green detritus, most likely a gift of her attacker, ringed the bite mark like algae on a stagnant pond.

I looked up from her wound as the car passed the final speed bump in the garage and slowed to a stop at the exit doors. Kate pressed a button on the access device in the front seat; the little white box taped to the windshield signaled to the automated gate device, and the rolled sheet metal gate hummed in response, chains set in motion by the electronics whining in compliance as twilight appeared in the crack between door and cement. Shadows cast by figures waiting on the other side extended into the garage as the gate rose.

"Well that just figures," I muttered.

"If there are seat belts back there ... you might consider using them," was the response from the front seat. I felt her foot slam against the floor board as the accelerator was flattened against its housing, and the sedan moved forward as fast as its fuel-efficient four cylinder allowed. The garage sat below ground, and we were met by a steep incline and five creatures, all having been called to the opening door as it opened.

She swerved to the right, where resistance was slight, clipping an outstretched arm and shuffling hip in the process. The creature spun off the hood against the retaining wall as the small vehicle took the second pedestrian in the torso. It lay flat against the hood, torn, bloody, bearded face upturned in vacant malice, mouth moving silently and eyes locked on Kate's face as the car crested the top of the incline, and she yanked the wheel to the right. Our hitchhiker slid off the left side of the hood, making a final grasp for the car but seizing only air as it was dashed to the macadam roadway.

We were on a narrow driveway, most likely originally designed for horse-drawn buggies, and were passing by poorly kept hedges to our right. Zombies—I supposed I should come to grips with what we were dealing with here—wandered aimlessly through the open campus to the left. From the distance, the sporadic popping of what sounded like gunfire was a welcome signal that we were not alone. Twilight was rapidly passing to night, and Kate switched on the lights, only one of which was apparently still functional. The solitary path illuminated before us made the dwindling daylight around the car a miasma of shadows.

Several times before we reached the main gate, which we luckily found open, the car was forced abruptly to one side or another by a creature in the road. The car performed like a champ, engine continuing to run, imploded front and all.

As we got closer to the tree-lined street running perpendicular to the entrance, we encountered them more frequently, individually and in mindless, roving packs. Once, across the gardens that until today had been tended by those inmates well enough to do so, we caught sight of a one-sided chase, as an elderly man fleeing slowly from a pack of creatures on foot was overtaken. He stumbled in apparent exhaustion, or perhaps succumbing to an injury, and a group of perhaps twenty fell on him in ravenous victory, arms moving quickly up and down as if pummeling the unlucky victim. As the gruesome scene disappeared behind a storage shed as the car moved onward, I suddenly remembered the news reports. And A-team. Fuck.

"We have to slow down," I said, already levering Erica's body against the door so gravity would take her away from the car without much effort on my part. "She's dead, and if the news reports are true, we don't have much time until she ... comes back." I couldn't believe I was fucking saying that.

Kate nodded, and the car slowed to a jogging pace as I reached the handle and pulled it toward me. The door came open and I pushed the body out of the car, Erica's buttocks sliding jerkily across the cheap fabric, and her head flopping messily to the side. The body fell heavily to the ground, and I quickly pulled the thin metal door closed. Her blood, already drying to the upholstery, was all that remained of her membership in our small group. I turned, watching her get smaller in the distance. I saw her arm move against her body, whether the body settling to the ground or already reanimated I couldn't tell, as her form became indistinguishable in the murky dark. I shuddered, and faced front.

We reached the street outside the facility, passing between the twin sentinels of stone that housed a now open but normally locked ten foot wrought-iron gate. A car sped by, too fast for the narrow space, risking collision with dozens of those things as it braked hard and hurtled away through the wooded area to the North.

Two helicopters flew by, low and fast, lights blurring in the sky, rotors thumping the air; in the dark, there was no telling if they were military or civilian. Row houses lined the street, parked cars intermittently abandoned

beside overgrown hedges and a narrow, cracked sidewalk. Several houses'
doors smiled emptily onto the now dark avenue, a front of civility standing
before leafless trees, branches swaying slightly in the dark air. Several
corpses — could I still call them that? — alerted to our presence, moaned
and turned toward our location. The street lights remained dark, a testament
to our new world, as Kate pulled the car into the center of the street and took
us toward the expressway.

CHAPTER 6

The Asylum was bordered on the East and North by Long Island Sound. Housing developments and neighborhoods were located to the South, and a small wooded area to the West, directly behind the row houses outside the entrance to the hospital. Recent development had encroached upon the trees, but most remained, guardians of a wilderness that had lost its battle of supremacy with the modern world.

Passing through the developed area immediately outside the institute, we turned South and drove slowly, keeping to the center of the road when possible. The hospital was far enough away from extremely populated areas to afford relative ease of movement, but as we had witnessed before, wherever there were people, there were zombies. The Park had, in the not so distant past, been somewhat isolated from the rest of King's Point, but a shortage of land on Long Island had pushed development closer and closer, apparently resulting in the encroachment of row houses and McMansions, all occupied by the suburban elite.

Well, not any more.

It was probably a nice place to live; quiet and green, far enough from the city to be suburban, close enough to be a livable commute. Maria and I had a house not too far from here before. Now it was probably, like me, property of the state. It was a nice place too, on the beach, overlooking the ocean. All the bare necessities: four fireplaces, a bathroom you could play tennis in, and a kitchen the size of Lincoln Center. Even a boat. What a life.

And it's all gone twice over, I thought, staring at the otherworldly dark outside the car.

Kate drove slowly, guided by the singular headlight, which illuminated living and dead alike. We dared not stop, even if we were inclined to do so, as we moved steadily toward the Expressway. There were so many people, some alive, most dead—all ambulatory. Too many to slow. It was our speed and momentum that kept us alive. To slow or to stop would be a death sentence. Creatures swarmed the few living we encountered. They streaked past the car, to the front and to the rear, in more numbers than I could count.

One young man—one of the few survivors we saw escape—dragged a duffel bag behind him. He had the headphones of some sort of music player hanging from his ears, and actually jogged beside the car for several paces before being diverted by three oncoming zombies, all wearing the uniforms of a high school baseball team. He sprinted off to the row of homes to the right, hurdling a fence and abandoning his duffel in the process.

I still have nightmares about the faces we passed in that time. It felt like each person we left behind was another soul we had personally condemned. It was a heavy burden to drag through the coming days.

We passed a used bookstore, windows full of gently used books that no one would ever read again. Ironically, the name placard showing the name "Read It Again" hung from one tattered chain, swinging fitfully in the wind. A small creature, probably female, crouched almost forlornly on the ground over a half-eaten carcass in front of the store, staring into the distance. A red smear on the cement in front of the store led deeper into the dark inside. Shadows moved within, slowly and deliberately.

Several blocks further on, a drug store sat on a corner, windows boarded up but with the front door hanging from its hinges. An advertisement for generic shampoo and conditioner still festooned the street sign, their black block lettering illuminated sadly in the gathering darkness.

Further on, an electronics shop, windows shattered and debris strewn in front as if looters had come and gone, was a testament to the initial misunderstanding of the true seriousness of the situation.

Amazingly, one television remained illuminated, showing only electronic snow to the few passersby. A solitary zombie stood before the window, head cocked to the side, staring at the snow. Its head moved as we passed, but its attention soon reverted to the window, seemingly fascinated and transfixed by the screen.

At the corner of two small streets running through a stretch of strip malls, and after carefully detouring around a crashed station wagon blocking most lanes of the road and slowly leaking gasoline on the concrete, we saw a door flash open behind us from a small office building and a young woman emerge, running fast and carrying a small object in both arms. She had bolted out of the door to a small insurance agency three yards ahead of two young men, both of whom were clearly members of the recently deceased and reanimated. More joined the chase as she streaked along the roadway, making a beeline for our car.

We kept moving as she fled, hoping she could outdistance her pursuers but unwilling to stop. We maintained our detachment as we moved away— right up until the time we recognized the baby.

Kate was the first to realize what the woman was carrying, slamming the brakes and turning her head.

"Sonuvabitch, she's carrying a kid!" she said in dismay and frustration, eyes glued to the rear view mirror and slamming the vehicle into reverse. I followed her eyes and confirmed what we had missed at first glance. The woman was running toward us, her burden in both arms. Her eyes were filled with terror as her legs pumped feverishly to reach the car. We stopped as we reached the slowly burning overturned station wagon, wheels facing the sky like the legs of some gigantic metal beast.

"I can't get around that thing in reverse!" Kate slammed her hands against the wheel in frustration.

I jumped out of the car, knowing that we were surrounded; at least ten zombies were converging on our location, breathy moans barely audible over the crackle of burning paint and rubber. A window in a small convenience store broke to my left, and several creatures stumbled through the broken pane, ignoring the shards of glass that lacerated their arms and legs as they moved forward.

"Run, you're almost there!" I gestured wildly, urging the young woman on. I moved toward her, thinking to help. From in front of the car, ten had turned to twenty, and more were shambling forward, not twenty yards from the car. I got as far as the trunk of our car before realizing that she had been cut off. Five or six zombies had emerged from a movie theater on the right, moving unknowingly between her and us. Stricken with helplessness, I froze.

Suddenly, from under a large SUV parked on the side of the street, a blistered, dirty arm snaked into her path, clutching wildly for her legs as she passed. Her foot caught in the twitching fingers and sent her sprawling to the ground. She twisted wildly in mid-air, desperate to cushion the impact for her child. I moved forward instinctively, although she was still fifty yards away. Any attempt to reach her was certain death, surrounded as she was by milling, shambling forms.

She came down hard on her back, knocking the air out her lungs. I could tell from where I stood that she was in pain. She struggled to stand, but collapsed in agony, her leg clearly injured. They were everywhere, and they moved with deliberate urgency. Hungry moans were in the air, and she knew she was doomed.

Her eyes met mine. I had nothing to give, and she knew it. We were separated by distance and circumstances, drawn together only by those last shards of humanity that had survived the initial outbreak of the disease.

A look of anger and determination crossed her eyes. Whether the anger was directed at me or at God is anyone's guess. Her head turned slowly, taking in her fate. She was surrounded, and they were only yards away. I saw her take a deep breath as she pressed her baby to her chest, in a last protective, loving gesture. The child's arms were moving slowly, as if weak with hunger or exhaustion. It cried once, meekly, and fell silent. As they neared her, a single tear tracked a line through the dirt on her cheek. Through a throng of undulating and shambling bodies, I could see her arms tense, as she held the child harder, its face buried in her chest. As the creatures neared her injured and desperate form, the child's arms slowed. As they swarmed her under, covering them both with twisting, excited shapes, she sobbed once and the child's arms stopped moving. She was weeping as they took her.

I fell against the trunk of the car, tears escaping silently from my eyes. Kate's voice jarred me back to lucidity, my world having been temporarily converted to ashes. I stumbled back into the car, slamming the door as approaching creatures came within arms length from the vehicle. More were coming our way.

"Go." I said it softly, my voice breaking.

"If she—," she started to say.

"Go, goddammit!" I screamed in anger and frustration. She jammed the accelerator and we shot forward, barreling headlong into the horrid night.

Several times, we were forced to detour around cars left abandoned in the roadway, some burning, some with doors still open, lights still on. At the intersection of two small roads, a small foreign car was wrapped around a lamppost, blood staining the open passenger window and the door panel, streaks evidencing that the occupant had been pulled from the window. Several creatures bent over a shapeless mass on the pavement not far from the car, heads moving up to watch as we moved past, moaning but not moving from their meal. One of them, an older woman with graying hair and a turtleneck sweater, continued to watch us as we drove away, blood and other matter hanging from her open mouth, moan a gruesome accompaniment to a hideous sight.

When I look back on what happened next, I realize that our mistake was not fully comprehending the nature of people in crisis, without civility's check on human behavior: both our own selfish nature, and the base desire of others. I think we all suspect that others are really animals at heart, harboring those most primal of instincts that are only curbed by the mantle of society, mostly because we know what we find when we look inside ourselves.

Ten long minutes after our detour for the young woman, we were met by a police car rolling toward us with lights revolving slowly atop the cab. Having not met, or for that matter seen, any authorities but for the occasional passing helicopter, we elected to slow the car to ask for instructions and information. I was a little wary, but couldn't exactly speak up and reveal my unrest. Instead, I slid slowly down in my seat, mentally willing myself to be invisible.

For the moment, we could see none of the undead. We had made our way into a deserted access road serving several big box stores, including a Target and a linens store. However, the buildings obscured much of our visibility, and the path to the rear of us had born witness to several packs, less than a quarter mile behind, so we didn't have much time. Our car came to a rolling stop at the crossroads of two roads. Ahead was an avenue leading forward, but the streetlights had yet to flicker on, and the path was obscured by the night and the imagined hordes of creatures that prowled the darkness. Trees slowly moved in the wind behind each of the stores, shifting the glare of the full moon with each breeze.

The police cruiser slowed to a stop, windows remaining up, lights revolving slowly, casting a bright red and blue beacon which was a boisterously out of place glow on the pavement and the hood of our car.

Kate rolled down her window, gesturing to the cop to do the same; No-Name leaned forward to peer to his left, apparently interested in the bright lights and the new arrival. Fred had his face pressed against the glass of his window, eagerly waiting to see what came of this encounter.

The driver's window on the cruiser inched down slowly, revealing the crew cut, squared-off jaw of a state trooper, and black eyes staring hard at everyone in the car. Not a happy face, I thought.

"Where you headed, miss?" he asked, baritone voice staying even and slow, shifting his glare from No-Name, then to Fred, carefully observing the standard issue hospital scrubs on both. Despite my best efforts and total concentration on the task at hand, my cloak of invisibility failed me, and his last glance went to me, noting the janitorial garb. His eyes trailed off my clothing, past my face—that was key—and to the blood covering the back seat where Erica had expired.

"Where should we go?" Kate asked, her voice crackling with the competing emotions of tension and relief.

"We had heard the expressway was safe, thought we'd make for the maritime academy. Maybe some sort of shelter there? We were left behind at the hospital, and already lost one of our number to those things back on campus."

He chuckled, eyes hard and unblinking. The smile didn't touch his eyes. "Expressway's no good," he allowed, as his radio crackled. He slowly reached to his shoulder and depressed a key, silencing the intrusion.

He glanced back to the back seat, again passing his gaze over my face. The vestige of his smile slowly melted from his face.

Like a snake rising silently to strike from beneath a rock, a pistol muzzle appeared from his lap, the dark tip laying lazily on the windowsill. Pointed toward the car. His hand was bandaged around the palm, a dirty brown stain having spread and dried on the dirty gauze.

"I'm not sure I need to be telling you where you might want to go," he replied, in that same slow, deep voice. "Seems that we've had a heck of a time determining who might have been bit, and the orders came down a yesterday to do checks on people before sending 'em up to the shelters."

He grinned, his gaze traveling from Kate's face to her lab coat, which was unbuttoned and lay open, revealing her blouse. Not good.

Back to her face, corners of his mouth turning up in appreciation.

No sir, not good at all.

"Why don't you three," he gestured with the muzzle of the gun, "go ahead and get on out of the car, come around to the back. You stay right where you are ma'am." Fred reached for the door handle, but I grabbed his wrist. No-Name was still staring at the officer, not comprehending, or not caring, about what was going down.

"We haven't been bitten," Kate protested, urgency flavoring her tone. She glanced into the rear view mirror, meeting my stare, and seeing her worry reflected back to her. "We've lost one to a bite, but no one else was hurt. We're just trying to get to a shelter." Fred's wrist twitched in my grasp.

She was answered by the stiff metallic click of the gun being cocked.

She turned back to me, moving her head out of the window frame, and No-Name came into the cop's line of sight.

The window behind No-Name shattered into a thousand pieces as his head disappeared in a cloud of red and gray. My face was suddenly wet, and Fred was screaming.

Kate cursed and curled instinctively over the wheel, the jerking of her body, out of sheer luck, causing her to slam her foot against the accelerator. The car was still in drive and it moved forward on command. Her head was still hovering over the center console, arms sheltering her head, not seeing the Dairy Queen sign ahead of us.

"Turn the wheel!" I shouted, reaching forward to do it myself, but knowing I was too late. She turned forward, hands reaching the wheel and foot shifting to the brake in time to veer the car from a head-on collision, but slamming our left side into the pylon supporting the large red advertisement. Fred's head slammed into the window, shattering more glass; I slammed into Fred; No-Name's body flew against Kate, an orgy of battered, confused bodies.

From behind us, the sound of more gunfire and a sudden explosion of taillight and Korean trunk. Kate turned the key in the ignition. Nada.

"We've got to get out of this car, we're sitting ducks," I said, struggling with my seat belt. Kate extracted herself from her own restraint, opening her door. Again from our rear, the squealing of tires, a gunning of cruiser engine. A thud. Then more gunning, but no more squealing. I looked back.

Five or six creatures had emerged from behind the linen store and the adjoining neighborhood behind the tree line, dozens more trailing behind. The first few were already to the cruiser, and one had met its demise under the Ford. But its body was apparently caught up in the undercarriage, preventing the trooper from flooring it. His window was still open, and the pistol came out again, this time pointing away from us, toward the attackers. They swarmed the open window, arms stretching forward, reaching for the trooper.

I got out, dragging Fred behind me as Kate crossed in front of the car and took his other arm. I looked through the front passenger door window as Fred got his footing, examining No-Name briefly. He was as dead as ... well, he was really dead. The bullet had entered through the left temple, and had taken off the entire back of the skull. A bloody gray lump matted with hair stood out from the back of his skull, evidence of the exit wound that had resulted in the shattered window. Poor crazy bastard.

Before turning away, I noticed a bracelet on his arm. It was one of those hospital bracelets that are impossible to take off without scissors or a knife, and it seemed out of place considering neither Fred nor Erica had worn one.

But I did.

Recognizing the mark of my kind, I reached through the broken window, grabbing his wrist and turning the bracelet toward me. Identification number, and then name: Seymour Williams.

What the fuck? How did he make it out of the maximum-security ward? He was one of the new admits: a truly violent psychopath. How could he have found his way to Kate's group? He couldn't have, unless someone had let him out and locked the door behind him. This begged the uncomfortable question: had I been locked in?

"Let's go! Aim for the Target," Kate yelled at me, snapping me out of my short trance as I put my shoulder under Fred's arm and helped him forward. He wobbled unsteadily, but was able to move. Several creatures moaned behind us, recognizing our presence. Another blast. Loud cursing, engine revving, then another blast. And another. We crossed the empty parking lot in darkness, the glowing red target a promising Mecca.

Several parked cars, left in the parking lot for reasons unknown, cast shadows we avoided, as we moved as quickly as we could across the dark cement. Fred groaned, and Kate looked back.

"We can stay ahead of them, but if the doors are locked here, we may have problem," I said, also looking to our rear. The lights in the store were off. Not a good sign.

We reached the beige concrete wall between the garden center and the glass entrance doors and moved toward the latter, Kate supporting Fred as I grabbed the handle and pulled. Damn.

I moved towards the automatic doors, waving my arms like a wild man in front of the sensors. Nothing. Double damn.

I looked to the parking lot. They were moving steadily toward us, a fat woman in a moo-moo in the lead, hands opening and closing slowly on the end of outstretched arms, head cocked to the side, eyes staring forward, locked on our group. Behind her, a tall man in a tee shirt and jeans, a cell phone still clipped to his pants, bloody arm revealing his bite wound. Following him, a small child, mouth torn slightly open at the cheek, hair missing from one side of the head, where white bone showed through.

"Garden center," I said shortly, grabbing Fred by the arm.

"Pancake," was his woozy reply, as Kate hefted the other side of his inert form.

We reached the chain link fencing surrounding the mélange of peace lilies, paving stones, and brightly colored annuals. The door was no use, obviously, but the chain link was open on the top. No telling whether we had access to the store from the garden, or whether that way was locked too, but these things couldn't climb, so we might be safe for a short time if got up and over.

Fatty was about forty feet away, and getting closer. Her retinue followed closely behind, like a line at a buffet, all with a hungry purpose.

I looked at Fred, who still looked dazed and uneasy. "Can you climb, buddy?" I asked, as nicely and calmly as possible, gesturing to the fence. "We need to get in here."

Thirty feet.

"Pancake," he nodded, tripping forward and grabbing the fence. He started to climb, and I helped him up, boosting him to the top until he was bent over, his chest hanging over the other side, legs kicking toward the parking lot.

Twenty feet.

Kate went up next, and I levered her feet over the top. As she reached the summit, Fred fell heavily to the concrete on the other side, landing squarely on his buttocks and grunting in pain. Kate's lab coat flipped over her head and her hair veiled her face, as she twisted and came down on her feet.

Ten feet.

I jumped as high as I could, grabbing the links and pulling up hard. Cold steel dug into the soft flesh of my fingers, joints unused to exertion groaning in distress. My feet scrambled for purchase on the smooth steel, and my sneaker caught a break, providing enough traction for a final surge. Searching, erratic fingers brushed my ankle, as my legs were thrown over the top of the fence, the metal bar capping the links jutting suddenly and uncomfortably into my crotch.

I exhaled in pain as the crowd reached the fence. Dozens of bodies pressed against the web of metal and it shook, nearly jostling me from my perch. Catching myself, I quickly jumped to the ground, nearly missing a rack of neatly stacked spice plants for the home garden.

We again grabbed Fred and moved toward the sliding glass doors into the store. Behind us, the fence shook with the sounds of hunger and the moans followed us as we disappeared between rows of hydrangea.

CHAPTER 7

The double doors leading to the inside of the store were locked. Apparently, whoever had closed up shop here had had time to cross the T's and dot the I's, thinking perhaps that they'd be back later. The fence continued to shake, and the moaning was getting old fast.

"If we break the glass, and those things get in, we've got issues," I said, hefting the cement edging brick I had picked up, as Kate leaned against the wall and helped Fred to an Adirondack chair sitting in a display next to the door. Stating the obvious must be a symptom of exhaustion.

"And if we don't break the glass, and those things get in, we're fucked." She replied, jumping on board the obvious-statement express. This with a tired sigh and hands placed on hips.

"Fair enough," was the reply, as I lifted the brick to shoulder level. "You think this thing is armed, like that one at the hospital?"

"You think it isn't?" she asked sarcastically, clearly exasperated. "What the fuck does it matter? You think we need a better advertisement of our location than the 'free lunch' sign that our friends put up by huddling around that gate? I think in is better than out, and that's about it right now. Just break the goddamned door. I'm sick of hearing these fuckers whine." Her voice and her attitude betrayed her exhaustion, wits frayed after days of running.

I tossed the brick, and the top pane of glass on the left hand door shattered, a horn beginning to bleat in short, concise bursts. Jesus, I hope the front doors are stronger stuff, or our stay here could be really short-lived. I used a length of hose to knock out the shards from the frame, and climbed through. The lights were out, but accent lighting above the shelving provided enough to see our way.

Kate climbed in and gestured to Fred, who followed suit.

"I'll find the manager's office and get the lights up and the alarm off," I offered, "You guys might want to get something in front of this door. Try the furniture section, get a chest of drawers, a futon, something like that." Kate nodded, and grabbed Fred's hand, leading him down the aisle of fertilizer and gardening tools.

"Wait," I said, grabbing a shovel from the rack next to me and jogging after them. "Take this, just in case."

Kate looked at the shovel and sighed. "You're probably right," she said wearily. "I've still got this," patting her lab coat pocket, "but I've only got three or four shots left, and my aim leaves something to be desired."

I grabbed a shovel, and walked toward the front of the store. From the outside, the fence rattled and the moans continued, following me further into the store. Passing racks of chips, soda and candy, my stomach, long neglected, reminded me when I had last eaten. As if in sympathy, a wave of exhaustion hit me, and my legs weakened. Adrenaline must be running low, I thought, turning the corner, through the dog food, the shampoo and the soap.

I turned into a hallway leading to a break room and restrooms, and reached for the door to the manager's office. A poster on my right caught my eye and my hand paused briefly above the doorknob. It described the emergency exit procedure in case of fire, giving a map of the store, and I studied the layout of the place. Three other entrances: the front, a rear exit that only opens out, and a door into the loading dock, which looked to be protected by another, larger external door like the one we had to open out of the parking garage at Hotel Crazy. From the manager's office, the sudden, unmistakable sound of movement behind the closed door brought me back to the task at hand.

Backing away from the poster and staring at the door, I raised my shovel. I could hear my own breathing come in short spurts. My pulse throbbed in my temples as I strained to discern any more identifying information from the next room.

Could one of those things have been left behind? Cold, dead, inarticulate fingers leaving it bereft of the ability to turn a simple doorknob? Leaving it locked in an internal office until dinner came looking for it?

The alarm continued to blare its shrill alert, continuing to serve as an audible beacon announcing our presence. It had to be shut off. The more zombies that gathered at the fence, the greater chance they got in here. If it was human, it would respond to me if I spoke, right?

"Hello?"

Nothing. No more movement from inside, either.

"We're looking for somewhere to hide—we're not looters or muggers or rapists, and sure as hell aren't those things outside."

Still nothing.

"No one has been bitten, and we're just trying to get the lights on."

God, I hope this guy didn't have a gun, I thought, as I reached for the door handle.

Suddenly, the knob turned and the door flew open; I was staring at a small, middle-aged, balding man, wearing the uniform of a Target employee, complete with name tag that read Earl. My eyes strayed to the more important aspect of Earl's appearance: he was also holding an ax.

"What the hell are you doing?" I squealed, so surprised that I almost didn't notice how very unmanly my girlish shriek of shock had sounded. Almost.

"What the hell am I doing? What the fuck are you doing here! How'd you get in? You didn't let those things in, did you? Fuck!"

A shrill, nasal voice, as excited as I was, and much more high strung. He hefted the ax; I flinched and jerked my arm up, bringing the shovel into clear view.

"No! Hold on, just calm down!" Easier said than done. "Look, we were running from those things, a crazy cop just splattered our friend all over the interior of a compact car, and we narrowly avoided being the main course on a crazy mother fucker all you can eat buffet line. Put the ax down, and let's just talk for a minute."

Sounded reasonable. Well, under the circumstances at least. Reasonable was becoming a relative term these days.

The ax dropped a fraction of an inch. "Who's we?" he asked, looking nervously over my shoulder. "There are more of you?"

"Can we lose the siren and get some lights on first? My friends are trying to barricade the door to the garden center, and we're losing time here."

He looked at me, and then over my shoulder again. The ax came down all the way, and he backed into the office, eyes still on me, and typed in a code to a panel next to the doorway. The siren died. He diverted his eyes to the panel for a split second, and flipped a couple switches that I heard click home. Ah-ha; let there be light.

"How did you get in?" he asked again, his desire to deal with the open door apparently winning out over his distrust of me, as he moved past me into the store.

"Magic," I joked, following behind, looking for some amicable bonding. He glanced back over his shoulder at me, glaring briefly.

"A brick," I said shortly. And then, my smart-ass winning over my assessment of his personality, "a magic brick."

Fuck him if he can't take a joke.

"Dumb ass," He threw back, moving faster toward the garden center.

Nice come back, you clever bastard.

"Listen, we had about zero options, man. It was either brick our way in here and risk a barricade, or stay out there, strip to our birthday suits, baste ourselves with butter, and jump on one of those damn grills that are on special outside."

He didn't answer, but shook his head and turned toward the garden center doors. Kate and Fred were there already, struggling to upend a metal futon against the opening in the door. A particleboard chest of drawers blocked each of the sliding doors, and a couple metal Tiki torches secured the chests against the doors by lodging against the shelving units on either side.

"Who's this," Kate asked, understandably wary after our last human encounter, and unconsciously grabbing the end of her shovel.

"This is Earl!" I said cheerily, pointing in mock excitement at his nametag.

She stared at me briefly, questioningly, her eyes then moving to follow him as he passed her and looked outside to the fence.

"Jesus!" exclaimed Earl, his tone rising as he took in the scene outside.

I looked out again. There were more than before.

Many, many more.

We all chipped in, piling items on the barricade. The futon went against the window, then some bags of fertilizer to keep it in place, some more Tiki torches for stability, and some chairs from house wares. It looked strong enough to give us warning that they had gotten in. That's about it.

As an afterthought, we moved a set of table and chairs from the outdoor dining display, and put them behind our masterpiece pile o' crap.

"OK, Earl, so we're sorry for busting in here, but we just barely made it out of the hospital alive, almost lost our heads to a crazy cop outside, and are just looking for a safe place to crash and recharge. Are you alone?"

He looked at me inclined, I think, to tell me to fuck off.

But then he looked at Kate, who was pretty even in disheveled exhaustion, and his face softened. "I'm the manager of the store," he said, self-importantly, "and we sent everyone home when the crazies started appearing. I didn't approve of the decision but it came from corporate. Regional corporate, anyway. There's always some bullshit reason for people to go home: bird flu, AIDS, cancer, etc."

This guy must have been an absolute jewel to work for.

"I thought it would blow over, but the regional guys called and told me to close it up. I locked up and stayed about an hour and a half to do the books." He looked toward the barricade, scratching his nose.

"I went to leave a couple hours later, and the parking lot was already full of these things, most moving toward the linen superstore across the street, some milling around in my lot. A couple of them were clustered around a car out there, trying to get in, but I couldn't make out what they were after. Something was moving inside, but ... Anyway, it looked like a bunch were ganged up outside the linen place like they are outside the garden center here. Maybe some people like us were hiding in there and they knew it." He glared at me, as if revealing his presence here wasn't somehow inevitable.

"So I kept real quiet, turned off the lights, grabbed this," he patted his ax, "and locked my door. I had been listening to the reports on the radio until yesterday evening. Then it went dead."

"Your radio?"

"Not the radio. The radio waves. Nothing. Dead air, no emergency broadcast signals, no recorded message, nothing." He was clearly bothered by this. This bothered me too.

"How's that possible? I saw live news just this afternoon. Why would the radios be out but the television networks still be broadcasting?"

He shook his head brusquely. "What you saw wasn't live. They've been feeding loops of news through, cycling every hour the same stuff as before." His hand brushed wearily over his eyes as he yawned.

"Television has been out for two days now. Radio was the last thing to go. Well, 'cept for the internet that is. And even that has been shoddy. Networks goin' down, people playin' pranks and whatnot. The major sites, CNN, Fox, MSNBC...they were all up for the first two days, then started to drop off. Some bloggers think that the servers were in buildings that got burned up, or the techs that ran 'em ... well, can't run 'em anymore. Who knows."

His face was tired, but his eyes betrayed his fear. "All I know is that it's some fucked up shit out there, and it don't seem to be gettin' any better." Suddenly, an inquisitive, worried look on his plain, chubby face.

"What hospital you say you came from?" he asked, looking again at Kate's lab coat.

"We didn't — " I said, while Kate answered simultaneously, "King's Park."

He grimaced and turned away. "Of course."

Glancing briefly at Kate, who realized her error too late, I stepped forward towards Earl. I didn't have the patience or the time for the stigma scene. "Just point us toward house wares, and we'll go to sleep. You won't hear a peep from us the rest of the night, and we'll figure out what we're doing tomorrow, OK?"

I was very tired, and this guy's bitching was starting to wear on me. I tried very hard to loom imposingly, banking on his Napoleon complex to peter out in the face of larger size.

Besides, he wasn't about to try to kick us out, even if he wanted to, as we outnumbered him. As much as he probably hated it, we were all he had right now.

Earl shook his shiny head and stood up. "Go down this aisle, turn left. We don't stock beds, but the futon mattresses will work. Linens are two aisles over. I'm going back to my office. I've got security cameras in there that I can see our friends in the garden section on. I'll get on the intercom if they make a move."

He started to walk away, and suddenly stopped, turning and looking at me.

"Anyone ever tell you that you look like that guy from the movies, what was his name ... he had that line from that one movie ...

The voice inside was sudden and sardonic.

Aww, isn't that special? Someone knows who you are!

Shit, shit, shit.

"Yeah, I get that all the time, especially from the other janitors. Gets annoying," I finished, trying to sound pissed off so he'd leave it alone.

But he didn't.

"What was that line he said when he killed a bad guy ...?"

"Man, I don't remember. Look we're tired, so..."

"Yeah, yeah, okay. Damn, it's gonna bug me all night." He walked away for real this time, muttering to himself and shaking his shiny head.

Kate looked at me, but thankfully no glint of recognition. "I'm gonna check the break room for a shower," Kate said, grabbing her shovel and her lab coat, which she had tossed to the ground during the barricading.

"Sounds like a plan to me," I said, looking down at my jumpsuit, which was covered in the blood and fluids of Erica and No-Name, and thinking about my earlier close encounter with Conan. What a day.

What a damn, dirty, nasty, horrible fucking day.

Fred and I moved toward the house wares section, passing through the toy aisle and the electronics, and on through kitchen wares. As we passed a rack of cooking utensils, Fred's attention was diverted. I stopped when I realized he wasn't following, and walked back to the corner of the aisle, looking back at what had halted him. He was staring at a variety of frying pans, 6, 8, 10 and 12-inch varieties; stainless steel, cast iron and Teflon, all stacked neatly in rows. He slowly touched a 12-inch stainless steel job, almost caressing the handle. He pulled his hand back and started humming to himself, all the while staring at the pans.

"Fred." No response.

"Hey, Freddie!" Just staring.

"Pancake!" I said, and his head whipped around, eyes glaring at me in confusion—and was that suspicion? He softened his look almost immediately, but shot his hand out and grabbed the handle of the stainless steel 12-inch pan, and tore it from the rack. He looked back at me and nodded once, strongly and confidently.

"Pancake," he said, in a voice that, had he said more than that, would have brooked no dissent. As it was, there was little to disagree with. In a world seemingly overrun by zombies, the previously inane becomes commonplace.

Pancake, indeed. I nodded, smiling.

He walked past me to the vacuum cleaner rack, still clutching his new acquisition, and turned back, shooting me a look that said "let's go, what's the hold up?"

I shook my head, and caught up as we detoured through the clothes department. We each grabbed a new outfit, both of us taking a while to figure out what size we were, not having had the responsibility of clothing ourselves for years. I picked up a pair of cargo pants, a tee shirt, and a leather jacket, grabbing a pair of heavy boots and a knit hat as an after thought. Although the summer weather was still warm, I figured that the long pants and the thick leather might serve some deterrent to teeth and nails.

Fred picked out a pair of pajamas, which I replaced after laughingly dispensing with the mental image of him, his frying pan and his Winnie the Pooh PJ's facing off against the zombie hordes. We grabbed some jeans and a sweatshirt instead, and made it to house wares.

We each found a futon mattress and laid it out in the aisle. Kate found us fifteen minutes later, having quickly found and used the break room shower and a new change of clothes: jeans, a long-sleeved tee shirt, and a leather jacket. I smiled at the matching outfits. She also must have seen the advantage of boots over sneakers, carrying a pair in her left hand and her shovel in her right.

Fred and I took turns at the shower. He cleaned off first and headed for bed, and while I stood under the spray of the shower watching at least three different blood types head to the sewer, I couldn't stop wondering whether this was all a hallucination. I was, in fact, legally insane, was I not?

This was, in fact, an insane scenario, was it not?

I was, in fact, hearing a voice in my head, was I not?

Indeed you are. Or maybe I'm the one with the voice in my head? Ever thought of that?

God, what an annoying fuck I was. It all seemed so real, but didn't hallucinations seem real? Wasn't that what made them a problem?

Who am I to judge—all I can do is keep on and hope to outlast the creatures outside, or the one within, whichever is real. Fuck, what a trip.

I dried off, threw on my new clothes, and stumbled back to my futon.

Too tired to bother with sheets, I laid down and stared at the tiled ceiling, finally catching my breath after what could only be described as a difficult day. Beside me, Fred was already snoring. Kate had found a brush, and was trying to get her hair in working order. Really a beautiful woman, I thought, as she pulled the brush through her long hair in consistent, hypnotic strokes.

As I drifted off, I thought: too bad she's a shrink.

To which the voice in my head replied, softly this time: Too bad you're insane.

CHAPTER 8

"You mean like Goofy, and Mickey Mouse?"

She looked at me crossly, putting on the oven mitts and opening the oven door.

"No, not like Goofy. Not cartoons. We're talking about cells here, just little, tiny microscopic cells." She put the roast in and shut the door, her long blond hair falling over her shoulders as she leaned forward to examine the temperature.

"Reanimation. Just sounds funny. Like Goofy." I popped a tortilla chip into my mouth and sat down at the bar between the kitchen and the living room, watching her move to her next task.

"The word animation is not owned by those cartoons you watch on television, you know. It can be used scientifically too." She was washing lettuce now.

"When you animate something, you make it move, give it life. When you reanimate something, you're taking it from an inert or dead state and literally reviving it…bringing it back to life." She tore the leaves from the head, and tossed the stalks into the disposal.

"Just like new?"

"Mostly, yes."

"Mostly doesn't sound convincing."

She made a face and shrugged. "It's a very complicated process. There are issues, but the fact that it's possible lets us know that nothing is beyond our capabilities."

"How do you even begin to know how to do that? I mean, aren't cells really small? You guys must have really tiny needles."

The chips were really good. I wonder if we had salsa. I think we did, but that was weeks ago. Maybe months. Would it still be good?

Another dirty look. "Honestly, Michael. If I didn't think you were at least half kidding, I'd divorce you. I don't want idiot offspring running around the house trying to plug the dog into the electrical outlets."

"Ouch! Okay, so you don't use tiny needles to jab the tiny cells. So how, then?"

More tearing and crunching as she smashed the stalks into the disposal, reaching across the sink to flip it on. The kitchen hummed with the sound of disintegrating vegetable, and then went quiet again. The timer for the meat ticked away slowly in the background.

"We have a lot of expensive equipment," she said, shaking her hands over the sink and drying them with a striped dishtowel. "The scientific equivalent of your video game system—the Xbox or Playstation of the scientific world."

"So how do you know when they're reanimated?"

I walked to the fridge door, mouth full of chips. Opening the door, checking for the salsa. I think it was a red bottle.

Her voice rose excitedly. "They reactivate. They start doing all the things cells do when they're healthy. With some minor exceptions." Tossing the clean leaves into the salad spinner, she pushed the button to spin them dry.

"Minor exceptions?" I said, absent-mindedly.

Ah ha! Expiration date ... damn! Wonder if it's still good anyway.

"Like I said, we have had some issues. There are some ... anomalies ... in their functioning. But the fact that we've been able to get them back after they were, for all intents and purposes, dead, is mind blowing!" She was getting more excited as she spoke, gesturing with her hands, eyes wide and bright, and lettuce momentarily forgotten.

"Definitely not good." I grimaced, and shook my hand in the sink, running water over my finger, where globs of overripe salsa still clung tenaciously.

"Temporarily, no, it's not," she went on, "But we'll get them worked out eventually—we're making tremendous progress every day. The subjects are getting progressively more active and the cells are ... I mean, the biggest step has been taken." She slowed down and took a breath.

"Reanimation of dead cells is meteoric progress in this field. No one has ever gotten this far. Some hiccups are to be expected, but Dr. Kopland is the best in the field. We've been working on the problems, and we think we have a solution."

"I'm sorry, what's looking good?" I had missed something here.

She sighed, turning back to the lettuce and transferring it to a tossing bowl. She sprinkled dressing on it, and added baby tomatoes. She reached for the carving knife, turning toward me. The kitchen flashed in my mind's eye, and the scene became black and white; it stuttered in fits and starts, like a poorly buffered video or a choppily edited film.

Flash.

Suddenly, it was no longer Maria. It was something entirely different, but the same. Eyes lined in red, graying skin sallow on the bones of her face, mouth agape, she staggered toward me.

"Maria?"

Flash.

She was on me. I struggled, but she was stronger than she had any right to be. I threw her off and ran for the door. But my legs wouldn't move.

Flash.

I was back on the floor. My hand throbbed in pain, and I felt her convulsing jaws close on my throat. Dishes fell to the floor as our entwined legs slammed into the counter.

Flash.

I couldn't breath, and my face burned; fever was a furnace in my head. I thrashed on the ground, helpless. Her body lay prone nearby. In the hall. Not the kitchen. Even in my pain and disorientation, I knew this wasn't right.

Flash.

I awoke, sweaty and screaming, to the anxious stares of Fred and Kate, looking worriedly around, searching for the danger. I was sitting bolt upright, breathing hard. I blinked in confusion. It was one of those dreams that seemed so real, but felt so wrong. Wrong, but familiar. Like parts of a real story had been superimposed on a fiction.

Starling Mountain. Jesus, how had I forgotten? They were doing work on reanimating cells. That must have been why the name shot to my head after my black out. Could Maria's employer have had a hand in this? Walking corpses seemed a far fucking cry from reanimated cells, but the science seemed similar. Creepy as shit, but technically similar.

I told myself it was impossible. Maria would never have condoned something like that. The potential side effects and ramifications of that kind of science weren't her thing. She was always a cellular-level kind of scientist. She didn't even like using rats—no, it wasn't possible. It had to be just a coincidence.

"You OK?" Kate seemed concerned. But there was something in her eyes that was more than concern for me. Was she scared for me?

Of me?

"Yeah, " I responded breathily, shaking my head. "Just had a bad dream. What time is it?"

She checked her watch. "Quarter to 7. We've been out for about 8 hours." She glanced at my head. "Head healed up pretty quick; guess it wasn't as bad as it looked."

I touched my forehead, looking for the abrasion from last night. I searched, probing gently for the cut. Nothing. That was definitely weird.

My confusion was interrupted by a dose of concern. I could hear the rattling from the garden center in the distance. It seemed louder and more intense. Early morning daylight was visible toward the front of the store, and I rubbed my eyes, still struggling to comprehend my dream, struggling to separate reality from fiction. Fred laid back down, eyes open, staring at the ceiling. Kate stood up, putting her hair back and grabbing her shovel and her pistol.

"I'm gonna hit the bathroom, check in on Earl. Maybe you guys wanna find some food?"

My stomach answered her, growling in response. "Yeah, definitely a good idea."

I headed to the food department, grabbing boxes of pop tarts, chips, milk, and some sort of canned coffee. Adding a bottle of water as an afterthought, I headed back to the futons. Fred was asleep again, apparently not disturbed by my rude awakening. Kate rounded the corner at the end of the aisle, face anxious.

"You better see this," she said, glancing at Fred.

I didn't ask why, just rose and followed. She gestured with her other hand and turned around.

"You think Fred's okay?" she asked as we headed away, "I'd hate for him to wake up and think we left him."

"He looked pretty zonked to me—I doubt that will be an issue," as we reached the electronics department, where a bank of televisions against the wall contained the picture of a disheveled news anchor.

"Shit, is this news live? I thought Earl said it went dead?" I could hear the anchor talking, but it was too soft. "Do you have the remote?"

She reached into her pocket, pulling out a remote, and zapping the televisions. "It's not live. It's another recorded loop, apparently. He repeats himself three times, same stuff, cuts out, and it starts from scratch. But it was just done about 10 hours ago—about the time that Earl said the radio went out."

The volume increased, and we watched the haggard, clearly exhausted local anchor read from a wrinkled piece of paper, hands visibly trembling.

"...repeat, reports are still unconfirmed, but we have received indications that the cities of Boston, New York, Washington D.C., and Philadelphia have been overrun and are no longer safe. Additionally, rural areas from Maine to Virginia have reported outbreaks and incidents in smaller towns outside populated areas. I repeat, if you have loved ones in any of these areas, please do not try to reach them, and do not under any circumstances venture close to these locations.

"Surrounding suburbs of these cities are likewise not safe, and citizens are encouraged to remain in their homes, with doors locked. If you live in a multi-story home or building, remove yourself to the highest point, and barricade the stairwell. If you live in a one-story home, block your windows and doors, and stay hidden. Do not reveal your location. The creatures seem to be motivated primarily by sight and sound, and will congregate wherever a living person or persons are located.

"If you encounter any of these creatures, your best defense is to run away and attempt to find a strong, defensible position. If you are forced to confront them, remember that they are no longer like you, and no longer possess the capability of reason. They do not hear you, they do not listen to you, and they do not fear you. You can stop them only by massive trauma to the head or spinal column. Again, you must either destroy the head, or brain, of the creature, or sever the spinal column at the neck."

The anchor's head drooped for a moment, as people moved in the background, gathering equipment and speaking softly to one another in full view of the camera. He looked up as if, somehow, he had even worse news to report.

Turns out, he did.

"The government has been mostly silent in response, although there are indications that remaining federal officials are moving rapidly southward. The CDC has no indication on cause, and individual units in the field are uncommunicative. Although National Guard units have been deployed to certain locations, there has been no indication of any nation-wide or systemic response. The White House has released a statement that the President remains safe aboard Air Force One, and is closely monitoring the situation. We have further unconfirmed reports that the Capitol was overrun before evacuation, and the status and security of the members of Congress that were inside is unknown."

"At this time, our local reports indicate sporadic response from federal forces, with increasingly slow reaction times as the infection progresses. The military remains on full alert, but reports from local commanders indicate a severe shortage of troops. There has been no word from the military regarding any withdrawal of troops from the Middle East to respond," he took a deep breath, "but all indications are that any type of mobilization and relocation on a large scale would take more than two months."

He looked back down to the sheet of paper before him. "Again, I repeat, reports are unconfirmed...-"

Kate muted the reports, and we looked at each other. "Not something you see on TV every day, is it?" I asked.

"Not unless it's in a movie," she replied, looking at me out of the corner of her eye.

What did she mean by that?

"Don't watch many movies myself," I shot back, overly nonchalant. "Tend more towards books, really."

Not untrue, that. I had read quite a bit during my stay at the hospital: regional histories, fiction, non-fiction, even a big pamphlet on the history of the hospital. Amazing how much time you have to catch up on your reading when you have 13 hours a day to fill.

"I suppose you would, considering." Her eyes held the slightest hint of a question as she gave me a sidelong look, flipping the television off quickly.

"What does—", I started.

"Look," she interrupted, turning toward me finally, "I know who you are. Not only are you very recognizable, but I worked at the hospital, and yours was not exactly a low-profile case. I know you were in 13, and I'm not sure how you missed your bus or, even more questionable, how you got across campus, into a janitor's suit, and into my building.

"But you did. So here we are, doctor and patient. Patients, excuse me. Truth be told, yeah, I'm a little concerned about traveling with you, but I have limited choices, and I read your file. Actually, I was a student of your case when it came out. I was in med school then, and it was certainly," she paused, head tilting to one side as if choosing her words carefully, "an interesting scenario."

Okay, so she was being honest. I could give it a shot.

"So why aren't you scared of me? I killed my wife you know? At least that's what they tell me. I don't remember doing it, I can't even imagine doing it. But I can't tell you I didn't do it, because I can't remember a goddamned thing about that evening. Apparently the evidence was against me and a jury of my peers gave me a one-way ticket to the loony bin. So what gives? Why the bravery? I could do you in the same way, and not even remember it in the morning."

I backed up, realizing I had moved toward her in my frustration. My voice trembled, as I struggled to keep my sudden, inexplicable anger in check.

She looked at me, blinking once, shifting her gaze over my shoulder. She put the remote on the counter and leaned against a rack of DVDs casually.

"You see, that's where I'm not totally convinced." She crossed her arms and made eye contact with me.

"Not convinced?"

"Not totally convinced," she qualified quickly, "Don't get me wrong; for the moment I'm just gonna go ahead and continue to assume you're not right up there—self-protection you understand—but I have some doubts. I read the reports. All of them. Several times. Police report, psych evals, coroner's report, even the prosecutor's case and the defense response." Her tone changed, skepticism creeping in.

"There was something that didn't make sense about the police report and the coroner's report. Led me to suspect that there was something amiss. They didn't quite click. It was the timing."

"The timing? What the hell does ..."

Suddenly, from above us, Earl's nasal voice, shrill with fear, shot over the intercom. "Wake the fuck up! They're almost through the fence!"

CHAPTER 9

We raced back to the futons, finding Fred awake, looking worried, clutching his pan to his chest. We quickly gathered our weapons and jackets and bolted to the barrier.

I moved a chair close to the barricade and peered over the top. A huge group of teenagers in football uniforms had come from nowhere, their sudden arrival adding critical mass to the already sizable number of creatures pressed against the fence. The steel posts supporting the metal curtain remained standing, but were steadily succumbing to the external force, their structure weakened enough to compromise. The fence bowed inward from the pressure of the massed bodies, the chain link pregnant with their weight.

"We have about five minutes before those things are at this barricade." I turned and jumped down.

"Won't this hold them?" Kate asked, looking unbelieving at the formidable pile of sundry house wares and garden products we had piled in their path. "At least for a little while?"

I shook my head. "If that fence is any indication, this thing will be a road bump. There's just too many, all moving in the same direction. We need to grab Earl and figure out if there's a way out of here, maybe through the back. Hopefully those things are clustered at the fence because that's where they saw us come in. If so, the back might be clear."

We headed toward the manager's office, and he met us at the entrance to the hallway, walking quickly, face somber.

"You see them out there?" he asked, looking over my shoulder and back to me. "That group of pimple-faced meat-eaters came outta no where."

"Yeah, they're itching for breakfast and almost through. We're on kind of a schedule here."

He rolled his eyes. "No shit? I was gonna throw in a movie, maybe make some popcorn." He glanced at Kate with a self-congratulatory smirk. Was he looking for a laugh? Trying to impress her? Seriously?

What a jackass.

She ignored his attempt at humor. "Is there a back way out of here? I saw earlier that you've got a back door and a loading dock. You got cameras on those?"

He nodded, pursing his lips and squinting doubtfully.

"The back door opens into an alley, with a ten foot cement wall directly in front of it—it's a bottleneck. There are about ten or twenty of them milling around back there. It's no good."

"And the loading dock?"

Shaking his head, he replied, "Might work if the dock door wasn't jammed. There's even a truck parked in there from a late delivery a few nights back. But the automated gate mechanism went haywire after the truck made its drop. Wouldn't come up on automation. On manual, we could get it up part way, but not high enough to get the truck out."

"Jesus. So you're telling me we either sit tight here and wait for our new friends, head into the back alley dead end and try to scale a cement wall, or try to get your truck out of the dock with a screwy gate? Not a lot of options here. What about the roof?"

This wasn't turning out at all as I had hoped.

"No go there, either. Roof access is through the garden center." He grinned. "But you're welcome to try it."

"You first."

"Oh, real witty," he said, "they teach you that in janitor school?"

"Look guys," Kate interrupted, looking between us, the urgency in her voice matching the concern on her face, "I hate to bust up this cerebral debate, but we don't have a lot of time here. We need to pick a route and go with it. From where I'm standing, it's looking like truck and expressway or bust."

She looked to both of us.

I nodded.

"Good," she said, looking to Earl. "We need some supplies. Sleeping bags, that kind of stuff. Where to?"

"Camping supplies, in sporting goods. That's where I got this," patting his ax. "Canned goods back the way you came. Water too. I'll meet you at the dock door, past the fitting rooms in the back."

I grabbed Fred, nodded at Kate, and started toward the sporting goods section. Fred followed behind, straggling, but keeping up. Grabbing a large hiking backpack, a hunting knife, a hatchet and an ax, I sprinted back to the food. I threw cans, five or six liters of spring water, some cereal bars, and a couple boxes of wheat crackers into the bag. I cinched it shut and threw it over my shoulder heading back through electronics, pausing as I passed a display case of handheld radios. I grabbed a package of two-ways, and made my way back toward Fred. He waited for me anxiously in sporting goods and we went together to the fitting rooms, reaching the door to the dock as Kate rounded the corner by lady's lingerie, toting a similar backpack, having also switched out her shovel but choosing instead a softball bat to supplement the pistol she had in her pocket.

"Earl?" I asked, looking around.

"Behind me," she was breathless. "They're through the fence, and they're at the barricade."

Earl raced through the baby clothes section, tubby paunch exploding into the aisle beside her at a breathless jog.

"Move! They're in!" His exclamation was punctuated by the sound of tumbling furniture from the garden center.

I bolted for the dock door, slamming my hands into the bar across the exit door and throwing it open. Massive shelves stocked high with all manner of items surrounded a paved, three-sided indentation, deeper on our side, and inclining gently upward to a large metal gate. Parked in that bunker was our redemption; our vehicular messiah masquerading as a delivery truck. Its back door was open and it was partly unloaded. Twenty or so large cardboard boxes sat lonely and unopened against the cab wall.

Earl ran past me, breathing heavily, making for the driver's seat. Kate went for the passenger side, opening the door and tossing her bag in.

"Where's the manual crank for the door?" I asked through the cabin to Earl, who was grabbing the keys from the center console.

"Right side, top of the ladder," he said looking up through the windshield to a mechanical box at the top of a ladder attached to the cinder block wall. "You have to pop out the crank and pull up the gate manually, but there was a jam the other night that kept it from going up all the way. Mechanic said he'd get to it but ..." He shrugged. "I don't know if he did or not."

Great. Well, time to act like a hero. That's what I do, right?

Well, usually, I wasn't on the verge of wetting myself. But other than that, sure.

"I'll take the crank, you guys load in. If I get it open wide enough, I'll jump on the top of the truck and we leave, pronto. If I don't — "

"You'll get it—just make sure you don't miss the truck on your way down." Kate said sarcastically. She looked at me gratefully, but with a twinge of something else in her eyes. She took my gear from me and ushered Fred into the truck as the engine started, turning over with a satisfying roar.

Yeah, I'll try not to do that. Smart-ass shrink, I thought, grabbing the bottom rung and hoisting myself up. As I climbed, I vaguely wondered what she really thought about me. She was pretty hot. Probably has all sorts of theories about me, though. 'Schizophrenic glory hounding egomaniac' came to my mind. And I was being nice to myself.

From behind us, the sound of a heavy weight against the door and the crashing of bodies slamming into a heavy door. Earl revved the engine as Kate rolled up her window.

I climbed quickly, reaching the top as the store entrance door opened, followed by a flood of creatures. The fat woman from last night must have fallen behind, as a young woman dressed as a fry cook had assumed the lead. Her empty glare fixed on me after scanning the room, her left arm looking as if it had been gnawed at by her companions and was of little value, her right arm raised to me in a gesture of greeting. Or a beckoning. A longing for me.

And not in the good way.

I shook my head, and focused on the crank. It came free of its housing easily enough, and I started to turn, going faster as it moved, my arm burning quickly from the strain. Light crept into the dock from below the metal door, and several creatures from the store tumbled clumsily into the recession housing the truck. More followed, electing simply to crash over the lip than to maneuver to the stairwell. Most got right up, shambling toward the cab. Others were buried beneath the press from behind. They poured into the dock, an endless procession of former humans.

Keep cranking, McKnight. No time to waste, here.

Unless you're imagining this, you crazy bastard, said the sarcastic voice from the back of my skull. You could crawl back down the ladder and see if you wake up when your fry cook friend takes a chunk out of your thigh. If you don't wake up, congratulations! You're sane!

I cranked faster.

The one-armed fry cook had reached the bottom of the ladder, and the vibrations as she pawed against the metal rungs shook my feet and legs. The door moved quickly, past the hood, past the windshield, to the top of the truck.

And then jammed.

Shit.

There was enough space to get the truck out, but if I was riding coach on the top of the thing, I might be in for a tight squeeze. I bore down on the thin metal strip with all my weight. The handle moved grudgingly several more inches, and then stopped.

The creatures had reached the cab of the truck and were pounding against the doors and the windows. More streamed constantly from the store, falling into the pit like lemmings from a cliff, filling the dock with their moaning, tumbling forms—a comical sight at another place, in another time.

Giving the crank one more try, and hoping I had enough space, I leaped from the ladder through the ten feet of intervening air, landing on the center of the roof, but sliding toward the back. The incline of the ramp turned the burnished steel top of the truck into an oiled playground slide. As my feet reached the back end, I caught the ridge of steel rivets in the center of the roof with my fingertips. Quickly, I banged my fist against the steel cover twice.

The truck shot forward, and I briefly lifted my head, eyes locked on the half-open door. I flattened my head against the cold metal, fingertips straining to hold their ground.

The bottom edge of the door was a breath of air against my neck, then my back, and finally my hamstrings. Early morning sunlight touched my face as the truck turned to the left, accelerating past and over creatures in the alley, and into the parking lot, toward the road we had abandoned yesterday. Our car sat crumpled against the bright red and white Dairy Queen sign, and the police cruiser was an empty vestige of last night's nightmare, door askew, window broken. Streaks of red matter trailed out of the open door onto the pavement, and around the front of the car.

I experienced a sudden feeling of karmic satisfaction about the sadistic trooper's demise until a sudden bump and burst of acceleration sent me slipping again, off the truck, hands grasping in vain for purchase on the slick surface. I fell toward the pavement, grasping air.

CHAPTER 10

In a last grab for a hold on the roof, I found the lip where the roof ended and the door housing began. I jerked to a halt, my legs flailing behind the truck and then falling down and in to the open doorway. I let go of the roof and fell clumsily, my momentum sending me sprawling onto the floor of the cargo area, landing hard on my side but miraculously avoiding major injury. The truck powered on, followed by whatever creatures we passed and whose attention followed our progress, but whose legs, thankfully, could not follow suit.

I fleetingly glimpsed the bus that must have delivered the football team to us. A green and white monstrosity, it was wrapped around a trio of oak trees behind the linen store. Several bodies lay squirming beneath the overturned vehicle, but their futile efforts were wasted under several tons of steel. Many were missing limbs and all were covered in blood and gore.

I sat there, watching through the back of the truck, as we drove over roads that should be teeming with everyday life but were now occupied only by the undead. The eerie silence of what should have been a normal, loud day was occasionally touched by the sound of gunfire. The world unfolded in reverse, creatures appearing from the left and right, eyes already focused on the truck as it passed, and dead gazes unerringly shifting to me as we moved away, staying with me until we were out of sight.

In stark contrast to last night's sojourn, where every detail was wreathed in shadow and uncertainty, I could now clearly see the destruction that this plague had wrought in a very short time. The world was unreal, roads littered with stalled and abandoned cars, buildings either burning or marked by violence, windows shattered or pockmarked with bullet holes. There were bodies lying about, some half-eaten, some untouched by the zombies, clearly having been killed by human acts. Apparently they didn't eat the ones that were dead already. Must be something about the living, maybe the blood or the tissue.

We passed City Hall, which apparently housed the local police station, and observed first hand the results of mass hysteria. Bodies littered the stairs leading to the building and bullet holes peppered the exterior frontal wall. The doors to the hall were broken; jagged shards of glass littered the ground. A dead police horse lay near the entrance, a cloud of flies discernible even from a distance. I gripped the handle to the open door and stared back at the large building, imagining the scene.

Scared people, looking for authority. Authorities, just scared people trying to deal. Fear permeating everything. A shot is fired, and then another, and then more. Pandemonium takes hold, and fear takes over. I shuddered, turning away as the building disappeared around the corner.

The gray morning air did nothing to alleviate the surreal setting, as we passed increasingly heavy zombie concentrations. The truck was large, and moving quickly, every so often shuddering with an impact or a bump. Groups of them reined the streets, roving at will, some upright, some bent over. Those that must have been attacked by their own kind before turning bore larger, more severe wounds, often to the extremities. Legs, arms, hands, feet—often completely missing or severely mauled.

No class seemed unaffected. I witnessed a small group, feasting on what appeared to be a large beast of some sort, although it was unclear whether it was an animal or a very fat person. The group was composed, in true multicultural fashion, of a white construction worker, a Hispanic woman dressed in dress slacks and a sweater, and a small child, whose face was smeared with blood and refuse. Finally America had achieved a truly classless society, I thought wryly, shaking my head. And all it took to reach this equanimity was the shared desire for undeniably tasty human flesh.

As the truck inexplicably slowed, I looked around me for the first time, wondering what we were hauling.

"Hold on, we have a problem" came the muffled shout from up front, as the truck slowed even more. The streets looked newer here, more maintained, with wider and more numerous lanes. Had we reached the expressway already? Something about the cop's comments last night intruded on my thoughts, but I had no more time to consider as the truck came to a stop. We were stopped.

Shit.

The boxes occupied about half of the length of the relatively short cargo area, leaving me closer to the open door than I was comfortable with. I ripped into the box closest to me, looking for a weapon, as the head of a large black man appeared around the corner of the truck and turned toward me. Eyes widening slightly, most likely a physical reaction rather than a psychological one, he immediately moved in my direction, grasping for me from the edge of the truck, but lacking the coordination or ability to hoist his body to my level. One cheek was gouged deeply as if cut or scratched; his black, curly beard was matted with blood and gore. His checkered flannel shirt was open at the neck, revealing a stained t-shirt; his hands and arms pounded against the floor, mouth opening and closing as a low, deep moan escaped his throat.

The truck jolted as it was thrown into reverse, and I fell suddenly onto the floor, legs flying out from under me, feet splayed close to the door. His hand brushed my shoe, and I reached up, over my shoulder into the box and withdrew an item from within, swinging it hard at the creature's head as its finger caught in my shoelace.

The large, purple teddy bear hit him square in the face, thoroughly confusing me as a diminutive squeak erupted from the large toy, but fazing him not at all as he reeled my foot toward him, along with the attached leg.

An absurd beeping suddenly sounded from the cab, as the truck moved into reverse. I was suddenly and painfully jerked toward the open door as my assailant disappeared under the truck, the pressure on my foot suddenly releasing, leaving me with an arm, attached to a finger, attached to my shoe.

I was still holding the large purple teddy bear, which I held up in front of me briefly and then discarded, laughing despite myself. I stood up quickly, kicking my foot rapidly to dislodge the grotesque gift he had left me, shuddering involuntarily as the curled finger finally released the lace of my shoe. I reached for the handle to pull the door down, but it refused to move. As I checked the frame, I realized my weight coming over the edge must have warped the housing just enough to jam the mechanism.

Wonderful.

"Hold on," Kate's disembodied voice floated back to me, as the truck slowed again. This time, a rolling stop, as Earl shifted into drive, and shot forward again. As we moved away, I could see what our obstruction had been and realized why the cop's comment came back to me.

The entrance ramp to the expressway was a metal avenue of car roofs and hoods, potholes of broken glass and bodies interspersed the mélange of broken, discarded and motionless vehicles. The ramp curved up to the expressway itself, located twenty feet above the street level, and I could make out the bobbing and slowly moving heads of creatures shambling directionless on the highway, half hidden from view by the concrete barriers lining the medians. The roofs of several large, yellow school buses peeked over the edge, the only vehicles visible from below. Some creatures, having seen our aborted attempt to gain access, moved down the ramp even as we sped away, hopeful in a mindless way of jogging off the highway for a quick bite.

A helicopter moved quickly across our path behind us, flying low, but clearly with no intention of stopping or landing. I moved to the doorway, grabbing the frame with one hand, and waiving with the other, expecting nothing but knowing I had to try. The chopper bore unfamiliar markings, and I couldn't quite recognize the make.

Strange, I thought, given how many movies had required me to ride in, pilot, or blow up such vehicles. I was familiar with lots of makes and models, the Apache, the Chinook, the Blackhawk, even the Sky Crane, having once been dropped fifty feet from one on a zip line for a scene in "Reaction Man." Stunt double couldn't do it because they needed a constant shot of my face as I came down, and it took me a while to gather the courage for the shot. I focused on the landscape outside the truck as the chopper disappeared from view, and the surroundings again became more rural.

I wish I had my stunt double now.

We were moving back the way we had come, but more Westerly, maybe back toward the water. I pounded on the side of the truck, and raised my voice.

"You know, as exciting as it is back here, I'd love to join you all in the cab!"

"We're going to try to stop up ahead—hold on," was Kate's reply, as the truck slowed, and turned slowly to the right. Few creatures were in sight, but there were always some. Jesus this thing had spread fast. A truck blasted past us heading the opposite direction, bed loaded with boxes and an old hound dog, who barked feverishly from the tailgate at the creatures it saw as they moved on. More gunshots sounded, seemingly from somewhere ahead of us, but hard to triangulate from the three-walled cabin of the cargo area.

The truck came to a stop and the engine shut off. I checked outside, realizing we were at a gas station but seeing only a few creatures in the distance. I quickly jumped off the back, rounding the side toward the cab. Kate was getting out of the passenger's side.

"We need gas. This thing is on fumes and this place looked clear. Watch those behind us, Earl's gonna pump." She reached back into the cab and pulled out my ax, tossing it to me. I caught it by the handle, fumbling it slightly and almost braining myself in the process. I looked up self-consciously, trying in vain to effect "cool" and look as if nothing had happened.

She smiled and moved to the front of the truck to watch for more attackers.

Earl cursed from the driver's side as I reached the back of the truck again, looking for more of those things anywhere close to us. Only the few that were still more than four hundred feet away, moving slowly but steadily toward us along the two-lane road, past a grocery store and a burning yellow sports car.

"The fucking pump is off," Earl screamed, kicking the side of the yellow and red metal box, as if expecting gas to start erupting from the nozzle in fear of his wrath.

"Pump controls are in the station," I responded, trying to keep my voice calm, "Should be behind the counter, near the register. Likely they turned them off before leaving to keep people from stealing gas." I worked in a gas station as a kid, and got beat once by the horse's ass of a manager for leaving the pumps on one night. I wonder if he had been eaten. Dreams are free, I suppose.

Earl's nasal voice interrupted my daydream.

"I'm not going in there, there could be things in there," he whined, as he looked toward the station, where the windows revealed no movement, but afforded only limited visibility. It was a full-on convenience store, not just a normal station. Looked like it even had some sort of fast food place attached to the far side.

Yes, my fat, chicken shit friend, there very well could be things in there.

From the front of the truck, Kate shouted "More of those things, coming up from the other direction. Maybe about ten or twelve, and they've seen us. I figure about four minutes till they're here."

Fred's head stuck out from the cab, looking at me and then at Earl. He pointed definitively toward the road with his frying pan. "Pancake!"

Did I have to do everything?

"I'll fucking go," I said, secretly hoping I'd get points for it from Kate. "Earl, you watch for those things coming from behind us, unless you're too gutless to do that" I looked in that direction, realizing as I did so that four more of them had appeared behind the initial group of three.

"If I'm not out in three minutes, you guys get out of here," I said as I backed away from the truck, sounding a lot braver than I felt.

"No problem there, pal," he responded sincerely, staring at the approaching creatures from behind the truck.

What a prick.

I spared a look to the front of the cab and nodded at Kate, who watched me, saying nothing, simply nodding in return. I jogged to the door, and pulled on the handles, which were locked. The ax head went through the glass quickly and loudly, an alarm sounding from within. Nothing to be done about the noise, I reached in, unlocking the deadbolt and opening the door.

The register was against the back wall, next to a wall of coolers fronted by a display of chips and snack foods. A hot dog warming machine stood to my right, rows of candy to my left. Through doors on the far left wall, a fast food roast beef place, advertising an extra large pile of stacked meat on white bread for only 2.99.

Feels like I should have that sign around my neck, I thought, the voice in my head chuckling but saying nothing. I moved slowly but cautiously, checking behind each aisle as I moved toward the register. The shrill whine of the alarm prevented me from hearing anything, and I relied on my vision as the light faded toward the windowless rear of the store.

I reached the counter, and jerked as I caught my reflection in the panel of coolers, and reactively raised my ax to chest level. Feeling foolish, I turned back toward the register, moving behind the counter and checking for panels or switches that would activate the pumps. From outside, Kate shouted.

"We've got company!" Her voice was shrill and loud, but relatively calm. Over the whine of the alarm, I heard Earl curse loudly.

There it was! Beneath the lottery tickets, a line of switches marked 1-6. Not knowing which was ours, I turned them all on, and heard an electric response of some sort kick on. I sprinted outside, finding that we were no longer alone.

The ones we had marked before were still at least a minute away, shambling forward as quickly as their bodies could take them, feet shuffling, arms swinging stiffly. Three others had apparently rounded from the back of the store, maybe alerted by my window breaking and the consequent alarm. Kate was backed up in the cavity of the open door, pistol drawn as two of them made toward her. Her bat was nowhere to be seen. From the cab, Fred could be seen looking anxiously out toward Kate. The last creature was almost on Earl, who held his ax up and over his right shoulder as if the creature could appreciate the threatening gesture.

"Get in the truck!" I yelled at Kate. Instead of jumping inside, she raised her gun, leveling it at the chest of the closest zombie. From the back of the truck, I saw Earl swing his ax forward. It struck the creature in the chest, lodging somewhere near the sternum, the blow causing it to stagger backwards, hands grappling briefly at the polished wood protuberance now caught in its torso. It moved forward again, pushing Earl back.

From the cab, a gunshot sounded. The creature closest to Kate flinched as if slapped, a burst of air and cloth from its shirt flying into the air between it and Kate, causing it to pause only momentarily.

I reached the second creature. I heard me only as I was bringing my ax down. It struck at an angle, cleaving through most of the gray-tinged neck and the spinal column. I felt the jolt of bone vibrate through the handle as the creature simply collapsed as if deflated.

Then I remembered the news reports.

"The head!" I screamed at Kate, who had moved back as far as possible, but couldn't close the door, as the creature was almost touching her. The pop of a second shot and the rear of the creature's skull flew off, landing five feet behind it as it collapsed in a heap at her feet.

From the back of the truck, a scream pierced the chaos. I raced to the corner to find Earl on the ground and almost laughed, despite the circumstances.

A massively fat, naked, and refuse-covered man lay atop Earl, its hands grasping for Earl's face. Bits of grime, bodily fluid, and spittle dripped on Earl as the obese creature struggled to eat its next meal. From the road behind us, I could now hear the moans of the approaching zombies from the street as they reached the station property, leaving the road.

Reversing the ax, I slammed the blunt side of the ax head into the zombie's neck, feeling rather than hearing the crack of the spinal column as the blow interrupted whatever vital connection existed between the head and the body that allowed them to stay active after the delivery of otherwise mortal wounds.

The zombie fell to the side with the force of the blow, Earl's ax handle pointing skyward. Grabbing Earl's hand and pulling him to his feet, I threw one more glance over my shoulder toward the rear and followed him to the cab. He got in as I pulled the fueling nozzle out of the truck and, in a stroke of inspiration, locked the handle open, allowing fuel to pour onto the ground. The creatures behind us had reached the back of the truck. I satisfyingly sprayed them with the caustic-smelling fuel, dropped the handle and immediately jumped into the still open cab door, slamming it shut behind me.

I turned the key in the ignition and pulled forward, tires squealing on the cement ground that had been made wet by the still pumping gasoline. The creatures in front of us had reached the property and were moving toward the front of the truck, as I shoved the transmission into reverse, backing into a parking spot in front of the store, aiming the truck toward the road, shifting to park, and gunning the engine. As they moved slowly in our direction, moaning and shambling, I reached down and popped the cigarette lighter into its housing.

"What the fuck are you doing, man?" Earl shouted, looking from me to them to Kate and back to me. Fred caught the tension and bounced excitedly in his seat, pointing excitedly at the zombies.

"I'm a little sick of always being on the receiving end of this nationwide ass-mastering," I replied, gunning the engine again, tauntingly. They had all reached the pumps, and the first few were again only feet from the cab.

"Pancake!" Fred shouted, as the first one reached the passenger door and Kate flinched back, looking sharply in my direction.

"Yeah, buddy. Pancake," I said softly, shifting into drive and flooring the accelerator. The throaty engine roared, and the truck shot past the creatures, under the awning overhanging the pumps, and onto the street. Reaching a safe distance, I stopped as the cigarette lighter popped out dutifully from its recessed chamber under the dash.

The gently glowing lighter was a red and silver arc, tracing a slow, gentle decline into a pool of gasoline gathering at the foot of the pumps. The creatures, having turned to follow us, were now all clustered around and between the pumps, moving slowly in our direction. The graceful flight of the lighter ended abruptly in a yellow and orange roar, as the pumps, the awning, and the store erupted in flame, incinerating the creatures that had come for us, and throwing a sooty black column of oily smoke high into the air. The concussion from the blast rocked the truck.

We watched for a moment, quiet. Finally, satisfied that nothing had escaped, I pulled away from the curb. I felt myself smile, and allowed my new inner soundtrack to surface, humming softly to myself as I steered the truck to the middle of the road and headed west, away from the happily burning station.

CHAPTER 11

"Are you humming the fucking A-team theme song?" Earl asked, incredulous. We were moving through intermittently forested and suburban areas, neighborhoods flashing by on the right, forest on the left.

I kept my eyes on the road, not answering. I stopped humming as Kate spoke up.

"Earl, can you reach the radio knob? I'd like to see if anyone else is transmitting." She and Fred were crammed closely together against the passenger door, her back to the window, right hand still holding the pistol. Earl was practically on my lap, the four of us making the best of a three-person cab.

He reached forward and pushed the power button, the backlighting for the tuner coming to life. As static streamed from the speakers, I looked down to check the frequency as Earl was extending his hand to reduce the volume. His left wrist bore the unmistakable oval of a human bite mark. I shifted my eyes back to the road quickly as he shot a look in my direction. He looked back to the radio, twisting the tuning knob.

"Doesn't sound good," I said, as Earl cycled through the stations, using his right hand for the other dial and holding his left arm close to his body. Had he seen me notice the wound?

"Where are we heading, anyway?" I asked, unfamiliar with the area.

"I figured we'd be safer on water than over land," Kate replied, "So we were heading to the marina. I know it's a long shot, but those things were swarming on the highways and if you think about it, the roads are probably our worst option." She looked out the front window.

I looked at her, remembering the expressway entrance. She must have taken my look for questioning, so continued on.

"When this thing hit, everyone was directed to head for certain safe houses via the Expressway or the other major highways. But as fast as this happened, and as violent as those creatures are, all it would take would be one, maybe two stopped cars to stop the traffic on the expressway. Then everyone sitting in traffic becomes a target. Nowhere to run, and surrounded by other people." She shuddered.

"Those cars, those buses," clearly now referencing the evac buses from King's Park—she probably had friends in there "would have been cages, and the expressways would have been a killing ground. Just a few of those things added to a confined space like that..." She faded off, clearly in her own head.

I nodded, thinking. Not knowing the area, I trusted Kate's call. But now we had a situation with Earl. He was going to turn, we just didn't know when. A-team had gone pretty quick, but he was already dead. I had no clue how long it would take someone who was still alive.

"How far to the marina from here?" I asked, slowing as a cluster of four shufflers moved into the two-lane road. We were approaching a small strip of stores on either side of the road, a post office to the left and a drug store and laundromat on the right. Traffic lights suspended above the intersection swung slowly in the wind, flashing a dull, yellow warning of caution.

Yeah, no shit.

The creatures saw the truck and turned toward us; I pulled the wheel to the left, smashing one to the pavement with the right front wheel and clipping another with the mirror that extended out from the cab on a pair of steel rods.

"About one more mile to...Holy shit!" Her calm response was interrupted as her voice rose quickly in surprise. We had reached the center of town, following the road around a bend to the right, and a roadblock had come suddenly into sight. Composed of mostly cars and smashed-up furniture, it was nevertheless fully manned by at least twenty or thirty men and women, all armed with rifles and handguns. I slammed the brakes, bringing the truck to a stop in front of the pile.

Beside me, Earl slammed against the dash, cursing under his breath. Looking over, I noticed his pallor and the sweat beading on his brow. We didn't have much time.

Kate was rubbing the side of her head and Fred was looking intently forward, curious. His frying pan was at the ready, left hand rubbing the rim, right hand clutching the handle.

We stared ahead. The defenders stared back at us. A short, dirty man in a dark green jumpsuit that looked like a mechanic's uniform rose to the roof of a Dodge pickup and yelled in our direction. In his right hand he held an automatic rifle, in his left a bottle of beer.

"You can turn around right now, or you can join these folk," he gestured to the ground in front of the roadblock, indicating bodies littering the base of the barricade. I had assumed them to be creatures, but realized now that some looked human.

A man lay directly in front of the truck, face upturned to the sky, bullet wound marring the chest of his pink polo shirt.

No sign of infection, no gray skin, no bloodshot eyes, no gaping, half-chewed wounds. To his immediate left, a pretty woman in a pink sweater and jeans, maybe his wife or girlfriend, face turned to his, stomach soaked in blood, eyes vacant. I scanned the road to either side. Equal parts zombie and living humans, exterminated at the gates to this pissant village.

It took only moments of surveying the carnage to comprehend what had happened here. What would happen again.

"You're murdering uninfected people!" Kate yelled from the passenger side, rolling her window down two inches so that her voice would carry. "You're monsters!"

The bastard smiled. "Now how do we know whether or not they're infected? News said that people don't present sometimes until hours after they've been bit. All you folk are coming from the expressway, ain't ya? We know it's heavy round there." He spit, companions on either side of him nodding. A shot rang out from the far side of the wall, and a triumphant yell sounded. I flinched, my eyes closing and reopening to check the windshield for a spider web bullet hole. Another crack, another shout. I realized they were shooting creatures behind the truck.

"These folk here tried to get in when we told 'em to leave, and they got what's coming to 'em. We're not letting anyone in. We've gotta look after ourselves, seeing as we haven't seen the police or the national guard since this thing started, and we're gonna protect our families and our property." He turned to the side, spit again.

"The government will be out here sooner or later; you will be held accountable for this. It's only a matter of time," Kate said, the tone of her voice indicating that her statement was equal parts hope and determination.

He smiled again, his lower lip pulled in to hold his spittle. He looked amusedly at his compatriots then back to us. "You must be out of the loop, sweetheart!"

"Government," he spat that word out like he had expelled the last two globules of spittle, "is already pulling back. Can't handle this ... situation. I've got five different HAM radio operators from Vermont to Georgia tellin' me that the feds are drawing a line around the damn East Coast. Anything south of Maine and Northeast of Louisiana and Mississippi is considered no man's land."

I recoiled at the news. In three days? It was exactly like that Internet program—fast and almost impossible to get ahead of.

"Shit, they've already chalked up the initial sites as goners. New York City is full of these things, so is Philly and DC. Half of Congress likely got eaten—can't say I object to that—and the President's a no show, been flyin' around in Air Force one for almost 72 hours straight. Even the fuckin'

Canucks are shootin' people at the border. You think they give a shit about what we do here," he gestured to the bodies before the barricade, "in our little slice of heaven?" Shaking his head.

Another shot from the barricade, another yell. The sound of a beer can opening and laughter.

"Bottom line folks: we're on our own here." He raised his gun. He wasn't pointing behind the truck. "And you folk are too. Now, I'm going to ask you nicely one more time — "

I shifted the truck into reverse, not waiting for the end of the sentence, and not even checking the mirrors as I turned us around. A thump from behind could have been a zombie or a Kia; either way, we moved back the way we had come.

We needed to get somewhere safe with thick walls, and some locked doors. We needed to get somewhere that we could put some distance between Earl and us. Maybe lock him out or in a different room or something. I didn't know, but I knew he was going to pose a problem really, really soon.

I thought for a moment, finally turning to Kate.

"Where's the closest school?" I asked, surreptitiously looking to Earl. His eyes were closed and he was drawing deep breaths. We couldn't drive around with him in the truck, and we needed some time to regroup, maybe find another way to the marina. Besides, that pump hadn't been on that long before we had to bug out, and we were going to be short on gas again in the near future.

Why couldn't we have absconded with a hybrid?

She looked at me quizzically, and I shifted my gaze to Earl and back to her. She mouthed "what?"

I looked at Earl, his eyes were still closed. I brought my arm to my mouth and mimed biting my wrist, a fake grimace of pain, and a blank stare, looking back to her and then nodding toward Earl. Her eyes widened in understanding, hand instinctively tightening on her pistol.

Speaking, she betrayed none of the visual concern. "It's actually a half mile from here. Turn right at the second intersection and go about a quarter of a mile." She looked at me, and back to Earl. His eyes were open again, and as he turned to me, I noticed some redness in his gaze. He was very, very pale.

"What the hell you want with a school? You wanna try for your GED?" He smiled, pleased with his little joke, and laying his head back. He laughed to himself and suddenly coughed wetly, wiping his mouth with the back of his hand.

"We need to get to the water. Go trolling for dates on your own time." His voice was weak as he laughed again at his own cleverness.

Not much time, I thought, as we turned at the intersection. Woods surrounded the road on either side, wind stirring the branches in the gray morning air.

A station wagon sat on the side of the road, doors open, vacant. A bloody handprint on the driver's side windshield was the only evidence of foul play. In the field past the wagon, movement from the woods, and bodies could be seen passing between the trees. A deer bolted in front of us, passing out of sight into the opposite line of trees.

It was a small brick school, located across the street from a housing project and a small strip mall of some sort. A football field sat to the side of the gymnasium, a tall tower capped with an old cupola overlooking the front stairs. No sign of people, but the parking lot was mostly full. I pulled the truck up off the road, parking on the front lawn. Turning the truck off, and snatching the keys, I jumped down, ax in hand, and sprinted to the doors, pulling them toward me, hoping for the best.

They were unlocked.

I turned toward the truck and gestured to Kate, who grabbed Fred and their bags, and leaped from the cab. I could see Earl moving slowly out of the driver's side door. Kate and Fred reached the doors, and went inside.

The polished tile of the floor was a brilliant white. The neon lights reflected fitfully off the whitewashed cement block walls. Kate and Fred moved into the hallway, checking both ways. Kate nodded to me that it was clear for the moment. I turned back to the doorway, where Earl was reaching the open entrance. Grabbing the door and pulling it closed, I inserted my ax through the door handles.

Earl looked at me sharply, suddenly alert. He tried the doors, realizing too late what I had done. He slammed both hands against the glass. Kate moved to my side.

"What are you doing?" he screamed, looking over his shoulder, clearly scared now. From the woods we had passed coming toward the school, a virtual herd of creatures appeared. They moved en masse across the road, toward the school. Fuckers must have followed the sound of the truck.

"You've been bitten," I said through the glass, "You're going to turn, and you know it. How are you feeling? A little woozy?"

His hand went instinctively to his brow to wipe sweat from his forehead. "I've got the flu, you bastard!" he yelled, "And this wasn't a bite from one of those things! I have a nephew who bit me two days ago at the park!" He looked over his shoulder again, back to me, very scared now. Eyes bulging, he slammed his fists against the doors. "Open the god damned doors! Those things are getting closer! I'm not a fucking zombie! Listen to me!"

Kate's hand was on my arm, and I turned to her.

"Are you certain?" she asked softly, her eyes searching my face. The problem was, I wasn't sure. I wasn't certain at all. But I know what I saw.

"No. I'm not certain. But I know that the infection, the sickness, whatever you want to call it, I know that if you're bitten, you get it. And you can give it. He may be telling the truth, but he may be lying. He had one of those things on top of him for God knows how long before I got there. Are you telling me you believe his story? Enough to let him in here?"

She looked to Earl, who was now focused on the creatures coming from the forest. There were at least a hundred, mostly teenagers. Looked like half of the school. Looking back to me she shook her head.

"I can't leave him out there to die. If he turns, we can end it. If we leave him out there, he's going to get ripped up by those things whether he's destined to turn into one or not. I can't condemn him to that."

I looked at her for a long while before cursing once and lifting my hand to the ax handle.

"Come on, man, open the door!" Earl pleaded, no longer aggressive. Just plain scared.

They were on the lawn, passing the truck, and had reached the bottom stair before I could get the ax handle loose and manage the door open. He stumbled past me as I slammed the door closed again, threading the ax handle through, and moving back as the first creature hit against the thick glass. It was a young man, maybe all of fifteen. He wore a tee shirt bearing the name of a band in crazy cursive lettering. Vacantly staring eyes rimmed in red followed my progress as we moved back toward the hallways. Muddy leather sneakers shuffled in place as his hands moved against the glass, sliding on the surface as if it were ice. His mouth was a snarl, broken teeth evidencing his transgressions of the day.

Suddenly, a blinding pain in the back of my head and I was on the ground. Another blunt impact to my ribs, and more angry shouting.

"Mother fucker! Gonna leave me to die out there?" Another impact and I tried to roll away, a second kick grazing my calf.

"You can't get away from me, you stupid bastard!" I tried to push myself up and saw his leg moving toward me. I grabbed the foot and twisted it, catching him off balance and send him sprawling onto the stairs, left leg twisting awkwardly under his contorted frame as he screamed in pain. A jagged white splinter protruded from his pant leg, blood covering the site of the compound fracture.

He rolled over, screaming, as I pushed myself onto my feet, dizzy from the blow to the head. At my side, Kate was staring at the doors, mouth open.

"There's too many of them!" I looked to the left, and the ax handle was splintering, doors bowing inward from the immense pressure outside. Suddenly, from behind Kate, Fred sprinted forward, frying pan a silver blur as he slammed it against Earl's head, sending him spinning against the glass doors.

"Fred, no!" I yelled, my own voice painfully splitting my skull, ears still ringing. Fred jerked himself upright, stumbling back up the stairs in reverse, as Earl moved against the doors.

Blood streaming profusely from the deep gash in his head, Earl pushed himself back against the wall, trying to get up, trying to fight the pain in his broken leg.

Rising slowly, my vision blurred, I somehow managed to stagger up the stairs into the hallway just as the ax handle shattered, splinters of wood showering the floor. Earl tried one final time to get up. But hampered by his shattered leg, he was forced to the floor again by the weight of the incoming flood, bearing him down and burying him under an avalanche of gray, writhing flesh. I caught one final glimpse of him, writhing in agony as a teenage girl grabbed the splinter of bone in his leg and casually ripped it from his bleeding calf.

Several creatures that were unable to reach him through the rest of the crowd chose instead to shamble clumsily forward toward the stairwell, the progress of the crowd outside temporarily bottlenecked at the one open door.

As Earl screamed in pain, Kate backed up into the main hallway, arm crossing Fred's chest protectively, forcing him back with her. I stumbled toward them, doubled over as I tried to catch my breath. Kate must have felt Fred tense, as she suddenly tried to grab at Fred's shirt, shouting at him in anxious excitement. He bolted forward toward the first few creatures, frying pan aloft.

"Pancake" he screamed, as his frying pan whirled into the skull of the closest zombie, its head whipping to the side as the stainless steel shattered the cheekbone and the strength of the blow forced it into the bodies of the creatures behind. Even as he cocked his arm for another attack, Kate balled his shirt in her hand, pulling him back as we ran to the stairwell. He protested briefly, but allowed himself to be pulled, frying pan ever at the ready, face red and livid.

We sprinted upstairs, our shoes sounding hollowly in the empty stairwell as shuffling bodies followed close behind. Earl's screams echoed continued to reverberate against the tinny lockers lining the hallway until they ended abruptly in a wet, tearing cough. Then there was nothing; nothing but the sound of our running and the shuffling pursuit.

CHAPTER 12

We raced up the stairs, taking them two or three at a time. Fred followed Kate as I, by necessity as well as choice, played rearguard, still woozy from Earl's blow. Barely pausing to snack on Earl, the horde had followed us down the hall and to the stairs, haltingly jerking their collective legs over each step, slowly but consistently giving pursuit. Shoes and boots and bare feet and sandals, all shuffling and squeaking on the slick commercial grade tile that an industrious janitor had recently polished to a mirror-like sheen.

Reaching the second floor, I scanned the hallway, gaze flickering past rows of lockers, abstinence posters and a faded banner advertising a long-past dance. To our right was a set of restrooms, to the left a doorway to a janitor's closet. We moved down the hall, searching for access to the roof. From below, the moaning and shambling corpses followed us up the stairs.

This school had not been spared the violence that had marred the rest of the town; bloody smears and indiscernible patterns of brown fluid covered the wall to my left, seeming to converge on a dark spot further up the hallway. A water fountain covered inexplicably in blood and gore stood out from the wall and a forgotten backpack lay torn open below, books scattered in the red mixture of fluid and solid that spread out from the scene of the mutilation.

I began to get concerned as the first zombie, a teenage boy with a large, gaping red socket where his left eye should be, reached the top of the stairs. He tripped forward as the rush of bodies from behind forced his feet out from under him on the smooth floor. His single eye never stopped watching me as he was trampled slowly from behind until his face was pushed from view.

These things are certainly determined, I'd give them that.

Not that they know that they're determined, or intended to be, but you gotta give 'em props for following that instinct.

"Uh, I'm starting to feel a little like that last lobster in the lobster tank," said Kate, looking over her shoulder at the creatures shuffled forward along the hall, mutilated extremities leaving more blood and refuse streaked along the whitewashed cinder blocks as they moved toward us.

"What, appreciated?" I joked half-heartedly, even as I spotted the last door in the hall adjacent to another restroom a doorway marked "No Student Access" with a picture of a stick figure man scaling stairs to an open doorway.

"More like I'm sitting in a glass cage with my claws rubber-banded shut waiting to have my ass plucked out by the next middle aged balding guy with expandable pants and 19.99 in his pocket," she said dryly, moving past me into the stairwell. Fred passed me next, eyes busy searching the hall behind us. In his flickering look as he moved by, I thought I caught a hint of concern.

Jesus, we must really be in deep shit if Mr. Nonplussed is showing anxiety.

We reached the roof, sprinting out as Kate shut the door and peered through the chicken wire and glass window in the steel frame.

"They're following us in," she said, face glued to the glass.

I looked around, searching for something to reinforce the door, remembering the ax handle downstairs and the barricade at Target. It's amazing what a group of hungry, determined, flesh-eating zombies can do to a barricade these days.

"Is there a lock on the handle?" I asked, looking frantically on either side of the stairwell housing.

"Yeah, but it's a deadbolt and it's on the other side," Kate responded. "They're at the last landing and they're gonna be up here soon. If you've got a way to keep them inside, now's the time..."

"I left my duct tape and baling wire at home, cut me some slack," I said, searching wildly for something to bar the entrance.

"They're here!" she screamed, and turned around, backing against the door and bracing herself for their onslaught. Fred joined her, lending his slight frame to the temporary wall, legs clearly straining as the first hit slammed the door into their backs, a crack of space appearing behind them.

"Hurry up!" she screamed, composure lost, eyes wild, as Fred whimpered, door bulging against their backs.

There! Not perfect, but better than the alternative.

"Let it go and run toward me! Behind the stairs!"

They jumped away from the doorway as it flew open behind them, the darkened stairwell yawning into the bright light of day and virtually vomiting the creatures onto the roof, even as Kate and Fred sprinted to me. I pointed to a ladder attached to the side of the building that led to the cupola overlooking the front lawn. It was the highest point on the school, and only accessible by ladder. It also lacked another escape route.

In other words, once we were up there, we had nowhere else to go.

"This is it?" Kate yelled unbelieving, looking over her shoulder in anxiety as they appeared from behind the stairwell.

"This is your solution? How the fuck are we getting down from there?" Her face was flushed as she pointed to the white dome, her eyes blazing. Her hair, tied behind her head in a simple ponytail, shook behind her rapidly moving head as she looked first to me, then to them, and back to the ladder.

"We figure that out upstairs," I said, looking over my shoulder at the approaching creatures.

Cursing, she grabbed the ladder and lifted herself up. Fred, looking behind me, moved almost surreptitiously toward the approaching crowd as I managed to grab his shirt as he did so, pulling him back.

"Uh-uh. Not this time, Rambo," I directed him as I pushed him toward the ladder, hand on his shirt until he was on the rungs, climbing up. I followed quickly, getting most of my body up just as the first creature reached the foot of the ladder.

A hand grasped the leg of my pants, pulling my foot toward its mouth. It was a teenage girl this time, wearing the boisterous uniform of a school cheerleader, bloody legs appearing from underneath her skirt, scratches adorning a pretty face marred only by her vacuous, hungry stare. Her eyes greedily tracked my foot in her hand as I struggled against her unnaturally strong grip.

I kicked out clumsily and violently, my heel connecting with her jaw and forcing her head back. Grasping the ladder firmly with both hands, I brought my other foot down hard on her forehead while her head rocked backward, forcing her spine to bend further in a direction it was unable to accommodate. I could hear the neck snap; my foot flew free and the grip released as I jumped up the next two rungs, narrowly avoiding the remaining creatures, which now crowded below the last rung.

Reaching the cupola, I turned and looked behind me, seeing the roof awash in milling, gray, shambling bodies, shuffling persistently toward the ladder, moans a constant refrain as a chorus of the undead serenaded us in our ivory tower.

I sat down hard on the edge and caught my breath. Kate and Fred were breathing hard, Kate leaning against the railing, chest heaving, while Fred had plopped unceremoniously in the middle of the enclosure, legs crossed and panting like an exhausted dog.

"Well, shit." I said. No one answered. No one needed to.

That pretty much said it all.

We sat there for a while, mentally regrouping, not speaking. I rooted through my bag, pulling out the box of wheat crackers. Finding the two-way radios, I turned one on, and static rose from the speaker. Realizing that the handset was virtually useless, I turned it off again to conserve the battery. Kate simply sat, staring at the sky, engrossed in her own thoughts.

Finishing my crackers, stomach tight from eating too much too fast on an empty tank, I rose and circled the small space, looking down and out at our surroundings. Front lawn, complete with our delivery truck lawn ornament, was still covered in creatures, some streaming in, and some simply milling about. To the right, the roof extended five hundred feet to the edge, that portion also by now crawling with zombies. Behind us, a bank of air conditioning units and hoses rose from the narrow ledge, backed by a large square box—probably the main unit.

"Any ideas?" Kate, who was now squatting over her own bag, asked suddenly, her hand searching for something as she looked at me.

"Not at present. You?"

"Nope. Was kind of hoping you might be some sort of insane-savant. You know, crazy, but in an autistic, supernatural kind of way?" It sounded like she was smiling, but her head was down now, examining the energy bar she had located. Good.

At least she wasn't pissed at me anymore. Even though I probably deserved it.

"Not so much. But I played one on TV once." She chuckled briefly, and then was quiet for a moment. I stared over the side. The school was surrounded to the sides and the rear by forest, which gave way in a half mile to the roads we had been on. The strip mall across from us included a chicken wing joint, a cell phone shop, and some sort of small grocery store or bodega. It was backed by a neighborhood, houses looking empty and abandoned. A fire was burning steadily through one of the homes, and an overturned car stood forlornly abandoned in the middle of the road leading into the development. Randomly, a shuffling form would cross a yard or a street, searching in vain for food. But other than the undead, there was no movement, no sign of actual life.

The moaning from below had gotten louder, as the creatures' numbers were being slowly augmented by those from the ground level that were climbing to the roof for a meal. Talking helped relieve the pressure of what now seemed the inevitable: that we would die up here, absurd casualties of a bizarre mass-extinction event.

"You got family around here?" I asked, genuinely curious and desperate to hear something other than the moans, as I turned purposefully away from the edge and leaned against the railing.

She shook her head. "I have a sister in Philadelphia, but my mom lives in California. Dad died a few years back." She stuck a cereal bar into her mouth, biting off a huge piece and swallowing her first bite before she continued. "I was actually going to go visit her this weekend. My sister, I mean."

She looked down at our admiring throng. "So much for that plan. You?"

"Nah. My dad died when I was young and my mom left us when I was seven. Lived with our grandparents until we went to college. I've got a brother, but he's in the Air Force, stationed in Kuwait the last time I heard from him." I looked away.

"Got any friends around here?" she asked tentatively, as if she was sensitive to the peculiarities of my specific ... circumstances.

"Big movie star like you has got to have a bunch of friends, right? People to run around with in fancy cars, share the mutual aversion to underwear and classy behavior—you know, standard stuff?" She said it with a smile, trying to be nice.

I felt my face tighten, even as the forced smile came to my mouth. "Maria was my only family. And as to friends ... well, in my line of work— my former line of work, I should say—you don't get to know a lot of people. I mean really know. Sure, you're around a bunch, you talk to people, you have a ton of acquaintances, but there aren't a lot of real relationships there."

I grunted, looking up and squinting into the mid day sun. "And after the trial and everything...let's just say I didn't get a lot of fan mail."

She didn't reply, just looked at me briefly, then back to her bag. Fred sat up, looking at a flight of birds that had erupted from the trees and taken to the skies. A mile or so away, another flight followed suit. Funny, I thought. Haven't seen a lot of birds since this started. I wonder if they sense something. How could they not?

I grabbed the radio and turned it on again, moving the frequency dial around to the different locations, listening for any sign of life.

"So," I asked, hoping the attention I was paying to the radio masked the desire I had for an answer to the question I had asked myself earlier this morning, "can I ask again what makes you doubt my insanity?"

She looked up from her bar, chewing thoughtfully. Out of the corner of my eye, I saw her looking at me but refused to meet her gaze. She could probably read me like a book.

Yep. All sorts of theories, I was sure of it.

"The reports had timing problems," she started off simply, laying her bar on the ground and reaching up to unbind her hair, "specifically the coroner's report."

She pulled her hair back tightly, retying the ponytail.

"The police report said that cause of death was blunt force trauma to the left side of the head. Golf club, I believe?"

A question.

"Putter." I responded, resenting the memory.

"Right," nodding, arms now to each side, supporting her weight as she leaned back, "so she was supposedly killed by your putter around ... I don't remember the time ... let's just say 4 or 5. Well, the coroner's report indicated that her major organs had shut down hours before that, maybe four or five hours before. That's a big difference, wouldn't you say?"

Another question. "I suppose."

Four hours? I didn't remember that.

"So to the lay person, that seems to say that she was already dead, right? But the police report said that the death was caused by the blow, and that was corroborated by the evidence at the scene: the blood spatters on your shirt, the blood on the walls, the placement of the body, et cetera."

She stopped, looking over my shoulder into the distance. "Question is, how do we account for that?"

The mention of blood brought the familiar images to mind; the blood on the walls, the putter, the sounds from the bathroom. But another image, this one new: I was walking to the bedroom, calling out her name, wondering why she wouldn't answer. Seeing her jacket on the bed, a file folder, a name: Lazari? Larzos? Lazarus? I think it was Lazarus. Yes, definitely. I picked up the folder, curious. I turned around when I felt a hand on my shoulder...

"Mike."

I started, eyes refocusing on Kate, who looked at me with concern. "I'm sorry, maybe this is too much for you. I should have —"

"No, no. I think it helps. I'm getting new flashes, new images. It's been so long since I've had new memories, it's just a rush when they hit me like that."

Looking around, trying to shift the focus off of me, I looked at her hand, noticing for the first time she didn't wear a ring. She looked at me, noticing me noticing. She smiled crookedly. "No, I'm not," she said, looking away. "I was dating someone for a while. A computer guy. Did work for the Army at Fort Dix."

Hopefully, I looked up, trying to act neutral, suspecting that I didn't look it.

"For a while? Kind of implies 'not any more,' doesn't it?"

"It didn't work out. I realized after a while that the only way I could get him to pay attention to me was if I had monitors for breasts and a keyboard for an ass. You can't build a new relationship on that kind of foundation."

The mental image hit me and I couldn't stop the laughter from first bubbling out, and then pouring. She looked at me, maybe intending to be offended, but she soon joined in. I let the laughter come; it felt good, and I couldn't recall the last time I had laughed so hard my stomach hurt. When the last of it passed, I shook my head, part of the memory coming back to me, and turned to her.

"The name Lazarus mean anything to you?"

"Like the guy from the Bible?" She laughed a short, halting laugh. "Not really, other than the story about him and Jesus. Don't exactly have the good book committed to memory."

"Yeah, me neither." Random. Probably nothing. We needed to think of a way out of here. Enough with the reminiscing. I didn't think I could handle any more memories right now.

I picked up the radio, pressing the send button on each channel, speaking "Mayday" slowly and clearly on each. I repeated several times until realizing how infinitesimally small our chances of that finding anyone able and willing to help were. Kate scanned the horizon, waiving whenever she saw a plane or a helicopter, no matter how far off they were. Fred helped, waiving when she did, occasionally shouting "pancake" in excitement.

Putting the radio down, I moved to the rear of the cupola to scan the backfield, considering our limited options. At first, I thought it was Kate talking, or playing with the radio, the voice was so tinny, the volume so faint. I pounced on the radio when I realized what it was, twisting the volume up all the way and pressing my ear against the speaker. My eardrum almost burst when the next signal came through scratchy, but audible.

" ... is the HMS Liverpool of ... jesty's Ro... Navy ... have picked up your signal ... are in the area ... coordinates ... can arrange a .... copter rescue. I repeat ... this is the ....iverpool, please respond."

I crushed my finger against the button, virtually tearful as I spoke to the small device in almost devotional attentiveness. I desperately repeated myself over and over, eager to hear the voice of a potential savor.

CHAPTER 13

The markings I hadn't recognized earlier, in our flight from the expressway, were British. Apparently, the HMS Liverpool was anchored in the Upper New York Bay when this thing went down, and was running search and rescue operations in the area by helicopter. That was all I could glean before handing the radio to Kate so she could give them directions. I laughed when she used the gas station we had incinerated hours ago as a point of reference.

"Find the large oily column of smoke, go about five miles Northwest, and turn left," was her last directional comment before she signed off and we settled in to wait.

The day crept on, and, relieved by the thought of escape, we talked. Her dad was a military doctor, her mom a nurse, so her general profession had been more or less a foregone conclusion before she was born. Just a matter of specialty, really. She was still doing her residency in King's Park when it started.

As we spoke, I had more flashes. Not of that night, but of memories that had inexplicably been absent from my head until now. Maria and I eating dinner, scenes from my last movie, sailing my boat, stuff like that. Oddly, most of it seemed recent, like months of memories before her death had been suppressed or pushed to the back of my head, only to resurface now for some reason.

Kate explained in a little more detail the inconsistencies in my case, and I listened intently. The basic idea was sound: how could I have caused Maria's death, if her body had shut down hours before I got home?

This was never mentioned, was never brought up—to the best of my memory, at least—in my discussions with my attorneys. These memories were coming back piecemeal, but more rapidly, and still I had no consciousness of these flaws. Had they not noticed? Had I dropped half a million dollars on those empty suits only to have them miss this?

It seemed inconceivable, but there it was. I asked about the details, listening to the response and hoping for more memories. Now drinking them in, relishing their contribution to making my mind whole again.

As the sun reached its midpoint and she closed her eyes to join Fred in catching a nap, I tried to let the memories come. Some came, some continued to elude me. Maria was there when I got home, but she didn't respond when I called out. When I reached the bedroom, I had seen a file folder marked "Lazarus" with a red binding and full of paperwork, but I hadn't opened it. Just really picked it up out of curiosity while noting that the bed hadn't been slept in.

She had startled me when she put her hand on my shoulder, but the memory of what happened next was still a nymph, darting behind the trees of my mind, which I still couldn't see for the forest.

What the hell was Lazarus, and why hadn't she gone to sleep? Why had she brought the file home? That stuff was supposedly classified. Maybe something was wrong, maybe she had to bring it home to protect it. To destroy it? She had been working on cell reanimation—maybe Lazarus was a code word for that project. And she had said there were problems with the program. Hiccups, she called them. That they had technically reanimated cells but that there were glitches: problems that needed to be addressed.

I rubbed my eyes with the back of my hand, the constant moaning a tortuous reminder of where we were. Was it possible that this was a product of their research? That Lazarus, if that's what it was called, had escaped or been let loose? I shook my head mutely as I considered it. I still couldn't let myself believe that Maria would be party to such research: science with such destructive potential and such lethal and global consequences. Not Maria, whose eyes lit up with excitement when discussing mitosis, who loved to take walks and smiled so easily. No, not knowingly. She wouldn't have participated knowingly.

I took solace in that thought, and scanned my mind for more details. She had discussed remedying the problems; that a Doctor Kopland on staff was the best, was working on the abnormalities.

What if he succeeded? This was months ago; he had had time, if he continued to work on it. Could a cure possibly exist? Something that Maria had helped start, that she had tried to protect or save, and that he had finished?

Or this could all be a figment of your imagination, the voice appeared unbidden and unwelcome from the back of my mind.

Isn't it all just a little too convenient, it asked dryly, sarcastically.

That you, an insane person after all, would hold the answer, the road map to redemption for mankind's newest plague?

It—or I—was laughing, genuinely amused.

Isn't it just a tad more likely that you're back in your bed, strapped to the steel frame, frothing at the mouth?

No. It wasn't possible. That would be absurd.

Oh really? Can't you see why you'd create this story? You're an actor for God's sake, you know scripts. What better to redeem your deepest regret; your darkest, vilest hour, than a new story? One where Maria is a hero, and you—a washed out movie star—hold the answer to mankind's very salvation and can act in one final role as the goddamn savior of the human race! One where you aren't a certifiable whack job, destined to drool out your lonely, pitiful days in a state sanatorium and, with this, the tone changed from aggressive to sly, there's a chance that this little flame you're harboring deep down for Doctor Hotty might get stoked a little higher, a little hotter? Can you say happy ending?

More laughter, now, amused more at the joke than the concept.

My head was silent for a moment, my mind afire with the agony of this possibility; my confusion and my anger boiled inside me, guilt and weariness battling for supremacy over my tortured head. Doubt crept into an unwanted corner of my consciousness, perched just out of range but clamoring for my attention nonetheless.

Or, this, the voice said dismissively and effecting the verbal picture of a shrug, maybe it is real.

You could jump down there and find out. See if mind can really win out over matter.

My foot moved, and my arm was pushing against the floor—did I ask it to do that?—to lever myself up, when the torture of this internal dialogue was interrupted by the hiss of the radio, much clearer, much more intelligible than the last transmission. Kate started awake, eyes sleepy but alert. Fred grunted, still asleep.

"This is Lieutenant Hartliss of the HMS Liverpool, and I am approximately 3 kilometers from your location," the voice was loud and confident; I noticed in passing that he pronounced Lieutenant left-tenant. Ha. Silly Brits.

"You should be able to make my location. I am flying West Northwest and need a situation report prior to pickup. Please advise on number of party and infection status. Over." The British accent was much clearer with the radio in better form.

Scanning the horizon, I picked up the unmistakable insect-like shape of a helicopter flying low over the tree line. The same helicopter I had seen on our flight from the expressway. In my pain and self-doubt, I over-compensated with joviality.

"Tell him to hang a left, and look for the tower with the three jolly idiots parked on top. No nibbles yet, but our friends downstairs would love to fix that for us."

She relayed my comments, smiling out of the corner of her mouth, and we saw the helicopter bank in our direction.

"We'll need to lower a rope ladder to you, and each person should come up one at a time. We cannot land, given the infestation of your position. Confirm you understand. Over."

"That's fine Lieutenant," Kate replied. "We're just happy to see you guys and anxious to get off this tower."

As an afterthought, she threw in "Over."

The steady, low-pitched thumping of the rotors got closer. The helicopter circled the tower once, and lowered itself into position over our perch, about thirty feet up. A rope ladder came into view on the front side, over the lawn and our parked truck, whipping from side to side in the downdraft produced by the spinning blades. The creatures below, on the roof and on the ground, howled their displeasure at the whirling blades above their heads. I wondered whether they had enough cognition to realize they were being denied a meal.

Fred, having been awakened by the thrumming rotors overhead, was the first to go. He was also the most reluctant. Looking over the edge to the milling creatures below, which were aggravated by the activity above, Fred considered the rope ladder hanging precariously before the railing and promptly sat down. Head shaking, he crossed his arms and looked stubbornly to the distant tree line, frowning and not meeting either of our gazes. Finally, after much cajoling, and the offer of a candy bar by Kate, he rose, tentatively reaching out to the gently undulating rope, and climbed out.

Kate went next, packing up the radio and quickly reaching for and navigating the ladder as I held it steady, waiting my turn. When she reached the top, she turned, gesturing, and I caught the closest rung, stepping out over the abyss, the vibrating rope my lifeline above a mass of ghouls whose upturned faces and open, drooling mouths gaped wide. Shuddering, I gripped the lines firmly, and pulled myself aloft. As I reached the top and heaved my torso onto the floor of the chopper with the assistance of the crewman, I heaved a sigh of relief.

I sat next to Kate on the hard steel bench seat against the aft bulkhead, and looked back down at the school as the helicopter banked hard and away. The roof was a solid carpet of creatures, their bodies colliding against one another in their haste to feed, but their urges frustrated by our escape. The lawn and the football field were similarly covered, although the ghouls wandering those areas were milling with less purpose, shambling from spot to spot, brought here by the promise to feed, but denied the pleasure: now sentenced to a temporary purgatory of hunger and purposelessness.

The engine was a monstrous roar as we were instructed with hand gestures to don large, insulated headsets complete with microphones and muffled ear pads. We pulled upward and my stomach lurched, as the crewmember manning the ladder and winch turned to us, lifting his sun visor. He smiled crookedly as he grabbed the doorframe for support. He was a young man, probably no more than twenty or twenty-one, freckled face undisturbed by the scene he had witnessed probably dozens of times already.

He spoke, the upbeat English accent lending an Oliver Twist flavor to the event and rendering the moment slightly more absurd.

"Welcome aboard," his greeting crackled over our headsets. "You lucky chaps just caught the last taxi out of hell."

CHAPTER 14

"Last?" asked Kate into her mouthpiece, leaning forward, her comment coming through clearly in my own earphones as he nodded.

"The ship is at capacity, but we were on our way back out for one last patrol before wrapping it up when we got your call." He shook his head, still smiling at us. "You were very fortunate to have rung us when you did. Lieutenant Hartliss was already in his bunk drinking tea when we got your call; at least mentally" he joked, looking over his shoulder at the pilot, who was mostly obscured by the front bulkhead.

"Not that I don't appreciate the effort," I interjected, "but what is a British ship doing parked in the Bay and running search and rescue over Long Island?"

He frowned, with a sardonic twist to his mouth and eyes, "We just happened to be the lucky buggers picked for joint maneuvers with your Navy off the East Coast for the last month. We were fitting out for our return jog when all this mess started up." He looked out the open door, gesturing down as he did so, eyes squinting against the glare of the sun, small mouth tightening with what could pass for anxiety.

Fred was seated across the cabin from us, watching our interactions with an unusually astute expression. When the crewman gestured to the door and the landscape below, he sat up, watching intently as if something was expected of him.

"It's a right mess down there, no doubt. We've picked up twenty-six survivors so far, and we're not getting many more distress calls."

Kate looked to me and back to the crewman, hugging herself in the cold air. "Who's picking up the rest of the survivors? I mean, millions of people lived in the City, on Long Island and Jersey. There have to be more survivors out there. More people like us?"

The frown laced with sorrow was out of place on such a young face. He looked back to the door, shaking his head. "Twenty-eight calls. Twenty-six pickups. Like I said," he said quietly, "a right mess."

Kate was leaning toward the door, looking down as we traveled west over the Island, toward the Bay.

"Mike," she said, transfixed by what she saw, wisps of hair escaped from the headset batting against her face as the cold wind blasted the cabin, "you should see this."

I looked out the window on my right. Smoke from hundreds of fires made tunnels of black into the gray autumn sky. The expressways were packed with cars, none of which were moving. Zombies were everywhere, moving individually and in groups, threading clumsily between cars and buildings, over streets and fields - no reason or method to their shambling.

On a large, four lane road below, we were forced to watch as dozens of creatures converged on two people who had clearly just been dragged from the back of a motorcycle. A man and a woman, both in what looked from this height like leather riding gear, struggled and squirmed on the pavement as zombies pawed and grasped at their limbs and exposed flesh. Details from our height were blessedly indiscernible, but I could see enough to be sick.

Green woods and gray concrete made a patchwork quilt of civilization, the appearance of which was shattered when the mind imposed upon it the reality of the moving forms below. If you concentrated, you could almost make believe that the shambling forms, so apparently inhuman from above, were the same people they had been. Mothers, fathers, sisters, brothers.

Friends and lovers. Until recently, each of these shambling specks had lives; they had hopes, dreams and fears. Now they had no hope, no dreams. Their lives were forfeit to this plague. And they had become our fears.

How many people that used to live in these peaceful-looking homes, who used to work at these stolid, boring offices? How many of us had died in the space of days? Thousands? Millions? What the fuck was going on?

And is it real?

I had to admit, I had my doubts.

But as I watched the earth unfold below me, I realized what I had to do. Not just because it might actually help others, but because I needed to know. I had to know that I was sane; that Maria wasn't involved—that the dreams and the memories weren't coincidence, and they weren't inconsequential. I desperately wanted to believe that, somehow, I had escaped the first round of carnage with knowledge that might lead to finding a cure to this hellish plague. I couldn't ignore that possibility.

Unfortunately, neither could the fact that Maria's lab was miles away and that I was, legally speaking of course, insane.

That might impact my ability to convince people that my memories were real and that, in some huge convenient coincidence, I happened to be married to someone who may have contributed to causing this but who also might have possessed knowledge of the cure.

Well, I knew what I had to do. I'd deal with figuring out how to do it later.

Eastchester Bay was off the starboard side, and we were flying relatively low, maybe a thousand feet. From below, a car moving too fast careened into a mass of creatures, shattering against the side of a building and exploding in a sheet of flame. The creatures that were left standing moved to the car's ruined hulk, ignoring the flames and allowing themselves to become engulfed, turning their already dead bodies into moving torches with a singular goal of feeding. As they reached into the car, it passed out of sight, denying me the absurd pleasure of witnessing their disappointment at finding their meal to be well-done, rather than rare.

A massive fire was burning out of control ahead, looking like it had engulfed an entire town. The crewman caught me looking and followed my gaze. "Used to be a town there, about thirty survivors. We caught a distress call from 'em about an hour ago. Seems they had barricaded themselves in and were being overrun and couldn't hold off the you-know-whats."

"Did you help?"

He chuckled. "Bloody well didn't! Those bastards shot at us a day ago on a fly-by; Lieutenant held back after that. Besides, if we had landed, we would have been swamped. This bucket can only carry six." He nodded his head toward the fire. "But we were glad to oblige with some rockets when they were overrun."

We passed over the marina, most boats still attached to their moorings, some wallowing half-sunk in the shallow water. The Bay was relatively quiet but for those that had made it away and were apparently anchored not far off shore, confused and directionless. Bodies littered the pavement of the parking lot, but it was impossible to tell whether they were human or zombie. As we flew over the last pier, a moving crowd caught my attention, and I looked back to the crewman.

"Looks like a crowd—maybe survivors down here," I said, pointing. He stood up, crouching, and moved across the cabin.

"No, mate. Look closer. See how they move? See how slow they're walking? Those are zeds, right as rain."

Zeds? I did see, and the pilot must have too, as the chopper banked hard to the right, and a new voice—the voice from the radio—sounded in the headphones. "I think I make two at the end of the dock; get the ladder ready for a pickup."

"Aye, sir," as he moved back to the winch, checking the harness.

I looked out again. The crowd, there must have been hundreds of them, was moving toward the end of the dock where two people stood, looking from the edge to the crowd and back again. One waived at us as we banked in hard and accelerated. Not fast enough—we couldn't possibly get there in time. The zombies were going to beat us there.

"Lock the cabin," came a terse order from the pilot, a young voice: young but unafraid. The helicopter accelerated even more, pushing us against our seats, and moving fast and low toward the dock. I could no longer see from the side window, but was able to peer straight ahead from the pilot's viewpoint, as the chopper lined up right into the crowd.

"Aye, sir," again as the door was locked open, the ladder bound tight, and the overhead compartment housing the headgear was shoved closed.

Suddenly from either side of the cabin, twin bright flashes erupted in an epileptic's nightmare of white light roared out of the side-mounted canons with the impossibly amplified buzzing of millions of wasps. From the front window, twin rows of destruction sprayed a path of splintering wood and ruptured bodies before us as we moved toward the end of the dock. Reaching the end, the pilot banked hard, bringing the left side of the chopper almost horizontal to the dark water below, and then slammed the controls back to the right, the helicopter righting itself abruptly, this time facing the oncoming horde and hovering thirty feet above the surface of the wooden planking.

From the outside of the vehicle, a loudspeaker, apparently hooked into the com system on the helicopter, ordered simply "Get down!" and the two instantly flattened themselves obediently on the dock.

An angry hornet, the helicopter moved forward and down threateningly, now hovering ten feet from the deck, close enough to see the first line of creatures which was perhaps ten wide. They shambled forward, hungry and unafraid toward the cockpit. The leader of the pack was a man dressed absurdly in the outfit of a yachtsman, blue cap still fixed in place over a gray and bloody face, sunken red eyes highlighting the lack of skin over his jaw. The stump where his left arm had been was a rotten, brown mass, and his brown loafers shuffled forward, twenty feet away from our hovering form.

"Bloody gits," was the pilot's calm comment, almost under his breath, as he opened fire again, the turrets mounted on either side erupting in a vicious deluge of flying metal and flashing light. He slowly rotated the vehicle from left to right, using the movement of the helicopter in mid-air to train the 20 mm cannons and ensure the widest possible swath of fire as he adjusted the constant stream of heavy rounds to head level.

The skipper went first as the front row of creatures simply evaporated. They didn't collapse or fall; they didn't stumble backwards or crumple to the dock floor. They just disappeared.

A red and brown mist interspersed with chunks of clothing and gray flesh sprayed back into the following ghouls, who, having lost the cover of their front-running companions, similarly disappeared into a cloud of bloody debris. Chunks of wood dislodged from the planking of the pier by errant rounds flew into the air and settled on the oddly peaceful surface of the water below.

Those in the rear echelon stumbled and fell over the parts and piles before them, slipping on the now-wet and splintered surface. Their progress slowed as the fire from the guns became less accurate, the distance to target now variable. The cannons now severed legs and arms and bisected creatures at the waist and chest.

Incredibly, these were not killing blows, as the unique physiology of the zombies prevented death from these wounds. But it slowed them down.

Their progress delayed for at least thirty feet and the guns now empty and clicking hollowly against their housings, the pilot reversed and rose, over the two survivors and ordering the ladder down. A young black woman rose first. She was dressed in a business suit and sneakers, eyes wide and body shaking, powered by the dual stimulants of adrenaline and fear. She collapsed on the floor of the chopper as the ladder was lowered again.

A small Indian man followed, and as soon as he was safely on the ladder, the pilot moved the helicopter back over the water, turning toward the Bay before he was even up. Out of the side window I could see creatures that had reached the end of the dock right as was lifted up were now crashing off the end into the dark water, the weight of bodies from behind pushing each subsequent creature into the dark water of the bay. The forerunners were forced into the water over the edge, those in the rear not appreciating the peril of pushing forward. I chuckled to myself and looked back as the man made his way into the cabin, blue jeans covered in blood and windbreaker matted with dirt.

"That's it, we're back to the Liverpool," came the somehow lighthearted voice from the flight deck. "We're bingo fuel and ammo. Captain's gonna shit when he sees we have five more."

As we banked to the West again, the woman looked at me, headphones adjusting awkwardly over her head. She cocked her head and stared at me. I looked away, trying to hide my face.

This should be interesting. Maybe they didn't get my movies in England.

As her face lit up in recognition, and she revealed my secret identity to everyone over the intercom, I somehow doubted it. Why didn't Superman ever have this problem?

The glasses. That's it. Maybe I needed a pair of glasses to pull off the incognito gig.

Kate turned to me and smiled, reaching over and patting my leg in mock conciliation.

"Tough being famous, huh?"

The bay came into sight, and the large gray form of a warship rose imperiously from its calm waters. I looked at her for a moment, her still smiling, beautiful face reflecting the mischievous glint in her eyes, and sunk my head into my hands, staring at the floor.

CHAPTER 15

We landed in a vicious cross-wind, the tail swinging sickeningly to the side at the last minute before Hartliss pulled the vehicle straight and then quickly down, somehow accomplishing a perfect three point landing as the tires bounced slightly with the gentle lateral momentum of the ship. Crewmembers shot out from the hanger, securing the helicopter to the flight deck and making incomprehensible hand gestures to the crewman at the door as the engines were throttled down. The conning tower and massive radar and communications assemblies towered above us, the faces of seamen appearing and disappearing behind thick glass and dull gray metal. The flight deck was located at the very stern of the ship, and we were separated from the cold black water by a lower deck and a simple railing. Deck guns stood at attention on either side, their cold lethality useless against humanity's newest threat.

Disembarking, we were routed directly to a portion of the hanger cordoned off from the remainder of the vessel. Hartliss and the crewman waived as they entered a hatch on the port side of the hangar, followed by an armed marine. Large white curtains further divided the space we entered, and the women were directed to the left, the men to the right. A small, fine featured man in the uniform of a sailor but wearing a doctor's coat met us at the entrance, looking at each of us and scratching on a clipboard.

"Okay, gents. Let's lose the clothing and step this way. Line up against the far curtain and put your arms behind your heads," he said in a detached, almost bored voice. "Can't have that nasty bug coming aboard our little slice of paradise, now can we?"

Gladly shedding clothing that had again been covered in various bits of blood and gore, the evening chill of the outside air touched my skin as the last article dropped to the floor. Self-consciously, I walked to the indicated position, covering myself until ordered to put my hands behind my head and face front. I admonished myself not to drop the soap as banjos dueled in the back of my mind. I smiled to myself, quickly straightening my face lest my mirth be misinterpreted as Fred was lined up to my left, the Indian man from the dock on my right.

The doctor—I assumed as much given the coat—carefully scrutinized Fred. He started at the toes and worked up the legs, examining thighs, groin, buttocks, stomach, back, chest and very closely surveyed the arms and fingers before moving to a cursory glance at the face and ears before scratching on his clipboard again and dismissively gesturing to Fred.

"Clear," he said, finishing his notes, and moving to me. Over his shoulder, "You may put your clothing in the bin against the starboard bulkhead and you will be issued soap for the shower."

"Uh, Doc?" he looked back to me, paying attention to my face for the first time, "He's not quite there upstairs—best to let me show him when we're done." He glanced at Fred, who was unconcernedly looking around the room, examining the pipes and ventilation tubes running the length of the ceiling while shivering violently in the crisp air.

"Right, then."

He stared at my face again, and then the obvious question. "You know, you bear a striking resemblance to ... "

I sighed. "Yeah, let's just short-circuit the inquiry. I am him and he is me. We're both getting a little chilly here, so if we can get this intimate little appointment over ASAP, I'd like to mitigate the shrinkage as much as possible. I do have a reputation to uphold, after all." My teeth were chattering in waves, and I caught the marine watching the door chuckling.

The doctor smiled. "I was going to ask you to repeat that pithy line of yours, but I see you lack the patience at present. Perhaps later."

He began with the toes, and gave me the same once-over as he had Fred. Finding nothing, he waved me on, scratching on his paperwork as he spoke. "You and your friend will be escorted to the showers, where you will be issued a bar of soap and strict orders to disinfect. You will be monitored, and believe me when I tell you that we expect you to be thorough or we will assist in the process."

He looked at me from the clipboard, not lifting his head. "We're not as gentle as your mum when we help you wash, so make sure you pay special attention to a comprehensive scrub." That sounded ominous. Like if you missed a spot, a large man with a jumbo Q-tip was going to batter you senseless with a foamy bludgeon.

From the other side of the curtain, I heard Kate's voice suddenly rise. "Whoa, that's cold! You keep that in the freezer, asshole? Jesus! At least buy me a drink first!"

At least Fred and I weren't alone in our five star treatment, I thought, smiling.

I turned, following the second marine to a box of towels, which we were permitted to wrap around our waists as we were escorted to the door in the far bulkhead. As we reached the door, the sound of a commotion drew our attention back to the deck. The Indian man was waving his arms, shouting at the doctor, as the physician moved back in apprehension. The marine watching the far door moved toward the man, lowering his weapon menacingly.

The patient stopped gesticulating wildly, instead starting to inch toward the external curtain. Was he trying to escape? Where did he think he was going?

"I will ask you once more sir," the doctor said firmly and loudly, clearly reiterating the question that had occasioned the ruckus, "Where did you acquire the abrasion on your ankle?"

I looked down, noticing for the first time a small, semi-circular reddening on the apex of the man's anklebone. His eyes were wild, shifting continuously from the doctor to the marines, to me and back to the doctor. He looked at his ankle, jerking his head up abruptly as he realized what he was doing, his body language as incriminating as a verbal admission. Unfortunately for him, the doctor, having clearly processed many others, spoke that particular language.

"Gentlemen," he gestured to the marines, casually stepping back and calmly writing on his clipboard. I saw him make a linear crossing gesture, as if he was crossing out a name. Just that quick, his fate was sealed. In the single horizontal stroke of a pen, the disease had claimed one more of a dwindling number of survivors.

The soldiers on either side of the man, each dressed out in full combat regalia, complete with Kevlar vest and helmet, stepped forward and grabbed an arm each, pulling the still-naked man between them. He struggled in vain against their brute strength, kicking his feet so violently against the deck that he drew blood, leaving a crimson trail behind him as he was dragged screaming and shouting while clearly cursing in what I could only assume to be Hindu, maybe Urdu. They roughly pushed the curtain aside and pulled him through, the screams echoing against the high metal ceiling.

The screams turned to pleading, now in English. From a distance, we could hear his pleas. Begging, he offered up money, property, servitude. It availed him nothing. The single, sharp sound of a rifle being fired was his only response, and then there was no more noise, no more resistance. No bargaining with this disease.

"As you can see," the doctor read my mind, explaining in his now seemingly preternatural calm, "we maintain an infection-free status by eliminating the diseased carriers." He pronounced it state-us. "No other way to go about it, and really," he shrugged, "it's much kinder to them in the long run."

He turned around, gathering his med kit and moving toward the doorway where we stood, mute. Catching my gaze, possibly misinterpreting my stare as judgment rather than simple astonishment, he paused and explained further.

"All indications are that the mutation itself is painful, and we have no idea how much cognizance the mind of the infected individual retains in post-mutation form. If they were aware of what was happening, if they knew what they had become but could only watch, mutely and impotently from within the rotting prison of their own flesh as they became and acted as ravaging ghouls, feeding on the flesh of the living ... well, it's really a favor we're doing them, yes?" he said unconcernedly.

Behind him, the marines walked back inside, faces blank. One picked up a hose, spraying the deck where the man had spread his infected blood prior to being removed.

He opened the hatch door, cocking his arm in front of his chest, making a directional signal and canting his head toward the hatch. His small eyes were sad but his face was stone; his countenance, if not his disposition, clearly affected by the difficult position forced upon him by his occupation and intervening circumstance.

I didn't answer as I moved into the ship, stepping over the lip of the metal bulkhead and following him to the showers. I wondered: what do they retain? If their brains were the engines that continue to motivate the machine, wouldn't it be possible that those brains would continue to operate, at least subconsciously, on some level?

It was a nagging concept that was too impossible to imagine. Indeed, it was hardly something you could believe if you were to survive. To believe that with each killing blow or gunshot struck or fired in self-defense was destroying an actual human conscience trapped in its own body...that was too much. Whether it was true or not, it wasn't something I was ready to buy into. For my own sake.

We cleaned ourselves, as was suggested, quite thoroughly. My own actions were motivated by an extreme aversion to having several marines help me wash my delicates, and directed Fred to do the same, uncertain of how he'd react in such a personal situation. We were issued clothing and directed to the ship's galley.

I had time to draw a cup of lukewarm coffee from the stainless steel pot, grab one for Fred, and sit down slowly. My stiff muscles protested against the combination of physical activity, cold air, and cold water, as Kate and our friend from the dock appeared. They were similarly dressed, long hair still wet from the shower, shoes squeaking slightly on the spotless floor. They were allowed to grab some coffee before we were all ushered below decks to a large room, clearly designated as a refugee holding area.

There were more than twenty people, all in various states of sleeping, sitting, talking or playing cards. They all looked up as we entered, Fred first, then Kate and the other woman, finally me. Recognition lit the eyes of several passengers as I sat down on an empty bunk to the left of the door, resigned finally to allowing myself to be outed. Kate sat down next to me, not speaking. The lady from the docks—Nicole, I believe she had said—had moved into the crowd, talking and gesturing in my direction. None approached, but I could see various degrees of awe, admiration, judgment and disgust as they passed across weary faces.

I felt for the first time the heavy stigma of the criminal, of the outcast. Until now, I had focused on flight and survival, forgetting in the maelstrom of confusion and otherworldly events that I bore the burden of the criminally convicted and the feloniously insane. I had tried to hide my identity with Kate, more out of what seemed necessity than aversion to being recognized. But because of her peculiar background, and forgiving personality, that had worked out fine. Overall, though, I doubted that most would be so understanding. Judging by the looks being direct toward me in this small world under the deck of a ship, I was right.

Even as society disintegrated and hell on earth asserted its claim as the new status quo, I wore the mantle of insanity as plainly as if the first zombie has never risen. I need look no further than the looks directed at me as I sat quietly on the firm bunk staring at some sailor's poster of a model lying on a sandy beach. While it is true that some evidently discarded my criminal record for my civil fame, it was clear that fully half of those in the room remembered nothing past the final pass of the gavel and the perp walk into King's Park.

The hatch opened, groaning slightly as the metal was exercised outward. Lieutenant Hartliss's face appeared through the open crack, looking around and finally finding us and smiling. Although I recognized him from before, I was able to pay more attention to him now, in the light. He was a young man, maybe no more than thirty. His black hair, cut militarily short, framed a longish, handsome face with a crooked grin. Blue eyes flicked from me to Kate and back again.

"Cap'n would like to see you both," he said. "Every newbie gets to be debriefed, standard stuff." He stepped back as we rose and walked past.

"Besides," he said confidentially, smiling again as he shut the hatch, the heavy door clinking heavily against its frame "he's never met a movie star before."

Kate smiled at me and put her arm out as if to say "after you." I shook my head, following Hartliss as he walked briskly down the narrow corridor, up a narrow, low staircase, and through two more hatches, emerging into a medium-sized office.

Tastefully paneled in dark wood, and with a large desk against the far wall, it was reminiscent of a study that you might find in any mid-nineteenth century, New England colonial home. Various seafaring memorabilia and nick-knacks lined the walls, each apparently screwed or otherwise fastened to the shelving. A pair of evenly spaced portholes looked out over the bay, the statute of liberty a briefly inspiring sight that prefaced the entrance of the Captain.

He was a tall man, a slight paunch protruding over his belt line, but powerful shoulders evidencing that he came by his post after a lifetime of hard work. Cold, dark eyes trained on each of us, his large frame pausing in the doorframe before he extended his hand to Kate.

"Captain James, ma'am. It is a pleasure to make your acquaintance," he bowed forward ever so slightly as Kate took the offered hand.

"Dr. Kate Whitmore," she replied, reminding me again of her vocation, and causing his eyebrows to rise slightly.

"I was unaware that you were a physician," he said, crossing to his desk and sitting heavily in his chair, gesturing as he did so to take our seats in the two chairs across from him. "Your vocation could be a quite a boon to us, under the circumstances."

"I'm a psychiatrist," she replied. He nodded, turning toward me.

"And you, sir, need no introduction," he affirmed, now looking at me, expressionless.

"Is that in a good way, or a bad?" I asked, genuinely concerned.

"That, I believe, is yet to be seen. Tell me, if you will, how you came to be travelling with this lovely woman, and how you managed to be on the rooftop of a high school, surrounded by zeds, and, forgive me for saying, but all around bollixed if not for the good Lieutenant here," nodding to Hartliss, who smiled as he stood at ease, hands clasped behind his back, staring at the far wall, "who chose to ignore my last order and bring you in anyway." Hartliss's grin didn't fade, as James' face bore a hint of vexation but no animosity.

We recounted our story together, told of our flight from the Park, our loss of companions, our attempt at the docks. He nodded along, surprised at some points, interested at others.

"Bloody good for you that you weren't able to pass through that town to the docks. The marina is the nastiest place of the bunch. When this thing started, people crowded onto the highways, toward the marinas and airports, government buildings and police stations." His voice was somber, his gaze distant. As if he had been there, remembering it all.

"All it took was an accident, an attack inside a car, whatever, and the highways were jammed up within the first few hours, beltways around Washington and Philadelphia reportedly bumper to bumper cars, with growing packs of zeds moving from car to car, highway to highway. Marinas went the same way, crowds of people sinking boats in their drive to board anything that floated, fights breaking out between armed groups vying for transport. Police opening fire into civilians that were trying to get into the stations and government buildings. Add zeds into the right mess the humans were already making of it all, and it was a regular pandemonium. Nasty business." He turned to a cabinet beside him, drawing out a bottle of scotch and three glasses, not bothering to offer.

"I'm sorry Captain, but the crewman on the chopper and now you, you've said 'zeds'—I'm assuming your talking about the zombies?"

He tilted his head back and laughed, pushing our glasses across his desk toward us. "I suppose if I had said aluminium you would have deduced what I was saying? Zed is what you yanks call "Z." We've dispensed with the 'zombie' nomenclature. Makes it too unbelievable. We've reduced them to zeds. Takes away some of the ... oddity ... of the situation." He glanced at Hartliss and back to us.

"I'm going to be honest with you now, Mr. McKnight," he said, looking at me seriously across his desk.

Uh oh. Here it comes.

"I'm not overly fond of the idea of harboring a convicted criminal on my ship, especially one that just escaped from an institution for the criminally insane," he said slowly, holding his glass of whiskey in one hand.

I stared back, no clever response coming to mind.

He continued in a slightly softer tone of voice. "But I'm also inclined to believe that no one who was truly criminally insane could have made it as far as you did, while winning the respect of an honest doctor," a nod to Kate, "so I am going to permit you to remain and we will allow you passage to England with the remaining refugees."

I nodded thankfully as I geared up my courage for the next comment, which I knew might be inconsistent with his expression of confidence in my sanity. My conclusion earlier made in the helicopter ride to the ship was weighing heavily on my mind. I had thought about this over the last few hours, and was more confident than ever that it was what I needed to do. While I thought it might not hurt to ask, I suspected I would find little support from this venue. But I had to try.

"Thank you Captain. But I'm afraid I'm going to have to ask you one last favor," I gulped and pressed forward. He cocked his head inquisitively, eyes slightly curious, questioning.

"I'm going to need a lift back to shore."

He stared at me, then at Kate, then back to me. Believing, perhaps, that this was a joke that he had not yet been let in on, he smiled suspiciously. Suddenly, he erupted in deep, body shaking laughter.

CHAPTER 16

It was the laughter of disbelief. He paused, seeming to believe for the first time I was serious. Still smiling, he leaned forward, dark eyes severe and unblinking.

"Mr. McKnight. Do you fully appreciate what has happened here? Do you know why your arse is sitting on a British destroyer instead of an American Coast Guard ship or Navy vessel? Your country is disappearing, sir. Your military is stretched too thin, and half of the armed forces left in your country were caught in the initial wave. Bloody hell, man. Your entire Navy is on its way to Florida! We may be the only operative combat vessel left in the Northeast!"

"Florida?"

He stood up, moving to a map on the wall. Our eyes tracked his hand as he pointed at New York City. "First cases, New York, Philadelphia, Boston, D.C." his finger punctuated each city name, pointing to each in turn.

"Infection spread from there, very quickly. Moved out from the cities, into the suburbs, then into the rural areas." He traced a wider arc around each city. Moving his hand to the Western borders New York and Pennsylvania, he continued.

"Your National Guard tried to draw the lines at the state boundaries, contain the zeds to the initial outbreak states through impromptu blockades outside cities and on major highways, but that idea was a no go. Like I said, large numbers of your military and police were either caught in the initial wave before they could even report, or overcome at their initial positions because their commanders didn't appreciate, no one appreciated, how many they'd be dealing with or how fast." He turned back to us.

My thoughts wandered to the news reports I had seen back at the hospital. The barricades over the interstates, the huge crowds of creatures approaching the small military forces arrayed against them.

"Not possible to control that many, not as fast as they were multiplying. So they fell back again, even as reports filtered in of new outbreaks in the Western states: Arizona, New Mexico, Utah, Texas. What you call your Midwest was already seeing large uprisings in some big cities, but there were some that remained relatively calm or that allowed the authorities more time to contain isolated outbreaks. Typically smaller cities that didn't see as much air travel as the larger ones. This is your nation's plan "B" so to speak. They're fortifying the smaller Midwest cities, and attempting to isolate the outbreaks in the Western states, with very little success. And all in a matter of days." He moved back to the desk, leaving the map unrolled as if to drive his point home.

"These things are everywhere, and they're multiplying like bloody bunnies. Our satellites confirm that you have widespread fire, confusion and all out pandemonium in most, if not all, of the major cities on the Eastern Seaboard." He sat down heavily again, picking up his scotch and taking a long drink.

"But you mentioned Florida? What does Florida have to do with Midwestern cities?" Kate asked, as I nodded along.

"Apparently, the Midwest idea was local. Came from some enterprising local governments that had managed their own evacuation and emergency response tactics as this thing unfolded. They were on top of the isolated outbreaks as they occurred and had the foresight to shut down their airports and train stations, barricade their incoming interstates, and initiate body checks, as soon as it was apparent what was happening. The whole time, your federal government was caught flat footed, still holding their wankers in their hands a full 24 hours into the infection." He smiled and turned to Kate. "Forgive my British," he joked as she smiled in return.

"So what did the feds do?"

"Finally someone got their head on straight, and remembered their primary school geography. Zeds can't swim—at least not that we know of—and the outbreak started in the Northeast. If they could isolate outbreaks in Florida and cut them off before they spread ... "

"... then the peninsula would be the perfect stronghold against a Southward infestation." I finished for him, understanding. "But that strip of land is huge," I continued on, thinking out loud. "How the hell can they protect the whole strip between the two oceans?"

He shrugged. "Sounds impossible to me, but last I heard, they were moving all the military assets from Florida, Texas, Mississippi, Alabama, Georgia and Louisiana along interstate 10, and mobilizing all their air units from the state to patrol the I-10 corridor. I also heard a rumor that they were commandeering civilian cars and trucks to park on the interstate as a makeshift wall, but ..." he drifted off and shrugged.

"We only get sporadic reports, and lately they've been fewer and fewer. I pieced together the picture I just painted you from com chatter, refugee reports and radio intercepts, as well as reports from fleet headquarters. But we have little direct knowledge from later than 36 hours after the outbreak."

I tried to wrap my mind around such an extraordinary concept. The Eastern seaboard had been abandoned and overrun, government response was disjointed at best, hopelessly inept at worst. The zombies were in de facto control of almost half the country and threatened infestation of the other half despite our best efforts.

But it didn't matter, I reminded myself. If there is hope for a cure or a vaccine, if Maria's legacy was the salvation of mankind from the effects of Lazarus, I couldn't sit back and do nothing. We wouldn't be safe in Florida, or England, or even fucking Antarctica. This thing would take over the planet. It was just a matter of time. It had to be stopped.

"I still have to go," I said into the silence that followed his last comment. "I may know of a cure."

Now Captain James was interested. No laughing matter anymore. "How's that?" I could hear Hartliss shift behind me.

"My wife. She was a researcher, a biochemist, at a government facility outside the city. A place called Starling Mountain. When she died," I hurried past that point, "she was working on a project code named Lazarus. It was designed to reanimate dead cells. They had succeeded, apparently only to a limited extent, but were working to iron out the kinks."

Everyone's eyes were on me, their faces serious as I continued. Kate's face revealed something more, but I couldn't place the look.

"There was another doctor there, a Doctor Kopland, that was supposedly the best in the field. He was working on fixing the anomalies in the project. That was months ago. He had to have time to get it right." I looked around hopefully, searching for agreement, comprehension, or even the lack of conviction that I was insane.

Hartliss didn't make a sound, and Kate just looked at me, her eyes searching my face, concern evident on her expressive face. James sat back, smiling, shaking his head.

"I'm sorry, but I can't take your word on this. You have to realize how bloody insane it sounds. You, and forgive me for bringing this up again, a criminally insane ex-movie star—action movie star—want me to lend you my only helicopter and a pilot to go chasing down an ephemeral cure that might or might not exist, that your wife, who you supposedly murdered, may or may not have worked on, so that you can be humanity's last hope against the newest killer plague?"

His empty glass came down hard on his desk like a gavel, condensation from the bottom making a wet ring on the dark wood. I suppressed the urge to find him a coaster, as the voice in my head pushed into my consciousness.

He's on to you...he knows you're still crazy. You know how crazy this sounds - did you need to verbalize it to hear it yourself? You are mankind's hope. Just like one of your movies. You, and only you, hold the key to humanity's redemption. Just like one of your movies. Why don't you defecate on the floor, claw your eyes out, jump off the radar mast ... those would be clearer examples of your insanity than spouting off this ridiculous theory of yours. Silly crazy person, heroics are for movies.

And it was gone again.

Ignoring the voice, I pressed on, fully committed. "I know this sounds crazy, but it's true. I'm not asking for a loan, I'm just asking for a ride."

Before he could answer, the loudspeaker above my head interrupted in a metallic squawk: "Captain James, incoming message from fleet headquarters. Captain to the bridge."

He shook his head and stood up, acknowledging his page with his movements. Walking to the side of the desk and stopping, turning toward us, he took a breath, exhaling fully before speaking again.

"Every time I send Hartliss out there," he jerked his hand toward the window and my eyes followed, drawn again to the statute of liberty, eyes focused on the torch. On the promise of hope, the very epitome of new beginnings, "I risk his life, the life of his crewman, and my only chopper. I don't have the luxury of authorizing fanciful trips like this, and the answer must be, and is, an unqualified no. I'm quite sorry." He strode quickly past us, turning only after he passed through the open hatch, past Hartliss. He looked at his watch.

"The Lieutenant will show you back to your quarters after you have a chance to eat with the first shift of refugees. It was a pleasure meeting with you both." He continued on, the clanking sound of his footfalls fading down the corridor.

I hung my head, disappointed and not a little embarrassed at revealing my theory to Kate. The sudden touch of her hand on my back, comforting and reassuring, brought my head up and my eyes to hers. Hartliss spoke first, surprising us both. More surprising was what he said.

"I have some people I think you should meet." No smile but a suggestive glimmer in his eye as he motioned to the door. "Sounds like you chaps might have something in common."

As he led us down the corridor and back to the mess hall, I spoke to Kate. "I'm sorry I didn't share this with you before. You could see for yourself how crazy it sounded and the last thing I wanted while we were out there was for you to think I deserved to be in that place."

She paused for a moment before replying, ducking her head as we moved through an open hatchway. "Did you?" she asked, suggestively, "deserve to be there, I mean."

"I used to think so. Now I'm not so sure. I have flashes of memory, like I had on the tower, but there are still blanks. It's the blanks, the gaps in my mind, that make me wonder. I don't know what fills those voids, and I can't assume the best. I won't."

I glanced in her direction, stepping carefully now, not wanting to reveal the voice that had plagued my consciousness since I left the Park, not convinced it was incriminating, but not persuaded that it wasn't.

She stopped, turning to me, and causing Hartliss to pause as he led us down another flight of stairs. "And you think these flashes, that they're true? That you're not filling the gaps yourself with what you want to believe rather than what is real?" Not waiting for an answer, she started down the steps; as if it was a question she wanted me to answer for myself before responding to her.

Oh shit, hotshot, she's on to you too! These people can see right through you! That's it, game over. Go home. Back to the loony bin. Rubber rooms and nailed down furniture for you for the rest of your miserable life.

With great effort, I shut the door to the voice and replied as best I could to both.

"These are real memories, as real as anything else I can remember. But you're right, who's sure of anything in their own mind, in their own head? Who of us knows at any given moment what facts, feelings or memories we

create to make ourselves feel better, to motivate us, to give us hope? All I
know is that I remember these things, and they're as real as you are."

Ah. And how real is she?

I sighed, knowing it was all too much. Knowing that were I her, this
story would be a far cry from believable. We passed into the mess, where it
looked like about a third of the refugees were seated, eating a small meal on
metal trays. They looked up as we entered and the looks returned, in all their
splendid variety. Hate and awe, judgment and forgiveness. A confusing
mass of emotions from people who I had never met, but who felt they knew
me nevertheless.

I lowered my voice to a whisper, grabbing her arm firmly and turning
her toward me, needing her to understand, to believe. "Look, I know it
seems unfathomable and an incredible coincidence, but I think we have a
chance here. A chance to set this straight, or at least keep it from getting too
big. If I don't try, I'll never know. If I try and fail, no one's hurt. No harm
no foul. If I succeed..."

"...a big if..." she interjected, "even if you have your facts straight..."

I continued over her objections, "...If I do, we have a chance.
Otherwise, the rest of world's going to go the way of the U.S., it's only a
matter of time." I finished my appeal quickly, needing to stop the flood of
words that wanted to come.

I moved to the counter alone, serving myself dinner, feeling her follow
me to the counter and recognizing again how little I had eaten recently. I sat
alone at the end of the last table, away from judging eyes. Away from her,
ashamed and saddened by her judgment.

I shoveled a bite of some sort of potato mash into my mouth, staring at
the oily gravy pooling in the center of the mass of starch on my plate. Peas
clung to the side of the mash, forming a green necklace around the white
mass, reminding me of Erica's infected neck. In a rush of disgusting
memories from the last two days, I pushed my tray away and stood. Beside
me, the sudden warmth of another body and her voice.

"You're going to need your strength for our trip," she said softly, pulling the tray back in front of me.

"Our trip?" I asked.

She looked at me over her tray of warm food, fork poised halfway to her mouth, "You didn't think I'd let you go alone, did you? Shit. Where else would I go? Besides, I get sea sick." She grabbed my fork and handed it to me.

"Now eat up." A full smile this time, lighting up her sparkling eyes. "Might not be a lot open where we're going."

CHAPTER 17

We got through half of our dinner before Hartliss sat down, accompanied by two friends. One of them was, quite simply, the largest man I had ever met—ever even seen. He towered head and shoulders above Hartliss and his shoulders extended at least half again as wide as the Lieutenant's. Gargantuan arms fought to break free of the oppressive confines of his thin tee shirt. The black markings of tattoos, clearly some sort of primal art, rose out of the neck and sleeves of his shirt, covering his arms to the wrists and his neck to the collarbone. Large black eyes gleamed with a disarming humor out of a friendly face, pearly white teeth flashing a quick smile as he sat down across from me. I could almost hear the bench cry out in agony as his massive weight settled down.

Beside him and in stark, incongruous contrast to his dominating figure sat a small, slight woman, face serious with large, bright blue eyes searching the room behind us, as if assessing potential threats. Her black hair was pulled up tightly in a severe bun that sat against the back of her head like a beetle nestled in a tree limb. Her sharp features accentuated her almost diminutive size, her full lips and fairly ample chest emphasizing her femininity.

"Never met a movie star before," came the deep voice from the monster across from me, still smiling as he extended his hand. "My name's Anaru." Seeing the question on my face, he finished, "It's Maori."

"Mike," I said, "it's ... shit, I don't know. Let's say Flemish." He laughed.

Jesus, his hand was the size of a 48-ounce porterhouse! Had he ever eaten a movie star before? Then again, would he have even noticed? I grabbed his hand, afraid not to.

"Ever met an insane felon before?" asked his companion, looking hard at me. No hand extended from her.

"No, I don't think so," he answered with a thoughtful look as he leaned across the table, shaking Kate's hand, "But I took a tour of the Capitol building once a couple years ago, so it's hard to know for sure." Straight faced, he looked at me and winked slowly as he returned to his seat. I smiled in return.

She apparently lacked any visible sense of humor. "I don't even know what we're doing here," she said, rising from the bench across from Kate and looking at Hartliss, eyes blazing. "I don't need to talk to a crazy person. This is bullshit."

Hartliss grabbed her arm. "Calm down, Sam. There's something you need to hear. It's about Lazarus." That got her attention. She stared at him for a moment before sitting down again, competing emotions evident in her stormy demeanor.

"Mike, Kate, this is Sam," he said by way of introduction. Turning to me, "I plucked each of these blokes out of harm's way a day back, and gave them a brief run down of your little talk with the Captain—told 'em you wanted to go back into the mess onshore."

He grinned as if it were funny. It was funny. Not funny ha-ha, but funny in the same way that a banana and mayonnaise sandwich was funny. A really sick, backwards kind of way.

"Thought you might want to meet, seeing as you have something in common. I know a lot of the stories hereabouts, and there's something sounds similar in what you were saying in the Captain's office. Why don't you tell them what you told him?"

I hastily recounted my story, detailing as much as I could remember as Sam and Anaru looked on. Despite her aversion to me, she was clearly interested, asking questions at times. Anaru simply listened, eyes intent, dark brown hands crossed on the table in front of him.

"Where is this facility?" asked Sam as I finished.

"How do you know about Lazarus?" I asked instead, feeling I had disclosed enough and was due some information in return.

She looked to Hartliss, who stood behind Kate and I, and then back to me. No response.

Hartliss spoke up, speaking for her as he continued to stare at her, as if disappointed.

"Sam, or should I say agent Samantha Courtney of the United States Secret Service, was picked up at Fort Dix after it was completely overrun. We took her off the roof of the base water tower yesterday evening. She was the last of four agents that had made their way by Army chopper to the base after D.C. was evacuated."

He stopped, looking to us and back to her. "Would you like to continue?" This was directed to her.

She glared at him for several seconds before turning her eyes to Kate, as if she was the only one being addressed.

"We were part of the President's protection detail, and were at the White House with him when this started. Those things started getting heavy at the gates and fences within 6 hours of the initial outbreak. Agents at the gates had been compromised by the time the evac chopper got to the lawn, and we got POTUS to the helicopter in time for a safe dust-off. We were on board and preparing to lift off when he realized his damn cat wasn't on board."

She looked down to the table, and back up, shaking her head slightly with the memory.

"He ordered myself and another agent to get the damn thing. We went back in while those things shambled through the Rose Garden and into the main entrance. The cat wasn't in the residence, and we radioed back to the chopper to report that it was a no go. Next thing we knew, the chopper was in the air. We weren't."

"They left you behind? For a cat?" Kate asked, incredulous.

I chuckled, before thinking better of it. I couldn't help it. I thought that was some funny shit.

"The President's safety is the primary concern," she replied, glaring at me with white hot contempt.

"Yeah, especially to him," said Anaru, chuckling. She didn't return the smile.

Kate was curious, and kept with the story. "So you made it to Dix? How'd you get out of the White House?"

"Myself and four other agents, five staff members and a cook made it to the roof, where we caught one of the last Army helos out of the city. It had been called in to support Marine One, but no one had called it off after POTUS made it out." She added, shrugging, "We were lucky."

"And Lazarus?" I asked.

Ignoring me, she turned again to address Kate. "On our way to Marine One, POTUS took a call from the Secretary of Defense. I heard him ask whether this was a Lazarus situation. I couldn't hear the response, but he was mighty pissed when they finished answering."

I was dumbfounded. This seemed to confirm my suspicions about the cause, and could substantiate my theories about the cure.

She lost some of her defensiveness as she clearly thought hard about what she followed with, her eyes narrowing and her voice lowering. "And then he said something really weird. He told them to deal with it by following the 'Baghdad protocol.' No indication on what that is, but he sounded pretty damn pissed."

Hartliss chimed in, "That was the last she heard before getting booted off the chopper and after the Army got eaten at Dix, she became our guest here." He smiled disarmingly.

"You really supposed to be telling a bunch of people you don't know what you overheard the president say? Isn't that some sort of national security breach of something?" I just had to have the last word; besides, I didn't like her attitude.

"Not if I kill you after I'm done talking, wiseass."

"So this is good, right?" asked Kate, face alight with interest, ignoring our banter. "This proves that your memories of Starling Mountain are real. Now all we need is a way in."

"How do you play into this?" I asked Anaru, recognizing why Hartliss had brought in Sam, but curious as to why he was here.

He smiled back. "I don't like boats," he said simply.

"Anaru here has been asking me since he arrived how he could help out in the rescue efforts. Poor chap is going through occupational withdrawal," Hartliss joked.

"I'm a firefighter," he said simply, explaining the Lieutenant's joke. "And no offense, but if you don't mind the company, I think you could use some help." I looked at his massive form and nodded mutely, imagining the damage he could do with a baseball bat. Or a pipe. Or a fricking slinky on a stick.

"But we still have the problem of transport," I said, looking sideways at Hartliss. "Starling Mountain is inland, almost a hundred miles over decently dangerous territory, and I'm guessing by land we wouldn't stand a chance...."

"Which leaves me to break orders and give you a ride, right then?" finished Hartliss for me. The other refugees were getting up from the tables. It was time for the next shift of eaters. He stood up.

"You chaps get some rest, and you leave the details to me. In a few days, I should be able to get you on an inbound flight. What the Captain doesn't know won't hurt him, yeah?"

"Why would you do that? James is going to be pretty peeved, I would imagine."

He looked down at me, losing the smile. "That shit out there is right scary, okay? I've got a wife and a kid at home and I don't fancy returning to Portsmouth to a brood of zombies. You may think this is your country's little problem, but the way I see it, if we don't get this bloody thing under control, it becomes everyone's problem real soon. I've seen those things tear a child to pieces and eat the remains. I never thought I appreciated real evil 'til then. Well I bloody well do now."

He paused, not really looking at anyone. "I'll try to get word to you before we need to leave. Keep your heads down 'til then."

The rest of us stood, looking at each other. "How about you?" I asked Sam.

"If there's a chance this thing can be stopped, I'm going with you. But you can damn well rest assured that I'm not going to let you out of my sight."

I muttered under my breath in response to her parting shot, but safely out of her earshot as she turned and moved out the door. Anaru smiled to me and followed her, trying to talk to her as they stepped out of the hatch.

"I heard that," Kate said, softly.

"What?" I asked innocently.

"I don't think I've heard a 'your mom' retort since grade school. Very nice." She smiled, standing up.

I wasn't above such things. I was crazy, remember?

I turned to Hartliss. "What about Fred? Will he be OK here, with the others?"

He nodded. "There's a kindergarten teacher that I think he's already taken a shine to. He'll be as safe as any of us." He gestured to the door. "Now you really need to get some sleep. You all look like crap."

I laughed. "Then I already look as good as I feel."

He ushered us through the door and we followed the rest back to the general quarters as the next shift of refugees passed us toward the mess. I shuffled wearily behind Kate, exhaustion hitting me like a freight train as my mind and body, finally given permission to do so, slowed to a crawl.

I thought about the situation. About our "mission." I tried to remember Starling Mountain. I had only been there once, driving Maria to work in an attempt to get a little more time together in an otherwise impossible schedule. It was a secluded location—pretty isolated. In truth, it was really only accessible by one road running north from a medium sized town. I think the name of the town was Kearny. I needed to look at a map.

Waving to Fred, who was apparently much enamored with a young woman across the room, I collapsed on my bunk, the chatter of others droning on in the background. I stared at the ceiling, wracking my brain for as much information as possible, for as many memories that would surface about Maria and anything that she told me. Barbed wire fencing, key card controlled access, and a whole bunch of guards. That's what I remembered. That, and signing an autograph for a groundskeeper on my way back to civilization.

My mind came back to Maria.

Jesus.

Had I killed her? I still didn't know. I couldn't make the memories come; I couldn't force myself to recall. The blood, the noises, the sounds. Sitting at the counter, covered in blood. Covered in her blood.

My mind suddenly exploded, recognition and understanding burning inside, a hot fire of sadness and relief, warring with one another in an emotional battle for my approval. The noises I heard when I got home weren't Maria. I mean, they were, but they weren't.

She must have been infected! That's why she brought home the information, and that's why she didn't answer when I called out. It was why she hadn't slept in the bed; why no tea was boiling. The bastards had infected her! Or allowed her to infect herself. That's why the reports didn't match up. The autopsy, the coroner's report, the cop's reports…they didn't match up because she was dead when I got home. My Greg Norman attack did kill her, just not in the traditional sense.

She must have come at me, startled me when I picked up the folder. Somehow, I got to the putter and scored a lucky shot to the head. It felled her, she "died" and I went into some sort of catatonic shock. It was all making sense now.

But why had she escaped, or left, knowing she had been infected? Why would she risk putting others in harm's way?

You can't imagine the frustration of knowing a memory is in there, rattling around just outside of your grasp. I knew I knew, you know? It was just ... like trying to catch water as it came out of a faucet. It looked like you could grab it, but when you close your fist around it, the water pours out over your fingers and you end up with nothing. That was my battle; my memories were present, just not accounted for.

My last remnant of fleeting concentration was broken as I noticed Kate walking toward me from the other side of the room, where she had just checked on Fred. Her hair was down again, eyes and mouth smiling as she caught my gaze. They had issued us each the dark blue jumpsuit that was the uniform of the crew. Hers was bound tightly around her small waist, the legs too baggy and the top virtually hanging off her slender frame. She had the sleeves rolled up to the elbows, exposing smooth, sleekly muscular arms.

She sat down on the bunk and I moved back quickly to allow her space to sit. She leaned against my curled up legs, her warmth a pleasant feel against my thighs as she turned toward me, pulling her feet up onto the bunk. She hugged her legs against her chest and locked her hands on each opposing elbow, cocking her head to one side and looking at me. I could smell her freshly washed hair, still slightly damp from the showers. It was a nice smell. Comforting.

"I just spoke to Fred's new friend. She's sweet, and doesn't mind looking after him," a haunted look passed her eyes like a storm cloud driven in a blustering wind. "She was at school when this broke. They were in the classroom until midday, waiting for the parents to come to pick up the kids," she shuddered, closing her eyes.

"The parents didn't show, but the creatures did. Only a few, but she couldn't keep them out. She got as many of the children out as she could, but the kids couldn't move fast enough. She eventually lost all of them. Some reanimated so quickly that she was running from her former pupils."

She sighed, opening her eyes and looking at me. "This has to stop. We need to put an end to it. We can't let it spread."

A single tear traveled down her smooth cheek, glistening trail reflecting the fluorescent light from the ceiling. She didn't wait for a response, but uncurled and laid down on her back next to me. Staring at the ceiling, she sighed, voice thick with emotion.

"I have a daughter. She lives with her father in Vancouver. If ... " She couldn't continue, but she didn't need to. She started to sob quietly, eyes closing as her body shook slightly with each gasp of air.

I lay there quietly. I didn't know what to say, but I didn't think there was anything to be said. So I stayed quiet, eventually searching for and finding her hand. She didn't pull away. I drifted off, the light touch of her fingers in my palm the last sensation I felt before sleep took me.

CHAPTER 18

We were on the ship for three days, killing time and waiting for a signal from Hartliss that our departure was imminent. He kept us informed as much as possible, but was constantly busy. We used the time to recuperate and recharge. God knows we needed it.

They kept us fed, despite what I knew must be a shortage of food. I ate almost constantly; my stomach felt as if it hadn't been full for decades, and I couldn't get enough. Good, bad, undercooked, overcooked; it didn't matter, I'd eat it. Kate said that I was probably going through some sort of withdrawal from the drugs I had been on at the Park. I didn't much care, as long as I ate.

I slept, but only fitfully. My rest was constantly interrupted by dreams. Most of the time, they were nothing consequential. At least, nothing that wasn't to be expected after fighting your way through zombies, watching people get eaten, and more or less witnessing as close to the apocalypse as you thought you'd ever see.

We were anxious to do something and it was tough after the first day to sit on our hands. Reports came in slowly of various radio chatter and news reports. They were fewer and farther between as the hours passed. The short story was that cities were falling and the infection was spreading. People were panicking, the government was ineffectual, and we were mutely watching and listening to the slow and steady collapse of our civilization. All in all, not a great way to spend some enforced down time.

There were rumors about messages from British command, whispers of secret plans and orders, but it was hard to separate wheat from chaff. The soldiers and sailors on board didn't share much past news from the shore, and Hartliss wasn't terribly disclosing in our brief conversations.

The real bitch of the stay on the boat wasn't the dreams, and it wasn't even the sickening rocking of the ship—although I have to say, a windowless room in the middle of a boat is not a great place to be disposed to seasickness. No, the real rub was the people. Half of them seemed to despise me, the other half adore me. There seemed to be no way around the judgmental looks and the sharp whispers of condemnation. Most had seen the trial or had caught the surrounding publicity in passing and, in the way of our digitally enhanced, 24-hour news, rush to judgment society, had either acquitted or convicted me without considering the case. Not that I really gave a shiny rat's buttock, but the burden of their attention, especially under the circumstances, was very trying.

The worst—the absolute worst—wasn't the bastards that called me a murderer or left me hate notes on my bunk. It wasn't even the prick that tried to trip me as I walked by his chair in the mess. No, it wasn't even the haters. It was the lovers—or should I say, the line-lovers.

Schwarzenegger was caught up by "I'll be back." Stallone had "Adrian!" I had the cheesy one-liner that that had been my own personal banner ad for five years.

The scene was shot in a cafeteria. Hence the infamous line.

I had valiantly chased a group of terrorists through the streets of New York City, up escalators and stairwells, down alleys and trash chutes. They possessed a nuclear detonator and my daughter. Although one would think that either of those would be sufficient justification for my character's urgency and tenacity, the writers apparently theorized that today's theater-goers needed double the suspense to justify twenty dollar tickets.

There had been gun battles throughout the movie, and violent tumbles galore. The set was top-notch, and I always wondered why they settled on a cafeteria as the grand finale. It was a nice cafeteria, all glass and marble, set on the fiftieth floor of a huge office building. But it lacked the gravitas of many other action movie finales. Take Commando and Rambo for instance, with the pipe room and the rain forest, respectively. Those were great finale scenes. Classics.

I, however, got the food service room in a Canadian insurance building.

But it worked. Incredibly well, it turns out. Well enough, at least, that the last line in the scene became "mine." It became the thing associated with the person. Emblazoned on shirts, hats, coffee mugs, the cover to the DVD, the poster for the film. You name it, that line was the linguistic alter ego of my professional career.

Despite my repeated indications that I was exhausted, they pressed me to the point that I fled when people were about. In other words, I started to hide.

The one bright spot of that time was that I got to know Kate better. Despite my Houdini acts, she always seemed to be able to find me. After that first night, she wasn't anxious to talk about her daughter, and I didn't press. She seemed to have said what she needed, and was happy to talk about everything else: my case, her school, my family, my movies, her job at the Park. Just not her daughter. If I had kids, I probably wouldn't want to have to think about what they were going through thousands of miles away either.

It was at the end of the third day that Hartliss found us in the mess again, as I shoved down a third helping of some sort of meat with what appeared to be potatoes. Kate was sipping a cup of coffee that, given the amount of time she had been nursing it, must have been tepid at best.

"Tonight looks good, chaps." He looked around, making sure no one was within earshot. "Can't say when, but be ready. I left some clothes in your bunks for you; don't put 'em on til I come for you. Don't want our secret to get out, eh?"

He got up quickly, looking down at us seriously. "It's gotten right nasty out there, just so you know. I've been out twice, and there's nothing on the ground moving faster than a crawl, if you get my drift. Don't know about your landing site, but can't imagine it's much better."

He paused, smiling. "Not that I thought I'd deter you crazy blokes, but just thought you should know." Still grinning, he threw us a fake half-salute and slipped out.

Making our way back to the cabin, we tried to get some sleep. I moved the clothes surreptitiously under the bed and laid down, watching Kate make her way back to her own bunk. She waved at me with a half smile as she laid her head down, and I smiled back.

Sleep didn't come easy that night, but it came. There were no dreams.

I awoke to Kate's urgent whisper.

"Mike! Wake up! Time to go!"

An alarm was sounding, consistently bleating out some sort of alert tone, red light twirling above the hatch casting a Hades-like glow about the shared room. She stood over me, eyes quick and darting.

I bolted upright, still in a daze.

"Is it time?" Jesus I was tired. My eyes would barely open. Sam and Anaru stood behind her at the open hatch door. They wore the black and white camouflage fatigues that had been left for us, identical to the ones worn by the marines on board.

Kate reached under my bed and tossed me my clothes and a pair of boots, glancing toward the open hatchway as she did so. She ducked back into the room and pulled off her standard-issue refugee shirt as she spoke, unconcerned with modesty as she stripped down to her skivvies in front of everyone in the room. I couldn't help but notice that she had nothing to be ashamed of.

"Some sort of drill or something. Apparently Hartliss thought this would be a good time to take a ride in all the confusion," she answered, her voice briefly muffled as she pulled the new shirt on over her head and hastily pulling on the matching pants, pulling the belt through the final loop as she moved close to the open door again. She watched crew pass the cabin through the crack in the door as I followed her lead, tossing my pants and shirt in a pile on my bunk and quickly pulling on the fatigues.

The others in the room watched us mutely and curiously, unsure as to what was happening.

As I tied my boots over the heavy pants, I wondered what kind of drill they would be running under these circumstances. Anti-aircraft? Anti-submarine? Damn military always has to drill something.

I rose from the bunk as a man from the back of the room got up and spoke to Anaru. "Where are you going? Is there something wrong with the ship?"

Anaru shook his head. "Nothing wrong with the ship. Something wrong with him, though. He wants to go back to shore." He paused, then said to the man, "Wanna come?"

The man backed off, shaking his head at me as he did so.

"You are crazy, you murdering SOB! Good riddance!"

Ignoring him and the looks his comments brought, I followed the others out the hatch and quickly down the hall. Crewmen rushed past, but our presence went largely unheralded in the commotion. Everyone had a place during the drill, and nobody's place was checking on us.

The chopper had been pushed onto the flight deck and the rotors were already spinning slowly, getting ready to start in earnest. Hartliss was in the cockpit, speaking heatedly with a crewman through the open front door. He slammed it shut, still yelling into his microphone. The crewman turned quickly, sprinting past us into the ship. Kate's head appeared from inside, hand motioning insistently toward us.

"Come on, we don't have a lot of time!" The crewman must be alerting the Captain.

I jumped on board behind Anaru as the rotors spun faster and faster, kicking up wind and sound. I pulled the headphones over my ears as activity from the hangar deck caught my attention. The hatch had opened and Fred came lurching out, having tripped over the edge. Seeing my face from the open door of the helicopter, he sprinted toward me as five marines emerged behind him.

"Pancake!" he screamed as I felt the chopper lift off. He reached the open door as we hovered inches from the ground. He jumped into the cabin as Hartliss pulled up and back quickly. Fred's feet still hung precariously out over the side as we moved over the water behind the ship. Marines gesticulated wildly as our headphones came to life and Fred threw his leg over the edge of the floor, pulling himself on board with Anaru's help.

"Helo 1, this is Liverpool Actual, respond." It was the Captain.

"Cheers, Cap'n," responded Hartliss over the radio as he rose and banked to the North. "Just taking care of your overcrowding situation, sir. Be back soon."

"You will return now, goddamn it. We have— " It was cut off as Hartliss terminated the connection, leaving the intercom open.

"I think I bloody well know he's not a fan of this idea," he said calmly, pulling us to a level thousand feet.

Suddenly from the starboard side of the ship, six bright trails of light followed by massive columns of smoke filtering into the night sky.

"They're shooting at us!" I screamed into the microphone, having been in enough military movies to recognize the look of missiles being fired.

"Those are cruise missiles, mate. Ground to ground; not ground to air. They're firing on a ground target." Hartliss spoke resignedly. His tone indicated agreement with the course of action but disapproval of the cause.

"You knew about this?" I asked, incredulous.

"What better way to get you chaps off the boat than during a live fire?" he said, banking to the left.

Made sense, I suppose.

"Orders from the fleet," he explained, "Take out the heavily infested areas before it spreads. Other countries don't want your disease, and nobody's itching to help you folk right about now. Not a lot of friends in the world right now, apparently. 'Cept me of course," he finished. His jaunty tone was heartily out of place at a time like this.

"There were almost a million and a half people in Manhattan before this thing hit," he explained as we banked slowly away from the ship. "Fleet figured this is a bloody good way to destroy a bunch of those wankers in one shot. Million and a half fewer carriers to worry about."

I glued my face to the window, watching the six streaming trails of fire lift awkwardly into the air and arc toward the city, each of the six breaking off slightly in various directions, all staying on target directly into the heart of a city that had already witnessed so much pain and devastation.

Despite the nagging feeling that this was the right course of action to be taken, I was unable to believe the signals my eyes were sending to my brain.

"Holy shit," this from Sam who, ignoring her dislike for me personally, had pressed her face next to mine against the window in a farcical semblance of intimacy.

It was as if we were moving in slow motion, the glare of the rockets bright in my eyes as they ascended, reached their zenith and turned to plunge quickly and purposefully to their nadir, six streaks of bright light heading for six minutely different targets within New York City.

Suddenly, six more bursts from the Liverpool in sharp succession. They were firing again. This time, however, the rockets reached about three thousand feet and veered sharply to the South, leaving a trail of fire and smoke in their wake.

Flowers of fire blossomed between buildings, illuminating the early morning skyline. Between one second and the next, vast swathes of the city were transformed into raging infernos of roiling heat and destruction. We could make out very little detail from our vantage point, but as we turned upriver, we were afforded a front row seat to the final destruction of the center of the world.

Buildings bearing the initial brunt of the explosions toppled against one another, causing a series of collapsing structures. Dust, debris and fire fell from above, blanketing the ground and infusing the air. In the streets below, creatures boiled out from the shadows of the demolition, ignorant of the fires burning around them, but pushed out by the sheer force of the blasts and the pressure of other zombies.

Avenues full of cars, trucks, buses and bodies became moats of flaming death as the city now destroyed itself from inside, the proximity of its structures now condemning itself to incineration. Flaming bodies could be seen running, shambling or collapsing in mute supplication, marked as undead by the speed with which they fled from the flames and debris.

The reasoning behind the strike was clear as we moved along the shoreline, crossed over where I knew the Holland Tunnel to be, and moved West, away from the inferno. There was no sign of life in the pre-dawn hours-no humans running for cover or crying out in agony. It was a city of the undead, and it was now burning in a hell befitting its occupants.

Over the intercom, no one spoke. There was nothing to say. We knew that this was only the harbinger of more to come.

From my side, a hand sought my own and I squeezed tight, knowing it to be Kate. We flew away from the light of the rising sun in silence.

CHAPTER 19

We flew over city and then suburbs, all touched and infected by the same plague that had decimated Long Island. Buildings burned as testament to human fear and folly.

Kate was the first to speak, more to me than anyone else, although there were no secrets over the intercom. Her voice crackled over the headphones. "He was able to get us some weapons from the Royal Marine stash on the ship. Only side arms and a rifle each with some ammunition, but you know...beggars and choosers and all that."

From across the cabin Anaru handed me a pistol in a holster attached to a thick, military belt, followed by a short, stocky semi-automatic rifle and several additional clips for it, which fit handily into pouches attached to the belt.

"SA-80," he said briefly, referring to the make of the rifle.

"Better than an ax from the sporting goods section, huh?" I said to Kate, holding the rifle up and examining the stock and barrel. She nodded in agreement, concentrating on and handling her pistol with more than a modicum of familiarity.

"You know how to use those?" Sam asked me from across the cabin, the sneer as evident in her voice as it was on her face, "Or are you going to shoot yourself in the ass before you can cap one of these zombie fucks?"

Although the make was unfamiliar, the rifle was similar to ones I had handled in previous films and I knew the basic handling procedures. Enough, at least, to prevent myself from serious harm. Voiding the chamber and sighting the piece in demonstrative fashion, I looked up at her, sounding more confident that I felt.

I had been trained in several different types of weapons, although rarely using live ammunition. As an action movie star, one was rather compelled to know the workings of the tools of the trade. A friend of mine from college lived in Montana, and although I rarely ever saw him anymore, when we were just out of college, he forced me to go hunting with him in Canada.

I had never been so cold and miserable in my life, but I learned how to fire a gun with real ammunition. Come to think of it, that was one of the reasons I jumped on my first action movie part. It was kind of exhilarating. I know that as good Hollywood liberal type I wasn't supposed to enjoy the phallic American obsession with guns, but God help me, I liked shooting. Although, truth be told, when I saw a moose, I aimed high. Couldn't bear the thought of shooting something so fuzzy.

Didn't think I'd have much of a hang up about wasting any of these flesh-eating ghouls, though.

"I'll be fine. If I shoot myself in the foot, you have permission to finish the job. But until then, try to play nice." She smiled a fake smile, venom dripping from her gaze. Jesus. I wondered if she'd ever be laid. I wondered if she liked guys.

Better warn Kate, just in case.

From beside Kate, a meek, quiet voice. "Pancake?"

Fuck! Fred! I had almost forgotten him!

What the hell did he think he was doing, following us out like that?

Ah, yes. He wasn't thinking. Mind of a child. Right. I looked at him and smiled, trying to reassure him. As I smiled, I spoke into the headset, "Hartliss, can you give Fred here a ride back to the ship after our drop?"

"Can do, but you have to make sure he stays put. Can't babysit and fly at the same time."

I wound the belt around my waist and made sure my weapons were loaded. I examined the rifle, finding the switch and selecting semi rather than full automatic. From what we had seen, we needed to take them in the head or not at all. Spraying twenty rounds into the torso wasn't as effective against the undead as it was against their human counterparts.

I looked out the window, watching interstate and suburbs turn slowly into forest and towns. We rarely saw signs of human activity. What little we witnessed appeared frantic and panicked. No organized fighting, no fortresses of holdouts. Merely a week after the outbreak, the land appeared calmly destitute and abandoned to the undead. I sighed heavily. It may already be too late.

I heard Kate shift behind me.

"I was 19." Kate said suddenly, peeling my headset from my left ear and speaking to me directly.

I chuckled, not understanding at first. "So was I. It was a good year."

She made a face. "That first night on the ship, what I told you. You had a look on your face like you were confused. I had her when I was 19. Her father and I met when I was in college. A one night thing, but then nine months later ... We share custody, every six months."

"Good thing it was his turn," I said, not knowing what else to say.

"Yeah, good thing." She turned away, looking out the window.

"Can I ask you something?" I said, realizing only after I had said it that I hated that question.

"You just did," she said, smiling crookedly without turning around.

Yep, that was why. I smiled anyway.

"Why?" I asked.

"Why what?"

"You have a daughter who I know you care for. Why go with us on this crazy jaunt? You must realize as clearly as I do that the cards are kinda stacked against us. Even if I weren't crazy, this plan definitely is. Hike off into the mountains through zombie hordes to find and break into a secret government lab where there might be a cure to a disease that appears to have won already? Definition of bat-shit crazy if you ask me."

She looked into my eyes, face serious. "There are a lot of people out there that don't have a chance to do anything to save their loved ones from this—not to mention from four thousand miles away. They may lock their doors, stockpile food and load their guns, but you and I both know that this kind of sickness gets exponentially worse. In two more weeks, the planet could be irretrievably overrun, and humankind—at least the humankind we know—could be very close to extinct. No one can hold out against that forever."

She turned away, looking out the window. "The only hope for anyone, my daughter included, is finding a cure."

Suddenly, the radio came to life, a frightened voice coming through clearly, the sounds of commotion and shouting loud in the background.

"Mayday, mayday. This is the HMS Liverpool. We are anchored in New York Bay and have been hit by an inbound freighter. We are taking on water, and abandoning ship. I repeat, we are taking on water and abandoning ship."

This was incomprehensible. We all looked at each other in shock as Hartliss spoke rapidly in response.

"Liverpool, this is Lieutenant Hartliss, what the hell happened?"

"Inbound freighter, loaded with zeds. Must've killed the crew or something. They're all ... what the bloody ... Jesus!" his voice escalated to a frightened tenor, ending in a shrill scream, as the radio squealed, transmission cut off suddenly from the ship.

They drive boats now? What next?

"Liverpool? Liverpool, come in!"

He tried several times, urgently trying to evoke a response. His pleas were met with the empty retort of static and dead air.

Hartliss cursed and checked his GPS read out, punching buttons and turning two dials quickly.

"I have to get back. There may be something I can do. Sorry, but I've got to let you down.

Before we could reply, the chopper jerked as it was buffeted by a gust of wind. "I'm going to drop you in a town about thirty miles South of the facility. According to the GPS, it's called Kearney. I can't take you the rest of the way. It's a medium sized town, but if you clear the inhabited area quickly, you might have a chance."

We started toward the grown, and I caught myself wanting to vomit as we dropped hundreds of feet within seconds. Small buildings flashed by below, and we crossed small town streets packed haphazardly with cars. Creatures meandered aimlessly below; some looked up as we passed. Not a good sign.

"I'm going to drop you in a football field. From there, you're on your own, but it looks like there's a car dealership across the street. Should be able to find transport there." Hartliss's normally calm voice was bordering on the frantic.

Mentally grappling with the potential loss of the Liverpool, I made sure my gear was in place. Across from me, Anaru read my mind, "Any idea how many of those things might be down there?"

"Negative. It's a medium sized town, but no way to know. Not as many as the city, but you should anticipate that they'll be drawn by the noise from the chopper, so be alert."

"What about Fred," Kate asked, grabbing my arm urgently. "We can't send him back to the ship if it's infested and sinking."

"We don't know that it's overrun or that it went down. They could have stopped the leak and could be mopping up the zombies as we speak. Either way, Hartliss has enough fuel to find somewhere safer than where we're going." It wasn't the best plan, but I believed it was true. There was no promise of safety in either direction, but at least by air, he had more options. "There's no way for us to keep him safe in this, you know that."

She looked into my eyes, doubt and uncertainty warring with her concern for Fred's safety. She finally nodded and turned away, grabbing Fred's hand and holding it tightly.

From the cockpit, Hartliss's tense voice. "Here's the drop. Get ready."

Out the window to my right, I could see an empty football field, surrounded by bleachers. On one side of the field, a banner hung limply from the stands, espousing support for the high school team. Behind the field, the school itself sat in dark, stolid silence. A Toyota dealership, bright sign illuminated brightly across the street from the field, corroborated Hartliss' satellite imagery.

As we banked and descended, I caught movement in the parking lot beside the field, and from behind the school. We definitely weren't alone here.

In a gut-wrenching change of altitude and pace, the chopper dropped suddenly to within twenty feet of the ground, bleachers disappearing behind us as we lowered the last fifteen feet. Then the last five, as the wheels touched the soft grass and the wind from the spinning rotors blasted off the ground and into the cabin.

"That's it. Everyone out. Good hunting and Godspeed!"

Sam jumped out, rifle up, head down but alert. Anaru followed, weapon similarly raised, then Kate. I was the last, and as I exited I turned quickly to Fred, who had been poised to follow. From behind me, I heard Sam's voice rising, Anaru yelling in response, and the sharp report of a single shot. I held my hand up and spoke quickly and loudly.

"You're staying, Fred. We'll be back, I promise!" Disliking the lie I heard in my voice, I kept my hand up in a 'stop' gesture, and brought the door shut in front of him. His face stared out the window, his hand pressed against it softly, as I slammed my hand against the metal wall three times in sharp succession and sprinted under the blades to where the others stood, backs to me and the helicopter. Another single shot rang out, as Hartliss made a thumbs up gesture and lifted off the ground immediately, obviously concerned about the ship.

I turned to see Sam crouched on the ground, sighting carefully over the barrel of her rifle toward a group of six zeds making their way across the field toward us from the open gate behind the far goalpost. Two bodies already lay sprawled awkwardly on the grass, limbs askew, proof of Sam's marksmanship.

From above and behind us, there was a sudden sound of metallic snapping and the arcing of electricity. We all looked back in time to witness Hartliss pull the helicopter back from an almost invisible line of electric wires that stretched between the announcer's booth and the main grid on the far side of the field. He had clipped one of the wires, which had struck the side of the chopper after briefly tangling with a rotor blade. He was perhaps thirty feet from the ground, and the chopper yawed wildly before coming to an even keel. Sam turned back to sight the incoming creatures, as the rest of us helplessly watched the progress of the ship.

He achieved a couple hundred feet in altitude before smoke started to pour out of the engine compartment directly below the spinning rotors. The engine whined loudly as the smoke got thicker and came faster. He kept the chopper moving forward, out of the field, past the outskirts of where I knew town ended and forest began. The tail suddenly skewed sharply to the side, and the chopper lost twenty feet in altitude. It disappeared from sight over the closest hill, smoke still streaming from the tail and descending fast.

As I turned to Kate, horrified but impotent in the face of events, a bright yellow ball of flame and smoke erupted from the crest of the hill that it had just topped. I ducked involuntarily, even as a secondary explosion lit the sky almost immediately after.

From behind us, Sam's voice drew us out of our trance. "We need to move, now!"

Anaru grabbed my arm, "Come on. We can grieve later. We need to get across the street and out of this fishbowl."

Sam sprinted past us, rifle in hand, held professionally at her hip. I slipped mine off my shoulder, checking the clip and following Kate. Anaru took the rear, as six more slouching forms shuffled slowly behind.

We passed underneath a metal archway that was topped by more bleachers and bore another banner of support. Motivational posters adorned the walls on either side, a solid wooden gate in front of us, chained shut from the inside. Sam fired a round into the lock, releasing the chain from the handles as we poured through. We were in a parking lot, which was half full of various vehicles, most likely belonging to those in the school that had shown up in the morning merely one week ago, and were dead by the time the afternoon bell rang.

From behind the various rows of cars, more forms were evident, the early morning light revealing only the shadowy outline of their slow-moving forms. We turned to our right, toward the dealership, as several more appeared from behind the field, much too close for comfort. They moved slowly toward us, too many and too close to allow a pursuit.

I dropped to a crouch, carefully sighting the first of the bunch. I squeezed the trigger, expecting to be rocked back by the kick. Instead, I was rewarded with an empty metallic click.

Shit!

I looked at the weapon stupidly, checking the magazine to confirm it was loaded. The first creature was ten feet away now, eyes wide-open, mouth yawning in hunger. It was an old man, cowboy shirt open at the front. He wore no pants, and the pale flesh of his thin legs was tinged with gray. His sun-browned face, in sharp contrast to his pale bottom half, revealed only the lifeless gaze of the undead.

The safety! I flicked the safety off as he reached five feet from my position. With no time to sight the weapon, I fired from the hip. The first round hit him in the chest, tearing a hole through the pocket of his outdated shirt and spitting cloth and dry flesh into the air behind him. I squeezed the trigger again as he fell toward me, angling the gun sharply upward. The second round found home, taking him under the jaw and removing the top of his skull from the inside. He collapsed lifelessly to my side as I sighted the next in line carefully.

This time, unprepared for the recoil of the weapon, I was rocked back by the force of the discharge, pushed back out of my crouch onto my ass. Reflexively, I threw out my hand, scraping several fingers severely against the concrete. I cursed at the blood now dripped from my hand as I looked up. The shot had flown wide, striking the cement wall of the stadium, and the creatures behind the cowboy were nearly on me. They were too close to line up a good shot.

I scrambled up, even as the head of the closest creature—a large black woman in the uniform of a postal worker—whipped back sharply, and collapsed on the pavement.

From beside me, Anaru spoke quietly as he next downed a woman in an expensive looking business suit with a carefully placed shot. "I won't tell Sam," he said with a grin, not taking his eyes off the last creature in the pack. His shot took it in the sternum and it stumbled back. It craned its head to the side and stared at Anaru before moving forward again.

I raised my rifle, prepared this time for the recoil, and squeezed the trigger. The zed's eye exploded as the round passed through the brain and out the back of the skull.

I turned to him, grinning like an idiot.

He patted me on the back with a massive paw-like hand as we turned to follow Sam and Kate toward the street. "Not bad. Like one of your movies, yeah?"

In front, Sam fired another single shot, hitting a slow-moving form that had materialized before her from the shelter of a large SUV. The shot took the man in the arm, pushing him back a step before he continued forward, unaffected. He was dressed in khakis and a polo, blood on his leg and neck indicating his wounds. Probably a teacher, I thought as a pistol shot sounded loudly in my left ear and he fell to the ground, bullet hole above this temple a dark hole. These things didn't bleed much, I noticed as I more surprisingly realized that Kate had fired the killing shot.

"Not Rambo, huh?" I asked, remembering her comment from seemingly years back in Target, "Where'd you learn to shoot like that?" I asked as we moved past her victim, reaching the last car in the row.

"Military brat, remember? Learned to shoot almost before I learned to walk." I noticed she was carrying the pistol in hand, with the rifle over her shoulder.

We were on a sidewalk along a four-lane highway. To our right, the edge of the football field and, further along, the entrance to the school. To our left, a shoe store and a gaudy, brightly colored Mexican restaurant that advertised one-dollar drafts and a three-dollar burrito. I was hungry again, and despite the carnage, my stomach growled unabashedly.

And I would kill for a beer.

Zombies shuffled and shambled toward us from both directions, converging on us as we crossed the street toward the car lot. We reached the property, and threaded ourselves carefully through the parked cars and trucks, the moans and hungry cries of our pursuers echoing in the early morning silence.

CHAPTER 20

As in any well-run car dealership, the salesmen greeted us as soon as we were in sight of the showroom. Shambling through open doors out of the glass-walled structure, they wasted no time in accosting our small group as we made our way through the parked cars and toward the building.

"Find a truck, we'll take care of the salesmen," Anaru said to me shortly, breaking off with Sam toward the shuffling pack. At least fifty more were now moving toward us from various directions, including those that had spied us on the street.

Kate and I ran toward the back of the lot. To our left, the large doors of the service department were open, and the movement of at least six creatures was visible from inside as hunching and slow-moving figures moved toward the sounds of our footfalls and gunshots.

We reached the back row of the lot, locating a crew cab pickup and quickly finding the VIN number etched on the windshield. I committed the last six numbers of the VIN to memory as Kate raised her gun toward the service section. One creature was visible behind a parked SUV, its gray wizened face peering at us from behind the glass of the rear window of the vehicle.

It simply stared, unmoving.

Kate kept her gun raised and looked at me in confusion. I returned the look, also uncertain as to why it had paused instead of coming right for us. I gestured to her in the direction of Sam and Anaru, and I moved into the open space between rows, bringing the creature into plain view, unobstructed by the glass of the window. It turned toward me immediately, feet dragging, mouth open. The skin of its bald head hung down from a massive gouge, the hanging flap almost covering one ear. It moaned, and the cohort of creatures in the service dock moved faster, goaded on by their friend's invitation.

My rifle spat in response, taking him in the chest. I cursed and sighted more carefully. Out of the corner of my eye, I saw Kate raise her pistol and glanced over, wondering if she was going to take the shot. But her gun wasn't pointed at the zombie; it was aimed at me. I was suddenly staring down the barrel of her pistol, unsure and petrified. I froze in terror and confusion, but before I could say a word, the muzzle flashed and my ears rang with the sound of the discharge.

Behind me, a dull thud and the body of a badly mauled teen boy in boxer shorts and a tank top fell heavily against my legs as I skirted to the side. I smiled at her in thanks, shaking my head. Suddenly, remembering the creature in front of me, I again raised my rifle, sighting carefully. This time, the shot took him in the cheek and passed through the back of the head, shattering the window behind his collapsing body and spraying dark gray and crimson matter on the waxed exterior of the SUV.

We jogged back to Sam and Anaru, eyes alert for incoming creatures and carefully watching those already on their way in. They moved slowly, shambling forward awkwardly. Some had arms raised in mute supplication. Others simply shuffled forward, arms at the sides and feet dragging like dead weight.

Anaru was reloading as Sam walked toward the downed creatures. Those from the street had reached the line of cars along the roadway and were clumsily shambling through the intervening spaces. There were more behind them; too many now to take down with single shots. We needed the keys to the truck, and we needed them fast. As confirmation, the creatures from the service bay came into view, moving around the corner of the building.

"Last one in is a crazy murdering bastard!" shouted Sam, as she sprinted to the doors recently vacated by the now motionless sales crew.

First one in is a self-righteous bitch, I thought, as I ran after Kate and Anaru, stepping carefully over the uniformed corpses lying prone on the ground.

A sports car and a large SUV stood in the showroom; wax glaring brightly as the rising sun streamed into the room from the east. I closed the glass door behind me, grabbing a chair from the waiting area next to the soda machine and jamming the back under the handle. Remembering the ax handle at the school and the barricade at Target, I moved back, unconvinced that this would suffice. Kate and Sam disappeared into the back, searching for the keys.

I looked around, checking for company in the break room and the bathrooms as Anaru watched the doors. Returning to the showroom, I shook my head and he nodded in understanding. From the manager's office, Kate yelled in triumph and I heard a shot ring out, sounding as if it the bullet had hit metal. They must have found the key box. "64873R!" I shouted over my shoulder, relieved to spit the numbers out so I could promptly forget them.

Several creatures had reached the glass doors, more of them close behind. Some clustered and pressed against the doorway, but an equal number pressed against the glass windows, soon creating a wall of living corpses.

Each one pawed and clambered against the glass like patrons at a mall pet store. I swore to myself that I'd never tap on the fish tank glass again as more of them arrived, soon blanketing the windows with the muted gray of their flesh, blood from recent meals still bathing the faces of several creatures.

As they moved against the glass, their greasy, bloody hands left smears of body fluids and dirt on the clear glass and their moans reverberated through the hollow acoustics of the polished floor and high ceilings. Sundry bloodless wounds gaped darkly from ragged tears in clothing and various stumps wiggled in vain where limbs had been rent from their hips and torsos. The rubbing of cold flesh on the windows made a high-pitched squeak that could be faintly heard under the din of their language. If hell had a brochure, this picture was certainly on the cover page.

To the left of the front door, a popping sound split the din of their clambering. A large, jagged crack had suddenly formed in the plate glass, running from floor to ceiling. Bodies pressed against the glass and pounded against one another, eager to intrude and frustrated by the meal that was so close but yet so far. The glass popped again as another crack appeared, forming instantly in the size and shape of a lighting bolt, stretching half the width of the glass section.

It was quickly becoming apparent that we needed to move. Much faster, in fact. Kate and Sam came out, skidding to a halt as they realized the enormity of the mass already outside the doors.

"You wanna go out and tell them we're closed?" I asked Sam, grinning like an asshole.

"What about the service section? We could see it from the truck when we were out there," said Kate, ignoring me. "If they followed us in the front, they probably don't know about the back, right?"

We all exchanged looks. We didn't really know what they could figure out. We were always running away in one direction, no real choice to be had in the matter. The doctor's comments on the Liverpool came to mind, and I wondered for the first time about the complexity of thought they were capable of. Given their numbers, if they ever learned to reason or—god forbid—to communicate, we were in some serious shit. Not that we weren't already, mind you, but it's all relative.

The glass popped again, and five more cracks split the overstressed panes. "One way to find out," Sam said, and moved back toward the office and the door to the service department. We followed, Anaru bringing up the rear. Their moaning followed us down the short corridor past the finance office and to the large, windowless metal door in the back.

Sam grabbed the handle, but Anaru moved up, gently pulling her back and grabbing the handle himself. "If they eat me, they'll be too full to eat you," he said jovially, pushing the door out and stepping through before any could protest.

Sam quickly lodged her foot in the opening and moved to follow. Before she could get through, Anaru fired three fast rounds before his gun went silent. A loud crash could be heard from the garage and a heavy weight fell against the door, pushing it shut again. We heard the sound of breaking glass, which was soon followed by the sound of another body falling. Sam cursed and slammed her shoulder against the metal door, but it wouldn't budge. Kate and I moved up, the three of us putting our shoulders against it as I counted quickly "One, two ..."

Suddenly, the door flew open and the three of us collapsed through, sprawling on the ground. I looked up to find Anaru standing before us, looking confused as he held the body of a zombie in mechanics' overalls in each of his huge hands.

"You guys could have waited until I moved these guys out of the way first." He smiled. "But I'm touched. Really, I am."

He tossed the now twice-dead corpses, one to each side, and picked up his weapon. He had shouldered his rifle, and now carried an ax in his enormous arms, which he had clearly liberated from a shattered glass enclosure next to the door.

"Figured we'd be in for some close quarters stuff," he said, shrugging dismissively at his choice. Looking at his giant form, I couldn't second-guess the decision. Stepping in front of an ax wielded by this monster would be like diving into a wood chipper headfirst.

From the showroom, the sound of shattering glass announced the expiration of our time inside. We bolted for the large blue truck I had identified earlier. A creature stepped in front of Anaru as we emerged into the daylight. He swung his ax almost dismissively with one hand—a single lateral swipe that passed through the neck of the oncoming zed without pause.

The detached head, eyes still moving, bounced once against the shoulder of its body and fell to the ground, where the severed neck hit wetly against the pavement, leaving a bloody spot when it rolled to the side. Anaru dispassionately kicked it under a dumpster full of used oilcans and moved forward, closely followed by Sam and Kate.

As the other three moved forward, disappearing momentarily between a couple of large sedans, two ambling forms appeared from either side of the narrow passage between two small SUV's to my right. With no time to draw my gun, I held my breath and simply barreled forward, lowering my shoulder into the first creature at a dead sprint. It was lifted off its feet as it fell backwards, hands grasping for me ineffectually as it dropped to the ground. The smell of carrion and rotting flesh nearly knocked me over as I righted myself, reeling from the impact.

The second creature hadn't been knocked down. Kate shouted from in front of me, but I was too close to afford her a clean shot, and the creature was too close for me to be able to step back and give her one. I swung my rifle up and around, catching it on the jaw. The jarring, muted feel of metal impacting bone and soft flesh traveled up the barrel and to my hands as the head jerked to the side. Behind me, I could hear the other creature moving, trying to get up.

I slipped between the two, creating distance enough for the killing shots that came from Kate's pistol. Sam hadn't stopped, but was in the driver's seat of the truck, slamming the door even as she turned the key. The engine roared to life as I got in the back seat behind Sam. Kate crowded in next to me as Anaru took the passenger side front seat.

"What say we get the fuck out of Dodge?" Sam asked, shifting to drive and pulling forward. She stopped abruptly as we turned toward the street. At least a hundred creatures stood between the four-lane road and us. They shambled slowly forward, moans filling the air. I turned my head, looking behind us to the low, solid wooden fence and the alley behind.

"You gotta go backwards. We can't go through that many," I urged. "This thing will make it through the fencing."

"The fuck it will, man. It'll hang up on the poles. We go forward through the soft targets, nice and fast."

"Look, we saw this before. Those things go down easy enough, but they jam up the undercarriage. There's too many—it's backwards or we're toast." The first zombie had reached the headlights. She revved the engine.

"Sam, he's right; they get caught up under the wheels. You have to go back. Now!" Kate was screaming as she finished the sentence.

Sam cursed loudly, whipping her head around and throwing the gearshift into reverse. Tires squealed as we moved backwards, distancing ourselves quickly from the first row of undead. The tailgate of the truck met the fence, and our heads jerked forward. Flattened by the impact of the truck, it slammed to the ground and we pulled out over the now horizontal wooden debris. Sam pulled the wheel sharply, straightening the vehicle and trying to pull forward. The engine whined and the truck jerked forward, moving a foot before stopping.

"Fuck! It's caught up! I god damned told you so!" We had gained a hundred feet, but they were still advancing, an implacable army of ugly, hungry motherfuckers.

Sam jumped out of the driver's seat, falling to the ground and out of sight to inspect the problem. Anaru opened his door, stepping onto the running board and setting the barrel of his rifle on the lower edge of his open window to steady his aim. He started firing carefully aimed shots at the approaching group. I jumped out, crouching and peering under the truck. A four by four support post had lodged itself in a gap in the engine shield next to the front axle; Sam was working on dislodging it manually, rocking it back and forth. I tried to help, but we didn't have the strength.

"Anaru, switch up with me," Sam yelled, rolling out and running to the passenger side of the truck. He stopped firing and came to the driver's side around the back of the truck, as she took up his position, standing on the outside of the door and shooting carefully into the crowd. I got up, hearing Kate's voice as I did so.

"Mike, watch out!" Even as I turned, I knew it was too late. Four zombies, their vacant staring eyes and drawn faces staring hungrily at Sam, had turned the corner ten feet away, shuffling toward her as she fired into the approaching horde. She couldn't hear their approach, focused as she was on the numbers advancing toward us and deafened by the sound of her consistently fired shots. I yelled at her and she turned to me; but she turned the wrong way, giving them the last few feet of distance they needed.

My hand shot out, pointing to them as the first creature, an ordinary woman of average height and build, left hand still clutching the remnants of her last wet meal, grabbed Sam's arm, bringing it toward her mouth. Caught off guard, Sam jerked her arm back, but the creature had leaned forward too far and it bit down hard on Sam's wrist, drawing a scream as blood rose from the wound and trickled out of the corners of the ghoul's mouth. Clutching the hand in its teeth, the creature shook the member from side to side like a dog with a chew toy, trying to detach it from her arm.

Amid her cries of pain, Sam's weapon discharged, splattering the head of the creature against the side of the truck. I reached her side, raising my weapon and firing at the remaining three as she moved back, cradling her wounded arm. She leaned against the truck, sliding to the ground slowly, face stricken and pale. The approaching crowd from the lot was forty feet away, shuffling steadily forward, moans louder as they approached.

I grabbed Anaru's ax from his seat and put my foot on Sam's shoulder, pushing her to the ground. This had to happen fast. Off balance from the unexpected contact, she fell down flat, back on the ground, arms splayed out to each side. I gave myself no time to consider or rethink; I simply acted on impulse, bringing the ax down with as much force as I could muster.

I briefly considered aiming for the neck, but allowed my initial swing to strike true. Her left arm lay flat on the ground with blood leaking from the bite wound and the ax cleaved through the flesh and bone of her forearm cleanly. She jerked and screamed, trying to raise her gun toward me. Suddenly the rear door of the cab opened, knocking the rifle from her hand as Kate looked down knowingly. Sam's eyes flipped back in her head as she fainted, head striking the pavement with a dull thud.

Nodding at Kate thankfully, I grabbed Sam by the vest, hauling her up to the passenger seat. Anaru appeared again from the driver's side as a loud thump resounded from beneath the truck.

"What happened?" he asked, looking at Sam and then to me. Her blood poured from her wound onto the seat, as I snatched her rifle from where it had landed. Taking the strap from the gun, I tied it hastily above the cut, stemming the flow of blood as much as possible. The horde was fifteen feet away and now fearfully excited by the sight of Sam's blood.

"Later," I said, pushing her in and slamming the door. I sprinted to the other side and dove into the truck. The kick from the powerful engine knocked me against the back of the seat as we shot forward, the first few zombies reaching the broken fence as we shot out onto the cross street.

I looked back and watched the mob descend on the severed hand, several faces converging on the dismembered appendage, mouths moving silently. They fought among themselves as the fingers were pulled from the palm, bloody trails following from hand to mouth.

"You should have shot her," Kate whispered softly, eyes riveted to the windows, intentionally avoiding my eyes. "She's going to turn. Like you told Earl, it's not a matter of if." She turned back to me, eyes uncharacteristically hard.

"It's a matter of when."

Silent in the face of her unexpected pragmatism, I stared outside, watching the town pass us by and listening to Sam's heavy breathing. Why could I so readily abandon Earl to his fate, but hesitate with Sam? Why hadn't I swung for the neck? There's nothing about the human condition at this point in time that cries out for mercy. No hand should be stayed by hope and compassion. These were not emotions at home in a world overrun by the living dead. Not when you're dealing with a killer as ruthless as this.

But why Earl, and not Sam?

You know why, you sentimental, cowardly bastard. You can't kill another woman, not if there's a chance. You killed Maria, and you'll be damned if you repeat that sin, won't you. Well son, congratulations.

We passed out of the alley into the main street we had just crossed. Creatures covered the pavement, alerted to the presence of food by the masses clustered at the dealership.

You're damned whether you sin or not. Like your cute little friend said, it's not a matter of if...

A zombie still wearing the habit of a nun wandered in front of the truck, shattering the illusion of safety as Anaru sent it spinning into the underbrush lining the highway, blood from the impact spraying onto the windshield.

Anaru pulled the lever on the steering column, sending blue fluid over the glass. It mixed with the blood, and the diluted purple liquid ran lazily down the slick surface before the wiper blades erased it in one quick, efficient pass.

No, sir. It's just a matter of when.

CHAPTER 21

Dependence on fossil fuels never seems like an urgent or imminent problem when you have plenty of money and there's a gas station on every corner; you just figure that you'll keep paying for it until there isn't any left, and by then, someone will have invented an alternative. It's a logical enough conclusion, until something completely random, like a zombie apocalypse, is thrown into the works.

"We have a problem, kids." Anaru said from the driver's seat. We were passing the main drag of the town, and a post office and hardware store disappeared to either side. A hastily erected barricade composed of sawhorses and parked police cruisers blocked part of the road ahead. But he wasn't looking at the barricade. He was staring at the damned dashboard. I knew what he was going to say, but despite my own tendencies toward the skeptically negative side of life, I couldn't really believe that it had happened again. Not really. Attempts at humor had always been my first defense mechanism.

"Lemme guess," I said, affecting the appropriate sarcastic tone. "We're running low on gas?"

He nodded curtly, eyes on the road.

Despite my intuition, I was incredulous. "What the hell? Doesn't anyone keep gas in their cars anymore? Why don't any vehicles in the apocalypse have any goddamn gasoline? It's like a really bad fucking movie! Jesus!"

I couldn't believe this. Second time in as many vehicles!

"OK, I'm just telling you now, if any of you mother-fuckers even think about going outside to check out the noise in the dark, or go to the dark room upstairs to find the virgin after hearing the strange sound, I'm shooting you myself!"

Kate was looking at me funny, so I cut short my offended rant, realizing even as the echo of my voice against the windows faded into silence that I had sounded like a blithering, crazed moron. But it was unbelievable!

"How much?" I asked, moderating my tone.

"I'd say another couple miles; we're below red."

Out of gas. Again. See? Case in point. I was neither out of money, nor out of fossil fuels-on a global level, at least-I was just prevented from accessing the fuel by thousands of the living dead. Completely random? Abso-fucking-tively. But I digress.

We moved through zombies, in groups and individually, wandering in front of the truck, driven to feed but uncomprehending of the danger the large moving vehicle posed. Their skulls and limbs shattered against the front grill, their torsos were ground against the pavement, but there were always more. As the truck began to shudder after barely a mile through town, Anaru turned back to me, sparing a glance for Sam, whose face was pale.

"We need alternate transport soon, I think," he said. "I see a sign for a fire station coming up. You wanna try for one of their trucks?" He seemed almost anxious to get into a vehicle he knew. I shuddered internally at the thought of fighting through more of these with a wounded woman in tow, but knew we needed wheels to continue.

"Why not? But can we please, pretty please, check to see if it has gas first?"

He answered with a brief smile, steering to the right as the station approached. One large door stood open, the other closed. No truck could be seen in the open bay, but as our truck started its own death rattle, we ran out of choices.

We stopped and I jumped out, watching the doors and the few creatures outside that had seen our progress into the firehouse. They knew where we were, and others soon would as well.

"Check it out!" I yelled over my shoulder, noting already that there was no truck in the bay next to us. The station was empty.

"They might have something out back, I'll be back in a minute!" He disappeared through a door in the rear of the building.

Kate's voice from the cab broke the silence a minute later. "We need to get out of here, Sam's losing a lot of blood; she's not going to make it if we can't get this bleeding stopped ASAP!"

The zombies from outside were getting closer, and more followed from the street, emerging from alleys and buildings, from the ether, it seemed. How many people lived in this town, anyhow?

Anaru burst in through the rear door. "I got our new ride," he said, "but we gotta find some keys."

"Shit. Okay, help me with the door. We need more time in here." I bolted to the side of the hangar and slammed my palm against the automated mechanism. Nothing. As I expected.

Anaru bolted to the manual crank, slowly pulling the door down. The window of daylight on the smooth concrete floor slowly shrank to a rectangle, then a line. As the bottom of the metal sheet reached the ground, ten hands suddenly flew through the last sliver of light, reaching for us from outside. I cursed and jumped back, watching the hands and forearms search frantically for purchase against the cold concrete as the door came down at last. Anaru's massive arms strained against the crank as the door closed the last four inches, trapping the hands beneath the padded door and the floor of the station.

They twitched incessantly, fingers curling and uncurling in automated response to being confined. It was creepy shit; a row of twelve zombie hands lining the floor, looking like those prank Halloween candy bowls that curled down on your hand when you reached for a Snickers.

I leaned back against the exterior wall, breathing hard. Kate jumped down, moving to the front seat to tend to Sam.

"Keys?" I said after I caught my breath, glancing at Anaru. He nodded once and we moved into the office between the two truck bays.

It was a small space, and it held a radio and a white board covered with various assignments and names. I shrugged and turned to Anaru.

"Uh, I got no idea where to look. Any ideas?"

He shook his head and opened a small, empty box resting on the dispatch table. "Should be in here, but they're not. We'll need to check the living quarters." He moved past me, toward a narrow flight of stairs. "Up here."

I followed his eyes, incredulous. "You mean up the stairs, into what is likely to be a dark, windowless attic? Where the firefighters used to live and could still be stuck, behind that very door," my voice raised an octave as I gestured toward the solid wood door at the top of the stairs.

I was indignant. "What did I just finish telling you? Did I stutter?"

He just smiled as he moved up the stairs.

What the hell was so damned funny? Did he think I was kidding? Why wouldn't anyone take me seriously? Must be the insanity thing.

I sighed. It was hard being me.

Anaru reached the top of the stairs and grabbed the handle carefully. He turned it slowly, gun raised in his right hand. Moments later he turned to me, shaking his head.

"Locked," he said.

"So try it the other way, big fella. Don't be afraid. You can do it." I was being a wise ass, but I didn't appreciate being ignored.

Shouldering his rifle, he grabbed the banisters on either side and slammed his huge foot into the door, directly below the handle. The door, a fairly weak affair made of cheap plywood, shattered on impact. Shards of wood blasted back into the dark room. I reached for the door frame to pull myself up, noticing as I did so that my hand no longer bore the deep scrapes from its earlier run-in with the concrete outside the stadium. Several thin scratches still ran across the back of my hand. But the deep gouges were gone. I just stared, confused, knowing that I hadn't imagined the injury—the profuse amounts of blood on my sleeve were testament to that.

Suddenly, a shrill, weak voice from within.

"Don't hurt us, we're human!"

It was a young voice. Female. Anaru turned back to me, nodding once toward the rectangle of darkness above our heads before responding.

"We're not going to hurt you, we're friendly. We're coming in." He waited ten seconds before stepping inside. I followed him up the stairs and to the threshold of the top floor.

She was maybe all of fourteen, and she was sitting next to a bed on a small nightstand. The room was dark, but sunlight made its way in narrow streams through dark drapes, stapled to the drywall at the sills to the windows. A musty, dirty smell pervaded the small space. Her dark, clearly unwashed hair framed a narrow face. The tank top she wore was filthy, smeared and blotched; her pants, torn and mangled, hung from a too-thin waist. But for all her look of destitution, it wasn't her that our attention was drawn to—it was the bed next to her.

A large form, clearly that of a grown man, lay covered to the chin in a narrow bunk. Her eyes followed our own as we approached slowly. I noticed the restraints first. It was then that I placed the smell.

"He can't hurt you," she said defensively, moving unconsciously closer to the body—and between us and the bed.

As she got closer, the body thrashed suddenly, covers coiling and falling to the floor as the limbs jerked heavily against the bonds that held it. A dull, aching moan escaped from its throat and the bed rattled in protest.

"Who's ... he?" I asked gently, searching in vain for a better pronoun as I walked forward slowly, trying not to move too quickly.

"My dad. He's ... sick. But he can get better. He hasn't hurt anyone!" As she finished, her voice rose slightly as I brought my pistol up in response to his renewed movement. He was a middle-aged man, slightly portly but with what I knew had been a kind face. He wore a polo shirt with the name of a real estate office on the breast pocket. A gold wristwatch gleamed in the trickle of sunlight that melted through the small gaps in the drapery.

I lowered my pistol, hoping to ease her anxiety. "OK, OK. I'm sure he hasn't," I said, glancing at Anaru who had also lowered his gun.

"What's your name?" I asked, trying to sound friendly and nonplussed. He jerked against the bonds once more. I noticed that he was secured to the bed with four leather belts, all tied so tightly around the contact points that dried blood flaked and crumbled around the straps, evidence that they had been tied before his blood started to congeal. Before he had turned. While he was alive.

"Tristan," she said, sounding slightly calmer. She looked back toward Anaru, who was scanning the room slowly, hopefully in a cursory search for where the keys might be.

"How long have you been up here, Tristan?" I asked.

"Si—since it started," she replied, wiping her eyes and sniffling. Her eyes darted back to her father—what used to be her father—and back to me.

"You've been here more than a week? Have you eaten?"

She shrugged. "I found some cereal bars when we got here, and there was some soda and Gatorade... I thought more people would ... I thought we'd be rescued." She sniffled again, collecting her breath. "I tried to feed dad, but ..."

"How did you get here?" I didn't want to upset her, so I thought to keep her talking while Anaru looked for the keys. She turned to the bed and reached for the sheet that it had thrown off when we arrived, her hand passing within a foot of its head. The creature that used to be her father sat up as far as it could in response, teeth clamping down on air in an effort to reach her arms. She jerked back, but kept out of range as she pulled the sheets up as close as possible to her father's head. He snarled in response.

"Dad was—is—a realtor, and was showing a house to a client near here. He works a lot, so as a treat, he fixed it so that he would pick me up from school on his way home and we'd meet my mom for dinner. That was the day that everything happened. People at school started to get sick, so they called parents to pick kids up. But most of the parents were sick too, so all the students had to stay at school. I didn't feel sick, and I didn't want to catch anything, so I thought I'd wait for my dad outside." She wiped her eyes again, pausing as she remembered. From across the room, I heard Anaru curse softly as he dropped something in the near darkness.

"He called my cell phone and told me to wait near the road. He sounded scared and anxious, so I started to get a little scared. I had thought it was the flu, but right after I hung up with him, I heard loud noises from downtown. Like fireworks. Then, Mr. Simpson came outside and he looked really strange. His eyes were really wide open, and he sounded funny and walked funny. I got scared and ran to the street. My dad got there right before Mr. Simpson made his way down the stairs, and we drove away, but as we were leaving I saw Mr. Simpson trying to wrestle with another student who had run outside." She was crying in earnest now, but her voice was steady, if a trifle hurried, like she hadn't talked in days. She probably hadn't.

"My dad, he tried the police station, but it was empty. All the police were busy or gone, or had run away. So we tried the fire station. The trucks were gone and no one was here, but those things were outside, so we came upstairs. We thought that more people would come here...but they must have gone somewhere else."

I looked at Anaru briefly, and we exchanged a look. It seemed heartless to tell the kid that she may be the last surviving resident of this town.

"How did he get bitten?" I asked, looking at him as lay there, unblinking eyes staring at his daughter, mouth opening and closing in hunger and desire.

She just shook her head, as she started to weep. Seconds turned to minutes as she composed herself. Anaru was rooting through a chest of drawers in the back of the room.

"It was my mom," she said softly. "He told her to meet us here and she did, somehow. He let her in, not knowing about the bite." She drew a deep breath. "It happened that same night...while dad was asleep. She was feeling sick, and he had stayed up with her, but somehow he must have fallen asleep. But we didn't know about the bites. She woke up, and ..."

"She bit him?"

She nodded mutely.

"Did you tie him up?" I asked, surprised.

She shook her head again. "No, he tied himself up. I did the last arm." She looked up, defensive. "But he made me do it! I thought he'd be OK!"

From across the room, "Found 'em! Bastard kept 'em in his sock drawer!"

"Look Tristan," I said gently, "We can help you out of here, but you're going to have to leave your dad." I paused, thinking of what she wanted to hear. "We can send someone back to help him after you're safe, OK?"

She trembled violently and stood up. "No! I won't! You can send someone back for me too! I won't go! I won't leave him!" She moved back, almost stumbling onto the creature itself as she retreated away from us. It bolted up once again, desperate and tantalized by the prospect of food so close.

I spared a glance for Anaru and nodded my head toward the stairs, signaling him back to the others. "Listen, it may be a while. You could starve up here, and if he gets loose...You should really come with us."

Eyes wild, she moved around the opposite side of the bed, so that the twitching form of her father separated her from me. "I won't, and you can't make me! Send people back; I'll wait!" She had squatted down now, virtually hiding under the bed. She was mere inches away from the creature's face; close enough to smell the rotten stench of decay. I wasn't going to change her mind, and if I tried to make her come, I might hurt her. Or vice versa. Save one by force and risk the many, or leave her to her own devices and condemn her to death?

My day wasn't getting better as it went along; I wasn't prepared for these kinds of decisions. Slowly, I removed my rifle from my shoulder.

"You know how to use one of these?" I asked, putting it on the floor at the foot of the bed.

She nodded, calmer now. "My boyfriend goes shooting with his friends on the weekends. He taught me."

"OK, I'm gonna leave this here with you, all right? We pulled the front doors down, so you don't have to worry about those things getting in. I saw some vending machines downstairs, so you might be able to get some food there. I won't make you leave, but if he tries to hurt you or gets out..." She just stared.

I moved toward the door. "You're doing good, kid. Your dad would be proud of you." It was what I would have liked to hear, if I were her. Her hand came up briefly in a small wave; she even spared a tiny smile.

"Thanks. You too."

I ran down the stairs and saw Anaru looking out the back window.

"How we doin'?" I asked as I jogged to the truck.

"Mostly clear," he said. "We can get to it if we move quick enough. It's right outside." He looked at me questioningly, sparing a glance to the ceiling. I shook my head, and he understood.

"Took you guys long enough," said Kate, who was stooped over Sam's still-unconscious form in the passenger's seat.

"Yeah, well. The guy hid the keys in his sock drawer, and far be it from me to violate the sanctity of another man's underwear drawer before trying the other options."

She smiled briefly and I breathed an internal sigh of relief. I'd tell her later; quite frankly, I wasn't sure she'd understand. I helped Kate get Sam out of the truck and we moved to the rear of the building as Anaru stood at the door, ready to push it open and sprint.

"What kind of truck we got back here anyway?" I said, not having bothered to ask before. Anaru just smiled and pushed open the door.

We moved through the door quickly and I started in surprise and elation when I viewed our new ride. I understood Anaru's smile, as one of my own appeared stupidly on my face.

CHAPTER 22

A snowplow sat before us, large steel plow attachment duly attached and secured to the front of the massive, treaded vehicle. It was like a big yellow tank with a cowcatcher. Perfect for clearing snow, ice, and the occasional undead army.

Moving toward the cab, Anaru casually brained a zombie that shambled out from in front of the plow, sending it crumpling to the cement of narrow alleyway. He jumped into the driver's side and leaned across, opening the locked passenger door from the inside. I could see several creatures turn their attention from the street to our little party.

"She won't move fast, but we got nothing to worry about while we're inside," said Anaru, helping Sam up and into the four-person cab. I nodded and, still smiling, jumped on board behind Kate.

After a moment's consternation with the ignition system, Anaru started the huge engine, and we rumbled forward. He maneuvered the huge machine out of the alley behind the station and onto the main road. As we rolled out of the alley and onto a side street, my thoughts flickered back to Tristan, and to the unnamed mother on Long Island who was going to be indelibly etched on my memory for years to come.

I remembered Earl, who knew he was bitten, but grasped for those last seconds of life, even though it put the rest of us in danger. It was a cruel irony that had been forced on mankind of late; only in the face of a disease that robbed us utterly of our capacity for reason and thought, what some might argue to be the defining characteristics of humankind—what some might claim distinguished us from the beasts of the field—were we forced to exhibit the traits that really made us human.

Compassion, self-interest, love, tenacity, greed. Hate. Fear. It was only in situations like this when you realize that what you consider to be civilization and society is only a front. Narrow confines within which self-interest motivates compliance. Once the rewards of compliance disappear—once self-interest no longer dictates civility, selflessness, or compassion, we see the true nature of the human being. At once selfish and brutal, they possess in the same shell a phenomenal capacity for love and sacrifice, a paradox that is only the more tragic for its singular revelation in times of abject misery, sorrow and terror. I shook my head in sorrow and confusion, brought back to reality by the cruel, grating feel of bodies disintegrating before us.

Creatures wandered in front of us but were shoveled to the side or plowed under. They were crushed and maimed, decapitated and severed. The steel plow spared nothing and no one as its large merciless teeth carved a path through their hordes as surely as a scythe through a cornfield. It took off feet at the ankles and smeared creatures into the pavement as they fell. Though we couldn't see the front of the scoop from the cab, we knew it bore stark evidence of its gory passage.

We reached the outer edges of the town after what seemed like hours. The plow couldn't move faster than 30 miles an hour, and the town was much larger than we had seen from the air, being in large part covered by trees.

That's when we heard the gunshots. These weren't only the sidearm discharges—the kind of shots we had heard in King's Point—or even the kind that we had fired back in town. Spread out between the popping sounds of pistol and rifle fire was the concussing noise of much heavier ordnance. And it was being used close.

We met the soldiers about eight miles North of town and came upon them on a narrow stretch of mountain road. An APC had just finished plowing down a crowd of ghouls with a 50 caliber top-mounted machine gun when we came upon them, firing several warning shots in the air before we came around the last bend.

It was a small National Guard unit: four Humvees, two Bradley's and about thirty men, all lightly if adequately armed. They were almost as shocked to see us, proceeding toward them in a snowplow covered with zombie parts and congealed brown blood, as we were to see them: a large number of uniformed, armed men stopped in the middle of the narrow road.

According to their commanding officer, they had been on a weekend training exercise in remote areas of the mountains, practicing mountain maneuvers for an eventual deployment to Afghanistan. No contact with the outside world was allowed to ensure realistic conditions, so they knew nothing of the outbreak until three days ago, when they encountered their first zed on their way down the mountain, back to what used to be civilization. At first, they thought it was some crazy mountain man, ranting and frothing at the mouth. Maybe rabid or just plain drunk. But he was bleeding, so they stopped to help.

Radios don't work well in the mountains, and since it was a small exercise, and they weren't expecting to have to be in touch with anyone, the satellite gear was left behind. Even cell phones were ordered to be powered off and stowed. No one questioned the order. After all, it was just a couple of days: the standard one weekend a month.

A soldier from the first vehicle had approached the creature as it slouched forward, completely unaware of what it was. He had stooped over to its head level, asked what was wrong, and was met with a moan and grasping hands. Amazingly, he hadn't been bitten. A young man, he fortunately had the reflexes to deflect that first attempt, and instinctively brought his fist to the side of the thing's face. It had dropped to the ground and the Colonel, particularly astute, had ordered him restrained and confined.

The medics informed him that the man might be contagious, and the Colonel ordered him tied him up. It wasn't until a few hours later that they encountered more; a group this time, and far more dangerous. Two men were taken down and severely injured, another one had suffered a bite wound. That's when the safeties came off. It had taken them days to make their way through similar small towns up and down the highway, and they were exhausted.

As I leaned against the side of one of their trucks, I could hear Kate and a medic conferring over Sam's arm. She had regained consciousness, and was lying in the back of a cloth-enclosed Humvee, jacked up on painkillers. Kate and the medic stood outside, out of her earshot. Everyone knew what it meant to be bitten. It had yet to be seen whether you could excise the infection if you moved fast enough.

"There's no way to tell," Kate was saying. "We've seen people turn in a matter of seconds after they died, and we've seen people get turned within twenty minutes of being bitten."

"Our guys, Sergeant Ames and Corporal Blunt, they turned within a half hour," said the medic, clearly still coming to grips with the nature of this disease, "but they were both bit in arterial areas. Blunt took it in the neck. There was blood everywhere. It could've got into his system real fast, ya know?" He was young, no more than 19.

"Ames took the shortest. He took a bite on the leg, near the knee. He shot one of those fuckers all to hell and walked past it, thinking it was down. I mean he almost cut the damned thing in half—its guts were all over the pavement. But it grabbed him by the leg, and hauled itself up real quick, using his pants and climbing him like a tree. He clubbed it off, but not before it got a bite into his thigh." His face was ashen, the pallor of someone who had seen too much in too little time.

Kate considered the information and spoke slowly. "OK, so we have two that turned within thirty minutes, both potentially receiving the infection through an artery. One potentially to the carotid, one potentially to the femoral. Both severe, both deep." She shook her head as she saw me looking at her. "That's why this damn thing spread so fast. If they hit a major artery, the victim turns within thirty minutes or less." She turned to Sam, eyes uncertain.

"It's been more than two hours since it happened, but there's no telling whether it was slowed or actually averted by severing the infected area."

"I trust your friend is doing better?" Colonel Sharp was a tall man with an imposing demeanor. His dark, short hair framed a rather wide, severe face. Bright green eyes peered out from above a bushy, yet neatly within Army regulations, mustache. He held a cell phone in one hand, and a pistol in the other. The former evidence of his attempt to contact his superiors, the latter evidence of the most recent engagement in the rear of caravan.

"She's stable," Kate said, "but we've yet to see what effect Mike's lumberjack impression is going to have, long term."

"That was quick thinking, Mr. McKnight. I must say, your reputation precedes you. Unfortunately, given that reputation, quick thinking from you seems as unbelievable as poetry from a baboon." He smiled and jumped up to sit on the hood of the Humvee and put the cell phone away.

I paused for a minute, making sure I heard right before answering. "I'd just appreciate the benefit of the doubt at this point, Colonel. It's been a long week so far."

"I can give you that, but not much else I'm afraid," he said, glancing at his men as they stared alertly into the surrounding forest. A shot rang out from the rear of the caravan, then another short burst of that impossibly loud 50 cal fire.

"If you're intent on moving up the mountain, you'll have to go by foot after another mile or so. We hit a large group of these things a while back and took out part of a retaining wall behind us in the fight," he nodded back the way that they had come. "Not passable by vehicle any longer."

"We'd sure welcome your company, Colonel. Like I said, this could be really important. A cure or a vaccine might be possible, and this facility might hold the information we need." We had given him the run down almost an hour ago, when we ran into them and brought them up to speed on the extent of the reigning apocalypse.

"Sorry, Mr. McKnight. We'll be needed down the mountain, trying to weed out survivors and terminate as many of these ungodly beasts as possible. We can't divert these assets to a wild goose chase." He looked at Sam. "But you're welcome to leave your friend in our care. I can't imagine she'll be better off continuing on with you."

He scanned his command. "Besides, my men will be wanting to check on their families soon. I can't keep them up here like this without more information."

I nodded in understanding, and looked at Sam. "It will be up to her. We don't know what her infection status is, but according to Kate, she might be ahead of the curve already. If it's been an hour and she hasn't gone to the dark side, we might be in the green."

"Suit yourself," he said. "Just be on the lookout. There are a lot more of these things in the forest than there should be. This is a pretty sparsely populated area, but we've already put down about fifty of 'em between the last town and this one. Leads me to believe something more serious is going on up here."

He looked at me quizzically. "Really odd thing is that some of these creatures looked really out of place ... I swear we've put down at least twenty creatures that looked like they were Middle eastern or something. You got any idea why that would be?"

"Shit, Colonel. You're asking the wrong guy. I'm just up here 'cause I've got some sort of insane death wish." I leaned against the door next to him. "Does seem kind of off though, huh? This area doesn't exactly strike me as the most multi-cultural bastion of the state."

"Tell me about it. Some of 'em looked really old too, like they hadn't just turned a couple days ago. Smelled really bad too," he chuckled softly, "But I guess that's relative."

"None of these things smell like roses, that's for sure." From the front of the caravan, a small explosion shook the air.

"Stupid SOB's—I told them to hold back on the grenades." He shouted an order into his radio.

"Why's that?" Kate asked.

He grunted a short laugh. "The short answer is that they don't work worth a shit. The long answer is that the effectiveness of a grenade is in its collateral damage; it's not exactly a tool of great accuracy. Explosions typically take out legs, arms, torsos. That's the kind of damage that a human body can't sustain and keep going."

"Well, these things keep going until you destroy the head, as you very well know. You take out the legs, injure the torso, what not, they can keep functioning: slimy little stumpy torsos draggin' on the ground, armless, legless fuckers that are still able to bite..." he cringed. "Let's just say you're not doing yourself any favors using explosives. They're next to useless when you're dealing with that kind of resiliency."

He jumped down, holstering his pistol. "Just in case what you're telling me is true, about the cure or vaccine, I'm going to send a soldier with you, get you past our little roadblock and help you find your facility. We passed the road you're looking for a while back, and he knows exactly where it is." Into his radio, "Sergeant Gary, send Corporal Lansing to the med vehicle. Get the rest of the vehicles ready to move."

Engines came to life around us as a young, red haired man jogged into sight, friendly face peering out from underneath a helmet and above his Kevlar vest. A rifle was slung over his shoulder and a pistol strapped to his waist. He came to attention in front of the Colonel, saluting.

"Yes, sir," he said sharply, voice deep and serious.

"Corporal, I need you to show these people past the rock slide and to the road we passed on our way down. They're heading to a facility in the forest that may have a cure to this disease we've encountered."

"Sir?" he asked, unbelieving.

"You're going back up the mountain, soldier," he said.

"You mean back up to where those crazy mother fuckers tried to eat us? Back to the hillbilly all you can eat buffet?"

"Corporal..."

"Just clarifying, sir." His tone said otherwise but his face stayed blank.

"Grab the rest of your gear and some MRE's. You're dismissed." Kate followed him to the med vehicle, probably to talk to Sam.

As Lansing and Kate walked away, a thought occurred to me. "Colonel, you do any time in Iraq?"

He looked at me hard, eyes like agates as he climbed into the passenger side of the Humvee. "Son, every person in uniform has done time in Iraq. Most of us a couple times. Why?"

"You ever heard of anything called the Baghdad protocol?"

He stared out the front window of the Humvee, face impassive, not responding.

The hum of the idling motor was the only sound, and then, "Where'd you hear that?" he asked, still staring forward.

"Sam heard the President use that term right before he left the White House."

He turned to me quickly, eyes searching my face for more information. Finding nothing, he turned away again as if he were ashamed to look at me as he explained, "I heard it a couple times. Nothing definitive, but it was thrown around once and a while after entire streets were destroyed in the war and during the occupation." He shrugged. "I never knew for sure, but I always figured it was some sort of total destruction order designed to take out large areas of hostiles."

This time he looked at me. "The thing is, it was total," his face was hard. "And when I say total, I mean terrorists, civilians, police, men, women, children, babies, pet gerbils...anything that breathed. We're talking massive, undiscriminating collateral damage." He turned away again.

He shook his head, closing the door. "Your friend must have heard wrong, Mr. McKnight, the president couldn't have given an order like that here. Not on American soil. Not even now."

He turned to the driver, "Move out."

I stepped back as the vehicle began to roll. His arm extended from the window, wrist flicking once in a wave, and then back inside.

As the caravan pulled away, Kate, Anaru, Lansing and Sam walked slowly forward. "Ready to go?" Kate asked, looking around nervously.

"Yeah, man. The last thing we need to do right now is stand around waitin' for more of those things to come chompin' around." Lansing was holding his rifle up, staring into the forest. Anaru helped support Sam, who spoke up as I looked at her.

"I finish what I start, and I'm going to see this through," she said, teeth grinding through the pain but her face serious. I nodded, respecting the commitment.

"Then let's get this creep show on the road," I said, moving toward the truck.

"Fuckin' A, man," Lansing said, helping Sam into the truck and then following her. "The faster we find your damn zombie headquarters, the faster I get off this mountain."

It's not just the mountain, kid, I thought as we walked toward the plow. The world is a big place.

CHAPTER 23

When you're a child, you don't really appreciate the beauty of summer camp. Part of the problem might be that summer camp is designed by adults, who have clearly created something that every adult very much needs in their lives once and a while: a retreat to nature, solace from the rigors of day to day life, and a general return to youth.

But as a kid, you don't need that stuff. Camp is just a different place to do nothing.

I remember going off to summer camp and being disappointed at leaving my neighborhood and all my friends. When you're a child, it doesn't matter where you are, you're still having fun. You don't have to remove yourself from society because your social interactions are uniform no matter where you are. You play, you eat, you play some more, you eat some more, you go to sleep. Beautiful stuff. And you can do that anywhere.

Don't get me wrong, once you're at summer camp, it's great; you're outdoors, you meet new people, you play games. You might even learn something. I learned how to eat shitty food just because you're hungry, how to sleep through incredibly loud and obnoxious snoring, and even how to kiss a girl—all of which prepared me for real life; especially for marriage. But it's not the retreat it is for adults. It's just a change in locale.

So it is that when, as an adult, you enter a summer camp, you do so with some dual sense of nostalgia and regret. You remember the times gone by, and you regret not appreciating them more and, frankly, not being able to return to that life. Such were my own feelings when we passed under the rough-hewn gateway to Camp Lillikanda.

Even when being chased by flesh-eating zombies.

Our good corporal got us past the rockslide. It was quite impressive. Apparently they had fired rocket propelled grenades—RPGs, he called them—into the retaining wall. Held in only by a thin layer of metal-reinforced fabric, the rocks behind tumbled out onto the road, creating a barrier of shattered granite and limestone that prevented carrying on by vehicle. It also covered a few zeds.

There was a small pathway slightly hidden to the South of the slide that Lansing knew of. We followed him down off the road, around the slide, and back up to the concrete. A small portion of the rock fall had intruded onto our passage, and as I climbed over a particularly large pile, an arm that lay well-concealed and half-buried in the small chunks of gray and brown stone grabbed my ankle.

It was just a hand, no gnashing teeth above ground, but it still freaked me the hell out. After what we had been through, I was understandably a bit jumpy. I wasn't willing to fire my rifle or pistol at it, but its grip was firm and merely pulling at it with my fingers availed me little. My admittedly pseudo-girlish shriek brought Anaru from the head of the line, and he chuckled at my predicament as he knelt down at my side. He tested the grip of the fingers, shook his head and drew his combat knife, pressing it to the gray flesh and sawing quickly.

"Can't you just ... ya know," I made an opening gesture with my hands, miming that with his great strength, he could just rip it off.

"Sorry, but this thing is on good. Best idea would be detach from the body first and then work on getting the hand off later." He chuckled as he sawed, "Cause the hand don't bite. The head buried down there somewhere probably does." He finished cutting, leaving a gray stump capped with a congealed brown liquid protruding from the pile.

When he finished, I got up, feeling absurd with a dismembered hand clutching my ankle. That, of course, is when they showed up.

There were at least twenty or thirty, and they came from the trees behind us. We had ditched the plow at the rock wall, making sure to point it back toward town in the event we could make it back this far.

They shambled out from the tree line, covered in dirt and dried blood. There were locals among them to be sure, but the Colonel's suspicions were accurate. There were definitely people in this crowd that were out of place on a rural mountain road: mainly Arabs and a few Asians, all dressed similarly in uniformly blue pants and shirts. Several of the creatures were in a more advanced state of decomposition than the others, indicating more age. This also seemed to corroborate the Colonel's comments, but how was it possible? The outbreak only hit a week ago, but these things had been dead for far longer than that.

We shot out onto the pavement, the sounds of our rapid footfalls echoing off the rock ledge that ascended vertically for hundreds of feet on our left side. On the right, the tree line ahead of us was clear, but they were emerging quickly out of the woods behind us.

"Up here on the right, it's the turn off," said Lansing, not even winded from the jog.

I remembered the way and how I had missed the turnoff when I came up with Maria, drawing her mock ire and a slight punch to the shoulder. It was an easy road to miss, obscured by trees and bushes. She had made a joke about asking for directions; I had made a joke about that movie Deliverance. We had both laughed. It had been a nice day.

Jesus, Maria. How did this happen?

"We go down a few hundred yards, past the camp, then up the hill into the facility," I said as we kept moving, huffing the sentence out in brief syllables, trying to keep up.

Anaru was watching Sam, who seemed to be recovering her strength now. Kate was in front of me and Lansing was in the lead, rifle held at hip level, eyes alert. I tightened my grip on my own weapon, the moans from behind spurring us forward.

The surface turned from pavement to gravel as we began down a narrow road, surrounded on both sides by tall, dark trees. Leaves of various shapes and colors littered the ground before us, causing our steps to be accompanied by the crisp crackling of broken fauna as we ran from our pursuers. The road dipped down through a gully and back up, water running through a small culvert under the graded path, as we topped the opposite side and moved forward. I was starting to lag behind, my inability to complete extended aerobic activity catching up to me, when the sign came into view.

KAMP LILLIKANDA 100 FEET AHEAD!
WHERE KIDS CAN BE KIDS!

Fall Semester Now Open!

The sounds of pursuit from behind us had faded, our sprint having temporarily outdistanced our slower moving assailants. I slowed to a brisk walk, still searching the trees to either side.

"Corporal, I think we're in the clear for the moment. I would suggest we hole up in a solid building in the camp until those things are off our ..." I was going to say scent, but it didn't seem possible that this virus would improve any of the normal human senses. They must track and hunt using the same faculties that we did: sight and sound. So if we hid well, they'd no more be able to track us than would any normal human.

"Mike?" Kate asked, looking for the end of the sentence.

"Let's get inside and keep our heads down until they pass. They must hunt and track the same way we do - so if they can't see us or hear us, they won't know that we're here. Even if they come through the camp, they won't know we're there unless we tell them."

"Fuck that, man. We need to keep going to your facility. If it's just ahead, we can get there now, before those creepy bitches can catch up." Lansing was calm, and his idea had merit, but we needed to be cautious.

"We have no way of knowing what condition it's in. It had a large, electrified fence and was heavily guarded. If it's still in business, we may have to talk our way in. If it's not, we may still run into the fence or a bunch of those things. We need to start off fresh and that means not being chased by fifty zombies, savvy?"

He looked back over my shoulder then back to the camp and nodded. "Yeah man, whatever. Let's just get inside nice and quick. I'd rather not be standing here waiting for them when they come around that bend."

We moved quickly but carefully into the camp, underneath the large wooden gateway, and past a totem pole, brightly colored in oranges and blues. A camp bus stood empty next to a small administration building to our right, dormitories in front of us set back against the lake. To our left, a cantina and a large cinder block building with a curved roof, probably the gym.

"What the hell kind of camp is this?" asked Sam, looking around. "It's early September—past time for kids to be in school."

"From what I remember Maria telling me, it's a 'study outdoors' kind of place. Parents from the city pay top dollar to send their kids to the mountains for a semester."

Sam just looked at me and scowled. I shrugged. Why the fuck'd she ask, then?

A soft, slightly high-pitched sound caught on the wind as we made our way toward the gym, made our destination by an unspoken agreement that it was likely the strongest choice of redoubt if we were discovered. We crossed the open space between the gate and building warily, eyes darting to windows and doors, every slight change of light or movement of shadow a potential threat. As we moved, the sound seemed to get louder, and I strode forward faster, thinking it to be the sounds of our pursuers, amplified and twisted by the wind.

From the lake, the solitary sound of a water bird echoed between the branches of the trees. A small animal, most likely a squirrel, darted up a tree to my right, causing my finger to tighten involuntarily on the trigger of my drawn pistol before I exhaled in relief.

As we reached the door to the gym, Lansing held up his hand. "Anybody else hear that, or am I fucking crazy?"

"Yeah, I think it's those things behind us," Anaru said, looking instinctively over his shoulder. "But it seems louder here than it was on the road." He shrugged. "Probably the wind."

"Maybe not," said Kate, moving toward the door, where Lansing stood, hand on the steel bar that bisected the double doors leading inside. She held her finger to her mouth in a hushing gesture, and pushed softly and slowly against the steel bar. It didn't budge. She squatted in front of the bar and looked closer.

"This is locked from the outside," she said, standing up. As she did so, the noise seemed to crescendo, a chorus of high notes joining in a mockery of the moans we had been listening to for days. A horrid thought occurred to me, and my heart thumped in my chest as I backed up, turning to the side of the building where I had seen a door with windows on our approach. From behind me, I heard Sam's voice ask where I thought I was going, but I didn't hear, hoping and praying in my hasty walk that I was wrong.

The doors were painted a garish purple, the kind of color people paint for kids under the belief that youth automatically equates with poor taste. A large red ladybug adorned the one on the right; a yellow butterfly to the left. I approached the window with dread as Anaru appeared on my right. I peered through, stomach in my throat.

"Holy shit," Anaru said from my side, his massive form doubling over and retching next to me, vomit spraying onto the door and oozing down to the dirty concrete walk. Some of it got on my boots, some covering the rotting stump of the hand still attached to my right foot. But neither of us cared.

I had been right.

God help me, I had been right.

CHAPTER 24

There were maybe a hundred of them, most clustered around the far doorway, pawing at the steel panels. They were between 6 and 10, but it was hard to tell. So many faces and bodies were mutilated or defaced that apart from size, clues as to age were difficult to come by.

It appeared that the only adult in the room had been too badly ravaged to reanimate, its bloody misshapen form lying prone against the far wall. Tatters of clothing lay strewn about and around the corpse as if tossed in frenzy by a pack of wild, hungry dogs.

Almost all of them wore the uniform apparently imposed by the camp, a khaki shirt bearing the logo of the place, as well as khaki shorts and tennis shoes of different makes and brands. Breaking my concentration, Lansing came around the corner, followed by the two women.

"What the hell, man? We gotta get inside ..." he stopped talking as his eyes focused in on the window and his face changed slowly from irritation to dismay.

"Daaaaaaamn," he drew it out softly and slowly, like a long drag from a cigarette. As Kate and Sam took turns at the window, both silent in the face of the unspeakable, I scanned the road behind us, which remained clear. But only for so long.

Trying to put the scene behind me, I spoke as I put the window out of sight. "Let's get to the dorms. We can shut the doors, hunker down, and wait for them to wander past." I stepped forward and away from the doors as Sam spoke up.

"What about them?" she said, her thumb jerking over her shoulder toward the pack of zombie children now moving toward the window, where our peering faces had been spotted.

"What about them?" asked Lansing before I could answer.

"We can't just leave them," said Sam, incredulous. "They're children."

His eyes widened in shock at realizing her lack of comprehension. "Yeah, fucking cannibal campers from hell, man. They ain't normal no more—they're monsters. We're leaving their rottin' asses here, end of story." Her facial expressions changed rapidly in response, from sadness to anger to despair and back to indignation. As she looked at each of us, it finally shifted to acceptance as she turned away and cradled her injured arm.

"Yeah, okay. Let's go then."

We moved quickly across the grounds toward the furthest dorm. They were low, long buildings, with dark roofs. Brown cedar siding covered the exterior walls, there was one door on each end, both doorways bearing a screen door backed by a solid wood interior door.

Lansing reached the closest entrance and pulled the screen back, signaling for silence as he moved in, rifle held at the ready. Moments later, he reappeared.

"We're clear—in a manner of speaking," he said, waving us in as he watched behind us for any signal of pursuit.

"What do you mean by that?" asked Anaru as he passed from daylight to the dark confines of the room. As our eyes adjusted to the dark interior, we understood.

A teenager, maybe sixteen or seventeen, hung suspended from the ceiling by a lanyard of belts and sheets. Bulging eyes searched the room, moaning made impossible by the constriction of the voice box by the attached belts around its crimson and gray neck. His feet kicked in a crude imitation of perambulation as its arms stretched forward, hands opening and closing in unrequited hungry desire. Sandals lay below an overturned chair below the moving legs, and a piece of paper lay folded neatly under a blue Nalgene bottle at the foot of a nearby bed.

"This place is a damn freak show," I said, raising my pistol toward its head.

"Wait," said Anaru, grabbing my wrist and looking out one of the dorm's two windows that faced the road into camp.

"Shit! Everyone down!" whispered Kate, hunching and moving to the side of the window, pulling the ratty, dust covered curtains slowly shut. "Anaru, help me with these bunks," she said, skittering under the window toward the door and grabbing a nearby bunk bed by the post. She and Anaru dragged it slowly and quietly in front of the door as Lansing and I did likewise on the opposite end of the room, taking careful steps not to be seen from outside through the narrow slit between the two pieces of fabric.

The first of the group from the road had appeared at the main entrance, shuffling slowly and mindlessly forward, apparently simply following the road into the camp. Others passed by the entrance, walking slowly up the hill to the facility.

There seemed to be no rhyme or reason to their shambling other than the vague notion of feeding, and the memory of their meals having moved this way. Though their steps were shambling and seemingly directionless, their unblinking collective gazes were searching, eyes within rotting, lifeless heads constantly moving from side to side. Their food was out here, somewhere. It was just a matter of finding it.

I crouched down, out of sight. I saw Anaru carefully approach the hanging teenager from behind, knife in hand.

You know, if you were a nice guy, you'd let them know where you are. You're not being a good host sitting here, fondling your big gun, hoping they just walk on by. After all, they've gotta eat too. At least throw 'em a power bar or something. Maybe a box of raisins?

It laughed suddenly, wildly, as if it had said something far more witty.

I had never spoken back to the voice before, but I didn't have time to bend over for its abuse right now. I needed to have control of something, especially right now.

Shut the fuck up. I don't need your bullshit right now, I thought back.

The laughter stopped suddenly, as if a door had been shut or a light had been turned out. My mind was silent, but for the lingering echoes of the laughter. Just for the record, hearing nothing but the disembodied laughter of an internal, unknown voice bouncing around between your ears while the living dead linger outside your door does not a fun time make.

Then, suddenly: You don't know what you need, you crazy bastard!

It had clearly been affronted by my belligerence.

What the hell are you doing here anyway? Trying to save the world? Dumb shit. What makes you think the world is worth saving? That you, of all people, are worth saving?

I didn't have an answer to that, I just knew that I had to try. As I finished the thought, I realized that had been my answer.

Not good enough! The voice was yelling, reading my thoughts. Not nearly fucking good enough! This shit happened for a reason, and you have no right to interfere.

The tone changed from animated disdain to outright anger.

You don't even deserve to be alive. You should have died back there in King's Park! You never should have made it out, and you know it!

I brought my hands to my head, squeezing my temples, trying unsuccessfully to disagree with that sentiment and quell the distempered voice, even as a whisper from my side caught my ear.

"Mike," it was Kate. From behind her, a heavy thump and a lighter one, in immediate succession.

I opened my eyes to find the body of the zombie on the floor, the head having rolled back underneath a far bunk. A dreadfully rotten, coppery smell permeated the dark room as I involuntarily wrinkled my nose in response.

"Yeah," I said, trying to suppress my gag reflex. The smell was getting worse. It must have come from the inside the body. The damn organs must rot inside the body, even as the nervous system and brain keep functioning. What a way to go.

"What do you think happened here?" she asked. Her eyes were red, and her whispered voice was unusually hoarse. I elected not to ask about it as I shrugged in response.

"No clue." I watched as Anaru dragged the body underneath a bunk and carefully extracted the head from the far side of the room, grabbing it by the hair and rolling it slowly under the bed like a bowling ball.

From beside me, the sound of someone sitting against the wall. "Looks like this guy," Lansing gestured at the teen with his rifle as he slid slowly to the floor, "locked the little ones in the gym and then took care of himself. Must've been bitten or something."

"We could just read this," said Anaru, holding up the piece of paper he had extracted from beneath the water bottle and handed it to Kate. "It looks like he left it behind." His loud whisper carried just as far as it needed to chill us at the thought.

I wasn't inclined to intrude on this poor bastard's last thoughts, especially since this note was addressed to people that were likely already dead as well. It seemed doubly wrong to read a note left by a dead man for dead people. But we were alive, and it might give us information on the camp up the road or shed light on how the infection made it here. I nodded.

Kate read slowly to herself, tears welling in her eyes, emotion torturing an already reddened face. Her mouth moved slowly with the words as she read, as if giving verbal shape to the written word paid it homage that it was sorely due. When she was finished, she handed it to me silently, looking away as she did and wiping a tear from her cheek.

"Lansing was right," is all she said before getting up and moving to a bunk across the room.

I looked down at the now crumpled and somewhat moist scrap of lined yellow paper.

Dear Mom and Dad,

I'm so sorry. I did what I thought was best, and I know I will become dangerous if I don't take care of myself. They were turning on one another, and I didn't know which ones were bitten. I didn't want this to get out. God help me, I locked them all in.

Two men came to camp one night. They came from up the hill. They looked sick and hungry, but acted strange. Mr. Davies went out to greet them and they attacked him and tried to eat him. After that, a lot of the counselors got scared and ran away. All the children were so scared. I tried to keep them safe, but those two men kept following us, and then Mr. Davies got up again, and he looked like them. We couldn't run any further and they bit some children. I killed them with a shovel after that.

The children that were bit kind of died but then they came back. I didn't know what to do, but after one of them bit me, I put them all inside the gym before I could get sick. I didn't want them to get out and hurt more people, but I didn't know what else to do. I'm so sorry. Tell the children I'm sorry.

I love you,

Jim

I closed my eyes and leaned my head back slowly against the wood paneled wall, hearing the shuffling sound of leaves crackling outside as more creatures moved about. This was all so fucking pointless. What was happening? I opened my eyes as a thought occurred to me—where had the one larger body in the gym come from? That was certainly odd.

I offered the paper to Lansing and he shrugged, refusing it. I folded it carefully and put in my breast pocket, realizing as I did so that the goddamn zombie hand was still firmly attached to my ankle. I drew my combat knife and started prizing the fingers back, taking care not to cut myself. The fingers were ice cold and as hard as steel. Knuckles crusted with what used to be blood stared at me as I worked, removing first one finger, then the next. The situation was so absurd, I had to fill the silence. I spoke to Lansing in a soft whisper.

"So what do you do when you're not stuck in the mountains killing dead people?" I asked.

He grunted in amusement, staring at the far wall vacantly as if daydreaming. "I'm a carpenter," he said, taking a swig of water from his canteen.

Nodding in respect, I returned to my grisly task. He turned to me, deep voice muted and his eyes flickering to the window and back down, "Hey, man. Since I know what you do ... or did ... and since we're not doin' nothin' right now ... maybe you could say that line from the movie? I loved that damn movie."

I stopped mid-chore, holding a cold white finger in one hand and a combat blade in the other, and looked at him for a long moment until a smile struggled to my face. I shook my head and looked away. "That's part of my past. It's not me anymore. Or maybe you didn't catch the news."

He smiled, and the words came out in a plaintiff groan. "Aw, come on. You can't get rid of it that easy, man. That's who you are. Don't matter what they said you did, or what you say you didn't do. You got a rep to uphold, you know?"

"Not anymore."

He chuckled wryly, shaking his head slowly from side to side and plucking a cigarette from his pocket. "Whatever, man. You've been branded, whether you like it or not. Like cattle. You can't ever get away from that. That shit owns you." He lit the cigarette.

"Say it, don't say it, I don't give a fuck," he took a draw, exhaling slowly so the smoke dispersed almost invisibly into the woody, musty air before continuing.

"I'm just trying to pass the time. But if you tryin' to get away from bein' that guy? You gotta run a lot farther and lot goddamn faster before you find people that don't know who and what you are. Til you do, you're always gonna be that guy." He looked at me with a smile on his face. "And we always gonna want you to say that shit."

I laughed despite myself and pulled out a snack bar, eating silently. Occasionally, a zed would wander close to the bunkhouse, but would meander thoughtlessly away when it wasn't afforded entrance. Not hearing or seeing anything, they apparently lacked the capacity for suspicion or dissemblance, and no alarm was raised on account of a locked door.

As the daylight slowly dwindled, the late summer sun now slanting in the house from the West, we sat in tense silence. Whispering at times to one another, the imperative was to avoid detection, so little talk was wasted as we attended the creatures' departure. At steady intervals, Anaru or Lansing would peer carefully into the main yard and quickly pull their heads back in, shaking them mutely. Sam drifted off sometime during the late afternoon, but had to be awakened by Anaru when she started to talk in her restless sleep, head turning from side to side and sweat beading her brow. When she awoke, she had developed a fever and her eyes darted nervously about, as if paranoid. Anaru and I exchanged questioning glances, uncertain of what to do.

The sun finally faded completely, and as the last of the daylight slipped across the dirty wooden floor we agreed in soft whispers to take turns on watch, while the others slept. We had been fortunate, and no zed had gotten too close or heard or seen anything, but we had to be alert.

As darkness fell, the steady and calming sound of rain on the roof was in conflict with the nervous tension I felt, sitting against a three-inch thick wall of wood that was the only thing separating me from the living dead. Kate was sleeping on one of the many short beds, legs curled to her chest, eyes moving beneath her eyelids. Sam slept restlessly, still in the grip of the fever, and still muttering softly under her breath. I stared at the narrow beams that met in the middle of the roof, thinking about Maria and remembering the girl I kissed so long ago in a camp not unlike this one. She had been impressed by my bravado and ego, and I had been impressed by ... well, the things that hormone-filled twelve year old boys are impressed by. I remembered diving into the lake, swimming to the buoy in the middle, and ringing the bell, all on a dare. A dare that ended in that first encounter.

Wrapped in that comforting memory of happier times, I slept in an abyss of darkest night, my mind and body for once too mentally and physically exhausted to dream. Like all good things in this world, however, that small respite from reality eventually came to an end. Not with a whimper, but with a moan.

CHAPTER 25

I awoke to the smell of fresh air, which I knew instinctively to be wrong. The soft whisper of a cool night breeze must have been so jarringly refreshing that my unconscious refused to accept it, even in sleep. The door to the cabin stood wide open, the dark shapes of the trees and the gymnasium beyond outlined by the soft glow of the moon.

I looked around the room, noticing after slow inspection that Sam was absent. Cursing myself for not anticipating some sort of lunacy inspired by her infection, I got up and moved to the door, peering out into the dark. Only the sounds of crickets and frogs. I squinted, trying to make out moving shapes. As my eyes slowly adjusted to the diminished light, I started to track what appeared to be a human shape. My hand tightened on my pistol before my brain reminded my hand not to get too slaphappy with the shooting. I nervously looked around, remembering that only six hours ago those things were everywhere.

It was Sam, and she was moving toward the gym. She was moving slowly, with what appeared to be a limp, but she wasn't shuffling. Besides, if she had turned, she wouldn't have tried to leave. She would have just started to eat, merrily enjoying the sleeping buffet around her.

Checking the tree line a final time, I pulled the door shut behind me and stepped off the wooden porch, trying to make as little noise as possible. She was within ten feet of the large double doors leading to the basketball court, and was moving determinedly forward. I caught up with her easily, jogging as much as possible on the soft, silent dirt, ever vigilant for movement or sounds from the trees. I caught up with her as she started toward the handle of the doors.

"Sam," I whispered as softly as possible, "What the fuck are you doing? Get back inside!" I put my hand on her shoulder and pulled her around to face me. What turned before me, however, was only a shadow of Sam.

Her eyes were sunken and red, her skin a pallid gray. Blue veins stood out prominently from her pronounced forehead, her hair still pulled back severely in a tight pony tail; there was a sour smell about her, almost like turned milk. She snarled at me, stepping back and raising her good hand, which held her pistol.

"Get the fuck back, you crazy bastard." Her voice was strained and dry, and the air rasped audibly in her windpipe, as if all the moisture had been sucked away.

"What are you doing? Where do you think — " She interrupted me as she suddenly started to laugh. Loudly. Her head moved on top of her neck in what must have been painful gyrations, back and forth as the laughter boiled out. Insanely, she looked back at me with those red eyes, a trickle of drool leaking from the corner of her slightly slack lower lip.

The crickets and the frogs had gone silent. Her hand tightened on the pistol and I knew I didn't have much time.

I lashed out at her with my gun hand, pistol-whipping her sidearm into the dirt. It discharged once, kicking up leaves and dirt as the bullet tore into the soft soil. Her eyes flared with rage, but she simply stood there. Her smile hadn't vanished and the spittle was now dripping to her chest. She looked at the weapon lying out of reach, and then at my hand, aiming my own at her chest.

"Come on, Sam. It doesn't have to be this way. Come back with me." As I said it, I knew that couldn't happen. I knew that it did, in fact, have to be this way. She knew it too.

She backed away clumsily, toward the gym. "Yes," she said, reaching toward the metal bar on the doors, "it does. It's time you joined the majority, you insane—"

My first shot took her in the arm she had reached forward toward the doors, and she looked up in surprise. She lifted the wounded appendage up, staring at the hole in her gray flesh that was oozing an odd amalgam of liquid human blood and congealed brownish gel.

"If you're going to be crazy, be crazy. Join the club." I leveled the gun again, this time at her head. "But I hate a hypocrite."

She snarled in response and fell toward the door as my second shot flew wide. The weight of her body collapsed against the door, forcing it open. The creatures inside, excited by the noises and voices outside, were waiting for the opportunity. They crowded outside as I leaped back, leveling my pistol once more. But there were too many. I tried for a clean shot on Sam, wanting to end it for her, but it wasn't necessary. They shuffled past her as if she weren't there, seeing only me. From the tree line, more sounds and movement.

It was time to leave.

The others, awakened by the gunshots, stood at the door to the cabin, geared up and ready to go. I burst past them and grabbed my bag.

"OK, kids. Party's over. Time to check out." I stared back at the gym, trying to distinguish Sam's form from the others, but it was still too dark.

They moved toward us en masse, as if directed by some morbid, undead general. Small faces gleamed in malevolent hunger, small jaws working feverishly up and down, teeth grinding audibly against one another.

"Yeah, we need to move," Kate said, grabbing her pack.

"No argument there," said Anaru, shouldering his rifle.

From behind the group of children, a taller shape moved into view, staggering forward awkwardly. Its face emerged from the shadows, the ruined stump of her left arm hanging uselessly at her side. Her face bore the now-familiar slack-jawed look of desperate hunger, as her feet shuffled forward behind her minions.

"Hey, she didn't have a lot of time anyway. Let's stay focused. We've got half-pint zombies on the way, and those things from before are still out there in the forest," said Lansing.

"The big ones might not have been able to triangulate our position just from those shots, but we need to keep the gunshots to a fucking minimum. That means use your stocks and your speed, got it?" He showed his rifle barrel, to which he had already affixed a six-inch bayonet. "I'm gonna use this here to keep me honest."

I nodded and saw Kate holster her pistol beside me. Lansing turned to Anaru, "That means you too, Bubba."

Anaru broke off his stare and flicked a dirty look at Lansing as he holstered his pistol and grabbed one of the ladders from the foot of a bunk bed. He swung it quickly against the wall, detaching a six-foot length of two by four and hefting it easily. Lansing smiled and vanished quickly into the dark.

Anaru followed as the first of the children came within feet of the door. A girl, maybe all of ten, grabbed his arm. He shook the arm violently, but was unable to withdraw from her vise like grip. Disgust passed across his face as he brought up a massive leg and kicked her sharply under the knees, taking her support from under her. As she struggled to reach his arm with her teeth, he leveraged that same foot down on her throat and pushed. The firm sole of his combat boot crushed the soft tissue housing her larynx, and the visceral snapping of her spine cracked like a gunshot as he twisted his boot abruptly to the side. He shook off the hand as he backed around the corner.

A small boy with a ravaged torso and bloody arms moaned at me as I followed behind Anaru and Kate and skirted the corner of the building, nearly tripping on a hidden downspout protruding from the structure. His braces gleamed brightly in the light from the moon, small particulates of what was most likely human flesh clung to the metal. I swung the metal butt of my rifle in a wide arc, striking a glancing blow to the side of the head but knocking the child to the ground nevertheless. The children behind him stepped clumsily over his fallen body and continued toward me as I moved away.

In front of us, Lansing had encountered a group of three. They came at him from behind the shelter of two large trees behind the cantina, surprising him as he jogged forward. He came to a halt, bringing his rifle up in front of him like a lance and smoothly jamming the long bayonet into the eye of the closest zed. Its body crumpled to the ground like a bag of rocks as he pulled the metal free and swung the butt into the face of a small Asian child that had reached for his leg.

The tiny creature was flung back onto the ground as he reversed the stroke, and again stabbed the bayonet toward the head of the last zed, a rather chubby girl bearing pigtails and a too-tight camp shirt. His stroke went wide and scored a dark, unbleeding line into her pudgy cheek. Having overextended himself on the stroke, Lansing stumbled forward and fell to the ground.

Before the large girl could capitalize on her small victory, Anaru was there. His two by four, an unwieldy weapon for the mortal man, was a whirling circle of death in his massive arms. The dense wood caught the creature under the jaw on the upstroke, snapping its head back severely and forcing closed its gaping mouth. Before it could adjust, the down stroke ended its campaign, crushing the top of the skull and forcing the head down several inches of the spine, like a shrunken skull atop a voodoo pole. Anaru helped Lansing up as Kate and I reached their position and we bolted into the tree line behind the last dormitory.

We soon left the children behind, their small, ungainly bodies unable to follow at our speed. We moved quickly and spread out in the trees, stepping carefully but purposefully through the dense green foliage. The high canopy of leaves and branches obscured most of the moonlight. I struggled to make out forms and shapes in the dark as shadows turned every bush and fallen log into a concealed creature. My heart beat quickly and heavily in my chest and I was soon gasping for breath as the slow but inexorable jog sapped me of what strength I had regained in sleep. I followed the sound of the others' passage, hoping with each footfall not to twist my ankle or break my leg in the utter dark.

Owls and bats traded positions on tree limbs far above us as we stumbled blindly ahead. Suddenly, the forest ended in a graded road. We turned up the road, eyes trained to either side. A creature appeared before Anaru as he jogged along the edge of the path, and he almost disinterestedly pummeled it into the underbrush, its body spinning twice before falling inert to the ground. Two more emerged from behind us, arms raised in wanton desire as they caught sight of us. From the side of the road, more could be heard rustling in the trees. We had caught up to the creatures that had passed us earlier in the night.

We followed the road around a bend for another mile, and were confronted with a chain link gate that stood half open. The signs on the fence and on the gate read "No Admittance: Authorized Personnel Only."

A "NO TRESPASSING" sign lay trampled on the ground in front of the open gate. I had to chuckle to myself, despite the circumstances.

As early morning light broke through the trees and bathed the road with its orange glow, we filtered through the opening. Kate turned to me, breath coming in ragged spurts after the recent jog. I bent over in pain, my sides splitting and my chest heaving.

The creatures from the woods were emerging in real numbers now. At least twenty or thirty straggled in from various emergence points along the tree line. We could hear more in the trees behind them, their moans filtering out from between the branches and behind the leaves.

"Up the hill. To the lab. Another quarter mile." I couldn't speak in sentences longer than three words. My lungs were going to explode. Was it absurd to crave a beer right now? Probably. But there I was and crave one I did.

"We need to get this gate closed first or those things are gonna follow us inside and trap us in the lab," said Lansing, grabbing the metal frame and struggling to move the section of fencing that normally would have slid easily into its housing on the opposite side. Normally being the key word. The closing mechanism had been disabled or damaged, and the motor wouldn't release the gate from its locked position. A gap of six feet remained unguarded. But it could have been six miles for all we cared. Even if we got in and made it to the vaccine or cure, or whatever was inside, we couldn't get out. We would die inside with it.

"I'll stay," said Anaru, tossing his two by four to the ground and lifting his rifle. "But I'm gonna have to use this, if you don't mind." His deep voice betrayed no fear or anxiety as he calmly stepped into the breach and lifted his firearm.

"It's suicide, man, you know that, right?" said Lansing, casting a nervous glance over his shoulder at the growing crowd. They were now no more than thirty feet from the fence. Anaru simply pointed up the hill and turned away, waving to us dismissively as he did so.

Lansing looked at him and then to the zombies approaching at an inexorable shuffle.

"Well fuck, I can't let you have all the fun..." He opened fire at the oncoming zeds, taking the first two he could sight in the heads and spraying more fire into those behind.

Lansing glanced over his shoulder at us as he found his next target. "Get up to the lab. We'll hold 'em as long as we can and meet you up there!" Anaru's rifle started to speak forcefully to the oncoming creatures, and we stumbled wearily into a slow uphill jog.

As we topped the rise and moved out of sight, I spared a final glance to the engagement below. Anaru stood in the six-foot breach, firing rapidly and carefully at head level into the horde of creatures that had materialized from the forest. Lansing stood behind him and to his right, firing between the links in the fencing at those that escaped Anaru's suppressing fire. There were more than a hundred now, and more streamed from the forest. There were too many. Anaru and Lansing didn't have long before they'd be overrun.

Where had they come from? We were in the mountains, far away from large populated areas. For there to be this many up here...for so many of them to be here in particular, of all places...

Suddenly, the pieces fell together. The Colonel's comments about some of them being older and not freshly turned, the kid's note about two guys coming down the mountain into the camp, the sheer numbers in the forest and along the road, the gap in the fence.

They hadn't come to us; we had come to them. They hadn't followed us or gone out of their way to find a meal. They were from the mountain—from the facility that we had just broken into. The week just kept getting better.

I turned from the carnage at the gate and followed Kate's gaze to the building before us. It was a squat, gray building with fencing enclosures stemming from the sides and obscuring the rear of the building. A large glass double doorway led into the lobby, the doors overseen by a small guard booth that stood empty to one side. The lobby was in disarray, papers strewn across the floor, a potted plant shattered against the slick, freshly polished floor. A trashcan had fallen into an open elevator door, causing the machine to open and close repeatedly against the obstruction. A metallic ding sounded each time the doors nudged gently into the side of the garbage bin, exacerbating the eerie silence.

From behind us, the constant rapid fire coming from the gate suddenly ceased, leaving only the sound of the elevator and our still rapid breathing from the climb up the hill.

"Think they made it?" Kate asked.

"I don't know," I replied. "But there were a bunch of those things out there."

"Where to now?" she asked, conspicuously terminating the previous line of conversation.

I moved forward to the receptionist's desk, which sat squarely in the center of the room. "Watch the door. Tell me if you see them or any of those things. I'm going to look for a directory."

I righted the overturned chair behind the desk and rooted through the top drawers. Finding a slim black binder, I threw it open and searched for an index.

"No Lansing or Anaru, but I've got a crowd of zombies coming up the hill," said Kate, worry creeping into her voice. "We're going to have company in about two minutes."

There. Kopland, West lab, office 300. West lab? I looked up. The elevator doors continued to open and close in an infuriatingly persistent fashion to my right. To the left was a small door marked UTILITY. Fuck, I didn't know. I had only been here once, and I hadn't even come inside. Should have come to the god damned Christmas parties. Wait, did they have them here? Didn't seem likely, did it. Probably had them in a hotel or a restaurant somewhere. I wonder if...

"Very close now!" said Kate, struggling to slide a couch in front of the doors.

Right. Zombies. Cure. Man, I was tired. And hungry. I would kill for a burger and fries. Concentrate, I thought. I shook my head, clearing away these absurd flashings of fantasy.

Must be through the elevators, I thought. And there wasn't a second floor, so they must go down. Of course. Let's couple zombie attacks with my claustrophobia.

"Elevators," I said curtly, as the first creature arrived at the glass doors. It was an old zombie, clearly having turned much longer ago than four days. Tatters of brownish gray skin hung from its arms and droopy, lifeless jowls sagged from its constantly moving jaws. Its bloody, dirty hands slammed against the doors with a power that belied its appearance. Kate shrieked in surprise as the doors shook, despite having watched its approach.

"Let's go," I said, kicking the trash can out of the doors and holding the entrance open with an outstretch arm.

She flew into the small space as I saw more creatures arrive outside. The sound of shattering glass followed the closing doors as I pushed the small round button happily emblazoned with the number 3, and the motors above our heads whirred into action. We dropped slowly, the elevator our chariot as we descended into what I hoped was not a hell of human making.

CHAPTER 26

Elevator music was a movie industry joke. Mostly because it was an easy gag. You take a suspenseful scene, with bullets flying and emotions at atmospheric heights, and you inject some Michael Bolton or Kenny G while your characters are riding an elevator. It always seemed cliché to me, but I know I always laughed anyway. Like I said, an easy gag.

I say this simply by way of illustrating why it was weird to be in an elevator with no music. Just the sound of the motors and the memory of the moans that seemed a constant and irrepressible refrain over the past four days. Given the choice, I'd take the Kenny G. But only by a hair.

With a jerk, the elevator stopped at sub level 3. The doors opened slowly into a brightly lit hallway that extended approximately a hundred feet in front of us. I remembered the Park as we stepped out, fluorescent lighting providing a sickeningly constant white light that fizzled overhead. Every three or four seconds, one light or another would flicker briefly with the abruptly-ending buzz of a mosquito meeting its maker on a bug zapper. We stepped out of the elevator slowly, hesitantly.

"You think there are any zombies left down here?" I asked Kate as I moved a trashcan in front of the doors to the elevator to prevent them from closing behind us. God only knows what kind of knowledge those things retain, but even a lucky hit on the "3" button from the top floor would bring us the kind of company that wasn't welcome right now. Best to keep this little Kenny G wagon with us for the time being.

"I think we've got to assume that the answer to that question is yes until we know otherwise," she said, moving forward into the hallway and peering carefully into the doorway of the first office we passed. Names were stenciled on the doors, marking their inhabitants or their functions, depending on the room. We passed three scientists' offices, two labs, and a break room before getting to Kopland's office. The name was still on it, but the door was locked. No light from inside.

"I don't know about you, but I didn't come all this way to have a locked door stand in my way," I said, pulling my pistol and aiming at the lock. Kate's hands shot to her ears in anticipation of the echoing boom from the gun. I depressed the trigger and the pistol kicked impressively against my palm as the bullet tore into the wooden frame around the handle. My ears were ringing as I gave the weakened door a kick. It swiveled smoothly in against the backstop, and we entered. Kate switched the lights on.

Suddenly, from the hallway outside, we heard movement. Cursing myself for not thinking of the sound the gunshot would make, I sprinted to the door behind Kate. I looked out toward the end of the hallway, away from the elevator. A door to a lab at the far end stood askew. The sounds were coming from that room.

I gestured to Kate to stay put and walked into the hall, pistol held up at head level before me, finger resting on the trigger. I moved each foot forward tentatively, as if a landmine waited for each step. Trying to make no noise as I approached, I drew in my breath as I neared the door. The door stood too narrowly open to afford entrance or a good scan of the room, so I nudged it ever so slightly with my right foot as I trained the gun on the slowly opening space.

The lights inside were off, but from the light in the hallway I could make out stainless steel tables and lab equipment. As I stepped into the doorway, a slight whiff of rancid air seemed to blow past me, but it was gone too fast for me to be sure I had really smelled it.

Beakers and test tubes lined the walls behind sinks and Bunsen burners; a pair of large, glass front refrigerators stood to my right. No sign of the noisemaker. I slowly scanned the darkness a final time and reached my left hand awkwardly across my body toward the light switch, intending on making a last sweep in the full light.

That's when I saw the monkey.

He was sitting against the wall to my left, below a rack of beakers and a cabinet full of glass jars. His eyes tracked my movements as I withdrew my hand without having switched on the lights. His dark brown hair and large eyes were intent but unblinking. Long arms sat still on either side of his body as his legs pushed against the floor and slowly drew him into a slouching stand. I laughed at myself, lowering my weapon as I threw over my shoulder to Kate, "It's just a damn monkey."

My attention was only diverted for a second, but it was in that time he started to cross the short distance between us. And it was as he moved, that I noticed that he moved differently, slowly. He lacked the normal simian grace, but instead strode forward in jerks and starts, eyes still unblinking. He left a puddle of some indescribable liquid behind, spreading slowly on the polished floor as he shuffled forward. As his mouth opened and closed compulsively, a high-pitched squeal carried from his throat. Like a moan, but in the language of the jungle.

This was not a normal monkey.

I backed into the doorway, slamming my hand against the light switch as I did so. The fluorescent flickered on slowly, casting the dead white light over the animal as it moved forward. His previously concealed undead features sprang into view, the reddened eyes and grayish-brown face glowing in the new glare. His yellowed teeth were broken at places, but whether due to his being a primate or owing to the disease, I couldn't tell. Too shocked to react, I waited too long to raise my gun.

He leaped from the floor toward my out-raised arm, which was still attached to the light switch by an invisible tether of surprise. I jerked back, but couldn't move my arm fast enough as his grubby paws caught hold of my sleeve. Stumbling forward, I shook my arm violently, trying to dislodge his tenacious grip.

In stark contrast to his human brethren, he still possessed a modicum of agility and pushed against my legs and torso with his tiny legs. He was a spider monkey of some sort, not a larger chimp or orangutan, so he was small. But he was a feisty little bastard.

As I fell back against the sink and counter against the far wall, he pulled his head and mouth up and lunged for my arm, shrieking all the while. Unable to use my gun in such close quarters, I chose the manual method. I swung my arm around as fast as I could, aiming for the six-foot storage cabinet on my left. He continued to shriek as I pummeled his rancid black and white head against the sheet metal door. The solid thunk of the metal was a satisfying sound, as the shriek cut off momentarily. The impact had left a red and brown smear on the door, but he was down, not out.

He continued to hold my arm, lunging for my flesh, and I swung again, shaking my hand violently and urgently, finally swinging him into the door again. And again. And again.

After repeated blows, he fell to the floor. His grip had finally slackened enough to shake him off, and his tiny little corpse made a pathetic splattering sound as it hit the smooth tile. His legs twitched, unable to die. As Kate appeared in the doorway, I leaned forward, thinking to confirm his demise, and his body twitched once again, small hand shooting out from beneath his body. He reached for my leg, and I remembered the gun in my hand. His furry little head exploded in pieces of grayish goo as Kate screamed in surprise.

"What the fuck?" she yelled from the doorway.

I kicked the body into a corner and wiped the blood from my cheek. Not quite believing it myself, I turned back to her.

"Zombie monkey," I said softly, walking past her and back into the hallway.

"Zombie ... monkey? You've got to be kidding."

"See for yourself," I replied. But the encounter gave me pause. I hadn't considered the potential for a cross-species infection. We hadn't seen any other animals infected, and it didn't seem a coincidence. Humans and animals rarely shared the same diseases. I know I never gave my dog a cold, and I don't think I've ever had a case of hoof and mouth. I did have a pretty severe case of athlete's foot once, but I don't think that was in the same league. I paused in the hallway and looked at her questioningly.

"You think ... ?" I started, but she interrupted me.

Her eyes were bright and curious, but she shook her head, almost disbelievingly. "It's gotta be the similarity between primate and human DNA. We're only a couple links off, and we know some of the nastier bugs of recent vintage were introduced to humans by monkeys in Africa and Asia," she sounded fairly confident, which made me feel better.

She cocked her head, looking slightly worried nonetheless. "But then again, we could be dealing with zombie dachshunds and undead koalas soon. This situation is so fucked; how the hell should we know?" She shrugged and pushed past me into the office.

Now that was an image, I thought as I followed her.

I moved into Kopland's office and looked around, taking in the room again. It was a large room, with a file cabinet against one wall and a desk against the other. Pictures of smiling children plastered the walls and papers lay in neat stacks on the oak desk. A bank of television monitors sat against the wall closest to us, and a computer hummed from some concealed location beneath the desktop.

"What do you know about this guy?" Kate asked as she examined the pictures on the walls: a collage of sickening domesticity. "Looks like the consummate family man."

"Also looks like he hasn't been here for a few days," I noted, comparing the state of his office with that of the others we had passed, each of which had appeared hastily abandoned.

"He worked with Maria on this Lazarus project. Apparently he was an expert in the field, and was close to perfecting the process. She didn't talk to me about this stuff that often, but she mentioned him a couple times. He was some sort of bigwig. We're looking for anything marked Lazarus or regeneration or anything like that."

She turned to the file cabinet against the far wall as I sat down in his chair, switching on the computer monitor and waited for screen to light up. A picture of a woman in her mid-fifties sat on a shelf at eye level. Behind that silver picture frame was a row of books. Several different versions of the Bible were visible on that shelf, as were some motivational Christian texts. Some of the titles caught my eye as the monitor flickered to life: Staying Right in the Face of the Left, How Would Jesus Vote?, Right to Choose is License to Murder.

Nice.

"This file cabinet is empty," said Kate, slamming the top drawer shut. "What do you think these monitors go to?" she asked, walking to the bank of dark screens and tapping one with her knuckle.

"Don't know. You see a power button anywhere?" I asked, only halfway paying attention as the computer was now prompting me for a user name and password.

Shit. Now what? I thumped the desktop in frustration and the picture in the silver frame fell from its shelf, landing with a conspicuous clatter on the keyboard. I opened a drawer in front of me, but before looking inside was diverted by her excited voice.

"Hey, I got something," Kate exclaimed.

She was squatting in front of the bottom line of monitors, which now held images of concrete pads and metal fencing. They looked like kennels, with cement flooring and small doors through which one could safely slide food. Each of the eight monitors switched to a different cage every two seconds. There must have been hundreds.

"What about the top ones?" I asked, after we had watched the top embankment for a minute or two.

"Hold on ... " she replied, as she craned her neck over and behind the row of screens. Then she reached in suddenly and I heard the flip of a switch. The remaining monitors came to life. Four showed static, two showed nothing. One of the remaining two bore the motionless image of a lanky, gray haired man in a white lab coat standing in front of a blue screen.

As curious as that image was, it was the last monitor to which our attention was immediately drawn. The cable was on, apparently brought in by a satellite feed. The first channel was inoperative, as were the next four. But as she scrolled through the networks, we eventually landed on the BBC. A small, distinguished young woman sat at a gray desk, pictures of what looked like mob violence flashing behind her on a small screen. She spoke to the camera slowly and distinctly, in true English fashion.

"...as reports continue on the ongoing crisis in the United States, we have confirmed reports of massive explosions in New York City, Philadelphia and Washington D.C. The British government has not disclosed their source, and the American government is still in utter disarray."

She looked down briefly to the stack of paper in front of her, and back to the camera. "Again, to repeat our story from the top of the hour, and the top of every hour for the last four days: it appears that a massive plague or infection, turning citizens to violent, deranged psychotics, has overcome the vast majority of the United States."

On that report, we looked at each other without speaking. Thirty-six hours ago, it had only been half of the country. Now it was the whole enchilada.

"Apparently originating on the East Coast, this infection, which appears to be spread through bodily fluid contact with the diseased, has now infested massive areas of the now quarantined nation. Populated areas were hardest hit, with the infection spreading rapidly between victims. Reports we now have from military, commercial and civilian air and grounds sources within both infected areas and non-infected areas indicate that vast swathes of the country have become no-mans' lands, inhabited and controlled by the living dead."

The amazing thing about this report was that, unlike the man we had seen in Target mere days ago, this reporter didn't pause when she was made to speak the name of the perpetrators.

"Safe harbors within the U.S. are few and far between, but limited contact from isolated strongholds within the besieged nation indicate that the State of Florida south of American Interstate number 10 is a confirmed safety zone. However, individuals approaching from the North or the West are warned to display identification of some manner indicating sentient status. Large signs, the firing of weapons into the air, or the honking of car horns are suggested."

I'm thinking a huge sign that says "Get out of my way. I'm going to Disney world."

"All indications are that the American President is safe in Florida ... "

Oh, now there's some happy news. I can die content now.

"Likewise, isolated cities and towns throughout the American West and Midwest are reported to still be infection free, but it should be warned that reports are sporadic, and the veracity of these reports cannot be assured. Our experts have warned, however ..."

Where the fuck did they get zombie experts?

" ... that as the infection progresses Westward, the vast numbers of creatures will have multiplied exorbitantly and these small outposts may be ill-equipped to survive such large numbers."

She looked directly at the camera, discarding the notes in front of her. "Survivors are urged not to take risks or expose themselves to the creatures ... they are not your friends or family anymore..."

Just as I was thinking that I had heard that before, the cable feed cut to static, plunging the office into a white-noise oblivion. Electronic snow covered the face of the monitor and despite her best efforts at wiggling cables and plugs in the rear of the embankment, Kate couldn't get it back up.

"What about this guy? He looks like he's got something to say," she said, nodding at the immobile man staring awkwardly at us from behind the last monitor.

"That thing got a play button?" I asked, looking around. She shook her head. I moved behind the desk and looked into the drawer I had opened before. A remote lay at the bottom, surrounded by packages of Twinkies and unused blue pens. I remembered the jokes Maria would make about Twinkies surviving the coming Apocalypse and chuckled briefly as I aimed the small black device at the television and pressed play.

"...briefing is an explanation of the Lazarus program and is designed for DOD use only." You gotta be kidding me. We finally got lucky.

I spared a glance for Kate, who was staring at the screen. She spared me a glance of triumph and excitement, which I readily returned. The speaking continued.

"All other uses are strictly prohibited by USC 17-36 and the Homeland Security Act of 2001." The man, clearly a scientist, seemed uncomfortable with the legalese, and looked slightly more at home after delivering the message. He was tall and slightly balding, with piercing black eyes and a deep voice. A small paunch struggled to break free of his pleated pants.

"My name is Doctor Derrick Kopland, and I'm a biochemist with the Starling Mountain Project in New York. As you know, a vast portion of our funding comes from DOD R&D sources, and this is a progress report on the project referred to here as Lazarus."

We looked at each other after he mentioned the DOD funding—was Lazarus supposed to be a military asset? A weapon of some sort? I didn't see how that helped us. Gee, the enemy wasn't hard enough to kill so we're going to zombify them and make them hunger for our man-flesh?

That's really bright.

Note to self: don't pay any more taxes until these idiots get their shit straight.

He went on. "As you can see in your written reports, Lazarus is a unique discovery, with historical and, some might say, religious implications. Although not scientifically relevant in the strictest sense, a short historical summary would be helpful to understanding the true genesis of our research.

"In 1989, archaeologists from the University of Chicago unearthed a hitherto unknown chamber that adjoined the tomb believed to have housed an individual named in the bible. Since the discovery of this tomb, hundreds of tourists had visited the chamber, not knowing that below their feet lied an archaeological and biological find that would rival that of King Tut's Tomb and penicillin, all rolled into one. A team from the University was doing standard excavation in the rear of the chamber when sonic resonance scans indicated a small, uncharted depression that seemed to be located behind a wall of solid rock. Upon boring into the rock, it was discovered that there was indeed an extensive series of caves that had seemingly been blocked off from the original tomb by walls of fallen rock. Over the years the rocks had shifted and gravel had filled in the crevices so that it looked like a natural wall."

He hurried himself along, realizing that he had digressed in his excitement to relate the story.

"Anyway, the theory is that the locals for some reason walled up the rear of the tomb to seal off the caves from the surface. When the team got into the caves, they realized why. After being under the surface for only hours, they began to feel strange. Eventually, within four hours, all five members had succumbed to vomiting, nausea, and extreme disorientation. Only when they were removed from the room did those effects dim and eventually abate completely."

He took a breath, slowing his speech. "As you can likely guess, the tomb was that of Lazarus: a man that Jesus raised from the dead in the book of John."

I noticed in passing that he didn't say "*supposedly* raised from the dead." Probably not a big surprise, given his office materials and the wandering hordes outside.

"After that, a team from the CDC was called in. Unique mineral deposits were found lining the caves, in large quantities. In small doses, they were virtually harmless, causing only a small headache or minor dizziness. In protracted exposure, cases were much more severe. As you know, we were able to secure almost 2 metric tons of the deposits, which were subversively extracted from the area under cover of darkness, and exported via military channels back to the U.S."

He smiled, and the blue screen lit up behind him, transforming from a blank screen to a video of several scientists bent over small Petri dishes, hypodermic needles in hand, wearing full HAZMAT regalia.

"Since then, for almost fifteen years, Starling Mountain Research Facility has been the home of the Lazarus Project. At first, we didn't appreciate the unique qualities of the compound. While we realized that it caused various physical ailments, we were intrigued by writings found on the walls of the tomb indicating that in other iterations, the compound might actually possess restorative properties. Of course, we had no idea what that implied. We assumed initially we were talking about a primitive Ibuprofen or similar painkiller. Maybe even an amphetamine."

He smiled again and shook his head, stepping aside as the picture behind him changed. The footage was grainier, the camera shaking.

"It wasn't until about ten years ago that the full import of the substance was realized." The camera was clearly being held by an amateur, and it followed the path of a stretcher as it wound its way down halls very similar to those through which we had come today. Exactly like, really.

"What you're seeing is footage of the medical evacuation of a scientist who suffered a massive cardiac event while working with the substance in lab 4 a decade ago. In his discomfort and pain, he removed his protective garb in direct exposure to very concentrated amounts of the compound. Since he was in obvious distress unrelated to the effects of the compound, no one thought much of it when he was removed from the room."

The camera had stopped and the image of a body on a wheeled stretcher was visible in a stark, dismal hallway. The paramedics had moved back from the gurney, and were looking at one another uncertainly.

"Quite by accident, we had been filming the degeneration of certain primate functions in laboratory animals when he became ill, and were able to catch the subsequent events on camera." His tone was thinly veiled excitement, a tone of wonder and marvel infused with anxiety.

On the screen, a white sheet stretched over the form of a body moved, as if the body below was no longer inert.

"What we discovered by pure accident," he continued, "was quite phenomenal."

The sheet rose up as if levitated, falling down again to reveal the now-familiar gaping maw and gray-hued skin on the face of an older man in a disheveled white coat. His teeth were bared and his hands were suddenly active, searching for the cameraman. The camera dropped to the floor; feet moved in front of the now cracked lens, and blood splattered on to the floor. The video feed terminated in a flash of motion. The screen froze on the last image: blood covering the dull linoleum, mere centimeters from the camera lens.

The video feed shifted back to Kopland, whose grinning face was morbidly out of place considering the scene that had unfolded on the blue screen mere seconds ago.

"We found that, for lack of a better description, we could now reanimate the dead."

CHAPTER 27

The screen behind Kopland now transitioned to a laboratory with bustling scientists clustered around a table. The object on the table was obscured by the bodies in white lab coats, but he continued to speak as the camera neared the table, slowly making its way forward.

"After the incident with Dr. Matthews, research progressed on the mineral, which we found had, to say the least, unique restorative capabilities. However, we also found that it was inherently unstable. Tests on subjects in the lab indicated that reanimation was possible, but only on a certain level. In other words, we weren't raising the dead per se; we were simply reanimating the corpse and reenergizing certain bodily functions and impulses. As we saw with Dr. Matthews, brain function past certain primal stages was impossible to restore due to the instability of the element. And as we saw with the cameraman that Dr. Matthews attacked, innate impulses to feed were inexplicably drawn to human subjects, possibly due to the high iron content of the blood or some sort of genetic response to other human pheromones; potentially even a primitive draw to the scent of human hormones or other bodily odors."

The crowd had been parted, and the camera was focused on a young, middle eastern-looking man strapped to a long, steel table. His face registered fear and pure anxiety; he quivered against the metal table and his hands and feet moved slowly against their restraints. Eyes like agates shifted constantly around the room; his voice was shrill and pleading. He was naked but for a pair of under shorts and the straps adorning his extremities. From the side of the table, a nurse approached him and coldly injected his arm with a milky red substance. As the chemical disappeared into his arm, the scientists around the table backed off. His face grew slack and his arms dropped limply to the table.

"The restorative properties of the chemical lead naturally to a drive to determine whether it could be utilized not only to safely reanimate dead tissue, as it had shown it was capable of doing, but also to make existing, living tissue regenerative or even impervious to flesh wounds or bodily injury."

"As you know, we were provided ample test subjects from our various Defense Department sources. All of them provided vital information for the project. The young man you see behind me was our first direct injection specimen."

The body hadn't moved.

"In its solid state, the element's restorative properties seem only to be applicable if death occurs in direct proximity. However, in the weaponized version, LZR-1143, the chemical was and remains highly transmittable through liquid contact. Fluid transfer and bites tend to be the most dangerous methods of contagion. Interestingly enough, there seem to be no similar effects from direct exposure to the chemical in its mineral form. Of course, other adverse reactions manifest, such as the nausea and headaches. But the chemical in its natural state has no transformative capacities unless the body in proximity is deceased."

The fingers in the right hand were now twitching slowly, as if the man on the table was having the human equivalent of a doggy-dream.

"We found, of course, that direct injection of the chemical into the blood stream causes death. But it also caused near instant reanimation. ETI—I'm sorry, Exposure to Infection—times varied depending on the location of the bite, but typically had run their course within forty-five minutes. Overall, an extraordinarily tenacious and aggressive infection."

Our assessment of the infection had been correct: infection timing depends on location of the bite. That must have been why it took Sam so long to succumb.

The man's eyes had opened, staring unblinkingly at those clustered around him. His mouth opened soundlessly in what we knew to be a soulless moan. Limbs jerked awkwardly against the leather restraints. The man we had seen before was no more. This was now, forever, his unformed substitute.

Kopland's voice droned on, untouched in affect by the reality of the horror unfolding behind him. "As of the date of this film, we have be unsuccessful in weaponizing this mineral in the manner mandated by our grant, or creating any version thereof that could allow for the creation of the desired "super-soldier." While we have determined both an aerosolized and liquid delivery system for 1143, we have not been able to determine how to counteract its less ... desirable ... effects in the event that the thirteenth apostle is located. However, advances are being made every day, and we feel that we are very close to achieving that goal."

Thirteenth apostle? What the fuck did that mean? And weaponizing? So this is how the human race was to destroy the world. I always thought it would be a nuclear war. But that was before the government really put their minds to it. This was much more interesting.

But it wasn't the world we were ending, was it? It was just us.

As I thought about it, I realized we were really doing the earth a favor. Eliminating the virile pestilence that had plagued the planet since we rose up off four feet and started playing with fire. We were doing in one fell swoop the work that the universe usually dawdled on about for millions of years: the mass extinction of an entire race of being.

And the thing is, we couldn't blame anyone but ourselves. It was appropriate to go down this way. As I watched this man speak so dispassionately and detachedly about a sickness so abominable that it lacked any appropriate descriptor, I knew we had created our own destruction. The bible came back to me in a fleeting moment of irrational whimsy.

And he saw all that he had made. And on the seventh day, he rested.

I guess it was time for us to take a rest.

The video had cut to one of the cages we had seen in the other monitors. A rifle had been laid to rest on the floor of the cage, and a female scientist with her back to the camera was miming the physical gesture of picking up the gun. The creature, knowing only hunger, simply clambered against the fencing, eyes on the human. She turned to the camera with a grin on her face, sighing in mock desperation: the picture of a naive scientist, ignorant of the macro-chasmal implications of their work, focused only on the end for the sake of the end; means be damned. I could have shrugged off the personal affront that this sort of arrogance entailed if I hadn't known the woman in the picture.

It was Maria.

Kopland continued on. "Continued funding is vital for our success. We urge you to continue to support this program. It is only through the Defense Department's continued commitment to this program that we can hope to ever perfect this process, create the weaponized agent sought by DOD, and provide a counteracting agent in the event the thirteenth apostle is located."

The video faded out, and Dr. Kopland's face dissolved into black. We sat there, stunned.

"I can't believe that something like that got out," Kate replied, still staring at the screen.

"Jesus, Maria." I said softly, still in shock at seeing her picture. I remembered her face, but seeing it so alive and vibrant in that video—even though she was involved in what might be the Armageddon of our millennium—brought back a rush of emotion.

"Yeah, well as personally devastating as that must be, we need to figure out where this guy could have kept any research on an antidote or a cure." It wasn't exactly heartless, but there wasn't a lot of compassion in her voice. And there was certainly judgment.

The wheels were turning slowly in my head, rust falling off slowly.

"In a minute. I'm still at the 'it getting out' part. You're absolutely right. How did something like this make it out of here? Despite our easy entrance today, this place was pretty locked down on a daily basis. Two separate guard booths, secluded location, barbed wire electrified fencing, the works. So are we supposed to believe someone stole this thing from the outside?"

I shook my head. Not likely at all.

"This had to be an inside job: someone from the inside knew how to get it out, how to spread it, and had the means to deliver it."

She looked incredulous, replying in an exhausted voice, "That's absurd! Why would anyone so arbitrarily sentence humanity to something like this? What is there to gain?" She flopped down tiredly on the chair facing me, eyes doubtfully cast.

Slowly they turned, step by step...I could hear the creaking of the giant wheels as they strained against the inertia of mental fog.

"This was no accident! Think about it! How could they accidentally release something from this location that spawned initial outbreaks in Philadelphia, New York, Boston and DC all at the same time! If it was an accident, the townsfolk down the street that tried to eat us a few hours ago would have been the first ones down, and the military, the police, the fucking boy scouts — someone would have eradicated the infection before it got too far."

As I spoke, it all made sense in the most perverse of fashions ... the facts were dropping into place.

"No, no, no. This was intentional. Someone meant to do this and meant to let this thing out. There's no other explanation. I'm not saying it was the government or the military; I wouldn't believe that if you told me. There's no possible scenario under which those guys win. If it was a coup, or an attack or something ... people take over governments to control people, not to kill them."

"Why does it matter?" she asked, interested but understandably circumspect. "Isn't the whole point that it's out? And that we need to try to stop it? What the fuck does it matter how or when or where or who let it out. It could've been Elton John and a troupe of trained circus squirrels for all it fucking matters. We just need to figure out how to put it back in."

She still wasn't following, and I had to make her understand. "That's just it! If we knew who let it out, we might have a better idea of how to stop it! There have to be logs, or journals or ... fuck! I don't know! Something! This is a god damned government lab! Shouldn't they have anal-retentive records or big brother spy cameras that can catch someone planning something like this — "

She interrupted me, still not a convert. "But who would do something like that? Why? Like you said, what is there to gain? Someone with a hard-on for survivalism? Some nerd that never got laid in high school looking for a reason to repopulate the earth? Who would do it?"

The lights flickered briefly, and the monitors reset. All now showed black screens. The computer I had been trying to access flickered off once more. From the end of the hall, toward the elevator, I heard a metallic thud and then the sliding of the elevator doors. We raced to the hallway to see them slide shut, the trashcan inexplicably lying across the room, far from where we had left it.

"Don't suppose there are more zombie primates in here, do you?" Kate asked, raising her pistol and inching out of the doorway.

"Not unless you brought them in with you," said a familiar voice from behind us. "I wouldn't turn around too quickly. Either of you. Move slowly, hands above your heads."

As I turned around slowly, I realized that I had my answer. He had lost weight since the film; his face was sunken and sallow. His eyes reddened by what I could only assume was a lack of sleep. The paunch had disappeared. But the black eyes were as hard as they appeared in the video. And the gun he held in his hand was steady and unwavering.

"I'd appreciate your discarding your weapons," he said politely. We stooped slowly to the ground, laying our guns on the floor.

"So I guess that answers her question," I said, understanding now. But the knowledge of the *who* didn't inform the *why*.

"What question?" Kate asked.

"Why, who would do such a thing, of course," he said, smiling. "That would be me."

CHAPTER 28

He ushered us down the hall to a larger laboratory. From the elevator shaft, the vague echo of pounding reverberated through the stone of the basement walls. The whirring of the elevator motor was an ominous indication that someone or something might have wandered into an open elevator door. They need only meander into the right button to join our party.

But then again, we had our own human problems now.

"Please, have a seat," said the good doctor, gesturing with the barrel of his snub-nosed revolver toward a pair of lab stools. We eased onto the cheap pleather upholstery as he leaned back against a tall cabinet on the opposite side of the room. A trashcan overflowing with food wrappers sat by the door; several cans of soda sat in various locations about the room, evidence of his occupation.

It was a large laboratory, with a door on the opposite side of the room that led to a marked stairwell. It was an exit door, with the stairwell only accessible from the laboratory.

However, the most conspicuous feature of the room by far was the gigantic window lining the rear of the room. Blank white walls, at times smeared with blood and other bits of zombie fodder, surrounded a white tiled floor that reflected the flickering fluorescent light of the room back through the window into the lab. A door to the chamber stood to the right of the window; an electronic keypad indicating it was a code-protected entrance.

A zombie stood immobile at the window to the lab, eyes searching endlessly back and forth, left to right. Its head was cocked slightly to one side, mouth agape. Grayish brown palms were pressed mutely against the glass, leaving smudges of oily, bloody residue on the surface. Ragged clothes hung from its limbs; clothes that used to be white, but were stained forever in the brown and red hues of its past meals, now congealed and pressed into the fabric. A security badge for this facility hung from the creature's lapel.

"Would you like me to introduce you to Doctor Mendez?" said Kopland, gesturing toward the zombie in the room, who hadn't moved or otherwise evidenced any indication it knew we were here.

"He's quite harmless behind the glass. Rather like a zoo animal; he's only provoked when I need samples or he is to be fed." Kopland flicked a switch on a panel close to the desk at the front of the room, and a small hatch opened abruptly on the other side of the small chamber. The thing formerly known as Mendez lunged across the room as if awakened from a deep sleep, shuffling with as much haste as it could manage toward the open hatch, moans filtering through the intercom system, which must have been activated by the hatch control. He reached the hatch, clutching in frustration at empty air, clearing having expected something more.

Kopland laughingly flipped the switch once more, bringing the hatch closed with a metallic bang as the creature moaned in hunger and fury.

"He must be hungry—I haven't fed him in days." He shrugged and looked meaningfully at me. "Maybe later though."

Punctuating the sentiment, Mendez threw himself against the glass as if he knew his tormentor to be present. As if he expected to reach Kopland through sheer force of desire.

I must have flinched involuntarily at the creature's staring eyes and moving hands and Kopland noticed, noting dryly, "Don't worry about him. He probably doesn't even appreciate that you're real. Funny thing about these creatures. If they see you moving behind glass, but don't see you actually go behind the glass, they don't recognize you. They're like dogs. I have a theory that their visual acuity suffers subsequent to the changeover, disallowing them from seeing in three dimensions. Fascinating stuff, really."

Ignoring the presence of the creature, which was now calming itself and resuming an immobile station against the glass, Kopland spoke unconcernedly.

"I'm curious to know whether you're alone," he said, distance between us giving him the luxury of folding his arms and pointing his weapon away from our heads. "Of course, it doesn't really matter, but I am somewhat appalled by the effort it would have taken to reach our little slice of heaven."

"We're it," I said before Kate could speak. I didn't know if she was inclined to let him in on the fact that there might be others out there, but I didn't want to risk it.

"Remarkable," he said, and stared at us for several long seconds before moving to a locked cabinet behind a desk, keying the lock, and removing several vials of a blue liquid. I wanted to ask if he had moved the trashcan from the elevator door, but if he hadn't, I didn't want him to know that someone—or something—was down here with us. It might be our only opportunity for a distraction.

"I'm guessing you came all this way for this?" he asked, placing the four vials on the counter in front of him. He still held the gun, now pointed to the floor, but he was too far away to reach for it. I couldn't believe our predicament. We travel a hundred miles over zombie-infested territory as part of what could have very well been a delusion-inspired nightmare, only to wind up the hostages of what appeared to be a mad scientist.

Still don't believe you're making this up?

That voice was starting to make more and more sense.

We didn't reply to his query. He smiled, knowing that he was correct and that no affirmative nod was needed.

"A shame, really. A hearty effort. But alas...too late. I'm supposing out of mere conjecture that you believe this to be a cure?" he said, holding up the blue vials. He laughed.

Apparently this was funny?

Ha fucking ha.

"You're not the first to make this mistake. In fact, Mr. McKnight, you are, or should I say were, intimately acquainted with the last person to embrace this belief." He picked up a vial of the liquid, removing the stopper and slowly tilting its open end over a sink. I jerked involuntarily as the contents slowly fell into the drain.

"What the fuck are you talking about?" Kate's voice was confused and troubled, as if she couldn't conceive of the type of personality that would have sanctioned such evil.

His smile faded not at all as he unstopped a second vial. "I would think that my previous admission would have answered that last question, so I won't entertain the inquiry except to say that my presence here was required to ensure that no ... complications ... interfered with my endeavor."

"Why would you do it?" I asked, hoping in vain that he would stop pouring to speak. "What could you hope to gain from letting this thing out and killing all these people?"

His voice rose and his eyes narrowed. "Oh sir, don't pretend to lecture me on morality. Not considering your acquaintances and their transgressions. Mine was a path divinely inspired; yours is one of degradation and Hollywood trash. Of those who were to suffer under this cataclysm, your kind was to be front and center." His face was serious as he slowly emptied the second vial.

"OK, you need to drop the Dr. Evil act and say what you mean. You're going to kill us anyway, right?"

He tilted his head momentarily and then nodded, the corners of his mouth edging toward another pleased expression.

"So what the hell does it matter?"

He nodded. "You're correct, what does it matter. You're also much more anxious for all the details of this little scenario than I would be, were I so intimately involved." He tossed the second, now empty vial into a trashcan and looked up at me again, leaning against the lab table in front of him. His face was cruel, his eyes hard. Small hands flexed compulsively on the counter in front of him.

"I wonder, Mr. McKnight...how much of your wife's death do you remember?"

The question hit me like a fist to the gut. What did that have to do with anything?

But in the back of my head, I suspected something. I just didn't know what it was. And that was what scared me.

"Did she seem different to you that night? A little off? Appetite was a little changed? Maybe she liked her meat rarer than she had ever ordered it before?" He was enjoying drawing this out.

"Go to hell," I said, feeling nauseous. I suddenly hated that he knew things.

"Mike?" Kate's voice filtered through a mist of confusion from somewhere distant.

My mind was on fire. Her face was there again, distorted and grotesque.

A flash and my hand was grasping hers, flinging her away from me as she pawed for my shoulder. Her arms flung wide as she tumbled backwards and I reached for her instinctively, trying to arrest the fall. A needle-prick of pain in my palm as I reached for her. She stumbled back clumsily onto the floor, but rose slowly again. Implacably, she moved toward me. In her right hand, a metal device of some sort hung uselessly from a stiff finger. She moved slowly, clumsily. Her mouth moved, as if she was trying to speak. But no sound would come.

In the corner of the room, behind the door, was my golf club. I had been practicing my putting. I was going to play on Saturday. I was down to a 13 handicap.

"Oh, I think not," he replied, bringing me back, sounding confident. "I think you remember enough, don't you?"

"She was infected." I stated, not a question but an affirmative declaration. This much I had suspected.

He nodded. "But you must wonder," gesturing around the room, "how that came to be. We took all the precautions, had all the necessary safeguards. It is absolutely true that the virus would not have been allowed to pass the threshold of this facility in its compound or elemental state." He affected a countenance of mock confusion.

Raising his hand to his chin and stroking it in a semblance of contemplation, he continued. "We wore protective clothing, and never handled the virus outside of a clean room. So she couldn't have been infected by accident, right? And the virus travels too quickly, has far too short an incubation period to allow for a two-hour drive back to the city ..."

"All seems impossible, or at the very least improbable, right?" He leaned back against the cabinets behind him, losing the mocking expression and getting serious. "Any thoughts, Mr. McKnight? Any ideas at all?"

I was mute. Kate's eyes were wide.

"She infected herself," he said flatly, tiring of the game. "She was trying to steal LZR-1143, and she infected herself to get the element out of the facility. It was the only way, you see? It wouldn't have made it out on its own, and she had apparently lined up a buyer somewhere. This would be a very valuable weapon in the hands of someone bent on reducing civilization to its knees." At this, he laughed uproariously, continuing on with laughter lining his words.

"Don't you see?" he asked, voice high, eyes wide, "She infected herself to steal the virus, banking on this," he held up the second-to-last blue vial, "to cure her of the virus once she had accomplished the theft. She somehow slowed the virus enough to get to the city—I must admit, I am still in the dark about her ability to do that—and injected herself with this after she had extracted a blood sample."

Unbelievable. Impossible.

Between thoughts of disbelief and feelings of betrayal, I thought I heard movement from the hallway. But my mind was a storm cloud of uncertainty and I ignored the nagging suspicion that had been spawned by the unexplained movement of the trashcan.

He was losing steam for the story, and had picked up the gun again. He was pacing now. But laughter still touched his voice as he continued.

"But what she didn't understand, what no one knew, was that I had indeed developed a chemical that counteracted the virus. I was successful in that work. But given security concerns, I made no one else privy to the details. Government rules, you understand. Very hush hush. She knew I had succeeded in my efforts, because I let it slip in a moment of triumphant bragging. But for all her planning and all her designs, she made a fundamental error in her calculations." Laughter had faded, but a smile remained.

"This isn't a cure, Mr. McKnight." He shook his head and held up the vial, unstopping it and emptying the contents into the drain. Only one vial now remained.

"It's a vaccine."

A world of expectations can crumble so quickly, beliefs and visions falling around your ankles like a wet pair of pants.

His statement shattered our hopes for sparing mankind and redeeming the lost and tortured souls that had already succumbed to the malevolent virus. Millions of people were doomed to walk the earth, endlessly hungering and constantly roaming a wasteland of dead and dying. None could be saved.

But a glimmer of hope remained. A vaccine could immunize those still within safe harbor from the threat of infection. Not the threat of harm, or being savagely mauled by their former friends and family. But from suffering a fate worse than death. Those people deserved that chance. I had to try to give it to them.

"Why?" I had to know. And I wanted to keep him talking while I inched slowly to my right, feigning an itch on my leg as I pseudo-stumbled several inches. A vial of unnamed chemicals stood two feet from my right hand.

"Why? Why?" He was incredulous.

I hardly believed my question to be worthy of incredulity, but he clearly believed the answer to recommend itself.

"Oh, I don't believe we have that much time, Mr. McKnight. My reasons are more than you can hope to comprehend. They are above what you can believe or may wish to know." His voice was haughty, his tone arrogant. Remembering his office, I took a chance.

"So you're so depraved, your mind so warped and sick, that you can't even explain yourself?"

Here goes. "You are one, twisted Godless bastard, you know that?"

"Mike..." This from Kate, who was understandably a little concerned about my provoking the crazy man.

His face contorted with rage, and for a moment, I thought he would end it. Appearing not to even realize what he was doing, he placed the last vial of vaccine in his shirt pocket as his hand tightened on the pistol as his arm shook convulsively in pure, distilled anger. Spittle flew from his excited lips as he sputtered to life.

"Don't you presume to talk to me about God! It was God's will that I saw done!"

I guffawed loudly, twisting my face with contempt. "God's will? To murder millions of innocent people? No God I know of would be party to that kind of act."

He moved forward, forgetting in his rage the strategy of keeping me at arm's length. "You know no God. You have no concept of the divine will!

He has inspired my every effort. Why else would I have been granted the privilege—the awesome responsibility—of discovering this exquisite device of judgment?"

He smiled, happy and content in his make-believe reality, thrilled to talk down to someone of my caliber. "You and your filthy Hollywood friends and your liberal gays; you of the abortions and the sodomy, the corrupt and the wicked. You think yourselves worthy of God's mercy? Judgment day is upon the world, and God has chosen me to be his tool."

I kept the smile on my face as I stepped slightly closer to the chemicals. "You're a tool all right, but you're not the hand of God. You're a sad, delusional little man who's responsible for the murder of millions of people. Dress it up how you wish, you're a murderer, plain and simple."

He continued to smile, my words repelled instantly from his force field of self-delusion. "I am a murderer, that is correct. But I am God's weapon, his arm of mighty vengeance upon a world of the wicked. I was blessed with the knowledge to facilitate His will and I alone was made privy to his great prophecy of Revelation."

Only six inches separated me from the vial on the table, and he had been keyed up by the Revelation talk. "You're telling me that the book of Revelation commands you to design a virus that turns people into the walking dead? You're cracked, pal. Certifiably insane. I should know."

He didn't like the reference to insanity. He raised the gun again, squinting in anger and disbelief that I could be so forward with one in his position. That would be the "on the handle end of the gun" position.

"God chose me to interpret His will...Revelation is a book of truth, but only to those with the eyes to read it. I was given the knowledge to hear His word and I knew what I had to do." Triumphantly, as he squeezed the trigger slowly, he spoke in words of unmistakable finality.

"I, the hand of God and the tool of his judgment, caused the mark of the beast to be in the world and brought about the end of days."

I moved toward the chemicals, knowing I wasn't going to be fast enough. At the same time, the door shook, and his head jerked to the side. Given the second I needed, my fingers found the vial of chemicals and I swung my hand toward his face. A surprised scream as the pistol fired. I recoiled instantly, moving to the side as I heard him crash to the floor. I heard a grunt from my left where Kate had crumpled to the floor. Blood pooled in a sickly crimson tide next to her.

And then things got interesting.

CHAPTER 29

The room was plunged into darkness as the power inexplicably cut out; a loud soullessly high-pitched beep pierced the darkness and a metallic thunk sounded from the rear of the room. It was pitch black, the darkness a palpable and oppressive shroud that nevertheless afforded some level of obscurity for us, the hunted. I moved to Kate's side and felt for a pulse. It was there, and fairly strong. There was a lot of blood, but there was nothing I could do for her if I were dead, and I was positive that the good doctor would do his best to bring about that end if he could. From behind the lab table in the front of the room, I could hear him moving quietly forward.

The silence was deafening in the pitch black, and my claustrophobia reminded me that we were forty feet underground. Suddenly, I could feel the walls closing in and the air around my head was a blanket of unbreathable gas. I gasped as the oxygen was sucked from the room.

Going to pick now to buy that one-way ticket back to crazy-land? Wonderful timing.

That's odd. It sounded almost disappointed this time. I snapped out of it when I heard the echo of my insanity, determined not to prove that voice right.

As I listened to the movement from the hall, to the things struggled to get through the locked door into the lab, I heard a very disturbing sound. A soft squealing of door against frame and a clear movement of feet against floor hit my ears. The door to the chamber that housed Mendez was opening, and he was joining the party. He moaned, heavily and deeply, and in my mind's eye, his mouth was open, his ears perked for movement. The potential that they hunted by smell made me conscious of my own scent, and I struggled to remain still and silent.

I crawled forward through the inky void as quietly as I could, my heart pounding against my chest, hoping that my movements weren't as audible as Kopland's. From his position, I heard him stop. From the back of the lab, beakers shattered as they fell to the floor and feet shuffled through the broken glass. As if the person moving cared little for being detected or observed. As if they cared little about anything.

At the sound of the shattering glass, Kopland's shuffling started again. Faster, and more audible than before, I could tell he was moving away from us, from the zombie, and towards the stairwell. I timed my crawling advance to coincide with his movements as best I could and hoped Kate would stay silent, hoped that these things couldn't smell blood. I could tell I was gaining on him when, surprisingly, he spoke.

"Stopping me won't change anything, you know." He sounded concerned. As if this turn of events was distressingly unexpected. "The wheels are in motion. God's plan has been executed."

Mendez moved toward the sound of Kopland's voice, feet shuffling forward, moan now loud and filled with hunger. I could smell him, the rotten stench always the precursor to the presence of the undead. I heard him hit a table and falter, a heavy thud evidencing he had encountered resistance; a frustrated moan confirming it.

Kopland was close. Very close.

From the hall outside the lab, the interlopers from the stairwell pounded against the door, providing audible cover for my crawling advance. In the darkness and despite our enmity, we listened in an uncomfortable unity for the approach of the unknown. I had to act, or my decisions would be made for me. I had had enough of that.

I shot forward, having taken my bearings from his previous comment and committing his position to memory. My shoulder struck the side of the table to my left but my right fist made contact with flesh. A grunt issued from Kopland as I bowled into him, and a deafening shot was fired. The flash from the muzzle illuminated his frightened face and I dove for what I thought was the gun hand, grasping the wrist for dear life.

He twisted and turned, his body writhing and his legs kicking. Something made contact with my jaw, stunning me for a moment. My hand almost slipped from his wrist as I pressed against the floor and drove my full weight against him. I felt the air rush from his lungs as my knee scored a lucky hit on his abdomen. The gun fired again, the flash this time muted, but joined almost immediately by a cry of pain and dismay. The gun clattered to the floor, but taken off guard by my push forward in the disorienting darkness, I tumbled over his moving body and into a wall.

Mendez howled his displeasure, still moving against the obstacle he had encountered in the pitch black, pounding its hands on the tabletop.

I could hear Kopland rise, disregarding his concern for the enemy without, as he clattered into a table toward the stairwell. I couldn't let him escape. He still had the vaccine.

Suddenly, the lights flickered. I was blinded briefly as the room was again thrown into sharp relief. Kopland stood in front of the door to the stairwell, hand on the handle, eyes searching the floor for the pistol. It lay next to me, inches from my left hand. Our eyes met briefly before I reached for the gun; he slammed the door open. Too late, I turned and trained the weapon on the stairwell, but he had gone.

Mendez turned to me, focusing on the prey that was mere feet away, and grabbing for my arm as I whipped the pistol around. His bony hand caught my arm as I turned toward him, not realizing in my haste to stop Kopland that the creature was so close. Kate watched in horror from where she lay hidden against the table to my left.

Bracing my leg against the table that separated us for the moment, I struggled to raise the pistol. The creature before me was strong, and its smell invaded my nostrils like a swarm of rancid fruit flies. All I could see in front of me was a rotting, putrid skull; flaps of black skin hung flaccidly from a slimy face with holes in the cheeks and jaw evidence of the decay that didn't wait for the corpse to sit still.

Eyes, bloodshot and milky, stared vacantly into my own, hunger its mute driving force. A mouth reeking of carrion and sporting yellowed teeth yawned widely in a desperate bid for my neck as he moved around the table, moved closer to me. Rotting bits of his last meal from days past still hung suspended in the cavity of its jaws. The grip on my hand loosened as it made a play for my head. I raised my gun hand quickly.

"Not this time, I've got a doctor's appointment."

I fired one shot, spraying the ceiling with the creature's head as fragments of bone flew into the air. I returned to Kate, who had moved into a seated position. I hastily moved toward her wound, which appeared to be just a deep graze.

"That son of a bitch shot me," she said indignantly. The locked door shook with more bodies. It was solid steel, but I knew that if we didn't leave the room soon, the stairwell would be compromised and we would be trapped.

"If it helps, I don't think he meant to hit you," I said, elated that the bullet had impacted her thigh instead of a more vital organ. She had lost a lot of blood, though, and likely couldn't move very fast.

"Glad to be your human shield, then," she said wryly, grimacing in pain as she shifted positions. I removed my belt, using it to staunch the flow of blood.

"Look, we've got to move before we're stuck down here. Can you walk?"

She tried to rise, but winced in pain and fell back to the floor.

"You've got to catch him. He's got the vaccine. I'll be fine in here. They can't get through these doors, so if the stairwell's clear you can come back for me."

I shook my head. "Not going to happen. I can't leave you down here, and you know it."

Her face contorted in anger. "You better fucking well leave me here, or you've dragged me out here to die for no reason. We need that vaccine—my daughter needs that vaccine—and it's up to you to get it. Now get the fuck out of here. Now!"

Taken off guard by her vehemence, I leaned back and looked at her face. She was serious, and I was wasting time. I nodded curtly and stood up. Taking a step toward the door, I paused. Moving on a combination of instinct and desire, I swiftly turned back and bent down to where she sat. Ignoring her surprised look, I pressed my lips against hers. Time passed too quickly as we said silently what couldn't be expressed in words. Slowly, I pulled away. Her eyes were still closed as I stood up.

"I will be back for you."

Without opening her eyes, she laid her head back against the side of the table. "I know."

I tore myself away from the picture of her beautiful face and moved to the door. I pressed my ear against the cold steel, listening for the sounds of movement. Nothing.

Pressing my hand against the steel bar, I pushed my shoulder into the door and moved into the stairwell. A minute trail of red blood led up the stairs to my right. Making sure the door was shut behind me, I followed the trail.

The stairwell rose for two floors before the trail of blood ended at the ground level door. The stairs rose one more level to what must have been roof access, but I slowly opened the door to what must have been the outside of the ground level. To my right, the door to what should have been the entrance to the facility through which we had come only an hour before.

I shoved the door open, and emerged into an open-air hallway. It stretched to my left, appearing to follow the contours of the building around to the rear. A canopy overhead protected the concrete ground from precipitation and the elements, and chain link cages followed the hallway until it disappeared out of sight to the rear of the building. These were the cages that we had seen in Kopland's office on the monitors.

As I moved slowly forward, following the small drops of blood on the gray floor, I allowed my eyes to flicker to the cages. Scraps of red and brown material were spread unevenly on the floors, against the walls, even between the links of the fencing. In some instances, streaks of bloody material bore witness to the savagery with which the creatures devoured their meals.

It became apparent as I moved past each cell that they had not been occupied in days. The bloody evidence of their last occupation was brown and crusted, and each door to the outside stood open, visions of the grounds peering through at me through rectangular windows. No ghouls moved in the rear of the building, outside these cages, nor were any of the interior doors opened. Whatever caused the exterior doors to open had thankfully left the interior gates locked.

I followed the pathway to the rear edge of the building, and stopped before turning the corner. Something told me that I should slow down. Kopland was clearly on his way somewhere, and he knew the place better than I did, obviously. I caught myself wondering which cage Maria had been in when that video was taken and in that same thought was disgusted at her involvement. How could she have been a willing participant in something so horribly wrong? How could she—how could any of these scientists—see what they saw on a daily basis, and go home to their wives and husbands? To their children?

To believe that these experiments could lead to any result but catastrophic seemed folly to me in hindsight, but as I looked into the cages and stared at the brownish red stains on the floor, I realized that I had the luxury of looking back over the results without ever having been encumbered by the burden of the dreams.

I still wanted to believe that Maria bore that burden.

Peering slowly around the corner, gun firmly in hand, I caught a hint of movement as the door to a large cage at the very end of the hallway swung shut. I moved quickly forward, as silently as I could, stooping over to reduce my visibility. Reaching the now-closed door, I looked into the cage. It was much larger than the others - indeed, it was the size of a small barn, with a commensurately large exterior door that sat closed against its frame on the opposite side of the enclosure.

Fragments of the now-familiar brackish goo were spread across the floor, chunks of more solid substance interspersed with the dried liquid. The stench was unbelievable; like a butcher's shop laid bare to a sweltering heat for days on end, the odor was almost visible.

As I brought my hand to my nose, I saw the bastard. He was moving toward the exit door; more precisely, he was moving toward a steel box located at chest level to the right of the door. He was trying to get out into the grounds, the crazy shit!

I grabbed the handle to the door, and it refused to budge. Kopland, alerted to my presence by the sound of the gate clanging against the frame, looked up and hurried forward, pulling a key from his pocket and inserting it into the gate controls. I leveled the pistol, aiming carefully at the locking mechanism.

The exterior gate hummed, as if awakened from a long sleep.

I fired, shielding my eyes from the sparks and the loose metal as the lock, warped and shattered by the bullet, loosened its hold on the doorframe. I ripped the door backwards and sprinted through, running toward Kopland.

The exterior gate was now opening, inch by inch, the gates sliding to the side slowly. He wouldn't be able to fit through before I got within range.

He realized this too, turning to face me and taking the last blue vial from his pocket and holding it up.

"I was really hoping it wouldn't come to this," he said, watching the gates move inexorably open over his shoulder and then looking back to me.

"I did intend that at least one sample of this chemical survive for the benefit of the believers that should be spared the full impact of God's wrath." He smiled a lopsided smile that didn't touch his eyes.

"But such is the nature of God's eternal damnation. Had He intended for this to be disseminated, He would not have put you in my path." As his hand moved toward the top of the vial, I noticed movement behind him.

The gunshot! Those things had been clustered in the front of the building, and had doubled back at the sound of the shot. Several creatures had appeared behind him, and I could see their rotting faces through the slowly widening crevasse between the gate doors. In twenty seconds they would be through.

Somehow, Kopland was ignorant of their approach, likely due to the noise of the grinding gatehouse gears.

I lowered the gun and crouched to the ground, placing the gun on the filthy floor. "You don't have to do that. I'll just step back, and you can go ahead. No one will stop you."

I was still thirty feet away from him. Too far to do anything in the short time it would take him to empty the vial.

"I think not; your interference has only proven that God's will is absolute. Had he intended for salvation to be available to the believers, he would not have delivered you to this place. I had thought to protect my plan by remaining here, but you have proven his will."

The first ghoul had squeezed through, its rotting hands pulling the emaciated remainder of its corpse between the large doors.

"His will be done," he said piously, clutching the stopper with his right hand and moving to pull it free.

The creature moved over the last few feet separating it from its clueless victim; it opened its mouth, tilting its head and bringing it forward against Kopland's exposed neck with a viciously quick jerk as its arms wrapped around Kopland's torso.

I had to move fast.

An earsplitting scream erupted from Kopland's throat as his neck was torn open, exposing severed, writhing red and blue veins that spurted blood over the face and head of his captor, whose jaws had clenched firmly on his flesh and were already moving against one another, chewing on the portion of his neck that it had dislodged. Its eyes were half closed, as in a semblance of culinary ecstasy.

The arms around his torso were apparently strong enough to prevent Kopland from resisting with his hands, and he shook his body like a dog trying to dry itself, but the creature clung on with an intensity borne out of raw, primitive hunger. It shot its head forward again, this time choosing the portion of the neck that joined with the shoulder, pulling eagerly back with strips of tendon and muscle streaming from its jaws. Kopland shook harder, his screams becoming sobs of agony.

I had picked up the gun and was running forward as the next zombie came through the opening between gates, clambering as quickly as it could toward what appeared to be a delectable feast. I raised the pistol and fired at the second creature, a small Asian woman in a hospital gown, but it suffered only a glancing blow to the shoulder and stumbled forward, immune to the wound. Reaching Kopland as the woman moved forward, I grabbed the vial, still clutched in his left hand.

He wouldn't release it.

The second creature moved toward me, and I raised the gun, sure of a head shot at this proximity. I pulled the trigger as the woman's head emerged from behind Kopland, apparently more interested in the free-ranging meal than sharing in her friend's.

The hammer fell, and an empty click echoed from the chamber. I looked to the revolver in my hand: all six chambers had been fired. Third and fourth zombies meandered through the constantly widening doorway as I struggled with Kopland, whose strength was ebbing as the creature on his back took a third bite, choosing this time to dislodge the doctor's left ear.

I kicked at the creature now grasping for my left arm, and stumbled as it moved against me from behind Kopland. Suddenly, the vial came free of Kopland's hand, as he was pulled to the ground by his assailant. His knees thumped heavily to the ground and I heard a sharp snapping sound, as if a sturdy limb had been shattered from a forceful impact.

Kopland screamed, clutching for my gun hand. Off balance from the combination of my own attacker's weight and Kopland's unexpected tumble, I fell toward the ground. Unconsciously, I stretched my hand out to stop my fall.

But the woman was there first.

Grasping my arm in both hands, she unwittingly used my momentum against me, bringing my wrist to her mouth before I could adjust.

The pain was excruciating. Her yellowed teeth knifed into my skin like superheated drill bits, each one piercing what felt like hundreds of thousands of nerve endings in their journey to the bone. My arm was on fire, and as she moved her head rapidly from side to side in an attempt to dislodge the flesh, I kicked out wildly with my leg, scoring a lucky shot that brought her to her knees and shook free from its tenacious grip.

I cradled my wrist in my arm as I stumbled back to the gate, unbelieving of the fate to which I had been so quickly damned. Looking down to my other hand, staring at the blue vial now covered in my blood; staring at the vaccine that I had acquired too late, I felt the hot tears of frustration burn my skin as they streamed down my face. Reaching the ruined door separating the cage from the hallway, I stumbled back to the stairwell. Kopland's screams serenaded me as I ran. I didn't look back.

CHAPTER 30

I had destroyed the lock. They would follow me inside, and there was nothing I could do about it. So I ran faster. In my delusion and my insanity, I thought I heard the steady thumping of helicopter rotor blades, but my head was a whirlwind of thoughts and images; my blood an imagined river of inky infection that coursed through ruined veins. In a panic and fear inspired delusion, I was convinced I was hearing things. But as I looked up, hoping for the best, I was rewarded with the impossible.

Hartliss's chopper was descending slowly, rotor blades beating the air slowly as it circled the facility. I didn't pause to ask how. I sped up, knowing I had mere minutes to pick up Kate and get her to the roof.

Slamming back into the stairwell, I cursed the inventor of the bar-handle door. That door that was ever so easy to open when you were carrying a latte in one hand and a cruller in the other also made a very accessible handle for the cognitively challenged ghoul bent on devouring your flesh.

I reached the door to the lab and slammed my open palm against it three times, shouting Kate's name. Seconds became days as I waited for a response, for the door to open. As I leaned my head against the steel in the hope of discerning movement or signs of life from inside, her face appeared. Wan and pale, but alive, she smiled. I didn't.

"I need a syringe," I said, pushing past her into the lab. Her confused look followed me as I pulled gauze and aprons out of a med kit fastened to the wall, breaking the seal on the sought-after item and plunging its needle into the vial.

"How much do I need?" I asked, pausing before pulling back.

"What are you doing? We don't know anything about that drug. We need to wait."

"Can't wait. The doc seemed to think this would be enough for a bunch of people, so I'm going to say a small amount will work."

She approached me, dragging her leg painfully behind. The bleeding had stopped, but the wound was in need of treatment. "You're not making any sense ... when did he say that? Upstairs? Why do you need to be inoculated right now? Can't it wait?"

I withdrew the needle from the vial carefully, gently inserting the sealed vial into Kate's tactical vest pocket and zippering it shut. She looked up at me curiously.

"No, it can't," I said, abruptly inserting the needle into her upper arm and stabbing the plunger forward. She yelled in surprise, jerking back instinctively. But not before the chemical had been delivered.

"Jesus! What the fuck?"

I held up my hand, turning my wrist toward her and plainly exhibiting my death sentence as I tossed the needle onto the floor.

"We don't have much time, we need to get you to the roof." I turned back to the door, asking as I did so, "Can you make it up the stairs?"

"God, Mike ... how? What ..."

"Never mind, I'll carry you." Time for the cowboy show again. One last time.

Before she could protest, I threaded my arm beneath her legs and behind her back and lifted. She was surprisingly light for her height, and she instinctively threw her arms around my neck as I moved forward.

"Where are ... where can we go?" she asked, not protesting her carriage but seemingly resigned to a fate she hadn't shared with me.

"The last time I had this idea, you yelled at me," I said, remembering the school.

"The roof. What is it with you and roofs?"

"I think some friends are here," I said shortly.

We reached the door, and we started up the stairs, moving slower than I would have liked, considering that I knew more creatures were making their way toward us from the open cage. It was just a matter of time.

We reached the ground floor and as I turned toward the last flight of stairs to the roof. As I stepped up onto the last landing, I knew I heard the sound of a single gunshot over the thumping of a helicopter rotor. I moved faster, my legs burning in protest and my injured wrist screaming its dismay. Kate held tight, her head pressed against my chest.

"Mike, I don't feel so hot," she said groggily.

From below us, the door from the cages slammed open, creatures stumbling through haphazardly, glazed reddened eyes searching for what they found above them.

Too late, I thought, as they started their slow progress up the stairs and we reached the door to the roof. I recognized the bitch that bit me and, for one irrational moment, thought about jumping her ass right then and there, with or without a gun.

Do it, you're fucked anyway. It'll make you feel better, you know.

"It's OK, I have a good feeling about this," I said to both of them, kicking open the last door and squinting against the daylight.

Hartliss's chopper stood in all its magnificent glory, blades slowing to a stop even as we emerged from the stairwell and slammed the door behind us. Beyond the vehicle, the gates of Hades had opened. The open fields within the grounds swarmed with the rotting, wandering forms of the living dead. Stumbling into one another in aimless, directionless oblivion, they moved individually and en masse toward the building, driven by an unending desire to feed. Knowing that their prey lurked somewhere behind those doors. I shuddered despite myself, keenly appreciative that only ten feet of cement and their lack of fine motor skills kept us safe.

But as I took in this scene, my eyes returned to the chopper and I recognized that all was not as it should be. In front of the open cargo bay doors, Hartliss was sprawled on the stone-covered roof, his youthful face contorted in pain and his hands clutching a stomach that was covered in crimson. He heard the door slam open and shut and turned toward us.

"Run! He's a bloody fake! He's not ..." I jerked in surprise as a gunshot interrupted his delivery. His shoulder spit blood into the air and he grunted, falling back to the roof. He was silent.

From his position inside the cabin of the helicopter emerged Fred, pistol in hand, heretofore innocent and retarded, face smiling in delight.

"Pancake, you stupid fucks," he said, leaping from the helicopter to the roof and training his gun on us.

My brain exploded, my inner voice a confusing firestorm of conflicting sensory signals. Fred had a gun? And he had added some words to his diatribe. Kate was laughing behind me, but for the life of me I couldn't figure out what was so funny.

"I'm supposing you succeeded in your little quest?" he asked. My brain refused to acknowledge that he was using non-breakfast cuisine-related words. All I heard was pancake.

Kate was crying now.

"Hey, asshole. I'm kind of on a clock here. Empty the pockets."

Fred was holding a gun.

How remarkable. I should get it from him before he hurts himself. Where was his frying pan?

Her voice breaking, Kate spoke, weakly. "Mike?"

Here, sir! That was me!

Why didn't I answer? My mouth wouldn't listen to my brain. Or my brain wasn't making sense. That was it; my mouth had it right, it was the brain that was off. I should try closing my eyes. I did.

I opened them again, and Fred was closer. But he was still holding a gun.

I cursed.

"I thought there was something unusual about you," I heard Kate say, her voice small and distant. "But I couldn't place it." She sounded resigned. "You were very convincing."

"Let's just say that my employer provides excellent on the job training. Or I should say ex-employer; I'm freelance now, given the degeneration of society, collapse of civilization, hordes of the undead, and all that. Looks like you had kind of a rough time of it down there. Find what you were looking for, did you?"

It was definitely Fred talking.

"Why?" It was the one word—the only word—I could muster.

"Didn't you ever wonder why you were kept drugged and secluded? Why rapists and serial killers were afforded more mental liberty than you were back at King's Point? Since you got out, been having flashbacks, have you? Fuck, man, get with it! You can see this is a government deal; didn't your internal conspiracy theorist come up with something?" He shook his head in disdain and amusement.

"You had seen and heard a little too much, if you get my drift. These fuckers," he gestured around him, at the grounds we could see from our vantage point, "they came from somewhere. Here in fact. But you think our government wanted this kind of dirty laundry aired in public?"

"I was set up." My head was clearing. My hand hurt like hell, but my mind was free of the blazing voices and the muddle of confounding disbelief. The pain in my hand reminded me of my fate. We didn't have much time.

"Fuck an A, man. You were set up to go in, and you were screwed once you arrived. We had you on so many cocktails, if you had been in there much longer, you wouldn't remember how to hold your dick when you piss, let alone that your wife was a living corpse when you got home. Best part is, even if you had, who would have believed you?" The bastard laughed.

"Didn't you wonder how you got locked in back at the Point? Wake up!"

And I saw her again, one painful, last time. And I saw what she held in her hand. A syringe. A steel syringe. Filled with blue liquid. I unconsciously raised my hand, looking for the long gone pin prick in my hand that I had felt when she attacked me.

"But I digress," he said, voice serious again. "Let's see it, and maybe I let you guys live, such as it is." He looked pointedly at the grounds, where hundreds of creatures swarmed over the dry grass. Their moans drifted on the cool air, the grunts and scratches from the door behind me lending the entire situation an air of surreal urgency.

I reached into my pocket, withdrawing a clip for my pistol, long forgotten in the passages below. Hiding it in my palm, hoping to buy just a little more time as I moved to the door, I gestured toward Fred, hoping he couldn't sense my dissemblance.

"What, you just gonna take it and sell it? You're going to abandon your nation, perhaps the world, for a few bucks to the highest bidder?"

"Come on, man," he said, cocking his head incredulously. "This place is fucked! Hartliss and I heard it after we got the bird in the air again. Caught some com chatter from an AWAC plane off the New York coast. Midwest cities are falling every day, they've reached the West Coast, and the Florida line has been breached in too many holes to count. Reports of infection in Canada, Mexico, Central and South America. Even Britain and France. Time to cut our losses and move elsewhere. I'm thinking a nice little Caribbean island somewhere. They can't swim, you know."

At the mention of Canada, Kate groaned in pain; whether physical or emotional was another question.

Behind me, the door shook from the constant impacts of corpses against its frame, seeking to follow us onto our last refuge. My hand still rested on the cool steel of the door handle; I felt it vibrate in my ruined fingers. I could smell them through the thick steel; imagined or real, their putrescence was a vile intrusion into the clean, crisp air.

"I'm sorry you had to suffer so much for something I'll profit from, but as they say in the biz, c'est la vie, right?" He seemed very amused at his reference to my line of work. Why did everyone find that so interesting and witty? Jackass.

He turned the gun on Kate, tilting his head and looking at me.

"Enough of this. You first, or her?" Her eyes were closed. She wasn't far from the door, so I'd have to move quickly.

Not being left much of a choice, I took the only path left to me.

"Neither," I said, and opened the door to hell.

CHAPTER 31

I rolled away from the door as it flew open. They poured from the opening as if someone had turned on a faucet. The wall next to me spit pieces of concrete and mortar as Fred fired at me in frustration, forced to move back by their sudden appearance. Because I had pulled the door open toward me, it proved an effective shield against their onslaught, directing them instead toward Fred, who fired at the flood of bodies in haste as he retreated, forced away from the door and the chopper, toward the low wall edging the roof.

The mass of creatures now separated us from Fred, who couldn't get a clear shot at me, even as he saw me move toward Kate and start toward the helicopter. In front of us, Hartliss had struggled into a sitting position and his hand was now clutching his side. Having seen his movement from my position before opening the door I was banking on the chance that he was well enough to fly the helicopter off this roof. If not, we were in for a shit storm of hurt.

He had pushed himself back against the aluminum door of the cockpit, but couldn't rise. Blood seeped through his blue uniform in copious amounts. He feebly motioned toward the chopper, even as Fred fired again toward the ghouls that still separated us from him. But he was moving parallel to the edge of the roof back toward the helicopter, and would soon have a clear shot at us as we neared the chopper. We needed to move faster, I thought, as I forced my tired legs to respond.

I moved forward as if in a dream. My feet moved but I didn't seem to get any closer to the helicopter. Each step was agony, my legs screaming in exhaustion and my arms threatening to drop my burden. Gravel crunched under foot, and the moaning from behind us nipped at my heels like a pack of invisible, rabid wolves. Every second I moved, I anticipated the hungry bite of a zombie in my thigh, or the sharp, piercing pain of a bullet tearing through my back.

Fred was backing slowly toward the helicopter. He fired carefully, not sparing a glance away from the group of creatures still endlessly pouring from the staircase. Heads exploded in a carefully measured cadence, congealed blood becoming a misty haze through which other ghouls had to shuffle to thrust forward in hunger.

Despite his efforts, they continued to move forward. Faster than he could dispatch them, they shuffled forth. Slowly and steadily, they ate up the distance between the stairwell and the helicopter. Even in the fresh mountain air, the stench reached my nostrils as I covered the last few feet to Hartliss, the stinking reek of carrion and rotting matter almost knocking me to my knees.

I placed Kate in the passenger compartment and turned back to Hartliss. He smiled wanly as I helped him to stand and opened the door to the cockpit.

"Not much of a hero act, eh mate?" he said as I boosted him into the chair and he flipped switches, his blood making the controls slippery and uncooperative.

"Listen man, you get this bird in the air, and I'll knight your ass myself." Grabbing his pistol from the seat next to him, I went to shut the door.

"You'll need a clip; the ponce tossed mine over the edge," he said, eyes livid. "Got a spare in the back. Good luck." Nodding, I slammed the door shut.

That, of all things, caught Fred's attention.

He was only feet from the first wave of creatures, and had paused to reload even as he continued to back toward the vehicle. It was the pause in constant gunfire that alerted him to our location; possibly, he assumed we had been overcome by the door and didn't realize we had evaded their grasping hands until he heard the commotion behind him. Possibly, his plan was to retreat to the chopper and fly himself out. Now, we had complicated the situation.

I reached into the cabin and grabbed a spare clip from a duffel bag strapped to the floor. Shoving the clip into the gun, I turned to Hartliss, who was igniting the engine. The blades started to turn slowly over my head, the air displaced by their motion driving away the putrid stench of the creatures.

"Get this thing in the air as soon as you can! Don't wait for me. If I'm not on board when you're good to go, get in the air!"

He nodded weakly, and turned to the dash, checking the gauges. I slammed the cargo bay door shut as a bullet hole appeared three inches from my right hand. Diving to the ground, I felt the hard stones cut my face and neck as I rolled toward the rear of the helicopter. I heard Fred's voice. Hoping he hadn't seen the pistol, I kept it out of sight behind me as I got to my feet.

"Give me the god damned vaccine, Mike! You can't win. I'll shoot your pilot right now, so help me! Give it to me now and we all leave. You don't, and it's just me!" He was shouting to be heard over the noise of the rotor blades, which were now ramping up to full speed. I moved out from behind the chopper, hands behind my head, hoping that he couldn't see the pistol held low behind my neck. Zombies shuffled forward, not far from Fred, who was almost to the cockpit door.

"Now or never!" he shouted, and realizing how close Hartliss had come to getting the helicopter into the air, aimed his gun at the cockpit door. The rear of the aircraft lifted off the roof by inches and Fred jerked his head to the side, giving me the distraction I needed. I pulled Hartliss's pistol from behind my head. The kick from the weapon jarred my injured hand and a lighting bolt of pain flashed up my arm.

Fred had caught my activity and had instinctively moved aside at the moment I fired, firing at me as he took my own shot in the shoulder instead of the chest.

His bullet took me in the right thigh, burning and tearing through cloth and flesh. I could feel the projectile lodge itself in my bone as I fell to the ground, crawling to the side instinctively as the tail of the helicopter rose into the air and swung about.

Small stones, kicked up by the rotors, flew into my face and hair and I closed my eyes against the debris momentarily. I opened them again as the tail swung out over the grounds and the helicopter lifted further into the air, and saw Fred rise to his feet slowly, closely pursued by the pack of creatures now further stimulated by the activity that had taken place. He stumbled forward and raised his gun.

I had no time to duck as the two, almost concurrent flashes of light from his muzzle left dizzying bright spots in my eyes. My shoulder and my injured arm exploded in agony, bullets tearing through the flesh of my bicep and my deltoid.

He continued forward, gun still trained on me but no more shots being fired. In the haze of pain it took me moments to realize his gun was empty. But still he came forward.

I lifted my own gun hand and moved to pull the trigger, noticing as I did so that Fred's shot to my arm had caused me to drop the gun.

There was no time to pick it up as he barreled into me, forcing me back to the ground. Creatures moaned and shuffled forward, not twenty feet behind us as we rolled, punching and kicking, toward the cinder block raised edge of the building.

My arm and leg groaned in agony as I struggled to throw him from me and to reach the gun that I knew lay tantalizingly close. I landed a fist on his ear, causing him to howl in pain as his foot unwittingly kicked the gun closer to me. I twisted sharply, throwing him off balance, and he tumbled to my left. Lunging for the weapon, I felt the composite grip slide into my palm as the wind was driven out of my lungs by his tackling body. Keeping my grip on the pistol, I rolled with him further away from the approaching creatures, which were now ten feet closer and gaining quickly.

Without the benefit of the rotor blades, their stench again sought to rip my nose from my face and drive the smell of living death deep into my brain.

Realizing quickly that this altercation needed to end, I had a flash from "the scene"—the one that had made my career. The one that had made me; that had defined me in the eyes of so many. The one that had pushed me into the mold I now realized I would forever struggle to break.

He was on top of me, his hand on my throat, his other hand clutching my gun hand with tenacious strength. His face was contorted in pain and aggression, the eyes that had seemed so simple and unwitting before were now narrowed in a hateful fashion.

I had to remember that this wasn't the man I thought it was. My memories of his awkward looks, those expressions that seemed ever so slightly out of place in his eyes, came back to me. My anger flared anew, enraged by the deception.

In a last desperate act, taking pages from a script that had been written and choreographed years before, I feigned a roll to the left, causing him to over adjust to his right. I brought my uninjured knee up quickly and solidly between his legs and simultaneously arched my back, causing his weakened shoulder to buckle under the new pressure. The hand on my gun arm faltered and I brought it around with all the strength that remained to me, cracking the grip against the side of his head.

He fell to the ground hard, kicking up pebbles and dirt as he rolled away towards the approaching creatures.

I didn't waste any more time with him. I knew I didn't have to.

I crawled to the edge of the roof as the creatures reached his barely moving form. At the first of their touch, he started groggily, bleeding head jerking up, realizing what had happened. Realizing that he was doomed.

Before he could get to his feet, they were on him. Four, five, six...then too many to count, hands plunging in, heads darting forward. His hands could be seen moving under the pile of rotting corpses, flailing about in a futile mix of desperation and agony. He screamed once—a pitiful, wailing, heart-breakingly painful scream. As it ended, his face appeared between the backs of two ghouls that were bent over his now open torso, streams of intestines spilling out from his body. Hands moved forward surprisingly fast to grasp them and pull them this way and that: dogs fighting over scraps at a table. His face was agonized, his eyes pleading. He mouthed the request I knew was coming.

In response, I raised my gun hand, pain still shooting up my arm into my shoulder. I aimed carefully at his head.

And then, remembering the deception and the hate; the death and the inhumanity, I dropped my arm to my side once more.

Even in his pain, his eyes narrowed in anger one last time, and he was gone, covered in writhing gray bodies, blood seeping between their twitching feet.

I stood on the ledge, and I looked down at the grounds. Four feet below me, hands clambered for my flesh, deadened rotting arms reaching up from the ground, from a nightmare of hellish proportions. Hundreds of creatures packed the grassy yard, an undulating carpet of decayed flesh and grinding jaws unrelieved by anything living. I looked back to the roof. The mass of creatures from the stairwell had moved past the remains of Fred's body, leaving a mass of wet, red flesh open to the light of day as they approached me slowly. What used to be Fred was a carpet of gore. Their dead, dirty feet moved past his corpse, tracking blood across the stones.

Their eyes, as always, were red and hungry. Their mouths, as always, moved in anticipation of their next feeding. Their legs, as always, shuffled forward slowly but surely, death an inevitable companion to their inexorable approach.

Again, my last film came to mind. This time, the fight scene choreography would avail me little. But in the end, I thought, why fight your own identity? Why battle against who you are—who you were, perhaps, meant to be? In the public mind's eye—at least, what was left of the public—I was never to be, could never be, exonerated of this crime. The television and radio, the internet and the email; everything that had so efficiently broadcast my guilt, were no more.

From above me, the sound of helicopter rotor blades and from the corner of my eye, a flash of color descended and was gone again. I thought I heard voices, but I was beyond that, beyond their help. I looked down at my hand and I laughed. Go figure, I thought, remembering Maria's final gift to me before her death; recognizing the humor of my condition despite all odds. A last minute reprieve at the knowing hands of a dead wife, and you die in the end regardless.

I raised my gun hand for the last time, speaking with an unsuppressed glee the line that had made me who I was today and firing steadily as the gun spat my defiance to the last.

"Eat me, mother-fuckers!" I shouted each time the gun spoke, noting with a detached amusement the incredible irony of the situation, but beyond caring. The gun fired too many times to count; heads exploded before me, gray and red mist coloring the clear air. But still they came. There were always more.

As the last shot left the chamber, I looked bemusedly at the gun as if it were a funny thing. Suddenly, the gates to heaven opened, and a rope ladder—the self-same rope ladder that had plucked us from the maws of hell on the rooftop in Long Island—fell to my feet. The voice of God spoke to me.

God sounded like Kate.

"Come on. They're almost here! Move!"

My vision blurred and my head swam but I somehow managed to wrap the rope of the last rung around my good arm. A gentle tug from the heavens and an anxious voice yelling to be heard over the rotor blades came close to snapping me out of my reverie as I was pulled toward the edge.

The hungry bastards had reached my perch, and were grasping for me in earnest. Dead paws with rotting skin falling from their bones clutched at my clothing, my face, my hair. I realized I hadn't left a bullet in my gun for myself. I must not have intended to die today.

And I fell off the ledge, flailing into space and away from my adoring fans.

I had lost a lot of blood, and don't know how I managed to reach the cabin. But I did. Kate was there, her face flashing in front of mine, tending to my shoulder, which was numb. I was in and out of consciousness, sounds and sights meant little to me. Light and darkness played across my mind. Sounds that I barely recognized. Reassuring tones from Kate for a short time, confused and excited words from Hartliss. In bits and pieces I could piece together what happened next.

A trail of smoke and a flash of light. A shuddering sound from the main rotor compartment and a sickening lurch. A shout of confusion and a cry of dismay. Kate's face above my own, worry streaking her beautiful visage. Hartliss's anxious words, his weakened tone, his confused shouting.

In the haze of pain and confusion, the voice spoke once more.

Ironic, isn't it, that she would go to all that trouble of inoculating you, and this is how you die?

But this time, it was detached and resigned. It wasn't angry or bitter, or even mocking. It was simply stating a fact drawn from our shared memories of where it all began. It was in this moment that I realized that this voice, this detached and haunting presence, wasn't the malevolent conscience trying to take me over from within that I had imagined. It wasn't an alter-ego, nor was it an insanity-induced figment of my own schizophrenia. It was the nagging, persistent voice of my own self-doubt.

Suddenly, a dizzying and rapid loss of height, and Kate was gone, disappearing into the lack of gravity and direction. I hit the bulkhead, and my world was again pain and darkness. I gave in to the blanket of peaceful black and ignored the world.

CHAPTER 32

I opened my eyes. Or my eyes opened of their own accord. One or the other.

I was staring at white; nothing but unrelieved white. It was the white of a blank computer screen or of a newly painted picket fence. Turning my head to the side slowly, I realized there was no pain. Given what I had been through, this seemed unusual.

My head felt fuzzy and disoriented, like it was packed in cotton. My tongue was covered in fur, and my hands and feet moved substantially slower than I asked them to. And that's why it took me so long to realize where I was.

Rather grungy white walls, complete with a low, stained white ceiling surrounded my narrow bed. Off-white sheets covered a lumpy mattress and a thin pillow, and a door with a small inset window stood to one side of the tiny room. The smell of mildew permeated the small space.

A nightstand stood next to my bed, a plastic cup full of pills neatly arranged next to a full glass of water. I turned, putting my feet on the floor and standing up, bracing myself against the frame of the bed to keep from collapsing in disorientation.

Something wasn't right here.

I carefully felt my shoulder and examined my hand, expecting a sharp stab of pain. Nothing; no pain, no bite wound.

I rolled up my sleeve, exposing my bicep. I tore at my pant leg, searching my thigh. My heart started beating faster. The blood that was pounding in my aching and swollen head was a kettledrum in an empty room. No wounds, no blood, no scars.

This couldn't be. Panic shot through my body and adrenalin chased away the daze. Where were Kate and Hartliss? Where the fuck was I? The room that my mind told me I recognized was familiar, but it was also impossible. I moved to the wall housing the window, set far above my head. I reached for the sill, but it was too high. I needed to know where I was. I needed to know that this wasn't possible.

Moving to the door, my hand paused above the handle.

Or did I? Did I really want to know the answer to this question? My hand hovered above the handle as my mind paused and the kettledrums quickened their pace. If what I had been through—or what I had imagined— had taught me anything, it's that knowledge for the sake of knowledge isn't always the safest thing.

But it didn't matter. I had to know. I had to see for myself.

I put my hand on the stainless steel knob of the door to the hallway, and turned it slowly, walking once again into a world that I didn't know.

###

A NOTE FROM THE AUTHOR

Zombies are fun, aren't they? Not just from the 'mindless walking death machine' angle, but from all the associated aspects that go with telling a zombie story. In point of fact, these creatures aren't terribly interesting, right? It's the action around them, supplied by the human protagonists and the backdrop of crumbling civilization that makes it a fun ride. But the creatures themselves—drooling, shambling, mindless carnivores—they're entertaining. They wander about in herds, they walk off roofs, and they shamble in front of moving vehicles. And they do it all out of an innate and primal hunger for flesh.

What is it about watching or reading about these things that captivates us? Obviously, we enjoy rooting for the good guys in their fight against something that can be loosely described as evil. We enjoy watching the automatic weapon fire play out in our mind; the thrill of bad guys disintegrating in a hail of righteous gunfire and the good guys walking away triumphant.

But it's not truly that simple, is it? Zombies aren't actually evil. How can they be? One requires sentience to formulate evil intent. After all, that's what makes some*thing* a zombie as opposed to some*one* a violent, cannibalistic sociopath. No, zombies aren't evil, just mindless and oblivious—bent on one thing, achieving one goal.

Like the guy who cut you off this morning on the freeway, blithely texting away on his mobile phone.

Like the lady that barely beat you to the front of the line at the grocery store, oblivious to the fact that you stood there in your pajamas, carrying two quarts of milk, while she carried several hundred pounds of items.

They're not so different, the zombies and the aforementioned normal folk. Oh sure, the guy from the freeway isn't trying to rip your throat out, but it's a matter of degree, right? To some extent, zombie stories are just that. A matter of degree. In the end, I would theorize that zombie stories are more real than we give them credit for. They're just every day life writ large and in more defined black and white.

While we may not be pursued by mindless automatons hungering for our flesh on a daily basis, neither is our reaction as extreme when we encounter mindless foes. The guy who cut you off? The lady at the supermarket? Both totally oblivious and mindless; neither truly culpable in intent. Which is why our reactions are equally mundane. In both circumstances, your reaction is likely to be what?

Inventive curses under your breath?

At most you actually honk the horn, verbally confront the transgressor. But you don't shoot them. You don't commandeer a shotgun or a pitchfork or a cleverly configured laser saw or any of the other numerous tools that get used in a classic zombie tale. It's because they're not chasing you hungering for your flesh.

Now if we take that mindless, selfish oblivion up a few hundred notches, remove hand-eye coordination and add a very specific preference for rare meat? That's a story!

So why am I talking about this? I suppose it's mostly to give you insight into why I enjoyed writing this book, and why I am continuing to enjoy writing the next one. Not that I need to tell you, obviously, since you're reading this, but this is a great genre, and one that I'm not only lucky, but privileged, to be a part of. Hopefully, you're enjoying my contribution to the art. If not, I'm sure your review will flesh that out in time. Sorry, pun definitely intended there.

Anyway…to avoid delaying further, I will make two last comments relating directly to the book.

This is my first full-length novel, and it was one that I enjoyed writing immensely. However, it is also not without its flaws, some or most of which are likely directly attributable to the fact that I enjoyed it so much. It was an interesting process, writing this book. When you set pen to paper (or finger to keypad in this case), you have an idea of what your work will be. You have an outline, you have characters, you have preconceptions. As you write, you realize at some point that your characters and your story begin to take control—that they are no longer your devices or your creation, but that you are now their tool. In short, the story begins to take control and the characters begin to live and breath, all without you. While some authors may disagree, I believe that this is when writing fiction becomes a truly interesting and rewarding endeavor.

I'll end on a note about endings. If you feel that the story was cut short prematurely, you are not alone. I myself wanted to follow further, to see what came next, and was somewhat disappointed about having to end where I did. I wanted to follow my characters further, continue to expand the plot, and take my story to new people and places. I grew so attached to my characters that I didn't want to stop writing the story. However, in my head, the story, which is really just the first round in more stories to come, had to end where it ended and the conclusion as it stands now is exactly where the ending happened, not out of design but out of evolution.

But it's not the end, just the end of the beginning. And to prove it, I've included a sample chapter from the sequel, *LZR-1143: Evolution*. I plan to have more fun with the sequel than I had with the first novel, and my hope is that the first chapter is evidence of that.

I love feedback, and enjoy hearing from anyone who has given me the honor of reading my book. If you feel so inclined, please drop me a note at lzr1143@gmail.com. Otherwise, enjoy the preview, and thanks for sharing this story with me.

Bryan

LZR-1143: EVOLUTION

A Zombie Novel

By:
Bryan James

CHAPTER 11

Truth be told, it was their fault for leaving it unlocked. If they didn't want people playing with their toys, they couldn't complain about me having some fun. Especially if it was the last thing I ever did.

I sprinted past the large banner lying trampled on the flight deck, ropes that used to hold it aloft lying prone on the canted deck like downed spider webs. Stumbling briefly as a portion of the paper tore under my boot, I looked one last time at the words printed on the roughly and hastily made sign: *U.S.S. Enterprise Welcomes Mike McKnight!*

Scrambling up the short metal ladder and slamming the cockpit glass down behind me, I settled in to the small seat, staring at the controls in front of me.

I had actually trained on one of these before, but I'd be damned if I remembered much.

Well, maybe 'train' wasn't an accurate word.

I had been given a day of familiarization training, which was essentially a pilot telling me what many of the knobs and buttons did, when I was filming "Airborne Assault" with Van Damme. I tell you, that guy made an awesome copilot. Nothing like a Belgian-French accent to strike fear into the hearts of a squadron of Libyan MIGs.

I sat down hard and looked at the cockpit display. How hard could it be to figure out how to operate the guns?

Oh boy.

There were definitely a lot of buttons. And dials, and knobs, and lights, and computer screens.

Okay, on second thought, this could be a little problematic.

Hundreds of creatures were clustered together and moving toward me.

I had grossly underestimated the number of them that had been able to get on deck after the helicopters took off.

Well ... at least the plane was facing the right direction.

Toward the bad guys.

I leaned forward, pressing a large button strategically located in a spot that could have been an ignition, or an 'on' button, or something similar. The aircraft shook suddenly, and for a moment I thought I had succeeded. Then I realized that it was just the flight deck of the massive ship shifting, its bow canting sharply forward as it took on water. With no one left at the helm to control the bulkhead fail-safes, the Enterprise was sinking fast. It was only a matter of time.

The airplane shifted slightly against its chocks, vibrating and then stopping. I scoured my head for any vestige of knowledge that I could apply to the situation. I vaguely remembered the pilot mentioning a touch screen something-or-other ...

The best I got was a blurry memory of playing Top Gun on the Nintendo.

Jesus. I was going to die on this ship.

I leaned back, craning my head to see over the nose cone.

Yep, they were still coming on strong. Nice to know something in this crazy world was reliable.

My attention snapped back to the chore at hand.

One button had to activate the onboard electronics. Without the plane being powered on, it wouldn't do anything, right? So if you're looking for an 'on' button, you can't do too much damage. Just press buttons.

When stuff lights up, you're golden.

Can't see anything wrong with that plan. So I started punching buttons.

Until one punched back.

The voice was small and feminine.

"Full weapons lock confirmed. Cannon disarmed."

Shit.

That was pretty much the opposite of my intent here.

Punch.

"HUD activated."

Okay, now we were getting somewhere. A heads-up targeting display appeared on the front quarter of the windshield, glowing letters and numbers flashing with electronic mirth.

Punch again.

"Unable to comply. Fuel insufficient." Useless piece of ...

Punch.

Suddenly a deep roar from the back of the plane. Engines were spooling up. Then lights, then computer screens. Finally, weapons dials. The little picture of a cannon on the computer screen to the right lit up green. It read 2500.

Bingo!

This part I knew. From years of playing arcade games and two different movies about hero-pilots, I was finally comfortable.

Once it was powered on, I knew the gig.

I grabbed the controls, inadvertently pushing the stick forward as I shifted my weight. The plane shot forward against the chocks abruptly, responsive to the movement.

Crap.

Didn't mean to actually move.

The zombies were close now, my incompetence in the cockpit allowing them ample time to play catch up. A group of seven or eight were in the front, all in some form of bloody disrepair or another.

The Enterprise shifted again. Valiantly she was holding herself afloat, seemingly by sheer will. Her forward compartments had to be full of water by now, and the middle of the ship was destined to follow. Sickeningly, I watched the bow droop again, and more water crash against the flat top of the flight deck.

It was now or never.

I slowly moved the stick to the right, lining up the target sight in the HUD with the first group of zombies. Purposefully, I depressed the safety switch and squeezed the bright red trigger.

"Weapons lock engaged. Please remove the safety before firing the Vulcan cannon."

Son of a *bitch*!

The bottom right corner of the screen had a picture of a lock, flashing red. It appeared to be a touch screen. From my periphery, I sensed the front rank of zombies were close. Close enough to reach the ladder.

I touched the lock and squeezed the trigger, hoping for the best.

"Weapons lock released," reported my new best friend.

Almost simultaneously, the twenty millimeter Vulcan cannon came to life.

It didn't just shoot the zombies.

It made them disappear.

Shambling forms suddenly disintegrated into clouds of red mist. Shreds of clothing floated to the deck, which was already slick with blood. I slowly guided the controls to the left, strafing the oncoming forms at close range. Tracers lit into the crowd, rounds pulverizing flesh and bone and traveling through ten or twenty creatures at a time before moving past and into the water below. Nothing stood a chance against that onslaught. It was a killing field for the undead, and I was in control.

After what seemed like years of fleeing—sneaking and crawling and watching people die—I wasn't prepared for my response. I quickly lost sight of the fact that these forms, these clouds of red spray and chunks of flesh, had been people not eight hours ago; that only mistakes piled upon mistakes had made them what they were now. No, this was not on the top of my mind.

I just wanted to destroy them all.

I slowly moved the nose of the plane from left to right, feeling the raw power of the twin turbines beneath me. It was a rush like none other. The cannon spewed large bore rounds by the hundreds every second, and I was powerless to stop myself.

Finally, the empty sound of hollow clicking tapped against the hull of the plane like a metallic woodpecker. The cannon icon on the computer screen blinked red, and I realized I was done. I grabbed the lever on the side of the canopy and pulled up, air hissing out of the cockpit as I rose on the seat, looking out onto the flat surface of the deck. Suddenly, I lurched forward, losing my balance and tumbling down the nose of the plane.

The Enterprise had started her final descent.

The blunt, square nose of the ship was fully submerged in the waves. Asphalt sunk into the angry sea as the stern of the massive machine emerged fully from the water, towering over me. Her giant screws turned slowly in the afternoon air, water streaming from the dark metal. The chocks holding my Hornet in place dislodged, and it slid forward as I rolled away, just missing getting clocked by a mounted missile as it glided past me and stopped ten feet further on, held up by the protruding edge of another restraint.

The flight deck was covered in the remains of zombies and slick with blood and rainwater. The clouds had opened up, cutting visibility. I searched the sky for my ride out and almost panicked. The helos were still AWOL, and I was running out of time.

The sound of shattered glass punctured the air as I watched, dumbstruck, as the glass from the control tower fell to the deck in a cascading, rippling sheet. The radar array followed suit, smashing through the remnants of a destroyed Hornet lying shattered against the conning tower. A stream of undead suddenly filtered from the open hatch, falling instantly on the angled deck, but struggling forward and away from the door.

Toward me.

I was alone, I realized suddenly and fearfully. They had left and I was alone.

Then I was sliding again, careening out of control as the flight deck tilted steeply, angling toward the cold sea. I reached out reflexively with my arms, searching for purchase against the slick surface. Blood and rain whipped against my face as my hand slapped against an errant protrusion and arrested my fall.

I was hanging almost vertically from a cockeyed railing, hands burning from the effort. Dark, angry blue waves crashed over the black tarmac, licking the dashed white lines. The gray form of my F-18 slid by in slow motion, the almost comical form of an undead crew member lodged in an engine cowl.

The port wing of the aircraft slammed into the water first, ripping it from the fuselage and changing the angle of descent, forcing the vehicle into the water headfirst. It sank quickly, disappearing deeper into the dark water. The crew member moaned once, the sound lost quickly in the tearing wind.

I hung, feet kicking against the slick deck. Zombies slid and tumbled past me, struggling for footing on the steeply canted flat surface as the ship sank slowly into the channel, the dark linear form of the Chesapeake Bay Bridge-Tunnel winding into the distance. Beside me, the conning tower loomed like a dark sentinel. It was an ethereal dark shape canting awkwardly over the crashing waves at an angle never contemplated by the ship's designers.

Despite my circumstances, I chuckled to myself in morbid humor. There were a lot of things happening right now that weren't contemplated by a lot of folks a little while back.

The popping of steel girders and breaking glass echoed the death throes of the dying ship. Rain pelted the deck, cold against my bare face.

A transport plane slid by my precarious perch, crashing to the water below and shattering open. Creatures spewed out into the water, thrashing in the water and trying to rise on the angled deck, even as it slipped beneath the water. The plane bobbed fitfully as the ship slipped beneath it, and floated dangerously closer each time the ship sank further. They slobbered and drooled, mad in their own special way. There were at least six. Maybe more. The rest were covered in water. But they were coming.

Three more heads appeared from the murky water, and pushed into the darkening twilight as I slipped farther toward them with the dying ship.

Oh yes, they were definitely coming.

There comes a time in every man's life when he realizes that his number's up; that in the game of man versus world, good versus evil, dead versus undead … that he was truly and honestly screwed. Here, hanging helplessly from the deck of a dying ship, surrounded by dead people that were trying like mad to eat me…well, let's just say I was beginning to develop some realistic expectations about my future.

I sighed heavily, recognizing that my grip on the wet, convulsing railing was going to give out. Soon.

Enjoy it? Buy the rest of LZR-1143: Evolution now, on Amazon.com!

Made in the USA
Lexington, KY
18 February 2013